ANOTHER EDEN

Recent Titles by Julie Ellis from Severn House

The Hampton Saga

THE HAMPTON HERITAGE
THE HAMPTON WOMEN
THE HAMPTON PASSION

BEST FRIENDS
THE GENEVA RENDEZVOUS
THE HOUSE ON THE LAKE
SECOND TIME AROUND
SINGLE MOTHER
A TOWN NAMED PARADISE
VILLA FONTAINE
WHEN THE SUMMER PEOPLE HAVE GONE

ANOTHER EDEN

Julie Ellis

This first world edition published in Great Britain 2002 by
SEVERN HOUSE PUBLISHERS LTD of
9–15 High Street, Sutton, Surrey SM1 1DF.
This first world edition published in the USA 2002 by
SEVERN HOUSE PUBLISHERS INC of
595 Madison Avenue, New York, N.Y. 10022.

British Library Cataloguing in Publication Data

Ellis, Julie, 1933–
    Another Eden
    1. Romantic suspense novels
    I. Title
    813.5'4 [F]

ISBN 0-7278-5663-4

Typeset by Palimpsest Book Production Ltd.,
Polmont, Stirlingshire, Scotland.
Printed and bound in Great Britain by
MPG Books Ltd., Bodmin, Cornwall.

Acknowledgements

I would like to thank the staff of the New York Public Library and of the Mid-Manhattan branch for their always courteous and helpful assistance in my research.

I would especially like to thank JoAnne Heiting, of the Admissions Office of the University of Carolina Law School in Columbia, South Carolina, who was so helpful and gracious in supplying answers to my endless parade of questions.

As always, thanks to my daughter Susan for her diligent research assistance and word-processing services, and to my son Richard, of Sentinel Copy, Inc., for so efficiently handling the myriad copyings and bindings that provided order for my masses of research notes.

One

The late-May afternoon was hot and humid, as could be expected at this time of year in Eden, South Carolina – just across the state line from Augusta, Georgia. Kara Jamison sat beside her grandmother on the rear seat of the 1987 Plymouth station wagon – its air-conditioner providing little relief from the heat – and tried to mirror the exhilaration reflected by her grandmother and by her mother, at the wheel. Both had taken the day off from their jobs to be at her law-school graduation.

She lifted a hand to sweep lush near-black hair from her forehead, for a moment closed the violet eyes – so like those of the father she'd never known. She was exhausted from the trauma of the day, the drive from Atlanta. A seven-year odyssey was over. The four years of undergraduate school, three years at Emory Law. She felt like an expatriate, returning home.

'This is the proudest day of my life,' Edie Jamison said with relish. 'My granddaughter an Emory Law School graduate – class of '98.'

'I owe you two so much.' Kara felt a recurrent surge of love and gratitude. College loans – though huge – couldn't have seen her through. Grandma had had to mortgage the house again.

'Seeing you stand up there and receive your law degree was the most beautiful moment in our lives.' Daisy's eyes left the road at a red light to focus on her daughter. 'Let this town see what a Jamison woman can do.' Kara understood that old-timers in Eden harbored little respect for the Jamison women. In truth, part of her hated this town – for what it had done to Mom and Grandma.

'I've got your first client for you.' Edie's love for her only

1

grandchild lent a charming radiance to her face. Her delicate features were repeated in daughter and granddaughter. At sixty-five Edie Jamison was still a lovely woman. 'Mattie hasn't much money – it'll be your first *pro bono* case.'

While her grandmother and mother exchanged grandiose conjectures about her future as an Eden attorney, Kara pondered her decision yet again. Was this the right move, to come home to Eden to set up an independent practice? Should she have accepted the fabulous offer from that prestigious law firm in Atlanta?

Her mind shot back to a conversation with Anita and Laura, early in their first year at Emory Law . . .

'Look, people choose law for a lot of reasons. For me it's money.' Anita prided herself on being up-front. 'If I land with a major firm – and I mean *major* – I'll break my butt for a few years. But then I can cut back on the insane hours, leave the office most days by seven thirty or eight, have some weekends for myself. And by that time I'll be pulling in a sweet three hundred thousand a year.'

'How many make it into the top-tier firms?' Laura countered. But Laura was not concerned. She would join her father and brother in a small but successful firm. 'Do you realize how many law-school graduates are out there fighting for those jobs?'

'I want an independent practice in my home town.' A hint of defiance in Kara's voice. 'I know I have no chance of landing with a major law firm there. They expect Ivy League colleges, Harvard or Yale Law School – or Old Family connections. No specialization. It's impractical in a town the size of Eden.'

She'd gone into law because she had an obsessive compassion for people in meager circumstances who were caught up in legal tangles. For them the need for a lawyer was panic time.

Grandma saw her mother robbed of a fair settlement when her father was killed as a laborer on a construction job because the contractor had cut corners. Grandma's mother settled for the money, to buy the tiny house that even today was the family's major financial asset. She knew how Mom's marriage had been annulled because Grandma couldn't afford to go to court to fight Roy Cameron, Mom's wealthy and powerful father-in-law.

'We're going out to dinner tonight.' Edie interrupted Kara's introspection. 'To Emily's. I made the reservation before Mom and I headed for Atlanta.'

'That's so expensive,' Kara chided her.

'How often does my granddaughter graduate from law school?' Edie's joy was contagious. 'It's an occasion to celebrate.'

'Tell me about my *pro bono* client. Provided I pass the bar exams,' Kara reminded them. No bar-exam preparatory courses for her – none available in Eden. She'd have to cram like mad on her own – every waking moment. Thank God, the exams wouldn't come up until late July.

'You're a shoo-in, Kara.' Daisy's conviction elicited an echo from Edie. 'You graduated in the top ten per cent of your class.'

'You made the law review,' Edie reminded her.

'Do you know how many grads have to take the exam at least twice?' The graduates who'd already been hired would be cramming for the exams with the help of lawyers in their firms. Laura was going to make the long commute to Atlanta for the prep course. *I wouldn't try to do it with Dad or my brother – that's as bad as having them teach me to drive*, she'd said. 'I hope this *pro bono* case can afford to wait.'

'Mattie's waited a few months in this situation.' All at once Edie's exhilaration seemed to dissipate. 'Ever since her husband died. I don't think you know her. Mattie Mason.' Kara shook her head. 'I know her from church. And she's a diehard mystery fan – like me. We belong to the same reading group. We exchange paperbacks.'

'Why does she need a lawyer?' Why did Grandma all at once seem so upset? And Mom, too. Mom always hunched her shoulders up that way when she was tense. 'I can't legally practice yet, but perhaps for now I can offer advice.'

'After Joe – her husband – had a stroke four years ago, he told Mattie he was the "hit man" hired to murder Eric Hamilton and Gerry Madison. He said he was blackmailed into killing those two kids,' Edie said with an odd, apprehensive glance at Daisy. 'When she married Joe sixteen years ago, she knew he had an unsavory past. He'd served time for theft and assault. But she prided herself on reforming him. He'd become a hard-working maintenance man at Cameron Insurance. He didn't make much money, but they got by.'

'Now Mattie wants to tell the police,' Kara surmised.

'After the stroke, he wrote and signed a confession and put it in a small metal box. He locked it and threw away the key. He told Mattie to take it to the police when he was dead. He didn't want her to know who hired him – it was in his confession. He said it would be dangerous for her to know. She was to take the box to the police and let them handle it.'

'But she was afraid to do that.' Kara was sympathetic.

'Mattie was scared what might happen to her. But she's a religious woman – her conscience said she had to bring out the truth about the murders. Now she's terrified that the police will try to jail her for obstructing justice.'

But now Edie's gaze focused on Daisy – and she seemed troubled again. 'Kara, you know about Eric and Gerry—'

All at once she understood her grandmother's anxiety. 'Mom's friends who were murdered the day after her accident.' This would bring the most traumatic event in Mom's life back into focus.

When she was old enough to understand, Grandma had told her how her parents had eloped, with his college roommate Eric Hamilton and Eric's girlfriend Gerry Madison as witnesses at their civil marriage. Her father was to leave in five weeks for his sophomore year at college. Mom had just graduated high school. He was determined to have her with him.

'*Tim and I didn't know I was pregnant,*' Mom had told her. '*He married me because he loved me and wanted to spend the rest of his life with me.*'

But coming home their car was struck by a drunken driver. Mom was injured but survived. Dad died. The lawyers for Roy Cameron had contrived to have his son's marriage annulled – and in doing so had smeared the reputation of a sweet, bright, outgoing eighteen-year-old. While 1973 was a period when many Americans pursued a liberal attitude towards out-of-wedlock births, most citizens of Eden considered this an act of lower-class families.

In truth, she thought, there were three Edens. The Old Families Country Club set, with Old Money. Grandma admitted to a malicious pleasure that Roy Cameron's New Money couldn't win him a place in that privileged set. The middle-class families, who struggled to pay their mortgages and their car loans and their health insurance policies. And the bottom rung, for whom life was a continuous struggle.

Grandma had been born to the lowest level, but through the years she and Mom had pulled themselves up into the middle class – though the scandal of Mom's youth still tarnished that standing among some residents. Grandma and Mom had convinced themselves that by her becoming a lawyer – a 'professional woman' – she would erase the stigma against the Jamison women.

In rebellious moments she'd asked herself why Grandma and Mom hadn't moved away – but she knew they were being realistic. Grandma had inherited the little house that had been her mother's settlement when her father died. This was their security. When her own husband walked out after several years of stormy marriage, Grandma had clerked in Woolworth's, taken in roomers. She'd hoped, somehow, to send her daughter to college. Mom had wanted to be a designer, Kara remembered compassionately – but there'd been no money for college after Mom's horrendous hospital bills.

They'd always managed, Kara thought with pride. Now Mom was manager and buyer for Eden's fanciest women's specialty shop. At Mom's insistence, Grandma had cut back to a part-time cashier's job at Smith's Pharmacy – her salary as of this year augmented by social security.

They were approaching the edge of town now. The lush greenery, the profusion of early-summer flowers evoked a sensuous pleasure in Kara. She was glad she'd come home.

Each time she came home from school she was conscious of new houses, new businesses, and most recently the new shopping mall – where Mom's shop had relocated just months ago. Smith's Pharmacy, though, was still on Main Street, where it had been for over eighty years. Folks insisted that most businesses would be moving out to the mall, where there was adequate parking space. Eden was behind the times in this.

'Daisy, instead of going straight home, why don't we drop by and visit with Mattie for a few minutes?' Edie suggested. Eager to relieve Mattie's anxiety, Kara interpreted. 'Our dinner reservation isn't until seven. I think it would make Mattie feel better to meet with Kara, to know she's here in town. The house is at Oak and Madison.'

'Sure, Mom. It's not much out of our way.'

'Kara, you don't mind, do you?' Edie asked. A touch of apology in her voice.

'No.' Kara managed a smile. Right now the last thing she wanted to do was to confer with a prospective client. 'I don't know how much we'll accomplish—'

'Just a bit of reassurance,' Edie soothed her. 'Mattie's had such a hard life.'

Daisy made a left at Oak Street, drove into an area of small, modest houses. Built forty or fifty years ago, most showed signs of loving care. Minute patches of grass were trimmed. Early flowers lined the narrow paths to front doors.

'Turn into Madison,' Edie told Daisy. 'It's the next right. Mattie's house is halfway down the block.' Moments later her voice grew shrill with alarm. *'What's happening?'*

Police cars sat at the curb. Ominous yellow tape closed off one house. A cluster of people huddled together on the sidewalk. Two cars from the local newspapers sat further down the block. Photographers were snapping pictures.

'That's Mattie's house!' Edie stared out of the window while Daisy drove past their destination to a parking spot on the opposite side of the street. 'Oh, my God!' A van was pulling out of Mattie's driveway. The coroner's van.

Before Daisy had drawn to a full stop, Edie thrust open the door, darted from the car.

'Grandma, wait!' Kara followed her.

'There's Jane Reynolds. She lives across the way.' Edie charged towards a white-faced, fiftyish woman, clutching the arm of another woman. 'Jane, what's happened?'

'Edie, you won't believe it! Mattie's been murdered—'

'Oh my God!' Edie's face was drained of color.

'She was stabbed to death,' the other woman added, flinching as she spoke. 'Her niece Val tried to reach her around noon. Val called her every day because Mattie's been so upset since Joe died—'

'I know,' Edie whispered.

'When Val couldn't get through on the phone, she came to the house, and—'

'Clara lives next door,' Jane broke in.

'I heard Val screaming, and I hurried over.' Clara paused for breath. 'There Val was, her little girl beside her. The two of them staring down at Mattie – lying there in a pool of blood. It's awful!'

'The police got hold of Hank at work.' Jane picked up the story. 'He came and took Val and Betsy home.'

'I gave the police a statement.' Clara's voice was unsteady. 'I never went through anything like this—'

'The police won't give out information about a motive just yet,' Kara began. 'It—'

'Oh, it was robbery.' Jane turned to Clara. 'Didn't you say the house was ransacked?'

'Everything was upside-down. I don't know what they took – but the living room was a mess.'

Not a routine robbery, Kara's mind pinpointed. Somebody killed Mattie to shut her up. He – or she – was after that box with the signed confession. She read this same conclusion in Edie's anguished eyes, and in Daisy's.

'Let's drive over to Val's. Maybe there's something we can do,' Edie said.

'Mom, do you think we should intrude?' Daisy was ambivalent. 'She must be in shock.'

'Let her see she has friends.' Edie was determined. 'Val and Mattie were very close. She'll want to know that Mattie's murderer is going to pay for what he did.' A wry smile appeared for an instant. 'Mattie was addicted to mystery novels. That and country music.'

'Val won't have a moment's peace until Mattie's murder is solved,' Jane said. 'Let's hope the police find who did it.'

7

'I'll buzz you later,' Edie told her. 'I'm anxious to talk with Val.'

'Mom—' Daisy struggled for composure while the three women settled themselves in the car again. 'You believe whoever killed Mattie murdered Eric and Gerry—'

'This wasn't just some intruder trying to rob the house,' Edie hedged. Worried, Kara interpreted, that they might be jumping to false conclusions.

'First thing tomorrow morning,' Kara said quietly, 'we'll go to the District Attorney and report what Mattie told you.'

Val's husband Hank greeted them at the door. Two neighbors were just leaving. Word circulated quickly in a small town like Eden.

'Remember, Hank, we'll be bringing over dinner,' one told him. 'And if you want me to take Betsy for the night, I'll be happy to do that.'

'Thanks, but Val will feel better if Betsy's here with us. We never know when she's going to come down with an asthma attack.' Now he turned to Edie. 'She's in the living room. Betsy's asleep – you know, all the excitement wore her out.'

Valerie sat huddled on a corner of the sofa. Her face ashen, her eyes red from weeping.

'Edie, I can't believe it,' she whispered. 'Who would do something so awful to Mattie? Everybody liked her.'

'You know Daisy.' Edie reached a hand out to draw Kara closer. 'This is her daughter Kara—'

'I'm so sorry,' Kara said compassionately.

'You're the lawyer,' Valerie recalled.

'Not quite. I still have to pass the bar exams. But your aunt was to be my first client.'

'Jane Thornton, who lives across the way, told us it was probably an attempted robbery – and Mattie walked in.' Edie was striving for calm, but Kara knew her mind was racing. All those mysteries she read. 'Did you notice what was missing?'

'Her TV was gone – and you know her collection of country music tapes? That's gone, too.'

Kara shot a warning glance at Edie. They mustn't discuss what they figured was the real motive for the murder. Not until they'd talked to the police.

8

'It'll probably be a while before the police release the – the body,' Edie warned Val. 'But if you need help in making funeral arrangements, I'll do whatever I can.' She hesitated. 'Did Mattie carry any insurance?'

'She had a small policy, with me as beneficiary. What she called her "burial money",' Val remembered. 'She always told me how she kept it in the drawer with her nightgowns.' Val shivered. 'I don't want to have to go there and look for it.'

'Right now the house is off-limits,' Kara pointed out. 'But I'm sure if you explain to the police, they'll allow someone to go in and find the policy for you.'

'I'll take care of that,' Hank promised. 'They'll realize we'll need the money for the funeral.'

The doorbell rang. Another neighbor had arrived with a casserole and words of sympathy. Kara marshaled her mother and grandmother across the foyer and out of the house.

'Tomorrow morning we go to the District Attorney,' Kara reiterated. 'He needs to know that this is something very different from what it appears on the surface.'

Edie was silent for most of the drive to the house. Daisy tried to alleviate the shock that hovered over them with talk about Kara's prospective law office. 'I know,' Daisy conceded, 'you haven't passed the bar exams yet.'

'I worry about Val's husband.' Edie dragged them back to the moment. 'I'm sure he had nothing to do with – with Mattie's death, but some problems might arise.' Kara's mind leapt into high gear. *What problems?* 'He and Mattie had an awful fight a week ago. Mattie said a next-door neighbor called to see if she was all right—'

'What was it about?' Kara probed.

'Hank and Val's little girl was born with a crippled arm. They'd just been told about some new surgery that could be helpful. But it's terribly expensive – and they have no health insurance. Hank wanted Mattie to take a mortgage on her house. He said he'd make the monthly payments. Mattie didn't see how he could do that.' She hesitated. 'Sometimes his temper gets the best of him—'

'If the police learn about that, he'll need a solid alibi for the time when Mattie was murdered.' Kara was grim.

9

'It wasn't Hank.' Daisy's hands tightened on the wheel. 'Whoever killed Mattie was after that confession Joe signed. Another hired "hit man" killed Mattie. She was murdered because she was about to identify Eric and Gerry's killer.'

'But who knew that – besides me?' Edie pondered a moment. 'Mattie was real close with Alice Evans—'

Daisy's shoulders tensed. 'She works for the Camerons! She buys at the shop now and then. She likes to talk about "working at the Cameron estate".'

'No,' Edie rejected the implied connection. 'Mattie insisted she'd told nobody but me. She was afraid to tell anybody else. Alice couldn't have known.'

'Why were Eric and Gerry murdered?' Daisy challenged. 'By a hit man from Eden – when they lived over in Salem?' Ten miles north of Augusta, Georgia. 'Eric and Gerry were coming here to try to stop the annulment!'

'How?' Edie was dubious. A question-and-answer game they'd played so many times.

'They knew something important – something that slipped past us. They had to be silenced.'

'How could they have stopped it?' Edie clucked in reproach. 'Daisy, you have to let go—'

'Kara, make the police discover who killed Mattie – and we'll know who killed Eric and Gerry.' Daisy paused for a deep, tormented breath. 'I know nobody in this town will believe it – but the trail will lead right to Roy Cameron.'

Two

Jonathan Cameron gazed out of the window as the Cameron Insurance Company jet approached Eden Airport. His father winding up a final phone call. His mother still engrossed in the copy of *Vogue* that she'd been reading since their plane took off at La Guardia in New York. It had surprised him that – with his father's hectic schedule – they'd flown up to New York for his law-school graduation at Columbia.

'*How could we not come up for your graduation?*' his mother had reproached him. '*This is a very important event in our lives. And you looked so handsome. I was very proud of you.*' Still, he suspected that she'd welcomed the prospect of several days of shopping at Bergdorf's and Bloomingdale's, plus several evenings of Broadway theater. And Dad mixed business with pleasure.

Why did he feel as though he was about to embark on a prison term? He was moving into a job other classmates would consider a plum. A high-paying spot on the legal team of Cameron Insurance Company that would entail trips all over the world. Ever since his second year in high school he'd known that Dad meant him to become an attorney.

'*Law's a great background for what lies ahead for you, Jonathan. One day you'll take over the company.*' Some years ago the company had gone public, but Dad made sure he owned controlling shares. Half the residents of Eden owned shares. To them the company was sacred.

Mom and Dad had been so good to him. They'd never hidden the fact that he'd been adopted at fourteen months, when he was abandoned at a police station in Augusta.

'*Those things leak out – it's best to be up-front,*' Dad had told him when he was about ten, though he'd known since he was four that he was 'special' because he'd been adopted. He knew about their son Tim, who had died in a tragic accident a few months before they adopted him. And they'd lavished all the luxuries on him that they would have given Tim. The best schools – including Columbia and Columbia Law. The finest summer camps. School trips to Europe at regular intervals.

Dusk was settling over the town as their jet came in to land. The Cameron Insurance Company's tiny tower – above the ten floors that made it Eden's tallest building – brilliantly lighted, a beacon that led into the town.

Sandra Cameron abandoned her magazine, pulled out a compact to retouch her make-up, ran a hand over the short, elegantly styled silver hair framing a face that would have been still attractive at sixty-six except for a ever-present aura of petulance.

'It's going to be a hot night,' Sandra predicted, gazing at the rose-tinted sky.

'I think you can bear it,' Roy Cameron said drily. 'Bart will meet us with the limo – that'll feel like suburb of Antarctica. You'll dash from the limo to the house, and that's air-conditioned to death.' A continual source of disagreement between his parents.

Dad and Mom never had any real fights, Jonathan thought – just these nagging, small exchanges. But longtime family friends talked about the storybook romance of Sandra Jennings and Roy Cameron – when she was nineteen and he was twenty-one and fresh out of college. He'd heard so many times the legend about how they'd fought her Old South family – the socially impeccable but financially shaky Jennings – who expected their only daughter to marry an aristocratic young man of similar background.

Roy Cameron had been the son of poor farmers, had worked his way through college. But from the beginning he'd had big ideas about his future. He'd seen what another ambitious hard-working young man was creating over in Columbus, Georgia – and there were dozens of others throughout the South at this period who were struggling to build insurance companies that would become powerful.

If Dad roamed at intervals – and there were snide rumors

that he did – he was smart about it. Mom wouldn't care as long as he kept it out of Eden, Jonathan surmised. They both relished the image of the perfect marriage, the perfect family. Dad carried his years well, his hair salt-and-pepper, his ruddy face exuding an aura of good health. Only a slight paunch hinted at an over-indulgence in rich food and a love for a nightcap. At odd – guilty – moments Jonathan asked himself if he'd been adopted to complete that image.

The plane rolled to a smooth stop on the runway. An airport crew rushed forward to facilitate their disembarking.

'There's Bart.' Sandra allowed herself a faint smile. 'I warned him to be here on time with the limo.'

Bart Jennings – years ago he'd told Jonathan to 'skip the Uncle bit' – was striding towards them. A tall, slender, silver-haired man who fought off weight gain religiously at an Eden gym. Something his sister taunted her husband with neglecting. Despite his constant posturing about being fit, Jonathan thought, Bart exuded a kind of physical decadence. Eight years younger than his sister, he'd never married, lived in a cottage on the family estate – his needs tended by a housekeeper who'd played that role for almost thirty years.

'You made great time,' Bart approved, glancing at his watch.

'That's what the crew is paid to do,' Roy snapped.

Bart exchanged a casual embrace with his sister, turned to Roy. 'We've had a little excitement in town today—'

'Like what?' Roy asked. Each time he came back home, Jonathan thought, he felt this covert hostility between his father and his uncle.

'A murder.'

Roy whistled. 'That's a rarity. It'll keep the police force busy for a while. Anybody important?'

Bart shook his head. 'A company employee – a cleaning woman. Brutal murder.' He grimaced. 'She was stabbed to death in her kitchen. I gather she walked in on a robbery.'

'Who was it?' Roy was curious.

'Mattie Mason. We gave her a job when her husband died several years ago. He'd been one of our maintenance men.'

13

'The name rings a bell, but I don't know her.' Roy dismissed this.

'Well, how would you know?' Sandra shrugged. 'Considering how many people you employ.' She was proud of the company's soaring success through the years.

'So, the wandering son is home for good,' Bart drawled. 'You'll miss New York. All that razzle-dazzle, living right in Manhattan.'

'I'll survive.' Jonathan thrust a hand through his unruly dark hair. A habit associated with tension. Why did Bart always make him feel defensive?

'You need a haircut,' Sandra told him while they settled themselves in the limo. 'You look like a fugitive from the sixties.'

'When do you take the bar exams?' Bart asked.

'In late July.' Now he understood that odd glint in Bart's eyes. Bart knew that Dad meant to train him to take over the company one day, but that was a long way down the road. Dad might be sixty-eight, but he'd be around a lot of years yet. Bart would like to see Dad step down and move *him* into the top position. After all, Bart had put in a lot of years with the company. 'Hopefully I'll pass on the first round.'

'Bart, what's the latest on the hospital scene?' Roy demanded, irritated by the small talk. He leaned towards the bar to pour himself a drink.

'I had a long talk with the lawyers this morning,' Bart said with an air of self-importance. 'It's coming along.'

'Set up an appointment for them to meet with me tomorrow.' Dad seemed testy, Jonathan thought. He always wanted Bart to know that *he* called the shots in the company's business negotiations.

'You know, Roy, you'll lose your halo in this town if the word leaks out you're behind it,' Bart joshed. 'And it *will* leak out.'

'That's your job,' Roy shot back. 'To make sure it doesn't – at least for the present.' He turned to Jonathan. 'We're moving into the hospital field. Right now we're negotiating to take over Eden General. That'll be the first in a chain of Cameron hospitals,' he added with relish.

Jonathan was startled by this new expansion. 'I thought Eden General was a non-profit hospital.' Sure, local people would be upset.

'A lot of non-profits are being taken over and run as for-profit hospitals. The old way isn't working. Too much waste, too much repetition. Eden General is in financial shambles. We'll go in and cut out the pork, run it with efficiency. And make a profit while we're doing it,' Roy conceded.

'How do you plan on doing that?' A hint of mockery in Sandra's voice.

'Know-how,' Roy said smugly.

While his father and Bart carried on a heated discussion about the future of for-profit hospitals, Jonathan struggled to mask his unease. Dad was almost revered in this town. But Bart was right. This hospital idea could tarnish Dad's image. People would see only that he was earning a lot of money. They'd overlook the way he brought efficiency into floundering hospitals. On the plane – before he became embroiled in telephone calls – Dad had talked about appointing *him* to handle a new division of the company. Could he have meant this chain of for-profit hospitals? He'd bone up fast on the laws against making deals with doctors. Dad just might be over-reaching.

'Roy, must we drown in shop talk the minute we're back in Eden?' Sandra broke in. 'Enough of this.'

'You won't mind spending the money a chain of hospitals will bring us,' Roy drawled.

'I was thinking we ought to give a dinner now that you're joining the company, Jonathan.' She frowned as he flinched at this prospect. 'You've been away at school so long. Let people know you're home to stay. I've had your room redone by decorators from Augusta.' Jonathan knew that his mother – despite being sixth-generation Eden – was contemptuous of local talent. 'If anything displeases you, just tell me.'

'Forget the dinner party,' Roy ordered. 'Jonathan will be studying for the bar exams.'

'Perhaps later.' Sandra shrugged. But the bitter glint in her eyes told Jonathan the party would be forgotten. She knew invitations – to people whom she would consider socially acceptable – would be politely rejected. She'd married beneath her. In the eyes of the Old Families that was unforgivable.

Mom refused to accept the fact that when she married Dad she'd lost her local society friends. Dad wasn't welcome in the lofty circle of Old Families. Even Bart had lost cachet, though he was invited occasionally to dinner parties when the hostess needed an extra man at the table. Nobody ever expressed this complaint to Jonathan – but even as a small boy he'd overheard his father's vitriolic comments.

'Hell, who needs those bastards? I can fly to the Capitol and talk to the Governor. Fly to Washington and talk to the President. Any time I want.'

New money opened no doors in Eden, South Carolina. In truth, Jonathan suspected, his father's enormous financial success was an affront to the Old Families.

Brooks, the longtime Cameron chauffeur – and bodyguard, because there'd been threats against Roy Cameron's life by vindictive policyholders – turned off the road, drove up the long winding driveway to the historic mansion that Cameron money had restored from earlier decadence. Built long before the War Between the States, Jennings Manor – renamed Cameron Manor – had fallen into decay by the time the beautiful nineteen-year-old Sandra Jennings had become fascinated by the ambitious, charismatic Roy Cameron – at twenty-one vowing to make his fortune in the county where his parents had been sharecroppers.

Within a dozen years Roy Cameron had restored the house to its former grandeur. A classic white-brick colonial masterpiece, with double galleries supported by Doric columns. To show their disapproval of their younger child's 'wild ways', the elder Jennings had willed to Bart the cottage on the grounds that in earlier generations had been the overseer's domain and later became the guest cottage. The cottage, too, had been restored – to coddle Bart's rancor at being denied co-ownership of the ancestral house.

'Oh, it's good to be home.' Sandra's smile was synthetic. Her husband and son knew she contrived to be away from

Cameron Manor on the slightest pretext. 'I don't know how people live up there in New York on a regular basis.'

Brooks pulled up before the house, hurried to open the limo door – his holstered gun visible as he pulled the door wide. Bart stepped out, turned to extend a hand to his sister. All at once Jonathan realized he was perspiring – though not from the heat of the day. He gazed out at Cameron Manor with a feeling – again – that he was about to begin a long prison sentence.

Three

K ara was conscious of a rush of anticipation as the car
approached the white Cape Cod – a towering oak on one
side and a sprawling magnolia on the other lending grandeur
to the modest house. She'd been home so little these last few
years. Ever since her freshman year at college she'd worked
each summer in Atlanta – where jobs in law offices had been
available.

She knew how Grandma and Mom hoped she'd settle
in Eden. So many local young people finished college or
grad school and left for big cities. But she'd never seriously
considered not coming home to stay. To be here with Grandma
and Mom. But it would be a culture shock, after college and
law school in the big-city environment of Atlanta. Eden's
population – even with all the retirees who had come down
here to live in the past few years – was barely 18,000.

'We'll have dinner at home tonight, all right?' Edie's voice
was apologetic. 'It's not the night for celebration.'

'Of course, Grandma.'

'I'll call the minute we get in the house and cancel our
reservation.' Edie shook her head with an air of disbelief.
'Today seems so unreal. A nightmare. One minute I was so
happy – and then we drove up to Mattie's house.' She closed
her eyes in pain.

'Tomorrow morning we'll go to the District Attorney's
office,' Kara promised once again. 'You'll tell him what you
know. That'll give the police something to work on.'

'I'll make dinner,' Daisy said, turning into their driveway.
'Kara, you still love spaghetti?'

'Sure, Mom.'

'There's salad makings in the fridge. And I defrosted a chocolate mousse cake,' Daisy continued.

It was tough for Grandma and Mom to focus on such mundane things – but it was the involvement in these that carried people through traumatic periods, Kara thought. Joe Mason's confession – and his wife's murder – catapulted Mom back into the most trying time of her life. Was Mom right? Was Roy Cameron involved in Mattie's murder?

'Daisy, turn on the air-conditioner,' Edie said when they were inside the house. 'It's so sticky.'

For a little while Kara was busy with transferring her gear – accumulated through the years at law school – from the car to her bedroom. She heard her grandmother canceling the dinner reservations at Emily's, discussing with the hostess the horror that had overtaken the town. Activity in the kitchen indicated her mother was busy with dinner preparations. Oh, it was good to be home.

Before they could settle down to dinner, the phone calls began. Grandma's friends kept calling to talk about Mattie's violent death. 'All you hear on the TV are reports about the murder. The town's in an uproar.' Everybody upset – even those who didn't know Mattie.

'Let the answering machine pick up,' Edie decreed at last. 'Until after dinner, at least.'

Kara was pouring coffee when somebody knocked at the side door, just off the kitchen.

'That must be Peg,' Edie surmised, rising to respond. 'She was on a private-duty case today.' Peg Dixon – their next-door neighbor since she and Edie were fourteen and high-school classmates – was a retired RN who augmented her social security checks and pension with some private assignments.

'Edie, I felt sick when I heard!' Peg declared without preliminaries. Her pencil-thin, wiry body stiff with shock. 'I came off duty, and right away somebody told me. I mean, that sort of thing never happens in this town!'

'It's happened now,' Edie said grimly, and Kara sent her a warning glance not to reveal what she knew. Not yet. 'Sit down and have coffee with us.' A familiar ritual.

'Oh Kara, this should have been such a wonderful day for

you,' Peg mourned, crossing to hug her. In the course of the years Peg had baby-sat for Daisy and then for Kara. She was considered a member of the family. 'But you look gorgeous.'

'You always say that!' Kara tried for a light mood. 'Have you had your glasses checked lately? I've got circles under my eyes all the way down to my knees.'

'This has been a bad day all around. I've been a wreck since lunch. There's an awful rumor floating around the hospital.' The others knew Peg was referring to Eden General, where she'd worked for thirty years.

'What kind of rumor?' Without asking Daisy brought over a slice of the chocolate mousse cake she'd defrosted earlier. She knew Peg's obsession with sweets.

'Well, you know things have been rough at Eden for the last two or three years. There've been weeks when they had trouble meeting payroll.' She took a deep breath. 'Now we hear whispers about maybe the hospital will be taken over to become a for-profit hospital. If that happens, will I lose my pension?'

'Not likely,' Kara soothed.

'Is that legal?' Daisy turned to Kara.

'It's happened in other towns.' Peg was grim. 'I never thought it might happen here. I don't know how much truth is in it – but folks are saying that maybe Roy Cameron and the company are behind it.' Now she retreated. 'Of course, some people think Mr Cameron has done a lot of good in this town.'

'Some.' Edie's face was an eloquent rejection of this.

'Edie, you know how I feel about Roy Cameron. But enough of that for now. Have Mattie's funeral arrangements been made?'

'It'll be a few days before the police release the body,' Kara explained. 'That's customary.'

'I feel so bad for Val. She and Hank just seem to have an endless run of bad luck. She hasn't been able to work since Betsy was born – except for that Sunday job she has at the supermarket, when Hank stays home to take care of the baby. And the doctor bills for the little one!' Peg whistled. 'Hank works two jobs, but they only just manage to get by.'

'I don't understand,' Kara railed – as many times before. 'In Great Britain national health insurance began in 1912. By 1949, thirty-six countries provided health insurance. We're supposedly the most enlightened country in the world – but we don't provide health insurance.'

'It has to come.' Edie sighed. 'If Congress would just get off its collective butt.'

'I hear the police think Mattie was killed by an intruder.' Peg glanced at the side door as though to reassure herself that all was well here. 'One thing's for sure, everybody's going to lock their doors – front and back – before they go to bed tonight.'

Kara awoke a few minutes past 6 a.m., after a night of broken sleep. Her mind focused on the somber hours before they'd gone to bed. She'd tried to relieve some of the tension with amusing stories of the last few weeks of law school – a time that blended exhilaration with fear.

They were all shaken by Mattie's murder, but for Mom there was more. She was reliving those horrible weeks right after her secret marriage. She'd spent her whole life since then under a cloud of disrepute. Many Eden residents still remembered her as 'that Jamison girl who tried to marry Roy Cameron's son by getting herself pregnant'.

Kara heard faint sounds in the house. Grandma was moving about the kitchen. Mom didn't have to be at the shop until a few minutes before ten o'clock, though – super-conscientious – she often went in earlier to make sure the shop was in top shape. There, Mom was up, too.

She waited until she knew the bathroom was clear. Grandma talked at intervals about installing a second bathroom, but there was never money that could be allotted to that expense. Not as long as she was in school. But that would change, she vowed. So she wouldn't be earning the kind of money the Atlanta firm had offered. She wasn't afraid of putting in long hours here. She'd bring in a decent income. Maybe not the first year, but she'd work up to it.

Showered and dressed, she headed for the dining area. Her grandmother and mother were seated at the table. A radio newscaster was reporting on Mattie's murder. The first murder in Eden in nine years – and the last had been a case of domestic violence.

'Did you sleep well?' Edie asked solicitously, ignoring the radio news.

'Fair,' Kara lied. Who in this town had slept well last night?

'They keep calling it a robbery,' Daisy fumed, reaching to turn off the radio. 'They have to realize it was more than that!'

'Grandma and I will be there when the District Attorney's office opens,' Kara soothed.

'We're giving them the motive. That's easier than working with a random break-in, isn't it?' Edie challenged Kara.

'I keep asking myself – why were Eric and Gerry killed by somebody who lived in this town? Somebody in Eden wanted to silence them. Tim's father – Roy Cameron.' Daisy was struggling for calm. 'He was afraid they'd come up with something that would stop him from annulling our marriage.'

'Daisy, you can't go around making accusations like that,' Edie warned. 'No matter what we believe.'

'But it fits into the puzzle.' Daisy was defiant. 'Somehow, Roy Cameron found out they were coming to Eden, was afraid of what they'd say. He tried to stop them—'

'I hold no brief for Roy Cameron – you know that, Daisy. But you can't go around accusing the man without proof.'

'Then let's find proof!' A vein throbbed at Daisy's temple.

'You know how people in this town feel about Roy Cameron.' Edie was choosing her words with care. 'He's provided a lot of jobs. Those who bought stock in the company bless him every night. He—'

'What about things we hear from other places?' Daisy challenged, and turned to Kara. 'Awful stories. How his sales force preys on the elderly and ignorant, frightening them into buying policies they can't afford. You know about the suits against the company. The national magazine articles. And a television network did an exposé three years ago,' she told Kara. 'They wouldn't dare do that if they didn't have damaging facts.'

'But Roy Cameron always manages to wriggle out of every ugly situation.' Edie grunted in frustration.

'People in town pretended those articles never appeared. They ignored the TV exposé. But it was out in the open for everybody to see,' Daisy countered.

'Mom, we're going to the District Attorney to make him understand the motive for Mattie's murder. We can't talk about our own suspicions. But once—'

'If Roy Cameron pops up as having hired a "hit man" to kill Mattie,' Daisy broke in, 'it'll be hushed up!'

'No,' Kara vowed. 'We won't let that happen.'

Edie's mind charged back through the years to that terrifying day twenty-five years ago. She was just about to finish her shift at the pharmacy . . .

'Edie, a call for you,' the manager said, his voice anxious. 'Eden General.'

'I'll be right there.' She gave her customer change and headed to take the phone. *Who's calling me from Eden General?* 'Hello—'

'Edith Jamison?' a crisp, impersonal voice asked.

'Yes.' All at once Edie's heart began to pound.

'She's in a stable condition,' the woman at the other end made an effort at reassurance, 'but your daughter Daisy Cameron has been in a car accident. She asked that you be notified.'

'I'll be there in ten minutes!' What did the nurse mean – Daisy Cameron? Daisy and Tim had gone to Salem last night for a party, stayed over at his college roommate's house, she remembered. At the hospital Tim must have given his name, Cameron, and somebody listed Daisy, too, as Cameron.

'Bad news?' The manager was solicitous.

'Daisy's been hurt – in a car accident.' She struggled not to fall apart.

'Do you want me to drive you over?'

'No, I'm all right—' *How can I be all right when Daisy's hurt? How bad is it?* She drew her purse from under the counter with trembling hands, fumbled for her car keys as she hurried towards the rear door to the parking area.

At the hospital she was directed to the room where Daisy had been taken after emergency treatment.

'She'll be a bit groggy,' the nurse warned. 'She's suffered a mild concussion in addition to a fractured collar bone and a broken ankle.'

'Mom—' Daisy was aware of her arrival. 'Mom, they won't tell me how Tim is—'

'Right now you just rest, darling.' The glance from the nurse – indicating something was horribly wrong with Tim – unnerved her.

'The accident wasn't Tim's fault.' Daisy's voice was slurred. 'That truck swerved out of its lane and hit us head-on.'

'We'll talk later, darling.' The nurse was moving towards Daisy with a needle. 'Just try to relax.'

Daisy cried out for an instant, then her eyes began to close. The nurse gestured to Edie to follow her out into the hall. Edie waited for her to speak.

'I'm sorry. Tim Cameron was severely injured in the crash. He died twenty minutes ago without regaining consciousness.' The nurse turned her head to a tableau just beyond. 'That's his mother being helped from his room.' Sandra Cameron was crying hysterically.

'He's nineteen years old . . .' Edie was cold with shock. He and Daisy so in love. *How am I going to tell Daisy?*

The following morning shattering news flashed around town. Eric Hamilton and Gerry Madison had been murdered on a strip of road just within Eden's town line. The two young people who'd been Daisy and Tim's witnesses at their marriage, Edie was later to learn. The town was in shock. The only child of the Camerons killed by a hit-and-run driver, and now Tim's college roommate and girlfriend shot to death. The *Ledger* referred to it as a modern-day Greek tragedy.

Later that day Edie forced herself to tell Daisy that Tim was dead.

'No—' It was shrill, agonized rejection. 'I don't believe it!'

'I know how much you loved him.' Edie reached for Daisy's hand. 'And—'

'We were married in Salem. We didn't tell you beforehand because we were afraid that you and Tim's parents would try to stop us – because we're so young. I want to see Tim!' she screamed, and Edie fumbled for the bell to summon a nurse. 'You're lying to me! Why? Because you found out we were married?'

A nurse rushed into the room, managed to sedate Daisy.

'There's no need for you to stay.' The nurse radiated sympathy. 'She'll sleep for hours. That's the best thing for her now.'

Edie arrived home as the *Ledger* delivery boy was tossing the evening's edition onto the front steps. She picked up the newspaper, read the headlines with a sense of having been thrown into an unreal world. CAMERONS ASK COURT TO ANNUAL SON'S MARRIAGE.

With the influence that Roy Cameron wielded in this town Edie knew the annulment would go through. But she was not prepared for the depiction of Daisy as a devious young slut out to marry the son of the richest man in the state. And three weeks later Daisy realized she was pregnant. The Camerons, as to be expected, refused to believe Daisy carried Tim's child.

Kara sat with Edie in the District Attorney's austerely furnished office. With growing unease she noted his reaction while Edie reported – in conscientious detail – what Mattie had told her. Harvey Raines was restless, almost impatient – but he made no effort to interrupt with questions. Finally, straining for composure, Edie concluded.

'Mattie planned on bringing you that metal box with Joe's confession this morning.' Had they found the box? Not likely. 'She was waiting for my granddaughter to arrive from Atlanta.'

'Is your granddaughter an attorney?' He cast a supercilious glance at Kara.

'I received my law degree from Emory yesterday,' Kara said. 'I'll be taking the bar exams in July.' She tensed before his air of condescension.

'Why did Mattie Mason feel she couldn't come to me alone?' He radiated skepticism.

'She was concerned that she might be accused of obstructing

justice because she'd waited months to come forward with what she knew,' Kara explained.

He reached for a buzzer on his desk, pressed.

'Mrs Jamison, will you please give a statement, repeating what you've just told me?'

'Of course.'

The door opened. A woman appeared, exchanged a glance with Raines in silent communication.

'Hannah, please take down Mrs Jamison's statement. Thank you for coming in, Mrs Jamison.'

Edie rose to her feet, exchanged a nervous glance with Kara. They were being dismissed.

Not until they were out of the building and in Edie's car did they dissect what had happened inside.

'He thought I made up the whole story!' Edie was out-raged.

'He didn't believe a word you said,' Kara agreed. Why had she been so surprised? After every murder, it seemed, the police were flooded with false leads. Raines considered this a false lead.

'Why?' Edie demanded, reaching for the ignition. 'Why would I make up a story like that?'

'He suspected we're after publicity for me. You know, the new young lawyer in town – hungry for clients. He was convinced we were trying to get my name splashed around in the newspapers.' She'd been too emotionally involved to anticipate this reaction.

'Lawyers advertise these days,' Edie scoffed. 'Right in the *Ledger* and the *Enquirer*.'

'He figured we were after big, splashy headlines.' Kara shrugged. 'I doubt that Mattie's metal box surfaced.'

Edie backed out of the parking wedge. 'What do we do now? We can't ignore Joe's confession—'

'You're sure Mattie didn't confide in anyone else?'

'Not even in Val – and they were very close. Mattie told me because of you – she was scared, felt it was important to have a lawyer to go with her to the police.' Her face softened. 'She couldn't afford to go out and hire a lawyer. She understood you wouldn't charge her.'

26

'The murder of Mom's friends is still on the records as an unsolved case,' Kara pondered. 'Harvey Raines wasn't pleased at the prospect of digging into a case that's twenty-five years old.'

Edie hesitated. 'I know it seems improbable that in some fashion Daisy and Tim's annulment is tied to Eric and Gerry's deaths – but for your mother's peace of mind we need some answers.' Her face tightened. 'And somebody has to pay for Mattie's murder.'

'We'll talk with Val,' Kara decided. But what could that do?

'When Joe died, it was sad – but to be killed through violence—' Edie shuddered. 'That makes it especially sad.'

They drove to Valerie's house. While Edie turned into the driveway, they saw the front door swing wide. Val hung there, waiting for them to approach.

'Edie, I'm so scared,' Val said. She frowned as the sounds of a children's television program filtered into the foyer. 'I know I shouldn't have television on at a time like this, but how can I explain that to Betsy?'

'Mattie would understand,' Edie comforted. 'But why are you so upset?'

'The cops came – they took Hank down for questioning—'

'That's routine.' Kara was guarded. 'It's just that—'

'You don't know,' Val broke in while they walked into the small, neat living room. She shot a nervous glance at Betsy, cross-legged on the floor before the TV set. Too engrossed to be aware of what her mother was about to say. 'Mattie had this nasty neighbor on her right—' She winced in recall. 'She's forever complaining that Mattie plays her tapes too loud – and she hates country music. Some mornings she'd call up to complain that Mattie had been playing her tapes at close to midnight – when Mattie was at work till one a.m. She told the cops that Mattie had a terrible fight with Hank just last week.' She took a labored breath. 'That's what they want to talk to Hank about.'

'You mean, when Hank asked Mattie to take a mortgage on her house?' Edie specified, and Val nodded. 'She couldn't bring herself to do that—'

'The new pediatrician over at Eden General – Dr Callahan, the head of the department – figured there's a good chance that a surgeon in Atlanta could repair most of the damage to Betsy's arm. Mattie loved Betsy like she was her own – but she was terrified of losing her house. Hank was so frustrated. He lost his temper and yelled.' She paused, her face etched with fear. 'And now I'll inherit the house.' To the police, a strong motive for murder. Val realized that. 'They can't hold Hank – can they?'

'He should have a lawyer present when he's being questioned,' Kara told her. *And Val will probably be questioned, too.* 'They have to allow that.'

'We can't afford no lawyer.' Valerie was fighting off panic. 'Hank gets so frustrated at times like this. He'll say all the wrong things.'

'Kara, what can we do?' Edie asked. 'They won't let you represent him?'

'No.' Kara's mind shot into high gear. 'What time did that newscast this morning say Mattie was killed? Between one thirty a.m. and four a.m.,' she added before Edie could reply. 'Val, where was Hank at that time yesterday?' Asleep beside Val wouldn't be an acceptable alibi. Not for either of them. Both prime suspects at this point.

'That was the night before last—' A sudden excitement in Val's voice. 'We were both in the emergency room at Eden General with Betsy. She was having an asthma attack. Dr Callahan said not to delay when that happened – to take her right over to Emergency.'

Kara exchanged a glance of relief with Edie. 'There'll be a record at the ER. I'll go to the police precinct, report this information on your behalf,' she stipulated. 'And if they want a written statement from the ER, I'll go right over and pick it up.'

'That'll clear him?' Valerie was anxious for reassurance.

'We're establishing he couldn't have been there.' In a corner of her mind Kara was uneasy with this simplification.

'Then he'll be able to go over to Mattie's house – if the police give permission,' Val said with relief, 'to pick up her life insurance policy. The funeral home won't make a move till they have the money up-front.'

'Let me rush over to the police precinct and take care of this. And while I'm there, I'll make sure Hank asks about going into the house.'

'Things are going to work out,' Edie said with a confidence that Kara suspected was contrived. 'Kara knows how to handle this.'

But, settling herself behind the wheel of Edie's Plymouth, Kara forced herself to face reality. She'd jumped too fast, hadn't she? Could she establish the fact that neither Val nor Hank could have been at Mattie's house at the time the coroner set the murder?

The coroner said the murder had occurred between one thirty and four a.m. *What time did Val and Hank actually arrive at the emergency room? What time did they leave?*

Four

Kara debated for only a moment. Go to the Eden General's ER, confirm the time slot when Val and Hank were there. *I'm not thinking like a lawyer. So I haven't been admitted to the bar – this is my case. Think like a lawyer.*

Pulling into the sprawling parking area at Eden General, she was conscious of a touch of nostalgia as she gazed at the three-storey white-brick structure, built thirty-some-odd years earlier and expanded through those years to accommodate a growing population.

At eleven I spent a night in the pediatrics section after a tonsillectomy. When I was fourteen, I waited – scared to death – with Grandma while Mom underwent an emergency appendectomy. When Grandma had a freakish accident with her blender, I rushed with her and Mom to the ER – and the doctors said Grandma had suffered a broken nose. Now there's talk about Eden General's being taken over by a for-profit group. That's awful!

She remembered a frequent pronouncement by Anita – her more cynical roommate: *'Kara, you can't stop progress.'*

All right. Enough stalling. Go into the ER and discover if I have sufficient grounds to demand that Hank be released. Was he – and Val – in the ER from one thirty a.m. to four a.m.?

She mustn't lie, she mustn't claim to be Hank's attorney – just use a play on words: 'I represent Hank and Valerie Thompson.'

In the ER – chafing at delay – she latched onto the head nurse in charge of records.

'I'm not sure I should give out this information.' The nurse was ambivalent.

'Call their home,' Kara said urgently. 'They'll tell you I'm

30

acting on their behalf.' No outright statement that she was their attorney – she couldn't say that until she had passed the bar exams. Now she spied the small local telephone directory on the counter at the nurses' station, reached for it, flipped to the proper page. The nurse was connecting Hank and Val with Mattie's death, she interpreted. Betsy was seen often here. Probably at times when Hank was at work, Mattie had accompanied Val and Betsy. 'Please, call Valerie Thompson. It's terribly important.'

The nurse crossed to the phone. 'I have to do this,' she apologized. 'This is confidential information.'

Kara waited while the nurse carried on a brief conversation with Valerie. She nodded in confirmation, brought out a record book, sought the required data.

'Betsy was brought into the ER at one twenty-five a.m. on the date you requested. She remained here until almost four a.m. Dr Callahan gave an order months ago to keep her here under observation for at least two hours when she was brought in – to make sure she suffered no recurrence.' Her eyes bright with curiosity, she wrote the date, the times of arrival and departure on a slip of paper and handed it to Kara. 'Betsy's a darling little girl – with such devoted parents.'

At the police station Kara talked with several layers of authority – scrupulously avoiding a reference to herself as Hank's attorney. A detective made a call to Eden General's ER to confirm what Kara had reported.

'This clears him for now,' the detective told her after conferring with others. But she was conscious of the stipulation 'for now'.

Several minutes later Hank was brought out from a questioning session. She saw his relief at being released, his gratitude at her presence. Not until they were out of the precinct and walking to the car did he verbalize his inner anxiety.

'They told me not to leave town,' he said. 'They said they might want to question me again—'

'That's routine,' Kara told him, but she understood: they had not dismissed the possibility that he had engineered Mattie's murder.

Hearing the car approach, Valerie was at the door when they

pulled into the driveway. Her face brightened when she saw Hank. She hurried down the few steps, darted across the tiny lawn to cling to him. 'Oh, Hank, I was so scared!'

'Hey, lady, what are you doin' to my lawn?' he joshed. 'I just seeded it again last week.'

Edie stood in the doorway with an air of tentative relief. It was time, Kara thought, to tell Val and Hank about Joe's confession, about the missing metal box.

'I have coffee up.' Edie smiled encouragingly at Hank. 'Val said you'd had only half a cup when you had to go downtown.'

'I need that.' But his air of levity was belied by the alarm in his eyes. He knew he wasn't out of the woods yet.

'Betsy's playing with Jennifer,' Val told him. 'She's going to have lunch over there, too. Everybody's so anxious to be helpful—'

'Where's my coffee?' He managed a grin.

'I'll get it.' Valerie hurried to the kitchen. Kara waited until Val returned with the coffee tray to brief her and Hank on Mattie's revelations about Joe.

'Mattie said she kept Joe's confession in a locked box – you know, one of those metal boxes people use for valuable papers,' Edie explained. 'I told the District Attorney about it, but I don't think he believed me. When you go to the house for Mattie's insurance policy, look around to see if you can find it. Though I'd take any bet that's what the killer was after.'

'Oh, I asked about going into the house.' Hank turned to Val. 'They told me I could go in with one of the detectives tomorrow mornin'.'

'I'll call the coroner then – to see about when he'll release the body,' Kara said gently.

'I still can't believe this isn't some awful nightmare—' Valerie hesitated. 'Kara, what'll happen when they discover the house goes to me?'

'There'll be more questions,' Kara admitted. 'But the ER records show you were there at the time of the murder.' No point in alarming them with the reminder that the police might suspect them of having an accomplice. They were already anxious about further questioning.

32

'The minister came over last night,' Val said. 'Such a nice man. He'll help with the funeral arrangements.'

'I think I ought to get back to work tomorrow.' Hank was troubled. 'At least, to the truckin' job. They get mad if I'm away more than a day.'

'Mattie would realize that—' Again, Valerie hesitated. 'The police will go digging for anything they can find. Mattie owned the house free and clear. The police will think that's a strong motive for murder—'

'It's a lot of money,' Hank acknowledged.

'Mattie never came right out and said it, but she never felt quite right about how Joe was able to own a house – and one without a mortgage. I mean, his job never paid much. He said something about being lucky with the numbers – but she didn't really believe that.'

'The house was probably his payment for murdering Eric Hamilton and Gerry Madison,' Edie said. 'But you and Hank wouldn't remember that.'

'But I do.' Val squinted in recall. 'I was about six, but it was all my mother and Mattie talked about for days. I mean, nothing like that ever happened in Eden. And now it's happened again.'

'You'll look for Mattie's policy tomorrow,' Edie reminded Hank. 'Then you can go to the insurance company and collect. And Kara will check with the coroner about releasing Mattie's body. I know how devastating this is for you, Val – but we're all here for you.' She glanced at her watch. 'I'd better get to work. Kara, drive me over and take the car for yourself. I'll catch a ride home.'

Jonathan slept later than he'd anticipated. But then sleep had been in short supply these past weeks. He'd have to put himself on a heavy cramming schedule, he thought – unaccustomed to the luxury of sleeping till almost ten.

He flinched at the possibility that he might not pass the bar exams the first time – despite his high placement in the graduating class. Dad would feel humiliated. He'd take it as a failure on his own part. But he had a job waiting. That was a plus. He wasn't facing the insane rat-race to win a spot as an associate in a good firm. No scrounging to set up his own office and praying that clients would walk in. He would have his own niche in the company in time. Dad made that clear. Yet the prospect was uninviting.

He glanced about his redecorated bedroom – designed by someone who meant to create a luxurious atmosphere for a prosperous young man, he thought with derision. At Columbia Law he'd shared a broken-down apartment on West 104th Street – where chunks of ceiling were constantly falling down and the hot water was dirty – when there *was* hot water. He'd worked too hard to worry about that – and, like his roommates, he'd had little time for a social life.

All right, enough of griping. Shower, dress, head downstairs for breakfast. Dad had breakfast three hours ago. Mom will have had breakfast in her room. That excessively feminine retreat that Dad had not shared within his memory.

As though aware of his footsteps down the lushly carpeted staircase, Annie Mae – who'd been the family cook and housekeeper for twenty-seven years – appeared with a pot of coffee as he entered the breakfast room.

'Good-mornin', Mist' Jonathan. Sure nice to have you home.' She carried one of the large mugs she remembered he liked to replace the delicate china cup and saucer at the one place-setting.

'It's nice to be home, Annie Mae.' The expected response, while she poured the strong chicory-laced coffee his father preferred. This had never truly felt like home. It was the place to which he came when he wasn't at boarding school or camp.

'What you be feelin' like this mornin'?' Annie Mae asked, her smile indulgent. She liked working for the Camerons. Dad always said, 'Be good to your help, and they'll be good to you.' Unmarried and with no children of her own, Annie Mae adored her youngest niece – who went off to college to become a teacher. Annie Mae boasted that her niece – 'wearing my lady's clothes' – was the nicest-dressed on the campus. 'I could make you some strawberry pancakes.'

'That'll be great.' In the years before he went off to boarding school, he remembered being spoiled by Annie Mae on those occasions when the governess was off and she filled in. Those were the times he'd felt almost as though he was like the other kids in town. Not 'the Cameron boy' – which somehow put up a wall between himself and the others.

'Comin' right up. And remember, it's gonna be a scorcher today. Not that we'll feel it here in the house.' She was proud of the central air-conditioning that had been installed – before her time – at huge expense.

Dad wanted him in his office a few minutes before two this afternoon. He'd have to dump the jeans, polo shirt and sneakers before he went there. He'd have to show up in one of the Brooks Brothers suits Mom insisted on his buying every year. Dad wasn't expecting him to start in at the company right away, was he? He needed to put in heavy studying for the bar exams.

Forty minutes later he left the house. He could steal one day away from the books, he thought in mild defiance. He'd take out the car that was kept for use by the domestic staff and for him when he was in town. He'd drive out around the lake, try to feel less wired. Heading for the garage, he felt a flicker of humor. Annie Mae never seemed comfortable driving the white Mercedes. *'I'd jes' die if I got a scratch on that beautiful car.'* Dad found pleasure in owning the three flashiest cars in Eden: the Mercedes, the red Jaguar, and the Porsche.

Annie Mae was right – this was already a scorcher. He welcomed the comfort of the air-conditioned car. No doubt about it, he thought, Eden was a beautiful town – especially at this time of year. The trees in full bloom, summer flowers everywhere, lawns an expanse of lush green carpeting.

That was one of the things he'd enjoyed at Columbia – a large campus set in the middle of Manhattan. All right, he corrected himself – not quite the middle but in the midst of the urban sprawl.

He'd drive out by the lake. Actually a pond in size, he thought humorously, but it pleased local residents to refer to 'Eden Lake'. Memories of coming to the lake with the governess of the moment to feed the ducks sprang into his mind. A treat he'd relished. Willows towered above the pond on one side. Flowerbeds in neat circles on the other.

Approaching the pond he spied a vintage Plymouth station wagon, its hood up. A very pretty young woman was staring – troubled – at the engine. He pulled alongside the wagon, stopped.

'Having problems?'

'I always knew I should have taken a course in auto mechanics—' Her smile was captivating. 'I stopped to look at the ducks—' She pointed to the large duck followed by a parade of tiny ones.

'After seeing them, how can anybody consider duck *à l'orange*?'

'Ooh.' She winced.

For an instant their eyes met in shared compassion. A strangely disconcerting moment, banished when she withdrew her eyes in sudden confusion.

'I turned on the engine, but all I could hear were weird clicking sounds—' She shrugged in frustration.

'Let me give it a whirl.' He left the Mercedes, crossed to the Plymouth, slid behind the wheel. 'It sounds as though the battery died—' He tried the key, nodded. 'Yeah, it's the battery. That click you hear is the engine saying, "I don't have enough energy to turn over."'

'Then I'll have to call a service man,' she said uncertainly.

'We may be able to handle it without that.' God, she was pretty. Eyes more violet than blue. Such an expressive face. 'There should be a jumper cable in my trunk. Let me check.' He strode to the trunk of the Mercedes, fished about, turned to her with a grin. 'One jumper cable coming up.'

'Oh, great! I'm furious with myself for knowing nothing about car repairs. And we should have a cellphone in the car.'

'Okay, both engines are off,' he said after a moment. 'Now it's a matter of connecting the wires.' He was conscious of her intense concern while he worked with the jumper cable. He managed a covert glance at her left hand – no ring; she was single. 'All right, try the ignition now.'

She slid behind the wheel, reached for the key, glowed when the engine turned over.

'That'll get you to your service station – but don't turn off the engine until you get there.'

'There should have been a jumper cable in the car,' she apologized. 'But I'm so grateful you came along.'

'It takes two cars to work this deal,' he reminded her. 'I'm glad I took this road—' Again – for a moment – he felt an exciting communication.

'I feel so stupid.'

'No,' he dismissed this. 'It's kind of paralyzing when the engine goes dead for no apparent reason. The first time it happened to me I was petrified. I thought the transmission was cooked . . .' Was she one of those women who figured she had to do everything a man could do? They were scary. He felt so drawn to her, yet ambivalent. Sure, she radiated charm – but she probably knew it. *Get a grip, Jonathan.* All at once he was anxious to be on his way. 'But it's a good idea to have a jumper cable – or a cellphone.'

'Again, thanks so much.' Her smile less outgoing now. Damn, he hadn't meant to sound so condescending.

'My good deed for the day.' He brushed this aside as inconsequential. *What the hell is the matter with me? Why am I feeling like a sixteen-year-old suddenly in love?* 'Happy driving.'

He drove away with a feeling of reluctance. Why hadn't he introduced himself? He didn't even know her name. Was she local – or visiting? Perhaps her parents lived here. The last few years so many retirees had moved to Eden. Was she here just on a visit?

Those last three years of almost no socializing were catching up, he berated himself. Every time a relationship seemed about to become serious, he'd moved on. He'd focused on coming up with top grades, graduating with honors. Dad and Mom expected that of him. It was kind of an obligation.

He'd move into a small place of his own as soon as he passed the bar exams, he thought with a touch of guilt. Dad and Mom would understand. He was twenty-five – too old to be under the familial roof. He hadn't been in full-time residence at the house since he was twelve.

Did she live here in town? Was she still in school, just home for summer vacation? She could be anywhere from twenty to twenty-seven. *Damn, why didn't I introduce myself? It would have been the cool thing to do. I'd like to see her again, spend some time with her. Am I overreacting – or is she very special?*

Kara followed the white Mercedes away from the pond. She read the bumper sticker: EDEN WELCOMES NEW BUSINESSES. What was his business?

Not many people in Eden drove a Mercedes. It wasn't his car, she realized – he wasn't sure if there was a jumper cable in the trunk. Did the car belong to his employer? Was he somebody's chauffeur – a rarity in Eden? Or maybe he was visiting.

She'd been too flip, she reproached herself. Why hadn't she told him her name? That would have been the friendly thing to do.

Why am I making such a production of this? So a very good-looking man – with a special brand of charm – helped me get the car moving. That's not the beginning of a great relationship. Focus on cramming for the bar exams. On setting myself up in an office once the exams are behind me. I don't need to be involved emotionally right now. That could become a hindrance. Be a realist. That's the road to survival.

Five

Changed into the requisite business attire, Jonathan waited for an elevator to take him to his father's penthouse office suite. The deferential smiles he'd encountered on the first floor of the building told him Cameron employees were aware that 'the son' was coming into the company. At intervals during the years he'd been brought into the company and presented to employees as 'my son, who'll one day replace me'. He'd never felt comfortable being the heir apparent – even before he realized the implication for Bart.

The elevator reserved for the penthouse floor – the realm of the top echelon of the company – had a museum-like quality. Persian rugs, the finest antiques, Waterford chandeliers.

Emerging from the elevator, Jonathan steeled himself for the royal welcome he knew he was about to receive.

'Jonathan, how wonderful to know you're going to be with us.' The white-haired, smartly frocked woman who'd been with Roy Cameron since the time when he'd operated out of two rooms in a run-down building came forward to welcome him. Cassie Bates had risen from lowly – underpaid – secretary to become the woman who protected her boss against all comers, no matter how lofty their positions. To see Roy Cameron, first they must pass Cassie Bates.

'I still have the bar exams ahead,' he reminded her, feeling strangely gauche in this situation.

'No problem there,' Cassie dismissed this, and frowned as others rushed over to greet the heir apparent. She waited a few moments before extricating him. 'Your father's expecting you. We have a meeting of division managers from all over the country in session already. Roy wants you to sit in on it.'

'Roy'. Only Cassie – of all the company's women employees – was allowed such familiarity.

The impressively paneled door to Roy Cameron's inner sanctum swung wide. He strode into the enormous reception area, dropped an arm about Jonathan.

'Right on the button. Let's go and join the meeting.' With his free hand he tugged at his necktie, loosened it. 'They've been at it about half an hour.' He prodded Jonathan in the direction of the conference room. 'Bart's got past most of the rough stuff by now.'

'I thought you said to be here at two o'clock.' Jonathan was apologetic. Why was he to sit in on a sales meeting?

'I did.' Roy pulled off his jacket, slung it over an arm. Jonathan understood: Dad liked to play the courtly Southern aristocrat in public, but he wanted to be 'one of the boys' with his division managers. On endless occasions he'd heard his father expound on the road to building a successful sales crew. 'I let Bart take them over the dull details before I come in. You know, point out how we've got to build up the sales so they can be sure of juicy Christmas bonuses. All that shit.'

Jonathan listened with a show of respect while Roy boasted about the healthy state of company shares.

'We've got a bunch of happy shareholders in this town. Most insurance companies pay back over eighty per cent of premiums.' He grinned in satisfaction. 'You know what we pay out? Less than forty-five per cent. That's why we're in top shape.' He reached for the conference-room door, opened it. 'Sorry to be late, guys,' he drawled while all faces turned to him with a mixture of welcome and apprehension. 'I was on a long-distance call – working out a deal with our Tokyo office. This is my son Jonathan. He's fresh out of law school and coming into the company. Bart, you go on with what you were saying,' he ordered.

'Yeah.' Jonathan read Bart's mind: *What the hell's Jonathan doing here? He's supposed to be on the legal team.*

Jonathan followed his father to a pair of empty chairs, sat beside him.

'I have to tell you,' Bart continued. 'Roy's not happy about the reports on the last quarter.' He shot an apologetic smile at his brother-in-law, and Jonathan suspected this was a set routine.

'My division's kept up with the last two quarters,' a burly man with a New England accent said defensively. 'We haven't—'

'You've stayed on a plateau,' Bart interrupted. 'It's like Roy always says. We're dead if we don't move ahead. In this field we can't be stagnant. Remember the heavy competition out there – with companies fighting like mad for subscribers. I expect you all to go out there and sell, sell, sell!' Bart's eyes moved from man to man about the huge mahogany table that had once graced the banquet hall of an eighteenth-century French palace. One of Sandra Cameron's trophies.

'Our fire insurance policies have increased twenty-three per cent in the past year,' a division manager whose speech indicated south-western origins pointed out.

'Screw the fire insurance!' Bart's face reddened. 'That's small potatoes. Today the real action is in our Health Maintenance Organization division. Do you know how many people right in this country carry no health insurance? They can't afford to see a doctor, be treated at a hospital. Remember, there's no national health insurance in this country.' He stared about the room with an air of triumph. 'All out there for us to pick off! You all go out there and see that our reps play their cards right.'

'We're telling them, Bart,' another division manager insisted. 'They know to ferret out the rural prospects. We tell them just like you told us. "Don't say to a prospective client, '*if* you develop cancer'. Say, '*when* you develop cancer'." And we don't let them settle on one policy – we've got at least a dozen that'll cover all the gaps for them. We scare the hell out of the bastards.'

'That was fine five years ago!' Roy broke in brusquely. 'These are new times. We've got to sell them full-coverage health insurance. We're an HMO today. Spend some time with the rural characters – but the big returns are out there in urban areas. I want you to sit down and study the sheets Cassie will give you when you leave. We've got all the statistics set up for you – all the approaches.'

41

'And you have to restyle your approaches,' Bart picked up. 'Your methods for dealing with rural prospects won't work with urban prospects. You need more polish, more finesse. Make them understand the thunderous bills they can pile up with four days in a hospital. Make them realize the high costs of specialists these days – and all the fancy tests hospitals and doctors are prepared to offer. We can't sit still and watch the parade go by. Damn it, let's *lead* the parade.'

Jonathan sat back in mental turmoil while his father continued his sweeping vision of the future of Cameron Insurance Company. At intervals he was conscious of his father's covert, appraising glances in his direction. Where did his law training enter this scene? He'd expected to become part of the legal team.

Now his mind focused on what his father had said earlier. *'Most companies pay back over eighty per cent of premiums. You know what we pay out? Less than forty-five per cent.'* Was it because the company was so efficient – or because it preyed on the most vulnerable of clients? Words he'd just heard tickertaped across his mind. *'We tell them just like you told us. "Don't say, 'if you develop cancer'. Say, 'when you develop cancer'."'*

Dad wanted him to hear the underside of the business, Jonathan told himself. Its worst side. The company sales reps didn't hang over prospective policyholders with a gun. When a claim came due, the company paid up. Didn't Dad talk with pride about the length of hospital time a policyholder was entitled to? He was proud of the care the company policies provided.

He was relieved when the meeting was over. This was Dad's way of bringing him into the business. Dad wanted him to know the overall picture. And yes, it was sharp of Dad to take the company into ownership of hospitals. Everybody said American hospitals – in many cases – were badly managed. Dad meant to get rid of the pork, put them in a sound state. So Bart went far overboard in his pep talk – the district managers understood that.

After a hasty lunch Kara had settled down with the law books.

Every law graduate knew the rough road ahead. Most of them were taking the prep courses. Those in cities where they were offered.

She was determined to pass the bar exams on the first try. But at intervals during the afternoon her mind trailed off to replay the encounter by the side of the pond. Who was he? A local resident or a visitor? Would she run into him again? *What's the matter with me? I'm reacting like a woman in some little sugar-sweet romance novel.* She forced herself back to the books until she heard her grandmother come into the house.

'I'm home,' Edie sang out, and appeared at the door to Kara's room. 'Would you like some coffee – or would you rather just stay with the books?'

'I'd love some coffee. I deserve a break,' Kara said with a lightness she didn't feel. *So much has happened so fast. Grandma and Mom are both more upset than they show about Mattie's murder. It's brought back such horrendous times.*

'I called Val to see how she was doing. She's awfully anxious now about arranging for Mattie's funeral. She spoke with the funeral home – they quoted her a shocking figure.'

'I'll go there with her if she likes,' Kara offered.

'Hank will pick up the policy in the morning. Val will go right over to the insurance company with it. You help her with the arrangements – let the funeral-home director know exactly how much she can spend. Val's so upset they might talk her into something way out of line. Mattie wouldn't worry about all the fancy trappings. She'd just want a simple, dignified funeral.' Edie waited while Kara cleared her desk, joined her.

In the kitchen Karen reverted to an adolescent habit of inspecting the contents of the refrigerator while Edie began the coffee-making.

'I made some low-fat lemon poppyseed muffins and froze them last week,' Edie told her. 'Little ones. Bring out four and throw them in the oven. We'll have them with our coffee.'

'Great.' Grandma had long ago indoctrinated this family with the importance of low-fat food. 'Oh, I had a little problem with the car.' Kara's smile was wry. 'It—'

'You're all right?' Edie broke in anxiously.

'It's just that the battery went dead and—'

'I should have checked it out,' Edie reproached herself. 'It's had a long run. You had to be towed?'

'No, somebody drove by and stopped to help me. He had a jumper cable.' *Would Grandma know who owns a white Mercedes? It's probably the only one in town.* 'He got the battery moving again.'

'You went to Mitchell's for a new battery?' Edie asked. 'I have a charge there.'

'I put it on my MasterCard.'

'Then I'll give you a check for—'

'Grandma, no.' Kara rejected her offer. 'I can pay for the battery – I'll be sponging on you for weeks, probably.' *When will I start seeing clients come in?* 'I'd forgotten how nice people are in a small town like this.'

'Was it somebody you know?'

Kara shook her head. 'But then I've been almost a stranger in town these past seven years.' *Does he live here? Will I run into him again?*

'It's so good to have you home on a full-time basis.' Edie radiated love. 'Your mother and I missed you so much.'

They were settling themselves in the dining area with coffee and hot muffins when Peg arrived via the side door.

'It's getting hot as hell,' she complained. 'I keep praying both my air-conditioners hold up a little longer. I had to go to my ophthalmologist this afternoon.' She sighed, then burst into a dazzling smile. 'Thank God for Medicare.'

'You're still seeing Dr Racine,' Edie recalled – and Kara remembered that her grandmother had labeled him as a 'greedy creep' who overbooked and kept patients waiting an hour to be seen.

'Yeah.' Peg's smile evaporated. 'I'm really pissed at him.'

'I thought you liked him so much. What happened?' Edie poured coffee for Peg, pushed the remaining muffins to her.

'Oh, I think he's a good doctor.' Peg reached for a muffin, bit into it with a murmur of appreciation. 'But I don't like the crap he's pulling.'

'Like what?' Kara was curious.

'Well, before I was on Medicare, he billed me seventy-five

44

dollars a visit. Then last year I went on Medicare – and the first time after that when I went in, Medicare sent me notification of how much they were paying. Now get this.' Her voice grew strident. 'The bastard billed my visit for two hundred and fifty dollars – as a new patient. I've been going to him for eighteen years! When I talked to his office, I got a bunch of double-talk.'

'But you keep going to him,' Edie pointed out. 'You didn't report him.'

'How can I ruin the man's life?' Peg was upset. 'I've known him all these years. But I'm pissed,' she reiterated.

'You hear a lot of that.' Edie was somber. 'Doctors who you've always thought were normal people with normal ethics. Jane was telling me. She's a mild diabetic,' Edie explained for Kara's benefit. 'And whenever she gets a tiny scratch, she runs to the doctor. Last month the cat got scared and scratched her. So she went to the doctor; he put on a little salve, and told her to forget it. And billed Medicare for "multiple lesions" at two hundred dollars.'

'The hospitals get a lot of blame for the state of Medicare,' Peg said, 'but some of the blame goes to the doctors. Look, we all know it exists – but we can't bring ourselves to report all these frauds.'

'Did you hear any more about Eden Hospital's being taken over?' Edie asked.

'Rumors are flying all over the place,' Peg reported. 'Most people are sure Roy Cameron's involved. But I didn't come over here to climb on a soapbox. I wanted to hear what's the latest about Mattie's death. The cops haven't latched onto the murderer yet, have they?'

Despite her announcement over dinner that they shouldn't waste a minute watching TV news, Daisy headed straight for the television set the minute dinner was over and the kitchen cleared.

'They'll keep throwing that hogwash about an intruder,' she predicted, and moments later this was verified.

'How can they be so blind?' Daisy railed. 'Mom, why do they believe you made up that story?'

'That could have been just a surface reaction,' Kara pointed at. 'They—'

'We have to do something!' Daisy broke in. 'We *know* why Mattie was murdered.'

'I'll do some back-tracking,' Kara said after a moment. Mom and Grandma expected her to come up with some action. She was conscious of a painful feeling of inadequacy. She'd had no real experience with criminal law except for the minor cases she'd been involved in in the summers, working in law offices. 'I need some thinking time,' she said gently. *I need to think like a lawyer.*

'You'll come up with some steps we can take,' Edie said with conviction. 'Mattie's murderer can't be allowed to run loose.'

As bedtime approached, the three women clung to the TV set while the late local news was broadcast. The lead item was a report of a vagrant seen in the area of Mattie's house on the eve of her murder. The police were trying to locate him. Thus far they had no real lead.

Waking in the morning after a night of restless sleep, Kara was aware of the muted sounds of the radio in the kitchen. Not likely there would be anything new, she surmised. Yet she felt a compulsion to become involved in the search for Mattie's murderer. Not just for justice for Mattie, but – hopefully – to put Mom's anguish about the murder of Eric and Gerry to rest.

Is Mom right in suspecting Roy Cameron is involved in Mattie's murder? That he ordered the killing of Tim's two friends all those years ago? Why do all my instincts agree with her? But so many times in these past three years Anita scolded me for making snap decisions. She said a lawyer couldn't follow instincts. Facts are what count.

Over breakfast the three women listened to what the newscaster called 'the latest report on the murder of Mattie Mason'.

'So Mattie's TV set and her collection of tapes are missing,' Daisy snorted. 'Can't they understand that's to make it *appear* to be a robbery?'

'Cool it, Daisy,' Edie soothed. 'Right now we have to get

through the pain of burying Mattie. We have to take this one day at a time.' But Kara knew that her grandmother, too, was steeped in frustration.

Daisy pushed back her chair, reached for her dishes and took them to the kitchen sink. 'I'd better head for the shop. We received a delivery late in the day yesterday – it has to be checked in.'

'When I talked to Val last night, she said Hank would be going over to Mattie's house before he heads for work,' Edie said. 'I'll call Val and see if she needs someone to stay with Betsy while she takes the policy over to the insurance company.'

'They'll probably want to see the death certificate,' Kara warned.

'Everybody knows Mattie's dead! And Val will need the money for funeral expenses.' Impatience at such red tape gave way to resignation in Daisy. 'I know – it's procedure.'

'I'll call the coroner to see when he plans to release the body. And ask when Val can receive a copy of the death certificate,' Kara promised. *I can't spend every minute with the books. Let me do what I can to help Val.*

'I'll call Val and tell her that.' Edie smiled in approval.

'If anything new comes up, buzz me at the shop,' Daisy said. 'It'll be a slow day again,' she predicted. 'Who in this town is thinking about buying clothes right now?'

Edie went to the phone to call Val. There was no reply.

'She probably went with Hank to Mattie's house,' Edie decided. 'She'll be trying to decide what clothes Mattie would have liked to be buried in.' She shook her head in anguish. 'I still can't truly believe this is happening.'

A little over an hour later – in her room studying while Edie vacuumed – Kara heard the phone ring over the thunderous noise. A moment later she heard Edie's voice raised in shock.

'Val, what do they mean – they won't pay off the policy?'

Kara hurried from her room to where Edie stood, phone in hand.

'Val, I'll be right over there with Kara. This doesn't make

sense.' Edie was indignant. 'Oh, it's all right – this is my day off.'

'What's the problem?' Kara asked while Edie put down the phone.

'The people at Cameron Insurance insist they're not obligated to pay on Mattie's policy. Because Mattie didn't die a natural death.'

'A clause in the boilerplate,' Kara interpreted. 'The policy pays off only on a natural death.'

'Then how's Val supposed to pay for the funeral?' Edie stopped dead, then sighed in relief. 'She owns Mattie's house now. She can borrow on that.'

'This won't look good for Val.' Kara was somber. 'The police will learn from Cameron Insurance that Val tried to collect on the policy. And they'll discover that Mattie's house – free of mortgage – goes to Val.'

Edie gaped in shock for an instant. 'You mean, this will make Val appear their prime suspect? Not that vagrant?'

'Probably Val and Hank – despite all that business about the vagrant they're trying to find. Here's a strong motive for Mattie's murder. An insurance policy in Val's name, plus a paid-off house in trust for her.'

Six

At Valerie's house Kara explained to her why Cameron Insurance refused to pay on Mattie's insurance policy.

'How will I pay for Mattie's funeral?' Valerie was shaken.

'You can borrow on the house,' Edie told her, and turned to Kara. 'Explain how the house doesn't have to go into probate.'

'Mattie was smart,' Kara told Valerie. 'When Joe died and the house came to her, she put it in trust for you. That means it doesn't have to be tied up in probate. I'll go with you to the County Courthouse, and the deed will be registered in your name.'

'Then you can borrow enough to pay for Mattie's funeral,' Edie pointed out.

'When do we do this?' Val was bewildered.

'As soon as you receive Mattie's death certificate,' Kara told her. 'It's just a matter of days.'

With Val less terrified about handling Mattie's funeral expenses, Kara went grocery-shopping with Edie.

'How did we survive without air-conditioning?' Edie asked when they left the comfort of the supermarket and walked in sticky heat to the car. 'Greatest invention of all time.'

'The next thing we get is a cellphone for the car,' Kara decreed. 'If the car breaks down somewhere on the road, at least you'll be able to call for help.'

'Oh, I was talking with the minister's wife when she came into the store yesterday.' Edie flipped on the air-conditioning in the car as she and Kara settled in, nodded with relief when cool air responded. 'She said her son and new daughter-in-law spent three days of their honeymoon in Columbia.' Where Kara was to take the bar exams. 'They stayed at Adam's Mark and

49

loved it. I want you to phone and make reservations for the time you'll be there.'

'It's great, but expensive,' Kara demurred.

'Darling, you stay there,' Edie ordered. 'Part of your graduation present.'

'Grandma,' Kara protested. 'You—'

'Don't "Grandma" me,' Edie scolded. 'Do it.'

They'd just put away the groceries bought at the supermarket when the phone rang.

'I'll get it.' Kara reached for the kitchen extension. 'Hello?'

'Kara, it's me.' Val was distraught. 'Right after you left, detectives came and brought me down here to the police precinct. They picked up Hank from his job. My neighbor's watching Betsy. They said I could make this call—'

'Cool it, Val. I'll be right there.'

Ten minutes later she charged into the police precinct. Right away she realized she was *persona non grata*. In their eyes she was a pushy recent law-school graduate – not yet admitted to the bar but trying to resurrect a twenty-five-year-old murder case for personal glory. Still, she contrived to have Hank and Val released, though with the stipulation that they not leave town.

'Where would we go?' Hank growled under his breath as the three of them left the police station. 'I'll be lucky if I don't lose my job after this nuttiness. Pullin' me off the job and draggin' me down here.'

'I don't want to think about anything but getting Mattie respectably buried.' Val's face was tense. 'That's what's important right now.'

'I'll talk with the coroner in the morning about your picking up the death certificate,' Kara soothed her. 'I'll go with you to the County Clerk's office, as I told you, and the deed to Mattie's house will be transferred to your name. Then you'll be able to borrow on the property,' she reiterated.

Hank's face brightened. 'That means we can move into the house. We've been rentin' for three years with a month-to-month lease. The landlord has some weird dream about how much he can sell for – but so far no takers. Instead of payin' rent, we'll pay off our bank loan.'

'I don't know what we'd do without you, Kara.' Valerie managed a shaky smile. 'Mattie was supposed to be your client – but now it's me and Hank.'

The next forty-eight hours were frenzied. Kara battled with the coroner to release Mattie's body. She went with Val to have the deed to Mattie's house recorded in her name, went with her to the bank to arrange for a loan that would cover funeral costs – a sum that stunned both Val and her.

'When I go,' Val said vehemently, 'it'll be in a plain pine box with no fancy trimmings.' But for Mattie she'd insisted on more, because that would show the townspeople her respect for her aunt.

On a humid, hot morning – the scent of flowers almost sickeningly sweet – Kara arrived at the funeral home with her mother and grandmother. Almost every seat was taken and more people were arriving.

'Mattie would be pleased,' Edie whispered, tears spilling over.

'Val's brought Betsy,' Daisy noted in astonishment. 'She's so young.'

'Val wanted Betsy to understand how much her aunt was loved,' Edie said. 'Betsy adored Mattie, and vice versa.'

But the police knew that Hank and Mattie had fought bitterly, Kara remembered. Mattie had been scared to mortgage her house. It was all she had if something happened and she was unable to work. She'd been too young to draw social security – and that would have been meager.

Jonathan swore under his breath at the lack of parking space. He'd have to drive further down and walk back. He felt uncomfortable on this first official assignment as a member of the Cameron Insurance Company.

'You'll represent the family at the Mason woman's funeral,' his father had explained at dinner last night. 'It's customary when any employee dies. Cassie sent a wreath of white roses.'

'I never feel human before noon.' His mother had shivered in distaste. 'I couldn't possibly go.'

'And I have to fly out to Dallas on business,' his father added. 'So you're elected. It's a family responsibility.' Bart, Jonathan recalled, had flown up to Washington D.C. this morning for a conference with the company lobbyists.

Jonathan parked five blocks from the funeral home, hurried back. By the time he arrived every seat was occupied. He took his place with the others who stood at the rear. The service had not yet begun, he realized with relief.

To his astonishment a woman sitting towards the rear smiled at him as though in recognition. He remembered her now, lifted a hand in greeting. She was a clerk on the main floor, had been with the company since he was a little kid. That's why Dad wanted him to come – so employees who took the morning off to attend the funeral would see a family member here.

He remembered her because she'd shyly slipped him a chocolate bar on a day when – no more than eleven – he'd stood by while his father gave one of his routine pep talks to her section. All these years later he remembered the sign of affection for a little boy bored and self-conscious at being there.

Now his eyes skimmed the assembled mourners, halted at the sight of the very pretty dark-haired young woman whom he'd encountered at the pond. As though feeling the intensity of his gaze, she turned, met his eyes, smiled. He lifted a hand in greeting. She returned the greeting. He felt a surge of pleasure at this encounter.

A moment later a woman across the room called out, 'Kara!' and waved. *She* responded. So her name was Kara, he mused. He liked that.

Now a hush fell over those gathered here. The service was about to begin. Bound to be emotional, he thought with compassion. It was clear that Mattie Mason had been well-liked in this town, the residents appalled by the violence of her death. And all were aware that a murderer roamed – undetected – somewhere in this formerly serene small town.

At intervals through the service his eyes strayed to Kara. Twice, it seemed to him, she turned as though to see if he was still standing there at the rear. When the services were over, he decided, he'd linger to exchange a few words with

52

her. Maybe ask her out for lunch. He waited expectantly for the moment when this could happen.

Then the last of the group of the friends who rose to speak about Mattie finished her tearful farewell. The formality was over. The crowd broke into small groups. He waited for the moment to approach Kara. Very casual, but not too light, he cautioned himself – this was a somber occasion.

Quickly he realized that Kara and the circle about her were to go on to the cemetery. No chance for him to talk with her, to take her off to lunch.

Disappointed, he joined those leaving the funeral home. But he suspected that she too would have liked to expand their acquaintanceship.

How am I going to arrange to meet her? Her name is Kara – that's a starting point. How many women in Eden are named Kara?

Kara listened with a polite smile to the conversation around her, then focused on beguiling little Betsy – bored and threatening tears. In a corner of her mind she pondered the reason why *he* – the man in the white Mercedes – was here at Mattie's funeral.

Maybe he's a reporter from a newspaper in a neighboring town. The murder is being covered throughout the county. But would a reporter be driving a Mercedes?

All through college and law school I steered clear of a serious relationship. Why am I reacting like this now? I can't afford to get emotionally involved. I've got too much on my plate already.

With her mother and grandmother, Kara drove to the cemetery for Mattie's burial. Afterwards – dropping her mother off at her shop and her grandmother at the pharmacy – she vowed to settle down with the law books. Yet her mind refused to cooperate when she sat at her desk and stared at the pages of constitutional law. When would the police drag Val and Hank in for further questioning?

Conscious that she wasn't to pick up her grandmother until four thirty, she made a sudden decision over lunch to go to the public library. Read up in the *Enquirer* and the *Ledger* on the two earlier murders. The library must have old issues on microfilm. But at the door – about to leave the house – she was halted by the sharp ring of the phone. She ran to respond.

'Hello?'

'Kara, I'm so upset,' Daisy's voice was shrill. 'Have you been watching the local TV news?'

'No. What's up?'

'We just heard that the police picked up some vagrant. They're holding him for Mattie's murder. I don't believe it!'

'Mom, he could be guilty.' Mom wasn't going to accept anything other than an accusation of Roy Cameron. But this would get Val and Hank off the hook. 'They must have some evidence against him—'

'It's enough that he's a vagrant!' Daisy paused. 'Kara, I have to go – a customer is asking for me.'

Kara hesitated. *Put a trip to the library on a back burner. Switch on the TV – see if there's any news.* She waited impatiently through a commercial. Now a newscaster was reporting on the arrest.

'A vagrant was picked up at shortly past eleven this morning. He was attempting to sell a television set that is believed to have been stolen from the Mason home. His story is that he found it in the woods behind the Jones Pants Factory, where he'd bedded down for the night—'

Kara flipped off the newscast. Her mind in high gear. Maybe he stole the TV set – or maybe he found it, the way he claimed. That would mean that the murderer had taken the TV to lead the police to believe it was a robbery and then ditched it. *It could have happened that way.*

But I'm not a detective. Right now my main objective is to study for the bar exams. Back to the books.

At four thirty p.m. sharp she was waiting in the parking area behind the pharmacy for her grandmother to emerge. From the set of her mouth as she approached the car, Kara knew her grandmother had heard about the arrest. Mom had probably called her.

'You know about that vagrant?' Edie said grimly, sliding into the front seat.

'Mom told me.'

'He's not the one.'

'We don't know,' Kara hedged.

'*I* know. The police are dying to close the case. They'll pin it on him.'

'He'll be assigned a public defender.' To the new law-school graduate, the equivalent of being shipped to Antarctica. 'If the PD can prove he didn't do it, then they'll have to release him.'

'This isn't just any murder case,' Edie rejected. 'It's not just that some monster brutally killed Mattie – and that's bad enough. But we know this is somebody who can't afford to have Joe's confession fall into the hands of the police. Joe was hired to kill Eric and Gerry – and you know what that means to your mother. We can't just sit back and do nothing.'

'Grandma, you've got an Agatha Christie complex.'

'For the last twenty-five years your mother has lived in the shadows – never a whole person. Haunted by the annulment of her marriage, ever shamed at bringing you into the world without your father's name. She made an existence – not a life – for herself by focusing on little things. She filled the crannies of her mind with your needs and the needs of the shop.' Edie's face softened in recall. 'She was proud to be chosen to buy for the shop, but she worries over every item, in case it's not right for the customers. *She doesn't have a life, Kara.* But we have a chance to give that back to her. Let her know – let this whole town know – that she was legitimately married to Tim Cameron.'

'There's no guarantee we can help clear this vagrant . . .' Yet Kara knew she must make every effort to do this.

'But if we do clear him, the police can't close the case.' An edge of desperation in Edie's voice.

'Call Val,' Kara said. Had the police found the vagrant's fingerprints in Mattie's house? 'Ask her if she's identified the TV as belonging to Mattie. One step at a time . . .'

At the house Edie immediately phoned Valerie. Kara stood by.

'Val, we heard about the vagrant. Did the police ask you to identify the TV set he was trying to sell? Was it Mattie's?

'It was?' Edie nodded to Kara. 'Oh, sure, I'll hold. There's some breaking news on the local TV channel—' she told Kara.

She waited, pantomiming her impatience, then was listening to Val again. Her mouth agape in shock. 'He confessed?' She listened a few moments longer. 'Val, I don't believe it. They probably just wore him down. I'll bet he did find the TV set in the woods! I'll talk to you later.'

'That doesn't give us much room.' Kara's smile was wry. 'He's confessed.'

'I don't believe it,' Edie repeated. 'You know how people confess to crimes, and then recant. For all kinds of crazy reasons. We have to prove he couldn't have done it.'

'Grandma, how?' Kara reproached. Then answered herself. 'We'd have to prove he was somewhere else at the time Mattie was murdered.'

'He was a vagrant, on foot,' Edie pointed out. These days people don't pick up hitchhikers. 'He must have been somewhere near here—' She waited expectantly for Kara to continue on this possibility.

'If we had a photo of him, we could make some inquiries,' Kara began. *I'm out of my mind. I have no time for this!* 'Maybe there'll be a photo in this evening's *Ledger*.'

'It's out by now, but ours won't be delivered for at least an hour. I'll drive over to the *Ledger* and pick up a copy,' Edie decided. 'You'll start dinner, okay?'

'Sure. What have you planned?'

Involved in preparing the chicken cutlets that were to be served at dinner, Kara chastised herself for plotting to try to clear the arrested vagrant. She needed to study for the bar exams. Yet she felt herself obsessively drawn into the case. Was it good for Mom to have the old wounds reopened? But those wounds had never truly healed . . .

With dinner made and the table set, Kara heard the car pull into the driveway. She strode to the door. Grandma's face was radiant.

'I have a photo of him being taken by the cops,' she called out in triumph. 'Of course, it's a little fuzzy—'

Kara moved forward to take the newspaper from Edie. Grandma was so convinced that she would know where to go

56

with this, she thought with a mixture of tenderness and unease. She stared at the newspaper photograph. A man somewhere in his thirties, unshaven, shabbily dressed. Just a vagrant, rare in this town.

Where do I go from here? Think like a lawyer who's fighting to defend his client. If he was my client, what would I do?

'We have to remember,' Kara warned while they walked into the living room, 'that he could be guilty.' Edie shook her head in defiance. 'We'll try to pinpoint where he was the night Mattie was killed. He could have been in jail or a hospital – or just shacked up in a shed somewhere for the night, with nobody to corroborate that. He did confess,' she reminded her grandmother, but again Edie shook her head in disbelief, and sank into her favorite armchair.

'He may be just some nut, or a drunk or a psychotic – but he didn't kill Mattie. He didn't steal the box with Joe's confession in it. Clear him, Kara. That's the first step.'

'I'll cut out just his face, have photocopies made – blown up. It'll be clear enough to be recognizable,' Kara plotted. 'Then I'll check in neighboring towns.' *Don't go to the police – to shops, fast-food places, hospitals.*

'You'll have time on your side,' Edie pointed out. 'He's not going anywhere. And he won't go to trial for weeks.'

'I'll start first thing in the morning.' Her mind began to plot. 'I'm a private investigator searching for the brother of a client. He's manic-depressive, hasn't been taking his medication. His sister believes he was headed in this direction. I may come up with nothing,' she warned. *And lose hours when I should be hitting the books.*

'I've got a map of the county.' Edie reached into a drawer of the end table flanking her chair. 'Here—' She pulled it out, handed it to Kara. 'Start with towns within a radius of twenty miles.'

'That's a lot of territory.'

'There's a lot at stake. Kara, we may clear him.'

At intervals in the course of the evening friends called Edie – all convinced that the police had nailed Mattie's murderer.

'He confessed, didn't he?' Peg said firmly on a late call. 'I was just watching the late local news. I hope he gets the death penalty!'

Grandma was convinced the vagrant was innocent – and instinct told Kara that Grandma was right. *But can we prove that?*

Seven

Kara awoke with an instant realization of what lay ahead of her today. *Grandma and Mom are so convinced I can clear this vagrant. They don't understand the odds against us. Why do I pretend such confidence? I don't feel that way.*

She'd leave just before nine, Kara decided, to arrive at her first stop – some place where she could have breakfast and ask questions – at a time when the morning rush was past. A flutter of the drapes at her bedroom window told her yesterday's heat had subsided. This would be a pleasant day.

She arose, showered – finding comfort in the sounds of the kitchen. The clatter of dishes, the sensuous aroma of coffee. She debated about what to wear. Not that her wardrobe was lavish. The blue linen/polyester pantsuit, she decided – bought for last summer's Atlanta job. For the low-key professional look. She dressed, headed out to the kitchen.

Edie and Daisy greeted her with good-morning smiles.

'Shall we live dangerously and have Canadian bacon and scrambled eggs for breakfast?' Edie asked. 'I'll cut back on the yolks. And we haven't had bacon in weeks.'

'Just coffee for me.' Kara chuckled at Edie's cluck of reproach. 'I'll have breakfast at a diner on the road – where I can ask questions.'

'You'll be having coffee in a lot of places,' Edie surmised. Kara intercepted the glance of approval exchanged by her grandmother and mother and felt a twinge of unease. They were counting so much on her to clear the vagrant. To keep Mattie's murder an open case. 'Switch to decaff somewhere along the line.'

'Take my car,' Daisy ordered. 'Mom'll drive me to work in the wagon.'

'Even with the new battery, I worry about my relic,' Edie admitted. 'Take your mother's car.'

On schedule Kara was on the road, *en route* to her destination of the morning. Beside her on the seat a dozen photocopies of the picture she'd ripped from last evening's *Ledger*. Outgoing traffic was light, incoming heavier. The countryside a spectacle of marigolds and cornflowers. Roses climbed everywhere.

All at once she tensed. Her heart began to pound. Was that a white Mercedes charging towards town? The driver was traveling faster than she. It *was* a Mercedes. Her smile was dazzling. She prepared to wave in recognition as the car drew parallel to her own. It was a white Mercedes – driven by a grim-faced, middle-aged woman. Disappointment washed away Kara's smile. It was the same car. Who was the woman driving it now? His mother? A fellow employee?

Oh, what's the matter with me? A good-looking man helps me out on the road, and right away I'm dying to meet him again? At Mattie's funeral I was sure he was coming over – but then I was caught up with the others. I turned around and he was gone. Why was he at Mattie's funeral?

She ordered herself to focus on the task ahead. Unless luck was on her side, this could be a long – possibly futile – chase. But she'd give it her best. She'd try coffee shops, fast-food places, the local supermarkets. If nothing surfaced, go to the library, read for the two days before Mattie's murder. Small-town newspapers often carried a police blotter column that mentioned vagrants picked up for some minor infraction. And all the while she felt guilty at deserting the law books for hours today.

On the outskirts of town she pulled off the road and into the parking area of a diner. Only a few cars, she noted – their morning rush was over. In the diner she ordered coffee and a toasted English muffin, questioned her waitress, showed the photocopy.

'Nope. I don't remember seeing him here.' She smiled apologetically and handed back the photocopy.

'Would you ask the others?' Kara offered an ingratiating smile. 'It's very important we find him.'

'Sure.'

But nobody recalled seeing the vagrant in the diner. Repeat performances in the course of the morning – over cups of coffee, small purchases at two supermarkets and a pharmacy, a visit to the emergency room at the hospital – elicited the same reply. Okay, try the library. Read the local newspapers.

'No, I'm sorry,' the sympathetic librarian told her when she asked if the man in the photo had been seen here. 'We rarely see a vagrant – except maybe in the dead of winter when one's looking for a warm place. I hope you find him.'

Now Kara pored over the local newspapers, found nothing. In a corner of her mind she remembered she mustn't ask questions at the police precinct. That would look as though she was intruding on the Eden police investigation. *All right, check off this town.* But there were seven more on the list she'd mapped out last night.

As Grandma pointed out, he was on foot. He must have passed through one of these towns before he arrived in Eden. *Can I dig up evidence that he was there on the night Mattie was murdered? The odds are not good. But tomorrow I'll try again . . .*

Jonathan sat at his bedroom desk on this third day in Eden and tried to focus on the page of the book opened before him. All morning – all afternoon – rain had pounded on the roof. Only now was the rain dissipating into a drizzle. It was strange how he could feel claustrophobic in this big house. But once the bar exams were out of the way he'd look for a place of his own.

'Mist' Jonathan—' Annie Mae's warm voice filtered through the door. 'Mist' Roy's home now. I'll be servin' dinner in a few minutes.'

'Thank you, Annie Mae. I'll be right downstairs.'

Mom had left this morning for New York. She'd spend a day there shopping, then leave on a three-week cruise around the Greek Isles. There'd just be Dad and himself at the dinner table, he surmised. But heading downstairs he heard Bart's voice. Dad and Bart would talk business all through dinner. Not much required of him, he thought with relief.

His father and Bart were at the bar in the living room. They'd dawdle over their drinks until Annie Mae summoned them to the dining room.

'What are you drinking?' Roy asked, a teasing glint in his eyes. 'Annie Mae says we have a couple of minutes before she can slice the roast.'

'Nothing, Dad.' He smiled. This was a routine they played whenever he was in the house. Dad knew he didn't drink, found it amusing in the face of his own hard-drinking habit. In Jonathan's mind, he'd got that out of his system his first year at Columbia. He'd never seen so many sick young drunks – including himself – in the course of the school year. The year of rebellion – grabbing at new-found freedom. But here at home he felt imprisoned. The school years, he thought wryly, were the good years.

'I'm puttin' dinner on the table,' Annie Mae sang out from the entrance to the dining room.

The three men took their places at the elegant Regency dining table. Roy and Bart deep in discussion about the thus-far covert acquisition of Eden General. Again, Jonathan felt qualms about this, though he knew his father's talent for bringing efficiency out of chaos. The company public relations man made sure this was circulated at regular intervals.

'Annie Mae, that looks sumptuous,' Jonathan complimented her as she set an over-sized plate before him. He doubted that his father or Bart – already digging into generous slabs of succulent roast beef with gusto – were truly conscious of Annie Mae's culinary skills.

'I don't care what the nurses say!' Roy grunted impatiently. 'They need to delegate duties to the aides. Hell, no business can make it big-time until the breakdown of duties makes economic sense. No business – not even a hospital – can allow employees making twenty-five dollars an hour to do work that can be handled by employees at the six-dollar level.'

Would locals be upset when they discovered that Eden General was to be reorganized, Jonathan asked himself – or would they realize Dad was trying to rescue a failing hospital?

Roy broke off the discussion with Bart. 'Jonathan, I want you to focus on studying right now. But you might find it easier to do that away from the house. Go over to the company and have Cassie show you your office. That'll be more conducive to studying than your bedroom here at home or anywhere in the house.'

'That sounds good.' It was perceptive of Dad to understand that. 'I'll go over tomorrow with a load of books.'

'And when you take a break for lunch, run over to Eden General and go up to the cafeteria on the third floor,' Roy continued. 'The people there will think you're either a resident or visiting a patient. Just sit there with your ears open.' He chuckled. 'Be my ears. I'd like to know what the staff members are saying about the takeover. It won't be announced officially for another two days – but I'm sure everybody there knows what's happening.'

'Sure, Dad.' Jonathan felt uncomfortable at this assignment.

Roy and Bart resumed their arguments about the takeover. Jonathan began to understand that this was a routine deal – for Bart to act as devil's advocate so that his father could nail the problems that might arise. At intervals in the course of dinner he was conscious of furtive, quizzical glances from Bart. Bart didn't just consider him the stumbling block to his own rise to CEO. Bart didn't trust him to be part of the Cameron team.

In the morning – well after his father had left for the office – Jonathan loaded books into a duffle bag, carried it downstairs and out to the car. At breakfast he'd asked Annie Mae if she'd need the Mercedes. She'd assured him she'd done her grocery-shopping for the week. *'It's all yours, Mist' Jonathan.'*

Arriving at the parking area beside the Cameron Insurance building, he parked in the visitors' area rather than the section provided for employees. He wouldn't be an employee until he passed the bar exams, he thought with a flicker of humor. But his future office here at the company would be a comfortable study area.

He left the car and headed towards the multi-doored entrance. All at once he felt a surge of excitement. He quickened his steps. That was the girl in the battery-dead Plymouth. Play this casual, laid-back. 'Hi. How's your battery behaving these days?' She paused at the door to greet a man leaving the building. He felt a rush of disappointment. It was somebody else.

Why am I so emotionally involved with a girl I've seen twice – for just a little while? Sure, she's great-looking – but it's more than that. I wanted to reach out and pull her into my arms, to protect her. Not just because the battery of her car went dead, or because she was grieving for a dead woman. I want her to be part of my life for always. Can it happen this way? Will I ever see her again?

The guys back at school would rib the hell out of him for this. 'Hey, we've been living like monks. You're just breaking out. Chill, old boy.'

He waited for the private elevator that served those who occupied the penthouse floor. Arriving at his destination, he sought out Cassie.

'Your dad's so proud of you, coming into the company,' she told him while she led him to the spacious corner office that was to be his. 'You should hear him carry on.'

Sometimes he thought Cassie was in love with his father, though he was sure it was platonic. And with a flicker of guilt he brushed aside the suspicion that his father received more love from Cassie than he received at home.

'Nice, huh?' Cassie interrupted his introspection. 'Your mother wanted to bring in her fancy decorator, but your dad overruled her. He said an office should be utilitarian rather than fancy.'

'It's great, Cassie.'

She beamed, telling him without words that she was responsible for the decor.

'It's real quiet here – you'll be able to concentrate on the books.' She smiled as he began to unpack the duffle bag. 'If you need anything, just yell. Oh, I forgot to tell you: I made reservations for you beginning on July twenty-eighth at Adam's Mark in Columbia. Your father worried they'd be booked solid if we waited. It'll be tourist season.'

At shortly past one p.m. Jonathan left the building and drove to Eden General. Feeling self-conscious – yet confident that nobody here would recognize him – he took the elevator up to the third floor, joined the line at the cafeteria.

There were few empty tables, he noted, anxious not to have to share.

The line moved slowly. He made his selections, paid at the cashier's desk, then headed for an unoccupied table for two. Tense and self-conscious, he sat down and began to eat. If someone joined him and started a conversation, how was he to explain his presence here without lying? His table was flanked by two occupied by nurses. The two young nurses to his left were avidly discussing a resident both had dated. The two older nurses at the other adjoining table seemed agitated.

'It's not just a rumor,' one insisted. 'Cameron's taking over here. And it's going to be hell. I know – everybody thinks he's a minor god for the way he's built up the insurance company and created so many jobs in town. But the kind of efficiency that works in an insurance company can only produce hit-and-run nursing.'

'We don't know that,' the other hedged.

'Oh, we know it! He'll come in and cut the nursing staff to ribbons. You've read about that – we all have. We'll be what's called "accelerated-care" nurses. We'll be drawing blood, learning to do ECGs—'

'Hey, that's kind of rewarding.' The face of the other brightened. 'It's sort of a promotion.'

'I came into nursing twenty-three years ago because I liked the prospect of helping patients. Getting to know them during whatever stay they needed. I like giving back-rubs and baths. That's when we notice things that need to be brought to their doctor's attention. I like soothing their fears, listening to their personal problems. I don't want to be a coach, telling aides how to do what we used to do. It'll be an assembly-line deal where we're rushing like mad – and I'll hate every minute.'

Somberly Jonathan listened. There would be trouble ahead, he conceded – even while he understood that aides could handle tasks that were part of a nurse's duty now. But aides wouldn't be trained to notice what a full-fledged nurse would notice. And in any assembly-line situation, there could be slip-ups. The accountants shouldn't rule in a medical situation. Yes, serious problems lay ahead.

*　　*　　*

65

Kara sat at the breakfast table and contemplated which town to approach next in her effort to clear the vagrant who'd confessed to Mattie's murder. He refused to give his name, was listed as John Doe. In the past five days – she'd abstained from her search on the weekend – she'd covered four towns and come up with nothing.

Edie and Daisy were talking contemptuously about the lead story on local radio this morning. Roy Cameron had announced that Cameron Insurance was taking over Eden General.

'He thinks he can do anything in this town and get away with it.' Daisy's eyes glittered with familiar rage. 'He's been doing that for the last thirty years.'

'We're living in an age of takeovers.' Edie sighed. 'Whatever happened to the anti-trust laws?'

None of the three at the table was surprised when the side door was flung open and Peg charged into the house without bothering to knock. They knew she regarded the hospital takeover as a catastrophe for Eden residents.

'Did you see this morning's *Enquirer*?' she demanded, sliding into the empty chair at the table.

'Not yet, but we heard the eight o'clock news.' Edie's smile was wry.

'And nobody's going to be upset about this?' Peg challenged.

'A lot of people will be upset,' Edie admitted. 'But it's a done deal. We'll have to live with it.'

'We're just beginning to relax with Mattie's murder solved, not looking over our shoulders every minute – now this.'

Pouring a mug of coffee for Peg, Kara tensed. *Mattie's murder isn't solved yet. Why are people so willing to accept that vagrant's confession? They must know that people confess – for no understandable reason – and then recant.*

'He won't go to trial for weeks,' Edie said, in silent communication with Kara.

Would the public defender assigned to the vagrant consider that his confession might be false? Kara asked herself. Not likely. *Would it make sense to approach him with what Grandma knows?* No. Harvey Raines hadn't believed her.

66

Nobody involved in local law enforcement would believe her without positive proof.

'I was so shocked when we heard how Hank had been questioned.' Peg brought her back to the moment. 'How could anybody have believed that he might be guilty?'

But if – when – the vagrant was cleared, Kara warned herself, then Hank and Val would be prime suspects. Not for committing the actual murder – because they'd both been at Eden General with Betsy when it happened – but for having hired the killer. Not until the real murderer was unmasked would Val and Hank be in the clear.

Eight

'It's going to rain – maybe pour,' Edie warned, following Kara to the front door.

'Will that light jacket be warm enough, the way the temperature's dropped?' Daisy called after her.

'I'll be fine,' Kara soothed them. She hurried to the car as the first raindrops began to fall. Bad weather was no excuse to stall on the job.

She backed out of the driveway, waved to Edie and Daisy, hovering at the front door. The weather was depressing, pushing her expectations to low ebb. *We know that vagrant is innocent – but what are my chances of proving it? I'll need an awful lot of luck.*

Within a few minutes the rain began to fall in torrents. Lightning brightened the sky. Thunder rumbled. Not a day for what she had in mind. But this case must not be closed.

Twenty minutes later Kara pulled off the road onto the parking area of a roadside restaurant. Rain was pounding the earth. She reached to open the glove compartment. Yes! A folding umbrella was there. With this meager protection she darted from the car into the restaurant.

She followed her set routine, with the usual results. Nobody here had seen the vagrant. All right, drive into town, play the whole scene. She approached fast-food shops, a supermarket, the local drugstore. Everyone listened with sympathy – but nobody had seen the man being held for Mattie's murder. One place left in town to check out, she reasoned. The hospital emergency room.

The emergency room was a quiet place this morning – in sharp contrast to the ERs depicted in television dramas. She was directed to the nurse in charge of ER records. She explained her mission, handed the nurse the blown-up copy of the newspaper photo.

The nurse squinted at the photo. Kara waited anxiously for a reaction.

'Yeah, he was here a while back. Kind of a nutcase, you know? Refused to give his name, talked about being involved in high-level spy investigations. Real delusional. He'd been brought in with head injuries from a fall. We kept him forty-eight hours, then released him.'

Kara's heart was pounding. 'Can you give me the dates when he was here in the hospital?' *Was he here when Mattie was murdered?*

'Let me check it out—'

'I'll be so grateful.' *Please, God, let the dates clear him.*

Moments later the nurse returned to the desk, placed an open ledger before Kara. 'Here, this is the entry.'

Kara took a deep breath, focused on the precise handwriting. He'd come in the morning before Mattie was murdered. He was released forty-eight hours later. No way could he have killed her.

Back in the car, Kara sat motionless behind the wheel for a few moments. Jubilant at this breakthrough. Her mind charged ahead. *Don't take this information to Harvey Raines.* It was important to keep a low profile with his office – she needed to practice law in this town without pre-established hostility. She mustn't appear to be trying to show him up. Ferret out the name of the public defender handling the case, she plotted. Turn over the evidence to him.

Grandma would get that for her. Then she'd call the PD at home, ask to see him. But now find a public telephone, call Grandma and Mom.

The rain had dissipated to a faint drizzle. Kara pulled in at a gas station, filled the tank at a self-service unit and then drove over to park beside the public phone. Impatient to relay her news. Her first call to the dress shop.

'Good-morning, Winston Specialty Shop,' Daisy's voice greeted her.

'Mom, I found the evidence.' Her voice deepened in excitement. 'The vagrant the police are holding was in a hospital

69

emergency room when Mattie was murdered. He couldn't have done it.'

'Oh, Kara, that's great news!'

'I'll call Grandma now. She won't mind, will she?' Normally Grandma disliked personal calls at work.

'Not for something like this. Call her right now.'

At home again, Kara aborted an urge to call Val and tell her what had occurred. No – this would throw suspicion back on her and Hank. Let them feel clear of that for the moment.

She must focus on boning up for the bar exams from this point on, she ordered herself. This was the most important hurdle in her life. Everything else must wait.

Grandma and Mom must understand – she couldn't perform as a lawyer until she passed the bar exams. And instinct told her that Val and Hank would need her legal services. For Grandma and Mom, finding Mattie's killer would be more than clearing Val and Hank. It would lead to finding Eric and Gerry's killer – and uncovering secrets that could change Mom's life.

Anita and Laura wouldn't believe that she'd allowed herself to be sidetracked this way. They were probably pounding away at the books – with the best of help. She was on her own – and spending too many hours on a side issue. Yet how could she have done otherwise?

Grandma and Mom must understand, she thought again, that every waking moment from now on must be devoted to study. Except that she'd track down the public defender, brief him on what she'd learned.

Grandma wouldn't be home for another hour, Kara told herself. *Settle down to study.* She reached for a book on anti-trust law, willed herself to concentrate on this. Totally engrossed, she was startled at the sound of footsteps in the foyer.

'Grandma?' She hurried from her room.

'Kara, I'm so proud of you.' Edie glowed. 'I knew you'd clear him.'

'I need to know the name of his public defender.' Kara walked with Edie to the kitchen to prepare the inevitable afternoon coffee. 'Can you dig that up?' Grandma's list of acquaintances was huge.

'I'll track it down for you right now,' Edie promised. 'Just put up the coffee.'

A dozen minutes later Edie came up with a name. 'You want to talk to Seth Rogers,' she told Kara. 'He lives just about five blocks from here, in an apartment his sister and brother-in-law set up for him in their house. A crotchety bachelor in his fifties,' Edie recalled. 'He tried practicing on his own for years, then gave up and took a public defender's job.'

'He won't live high on that,' Kara sympathized. 'I'll call him tonight, ask if I can come over and talk with him.'

'Hey, you're giving him his case. He'll greet you with open arms,' Edie predicted.

At an hour when she expected Seth Rogers to be home, Kara phoned him. As succinctly as possible she introduced herself, explained what she had to offer.

'May I come over and discuss it with you?'

'Sure.' But he sounded dubious. 'Right now?'

'In about ten minutes?'

'Why not?'

Kara walked to the modest, barnyard-red ranch house where Seth Rogers lived. He'd explained that his apartment had been created from the double garage and had its own entrance. She approached the door to his apartment – remembering that he'd sounded suspicious of what she had to tell him. Still, she knew he couldn't dismiss her without a hearing.

She rang the doorbell. He responded immediately. A rather seedy man with graying hair and cynical eyes. An attorney disenchanted with the profession, she evaluated him. A lot of those around, a professor had pointed out.

'I'm Kara Jamison,' she told him with a tentative smile.

'Come in.' He pulled the door wide. She walked into the small, book-littered living room. 'You're Edie Jamison's granddaughter,' he said with sudden comprehension. 'You live over on Maple.'

'Yes.'

'Scrappy woman, Edie Jamison,' he commented in approval. 'I remember meeting her at Civic Association meetings. Good-looking, too.' He ushered Kara towards a drab, threadbare sofa. 'So what did you dig up to clear my client?'

His face revealing nothing, he listened while she explained the facts.

'Okay, you say the guy didn't do it. You're telling me I can go over to the hospital and confirm those records?'

'The dates are there in the book.' Kara hesitated. 'You'll follow through?'

'That's what the court is paying me to do.' He shrugged. 'Poorly.' His gaze was quizzical. 'Why are you going to all this trouble when he's not your client?'

'In the name of justice,' she said after a moment, and smiled. 'I'm fresh out of law school. Taking the bar exams next month.'

'Welcome to the fold, counselor. But don't look for fancy pickings in this town.'

Within forty-eight hours local radio, television and newspapers announced that the confessed murderer of Mattie Mason had recanted. His innocence had been established. Again, local residents were locking doors and windows, glancing anxiously over shoulders lest the murderer be lurking and plotting additional mayhem.

Clinging to her resolve, Kara focused on preparing for the bar exams – constantly reminding herself of the urgency of this. She fought against guilt that she was abandoning her grandmother and mother by not trying to track down Mattie's killer. Watching the evening news with them a week after the official announcement that the Mattie Mason murder case was again open, Kara made yet another effort to explain her inactivity.

'I *have* to stay with the books.' Could anyone other than a recent law-school grad understand the pressure of these weeks? 'If I don't pass, I'll have to wait six months before I can try again.' An edge of desperation in her voice. Last night – conscious of the staggering phone bill she was running up – she'd talked with Anita and Laura about their progress. '*I'm working my butt off, but I'm getting terrific grilling here at the office. They're throwing everything at me so I'll be ready when I stagger into the exams,*' Anita reported. And Laura had gloated at having the help of her cram course. '*It's*

72

a life saver.' No cram course for her, no law-firm associates to grill her.

'We understand,' Daisy said, striving to sound convinced. 'The police are going to drag their feet on this for ages – but they can't close the case. Once you're past the bar exams, you'll be able to get back into it.'

A week later the Jamison phone rang while Kara was putting up morning coffee. 'I'll get it,' she called down the hall, and reached for the phone. 'Hello?'

'Kara, it's me. Val. We're so scared. It's starting again!'

'Val, tell me what's happening,' Kara ordered quietly. But she understood. Once again Val and Hank were prime suspects.

'Hank's buddy just called. He was nervous about telling us, but the police questioned him and two other friends of Hank's. They didn't mention Mattie's murder – just asked weird questions about Hank and me. Hank's buddy thinks we ought to get ourselves a lawyer—' Val hesitated. 'Will you be able to practice as soon as you take the exams?'

'It could be a month after the exams before the results are in,' Kara said.

'Oh, God! We know what sharp lawyers charge.' Val's voice was shrill with alarm. 'We could pay out everything we could get for the house – and still not have enough money. We know we'd have to pay you too, but you'd understand our situation, not expect it right away—'

'Grandma told you,' Kara said gently. 'You'll be my first case – *pro bono*.' Silence at the other end. 'Val, for you and Hank there'll be no billing,' she explained. 'But we'll have to wait until I pass the bar exams. I think,' she pursued, 'that we should play this by ear. The police can't bring you and Hank before a grand jury without some shred of evidence against you. They may eventually come up with something they think is enough for an indictment – but that could take months. By then I'll—'

'They know Hank and Mattie had a terrible fight,' Val broke in. 'That old battleaxe next door to Mattie told them.'

'They'll need more than that to face a grand jury,' Kara comforted her with a show of confidence she didn't feel. 'Time is on our side. Once the bar exams are past, I can dig into the case.'

Am I trying to play God? Should I advise them to go after the best lawyer they can find? Defense in a murder case can run into hundreds of thousands of dollars – they can't handle that.

But I'm sure they're innocent. I have to track down Mattie's killer – and Eric and Gerry's killer. Because they are the same. For Mom I must do that.

The weeks sped past, it seemed to Kara. The police kept Val and Hank in constant alarm – questioning and requestioning their friends. No arrest was made, yet Kara knew Val and Hank remained the prime suspects. Since they had not been placed under arrest, they were able to move into Mattie's house – the deed now transferred to Valerie's name.

'It gives me a creepy feeling,' Val confessed. 'I mean, knowing Mattie was murdered here. I just moved all of Mattie's personal things into one room and closed it. I can't do it just yet – but sometime soon I'll go in there and sort out her clothes to be given away. Give little things – like her tape recorder and her earrings and necklaces – to friends. Mattie would like that.'

'Mattie just had cheap jewelry,' Hank hastened to add. 'It ain't like she had the real stuff.'

'I knew that one day the house would be ours,' Val said softly, 'only I never dreamed it would be so soon.'

On the morning of Tuesday 28 July Kara awoke with instant awareness that in about five hours she would leave Eden to drive to Columbia. About a two-hour trip, once she was on I-20. All over South Carolina recent law-school graduates were feeling this same anxiety that was tying her stomach in knots. But she must be cool, go into the exams with a clear head.

Even at this early hour the weather was hot. From her bed she could hear the faint whirr of the air-conditioner that served the kitchen, dining area and living room. With her first decent check as an attorney, she promised herself, she'd buy air-conditioners for all three bedrooms.

In a sudden need for action, she tossed aside the sheet,

left her bed and hurried down the hall to the bathroom. She showered, dressed, headed for the dining area where her grandmother and mother were at breakfast. She felt her own nervousness reflected in them.

'Kara, you're not driving to Columbia dressed like that?' Edie was shocked. 'Those beat-up shorts and a T-shirt?'

'I'm not leaving until noon,' Kara reminded her. 'I'll change into something respectable. But what does it matter what I wear on the drive to the motel? The exams don't start until tomorrow.'

'You never know who you'll run into once you leave the house. And here you're going all the way to Columbia – you'll be meeting all kinds of people.' Interpretation, Kara thought tenderly, she'd be meeting young men. Deep inside, Grandma was such a romantic.

Before Daisy left for the shop, she insisted that Kara lay out her traveling outfit. 'I want to visualize you arriving at Adam's Mark.' Daisy's smile was radiant – her eyes filling with sentimental tears. 'I know you're going to do so well on the exam.'

Kara laughed. 'Just pray that I pass it.'

To her astonishment Kara realized her grandmother had taken the day off.

'I'd be making all kinds of mistakes at the cash register,' Edie said. 'I want to be here with you until you leave. And when you come home Friday night you'll be a full-fledged lawyer. My granddaughter, the attorney.' She glowed. 'Oh, sure – we'll have to wait maybe a month before the letter comes. But I know you'll make it.'

At a few minutes before noon – weekender in tow and her grandmother at her side – Kara headed for the car. This morning her mother had taken the old station wagon and left the less ancient Dodge Spirit for Kara.

'Drive carefully, darling,' Edie ordered and kissed her goodbye.

'I'll call you tomorrow night,' Kara promised. 'After the first day of tests. I know you and Mom will say a special prayer for me.'

'I have no doubts,' Edie said exuberantly. 'Friday night you'll come home a member of the bar.'

Driving on I-20 – which would take her directly into Columbia – Kara ran through in her mind details of the days ahead. The exams would be sat on Wednesday, Thursday and Friday, from eight a.m. to four thirty p.m., with a short break for lunch. They'd be given at the Canty building on the State Fair Grounds. About a ten-minute drive from Adam's Mark, she calculated. There was a restaurant at the Mark – Finlay's – where she could have dinner tonight and breakfast in the morning.

Traffic was light. She was making excellent time, she noted with approval. Now she was conscious of faint hunger. She'd been too uptight this morning to eat much breakfast. She began to watch for a pleasant place to stop for lunch. *Ah, there*, she decided at the sight of a diner, and swung off the road.

She lingered pleasurably over crab-meat croquettes with summer slaw, swigged iced coffee. The countryside so lush, wild flowers a sensuous delight. A young couple at the table to her right held hands under the table.

Her mind darted back to the encounters with the man who'd helped her with the car when the battery died and who'd seemed eager to resume their acquaintance at Mattie's funeral. Why did he linger in her mind this way?

During the years at college and law school she'd allowed herself almost no social life. Anita used to tease her about her one-track mind. Except in their most hectic moments Anita and Laura managed some social life. Laura called her their resident nun. But school was behind her now. Was she just overly susceptible now to friendly – charming – men of her own age? Her mind denied this. The man with the white Mercedes was special.

Shortly after three she arrived at Columbia – a sprawling, busy, modern city in the center of the state. Home of the University of South Carolina, with its famous tree-lined Horseshoe – both dating back to 1801.

As a high-school freshman she'd been part of a group that toured Columbia, where in early 1865 General Sherman had invaded, incinerating two-thirds of the city. Only a few early structures had been spared. The first Baptist church – the scene of secession – spared because, when Union troops asked directions to this spot, they were directed instead to the Methodist church. A few *ante-bellum* mansions and public buildings had not been razed.

Kara drove past the expansive university campus and into downtown Columbia – one of the first planned cities in the country, with streets that are among the widest in America. She turned off onto the parking area of the posh, newly renovated Adam's Mark and searched for an unoccupied wedge. A sea of cars met her eyes. Instinct told her that other bar-exam candidates were already ensconced in some of the hotel's 296 guest rooms and four suites. For all of them – including herself – the next three days would probably be the most traumatic of their lives.

There, she noted with relief, *an empty spot*. And then her heart began to pound. The empty wedge was flanked by a late-model white Mercedes. No, it wasn't *his* car, her mind derided her. It probably belonged to some CEO here for a business convention. But, parked and striding away from the car, she noted the bumper sticker on the white Mercedes: 'EDEN WELCOMES NEW BUSINESSES'.

His Mercedes.

Nine

K ara settled herself in her spacious room, hung away her clothes in the attractive armoire, piled the cluster of books she'd brought along for last-minute cramming on the desk. She was aware that the hotel amenities included an indoor pool, a hot tub and a health club – but it was unlikely that she would avail herself of these pleasures. She'd go down to the restaurant for an early dinner, she decided – before the crowd descended. Was *he* here – or had someone else been driving the white Mercedes? She remembered seeing a middle-aged woman behind the wheel of the car on another occasion.

Don't let my mind be derailed. I'm here to take the bar exams. She reached for a book. A pair of pillows at her back, she sprawled on the bed and tried to focus on a loose-leaf book of notes. But at errant moments she visualized the white Mercedes in the parking area. Was *he* here for some business conference? Could he be here for the bar exams? The possibility was exhilarating.

What is the matter with me? I'm a twenty-four-year-old professional woman – but I'm behaving like a naïve, madly romantic sixteen-year-old!

Shortly before six she headed for Finlay's. Self-conscious in the knowledge that she had wasted an amazing amount of thought and time on what to wear to the restaurant, likely to be sparsely occupied at this early hour. She was impressed by the spectacular atrium that housed the restaurant, the wood-wrapped columns. She was immediately seated, focused on the expansive menu.

As though feeling the weight of eyes, she lifted her head and gazed up at an arriving diner. Her face lit up. She felt a surge of anticipation. *He's here.* She smiled in recognition, lifted a hand in response to his own tentative wave.

She saw him indicate that he'd like to be seated at her table. There was nothing wrong about that, she told herself defensively. What was it about him that drew her to him this way?

Was he here for the bar exams? Was he going to be an associate at Condon & Jenkins, or Rogers & Langley – the two major law firms in Eden? Or was he just waiting to pass the bar and head for some major firm in New York or Chicago or Los Angeles, where the money could soar to over $400,000 for associates who made the grade? Or was his appearance here just a coincidence? Was he attending some business convention?

'Your battery behaving lately?' He paused at her table with an ingratiating smile.

'Perfectly.' This was like a meeting in a made-for-TV movie designed for romantic women viewers.

'Maybe I join you?' All at once a hesitancy in his manner that she found endearing.

'Please do.' With an air of relief he sat across from her. She felt herself in the midst of a dream sequence. 'What brought you to Columbia?'

His face was eloquent, expressing tension, anxiety and anticipation simultaneously. 'I'm taking the bar exams.' Now she saw a sudden realization in his eyes. 'You too?' An instant camaraderie in this suspicion.

'Yes.' It was a joyous confirmation.

'Are you as nervous as I am?' His smile charismatic.

'Oh, yes.' But she seemed all at once less nervous because she was sharing this trauma with him.

They paused now to concentrate on ordering, both pleased that the other also chose the sea bass with fennel, orange zest and Pernod. With ordering out of the way, Kara asked where he had gone to law school.

'Columbia,' he told her. 'And you?'

'Emory,' she told him. Not as prestigious as Columbia, she conceded, but still a top school. Graduates included Sam Nunn and Newt Gingrich. 'I loved it. I was able to intern while I was a full-time student. Of course, our major obligation was to school.'

'Columbia was great. I liked being right in Manhattan for three years. Though I don't think I'd want to live there the rest of my life.'

'I wouldn't want to work at one of those huge Wall Street law firms.' She shivered in distaste. 'Not from what I've heard.' But Anita prayed to make it at one of the super-firms.

'Wall Street is just a phrase.' He chuckled. 'Some of the major law firms are right in midtown Manhattan. I know, the money is great – but the pressure, the hours, are devastating. I want to be able to live a little, too.'

'A friend of mine is enthralled at being hired by one of those super-firms. She says for the ninety thousand they're paying her she'll handle hundred-hour weeks, even the over-nighters.'

'But there's a lot more to life than billable hours,' he said quietly, his eyes holding hers. Appraising, sensing with an air of pleasure that she agreed with him. 'I'm not interested in huge corporate lawsuits.'

'Not much of that pops up in Eden.' Where did his interests lie? Politics? Public service? Where would he be practicing? All at once she was impatient to know.

'I had my destination pre-ordained.' His eyes conveyed a blend of rebellion and resignation. 'Before I started college, my father made it clear I had a job – as an attorney – in his company.'

'In Eden?' Her heart was suddenly pounding.

'Right. With my father's insurance company. Isn't it about time we introduced ourselves?' he said with a hint of indulgent laughter. 'I feel as though we've known each other for ages. I'm Jonathan Cameron. Once I pass the bar exams, I'll be working for Cameron Insurance.'

'I'm Kara Jamison.' She fought for poise. Reeling from his disclosure. But the Jamison name would mean nothing to him, she guessed. It wasn't a subject the Camerons would discuss. *But he's the child the Camerons adopted when my father was killed.*

'Kara,' he mused. 'That means "dear one".'

'That's what my mother and grandmother told me.' She strove for lightness. Why couldn't he be just some ordinary person? Why did he have to be a Cameron?

'You'll be practicing in Eden?' His voice said he hoped she would. 'I was afraid you might just be visiting.'

'I'll be opening up an independent practice in town.' Her mind was in chaos. *Here I've met what Laura would call 'this wonderful man' – but such barriers exist between us.* 'I know it's hazardous.'

'I'd like to do that too,' he confessed. 'I'd like to feel that I was in a position to help people who truly need me. That I could provide a service.' He shrugged. 'Maybe one of these days I'll be able to move out on my own. But right now I feel I have an obligation to my parents.'

He didn't elaborate. She understood. He clearly knew how the Camerons had adopted him when he'd been abandoned as a baby. *I have an obligation, too. To Grandma and Mom – and now to Val and Hank. And to Mattie.*

'Of course, first I have to pass the bar exams.' Her smile was eloquent. 'Then comes the hassle of setting up my own office – and praying for clients.' She hesitated a moment. 'I was surprised when I glanced up at Mattie Mason's funeral and saw you there—'

'I was hoping we could talk – but right away you were swept up in what I gather were her family and friends. I was there to represent the company. She'd been an employee. Dad always makes sure that a member of the family is at the funeral of employees.'

'How nice.' She struggled not to sound sarcastic. What would he think if he knew that Grandma and Mom – and she – suspected his adoptive father was involved in Mattie's murder?

'I haven't spent a lot of time in Eden through the years—' He seemed to be apologetic. 'I was away at school an awful lot. But I want to settle down in the town now, feel I'm part of it. My friends from Columbia Law think I'm out of my mind to consider practicing here.'

'Mine too. But I know what you mean,' she said. 'You want to be part of a town. To serve it.' *But his father wants to rule it. What can there ever be for Jonathan and me? Be realistic.*

'In many ways I've been very lucky.' He knew she was aware of the Cameron fortune, she interpreted. 'I think I have a debt to pay.' *To his father – or to the town?* she asked herself now.

'I had a professor who used to say, "Everything in life comes with a price tag." For a while I thought he was such a cynic.'

'Now you don't,' he guessed. 'So the way to survival is to do what you feel is the right thing. I read somewhere that today there are twice as many lawyers practicing as there were in 1960. But the practice of law has changed.' He was somber, searching for words. 'It used to be that lawyers worked for the public good – now they're selling an expensive commodity. It's become a business, where values have zeroed downward and greed rules.'

'Not for every lawyer.' She felt giddy with excitement: he shared her feelings about the law. 'There are some of us who still have consciences.' She hesitated. She shouldn't be sharing what she was about to say, her mind warned her, yet she rushed ahead unheedingly. 'My first clients – if I pass the bar exams – will be *pro bono*. I'm already committed—' She laughed for an instant. 'Despite all those college and law-school loans hanging over my head.' But she hadn't named her prospective clients, she thought defensively – not that it would mean anything to Jonathan.

'When we're past this ordeal and back in Eden,' he said quietly, 'I hope we'll see each other again.'

'I'd like that.'

'We'll comfort each other during those weeks while we're waiting for the results,' he said with new lightness.

'Absolutely,' she agreed, following his lead. 'Who else in Eden will understand how we're feeling?' *Can I carry this off, knowing he's a Cameron?* Yet being close to Jonathan Cameron might lead to important revelations. *Can I do this without being badly hurt? I've never felt this way about any man. Can I handle myself in this situation?*

They lingered over dinner – both reluctant to part. Not an empty table in the restaurant now.

'We should call it a night,' Kara said regretfully. 'We have an important date at eight a.m.'

'Breakfast with me at seven?' His eyes an ingratiating plea.

'Great,' she agreed.

'I'll drive you to the Fair Grounds,' he said, and she nodded in acceptance. 'We'll bring each other good luck.'

She was conscious of heady exhilaration. This wasn't just a casual encounter at a traumatic occasion. Jonathan anticipated much more for them. She wanted that too.

Back in her room – feeling a need to touch base – Kara called home. A minor extravagance. She debated about telling her grandmother and mother that she'd had dinner with Jonathan. If it had been anybody but a Cameron, they would have been so pleased. *No, don't mention it. Not tonight.*

On Wednesday morning Kara met Jonathan at Finlay's for breakfast. She ate without tasting – geared herself to face the ordeal ahead. Jonathan made a determined effort to divert her mind with amusing stories of his years at Columbia Law. Both watchful of the time. They drove together in Jonathan's Mercedes to the State Fair Grounds, took their places in the Canty building – along with the huge group of other candidates – and wished each other luck.

At the end of the day they returned to Adam's Mark, met for dinner at six. Again, their conversation was dominated by discussion of the law profession. But their eyes carried on another conversation. He was warm, tender, intense. In her junior and senior years at Emory she'd allowed herself some casual dating – but there'd never been anybody that made her feel this way.

'Law is not serving people of this country the way it should.' Jonathan intruded on her thoughts. 'How many people can afford the hourly billing that's part of a serious case – civil or criminal?'

'My friend Anita told me her firm made it clear they avoided *pro bono* cases,' Kara admitted. 'She says that's a new trend.'

'You said your first case would be *pro bono*,' he remembered, his eyes questioning.

'It's a murder case,' she said after a moment. She shouldn't be talking about it yet, her mind chastised her again – but she continued anyway. 'My clients haven't been accused yet, but I'm sure they're the prime suspects.' She took a deep breath. 'If I pass the bar exams, I'll represent Valerie and Hank Thompson.'

Jonathan looked blank.

'Valerie is Mattie Mason's niece. Hank's her husband. Now that the vagrant has been cleared of the murder, I know the police will go after them. I just pray the results from the exams come in before that happens. And that I pass.'

'They can't afford to hire a partner from Condon & Jenkins or Rogers & Langley,' he surmised compassionately.

'They inherited Mattie's house. But even if they sell it they might run out of funds before the case is closed. You know how fast the billing escalates. No "dream team" for Val and Hank.' Her smile was wry. 'If they're lucky, they'll have me.'

It wasn't wrong to be discussing this with Jonathan. In the weeks ahead, she might pick up something useful from him – if his father *was* involved in Mattie's murder. *But I won't feel guilty about that.*

'You feel they're innocent—'

'Convinced.' Her eyes met his with confidence.

'It's great to be involved in a case that you're passionate about.' He squinted in thought. 'I'd like to be able to offer my services for *pro bono* cases – but I expect I'll be all tied up in dry, dull maneuvering. At least, for a while. My father's throwing me into a new venture of the company.' *The takeover of Eden General!* Didn't he understand what a rotten deal that would be for the town? 'I don't know a damn thing about it. With the exams out of the way, he'll expect me to join up with his legal team. You know I'll end up with all the grunt work. God, I'd love to have access to the Columbia Law library now.' He frowned, his gaze quizzical. 'Do you suppose you'll find time to see a lawyer caught up in dull, corporate negotiations?'

'I'm sure that can be arranged.' *Oh yes, no matter what, I mean to see much of Jonathan Cameron.*

*   *   *

Kara realized that Jonathan was disappointed when she told him on Friday morning at breakfast that she'd already checked out of the hotel, that her luggage was being held until her departure right after the exams.

'I was hoping we'd have dinner together tonight.'

'My family expects me home.' But her eyes told him she would have enjoyed another dinner with him. 'They're dying to hear about the exam—'

'We'll make it.' No arrogance in his statement, she thought with unexpected tenderness. Just confidence. 'We've made it through terrific law schools. I suspect some grads flunk out of sheer terror,' he said whimsically. 'We've survived without falling apart. Now comes the waiting period. And that,' he conceded, 'will be a bitch.'

'My grandmother and mother will be pushing me to look around for office space.' She shuddered in anticipation. 'Can you imagine having to sit around and wait for clients?' She'd talked a lot about Grandma and Mom, she realized now. Would he be shocked if he realized he'd been adopted by the Camerons because her father had been killed in that car crash? In a way, her father had brought them together. If he hadn't died, she wouldn't be sitting here with Jonathan.

'Let's have dinner tomorrow evening,' he said with an air of spontaneity. 'We've been through an ordeal together. It's over – let's celebrate.'

'Let's.' She'd been praying for this. 'We're survivors.'

Will Mom be upset? If she is, how will I handle it?

Ten

Driving up to the house, Jonathan noted that his father's limousine sat out front. Dad was home – and planning to go out later, since the limo was not in the garage. He walked into the house – the front door was never locked until bedtime – and headed towards the stairs. He heard his father's voice in the library.

Dad was angry about something to do with the takeover of Eden General, he interpreted. He'd have to bone up on the health-care situation. The bar exams were out of the way – now it was time to go to work.

'Mist' Jonathan—' Annie Mae's voice called to him as he headed up the stairs. 'I'm puttin' dinner on the table in five minutes. I know how you like fish – I made Dover sole stuffed with wild rice and mushrooms.'

'Sounds terrific, Annie Mae. I'll be right down.'

In his room he tossed his valise on the bed, hurried back downstairs. His father was striding into the dining room as he arrived there.

'The conquering hero is home.' Roy Cameron was jubilant. 'You go on the payroll Monday morning.'

'We won't have the exam results for maybe another month,' Jonathan warned him.

'You passed – I'm sure of that.' Whatever had angered his father earlier, Jonathan understood, had been dismissed for now.

'I'm hoping.' He held up crossed fingers as he took his place at the table.

'You'll start to work with Hoffman on this hospital takeover deal. Get your feet wet. And in time, you'll handle the whole set-up. There's a fortune to be made – and I mean to keep it in the family.'

'I know nothing about the field – except what I read in newspapers and magazines.' Again, he was conscious of discomfort as he considered what lay ahead. Some of what he'd read about cutting costs in health care disturbed him. 'I'll have to do a hell of a lot of digging.'

Roy shrugged. 'So you'll dig. You'll learn. We'll be able to provide better care at lower cost than the present administrators can ever imagine. That's our job. We cut every corner possible. Get rid of the window-dressing. Organize, get rid of the fat. Annie Mae, this fish is good,' he told her as she brought fresh-from-the-oven rolls to the table.

'Strawberry shortcake for dessert.' She winked at Jonathan. Since he was five that had been his favorite dessert.

'Now that you're home,' Roy joshed, 'Annie Mae'll be making everything you like. What I like won't count any-more.'

Jonathan waited until they were alone again to broach the subject that had been on his mind since he first arrived.

'Dad, I hope you won't take this the wrong way . . .' His smile was apologetic. 'But I think it's time for me to settle myself in a small apartment somewhere in town.'

'I get it.' Roy grinned. 'You can't have a real social life when you live at home. I understand,' he said indulgently. 'I was young once.' Jonathan knew the rumors that had circulated through the years about his father's and Bart's affairs with women – though Dad was cautious, unlike Bart. He remembered the time he'd stayed at the D. C. condo as part of a school trip – and saw the sheer black nightwear and lingerie that he couldn't believe was his mother's. 'Go to the brokers, find something you like. The furniture's on me. A graduation gift. That and your own car. Can't have you and Annie Mae fighting over the Mercedes. Go over to Gordon Motors and pick out what you like. No Lamborghini,' he joshed. 'Maybe a small Mercedes.'

'Thanks, Dad.' How could he feel such reluctance about getting involved in the family business when Dad was so good to him?

'Oh, for the record, it'll be a company car,' Roy said. 'That way the accountants can write it off as a business deduction.

Hey, the most important member of our legal staff deserves some perks.'

The newest, least experienced member of the legal staff, Jonathan thought. Uneasy in his father's blunt hint that his rise would be fast. He'd be facing a lot of hostility at the company.

'I still have to get that letter that says I'm a member of the bar,' Jonathan reminded him.

'You'll work closely with Bill Hoffman at first.' Roy brushed aside any doubts. 'He'll brief you on the basics, but I've told you – this hospital deal will be your baby. Before we finish, we'll have a string of hospitals across the country. It's the way to go, Jonnie.' Only in rare moments did his father use this diminutive.

'I suspect we'll encounter some roadblocks,' Jonathan warned. 'From what I've read, there's a lot of controversy involved.'

'The whole deal is cost. We'll know how to handle that.' Roy exuded confidence. 'We start here in Eden. Once we have the first one under our belt – and investors see how we're bringing efficiency to the scene, that the bottom line is healthy – then we're rolling. Oh, I'll have to cut out after dinner,' he apologized. 'A meeting with Bart and a few of the boys at the company. Nothing that you need to sit in on, though.'

While his father continued to talk about the burgeoning for-profit hospital scene, Jonathan's mind wandered. Tomorrow night he'd be seeing Kara for dinner. He knew – even now – that he wanted her to be a permanent part of his life. But he mustn't rush her – this was too important to derail. Yet he sensed that Kara shared this feeling.

Kara lingered at the dinner table – enjoying the air of euphoria that permeated the atmosphere, yet fearful that this was premature. Not until the letter arrived announcing that she was a member of the bar could she relax.

'I'm so pleased that you liked the hotel,' Edie said with satisfaction. 'And the restaurant.'

'It was a mini-vacation,' Kara said, then laughed. 'Except that I was scared to death.'

'Now that the exams are behind you, you'll be able to give some thought to Mattie's murder.' Daisy's eyes exuded hope.

'Right.' Kara was conscious of an urgent need not to disappoint her mother and grandmother. 'I think the first step is to back-track to the other two murders. Eric and Gerry's.' She felt a sudden tension in her audience. A rush of hopeful anticipation. 'I want to go to Salem and search the newspaper files of that time.' She paused. 'With luck I'll be able to talk with the parents.'

'Gerry's parents moved out west right after the – the murders.' Daisy was battling for calm. 'Eric's mother committed suicide a year later—'

'But Eric's father may still be there,' Edie rushed in. 'I'm sure he'll cooperate.'

'All right, that's where I'll start.' Again, she asked herself if she was sharp enough to handle this. Her lack of experience was scary. But those murders had never been solved. So they happened twenty-five years ago. They were clearly linked to Mattie's murder. The Eden police might not believe – but *she* believed. Mattie's husband had confessed to killing Eric and Gerry – and to steal that confession, Mattie was murdered. *I have no choice except to fight for answers.*

'Did you have time to try out the health club at Adam's Mark?' Edie asked, satisfied that Kara would pursue the case. 'I know how faithful you were to your health club in Atlanta.' Like her granddaughter, Edie was into fitness.

'All I had time to do was bone up on my notes and pray.' Kara laughed in recall. Now she hesitated. 'That and sleeping and eating.' All right, tell them about Jonathan. 'One strange thing happened. Remember the man who got the battery going when the car stalled? I met him at the hotel.' Edie and Daisy glowed. 'He was there to take the bar exams—'

'How lovely.' Edie exchanged a pleased glance with Daisy.

'We had dinner together.' *I can't back out now. Tell them.* 'You'll never guess who he is.' They waited expectantly. 'Jonathan Cameron.'

A stunned silence met her disclosure, lasted only a moment.

'He was adopted,' Edie said with an effort at casualness. 'He's not a Cameron.'

'I thought he might be useful. I mean, he might – without knowing its importance – say something that will help us.'

Daisy seemed distraught. 'Did the name Jamison mean anything to him?'

'No. But I don't suppose there's any reason it would.' Not likely his adoptive parents would have mentioned what had happened all those years ago. 'He seems very bright. He's nice,' Kara added awkwardly and paused again. 'I – I'm having dinner with him tomorrow night. You know, a kind of celebration for putting the bar exams behind us.'

'No reason you shouldn't,' Edie said, with a guarded glance at Daisy. 'Like you said, he might be useful.'

'You'd think he'd know something about Tim and me.' Daisy was ambivalent.

'Daisy, people have long forgotten that whole terrible period.' Edie contrived an air of confidence. 'Except maybe a few of the old-timers. It's not likely that Roy or Sandra Cameron would bring it up to their adopted son.'

Could Mom ever see Jonathan without being thrown back into the horror of that awful accident? Will she ever accept the fact that he's not a Cameron? I want to see Jonathan again. I want to see a lot of him.

Kara came awake slowly. Not a sound in the house, she realized. It must be late, she thought in sudden comprehension. Grandma and Mom both off to work. She peered at the night-table clock. Wow, it was only minutes before noon!

She'd lain awake until almost dawn – her mind in turmoil because of Mom's reaction to her seeing Jonathan. But she should have expected that. Yet she felt a stir of anticipation as she remembered she was having dinner with him tonight. Would Mom be home from the shop when he picked her up? Grandma would be here – she worked from eleven till four on Saturdays. But Grandma would be cool, she comforted herself.

In a need for activity – and feeling guilty that she had slept so late – she left her bed, headed down the hall to the bathroom to prepare for the day. No worries this morning – almost afternoon, she corrected herself – about the exams. That was over, thank God. She could pick up her life again while she waited to hear the results.

In shorts and T-shirt – aware that already it was a hot day – she went into the kitchen, found a note from her grandmother fastened to the refrigerator door with a fish-designed magnet: 'Pancake mixture in the fridge, with a dish of blueberries to add.'

She put up coffee, prepared the blueberry pancakes. She'd go over to Salem on Monday morning, she told herself again. Check out the back issues of the Salem newspapers, try to track down Eric Hamilton's father. Don't approach him right off, she cautioned herself – read the newspaper accounts first.

Grandma and Mom kept insisting she start to look around downtown for office space. It would have to be something small, inexpensive, she reminded herself. Grandma and Mom also insisted they'd pay the first three months' rent and furnish the office. Their graduation present.

They're so good to me. I have to track down Eric and Gerry's murderer. I have to give Mom's life back to her.

By the time she'd finished breakfast the morning sun had given way to clouds. The day would be hot and humid. Already perspiration dampened her forehead. What should she wear tonight? Go look through her closet, press whatever she chose.

Her mind trailed back to the business of setting up an office. Rent – if she found something right away – with the lease to begin on 1 September. By then she'd know if she'd passed the exams. She had two clients, she thought with an effort at optimism. That would kind of establish her as a new lawyer in town. Let the exam results come through before the police brought Hank – or Hank and Val – before a grand jury.

Feeling guilty at running up the electric bill, she settled herself in the living room and flipped on the air-conditioning. She sprawled on the sofa with a sigh of pleasure as the conditioner provided relief. How were Anita and Laura doing? Her mind traveled back to the night before graduation . . .

Laura slouched in the badly worn lounge chair – inherited from earlier law students, like all the furniture in the apartment –

and swigged down the last of her coffee. Anita sprawled at one end of the sofa – feet propped on the oversized coffee table – and made a final stab at the container of soggy fried rice, the remains of their last Chinese dinner in the apartment.

'You know,' Laura confided, 'I wish to hell we didn't have to go to graduation exercises tomorrow. I'd just like to sleep for the next forty-eight hours.'

'We can sleep late,' Kara consoled. 'We're almost all packed. Nothing much to do. I can't believe it – we've made it through the three toughest years of our lives.'

'Wait,' Anita drawled. 'This is just a respite before we kill ourselves cramming for the bar exams.'

'You're all set,' Kara reminded. 'You're going to join that great law firm up in New York. That's what you said you wanted from the first day of law school.'

'Yeah, that's cool.' For a moment Anita was complacent. 'They'll help me prep for the exams – they help all their new associates.' She shivered pleasurably. 'I can't believe I made it there.' She inspected Kara with an air of concern. 'Are you sure you know what you're doing? Going back home to private practice? That could be even worse than working as an assistant public defender or clerking for some low-paying judge.'

'It's what I want to do.' Kara fought off doubts. 'I didn't go into law to own the fanciest house in town and drive a Jaguar. I want to be a lawyer with a social conscience.'

'Hear, hear!' Laura clucked.

'You've both got your heads in the clouds.' Anita shook her head in mock dismay. 'Your problem, Laura – you've watched too many episodes of *Ally McBeal* and all those reruns of *L.A. Law*. But I'm starting at ninety thousand dollars a year – right out of school.' Anita's eyes were bright with triumph. 'I don't care how many hours a week I have to put in – it'll be worth it. My father's been driving a truck for thirty years. He never made that much in his best years, with all his overtime to make ends meet. I was able to go to college – and on to law school – because my mother was a beautician and kept a secret bank account.'

'And she's proud as she can be of you,' Kara reminded

92

her tenderly. Tomorrow was a shining day for most parents of daughters or sons receiving law degrees.

'We've all read the statistics –' Anita was smug – 'how you work your butt off for a few years as an associate, and – if you're one of the lucky – you move up to a partnership. Of a huge firm, of course. In New York a partner in a major firm can expect to draw around four hundred and sixty-five thousand a year. It drops to around four hundred and forty-five thousand in Los Angeles. They still do great in San Francisco and Washington D.C. – about seventy-five to ninety-five thousand less than in New York. Even in Cleveland it's over a quarter-million. I'm not sure what it is in Eden, South Carolina,' she joshed.

'You don't have to worry, Laura,' Kara reminded her other friend. 'You're going into a firm your father and brother control. You'll be okay.'

'You know the truth?' All at once Laura was serious. 'I want to work a couple of years – until I know my way around the field – and then I want to get married and have a couple of kids. Oh, after the kids I'll work three days a week, maybe – but being a lawyer won't be the center of my universe.'

'I want a criminal-defense and civil-rights practice,' Kara said. 'To handle the little guys of the world. I want the satisfaction of providing ordinary people with the kind of representation they need but can't afford. I won't worry about how many billable hours I'm piling up, about satisfying the partners. Oh, sure, I'll be doing wills and real-estate closings and the grunt work – but I want to know that some of the time I'm making life better for some people who'd be out in the cold if I wasn't around.'

'Oh God, shouldn't we all rise and sing "God Bless America"?' But Anita's jibe was colored with affection. The three of them had been through a lot together.

Kara prodded herself back to the moment. She'd received one brief, breezy letter from Anita, a longer one from Laura, and had replied to each with the message that she was happy with her decision to go into private practice here at home. Still, the future appeared uncertain – it would be many months before she knew where she stood.

She would find no friends at the local district attorney's office, she realized – nor among the local police. It was not the kind of initial reaction she had planned. But don't worry about that now. Tonight she was going to dinner with Jonathan. Like he said, it was time to celebrate.

Eleven

Kara inspected her reflection in the door mirror of her bedroom closet. Instinct told her that Jonathan wouldn't expect her to wear anything glitzy. The turquoise linen/polyester slip dress was flattering. The turquoise and green beads were from Laura's jewelry-making period, and lovely.

'Be sure you take the jacket with that.' Edie hovered in the doorway with an approving smile. 'You know restaurants set the air-conditioning for men in suits.'

'Right.' Grandma was being so casual about her going out with Jonathan. How did she feel about it deep inside? Grandma was better at concealing her feelings than Mom. 'It's not too short?' She'd been vaguely self-conscious about that each time she wore this, but Anita and Laura always insisted it was great.

'Not with your legs,' Edie said complacently. 'And wear it now, darling, because all the fashion magazines talk about long skirts coming in strong.'

'I can always shorten it and wear it as a top,' Kara said lightly, and picked up the jacket and her purse.

'Oh, I was talking with Val a little while ago.' Edie walked with Kara down the hall to the living room. Both women conscious that Jonathan would be arriving soon. 'She had Betsy at the hospital for a check-up.'

'Betsy's okay?' Kara was solicitous.

'This was just routine. She tries to keep the visits to a minimum, but she feels a little less pinched now that they're moving into Mattie's house and won't have to pay rent. Still, it's sad that they fall between the cracks in health care. Hank earns too much for Medicaid but not enough – even now that they have the house – to afford health insurance. Anyhow, this

95

new doctor in pediatrics – Dr Callahan – has been looking into some new procedure that might help Betsy's arm.'

'Val could borrow on the house,' Kara pointed out. 'To pay for the surgery. The house is in her name now.' If Val was indicted, would the government put a lien on the house? But with a little luck that wouldn't happen.

'Dr Callahan is going to let her know how much it'll cost, but she suspects it'll be some astronomical figure. Even stretched out over years, the loan might be more than she and Hank can handle.'

'I just can't believe that in a country like this – the world's super-power – people have to be terrified about doctors' bills!' Kara burst out. 'Even middle-class people can be reduced to destitution by one major illness if they don't have adequate health insurance.'

'And the situation isn't improving with all these HMOs putting up weird guidelines.' Edie's voice was acerbic. 'Peg's a nervous wreck about the takeover at the hospital. Nothing's happening yet, but she suspects some radical changes. You know Roy Cameron's reputation for efficiency – which means a lot of cost-cutting and firings.'

Kara glanced at her watch. Jonathan would be here any minute. She felt guilty at hoping Mom would be delayed at the shop. But with Mom here it might be awkward. She tensed at the sound of a car pulling up before the house. Jonathan or Mom? She hurried to check. Jonathan was emerging from the white Mercedes.

'There's Jonathan,' she said with relief and reached for her jacket and purse.

'Enjoy the evening.' Edie rose to her feet. 'I should start dinner—'

'Grandma, stay and meet Jonathan,' she said on impulse.

She waited for Jonathan to arrive at the door. Mom would have to meet him one day. No doubt in her mind that – barring some catastrophe – Jonathan would be part of her life. Mom would come to understand that he wasn't to be blamed for what the Camerons had done to her. Wouldn't she?

'Hi.' Her smile dazzling, Kara pulled the front door wide.

'Grandma, this is Jonathan Cameron. My grandmother, Mrs Jamison –'

'Wow! You're a family of beautiful women—' Jonathan extended a hand to Edie.

'Oh, this one knows the way to a woman's heart,' Edie chuckled, accepting his handshake. Kara felt a surge of relief. This meeting was going well.

In the car Jonathan explained that he'd made reservations at a new restaurant at the edge of town.

'My father says the food is great, and the service too,' Jonathan told her. Did he tell his father the name of his dinner companion? Kara asked herself, all at once tense. No, she decided – probably not. It wasn't that important. 'I feel almost a stranger in town,' he admitted.

'I know.' Kara understood how he felt. 'Everything has changed since my high-school years. All the new shops, new buildings, new houses.'

'I haven't been here to speak of since I was eleven,' Jonathan said somberly. 'From then on it was boarding school and summer camps.' He hesitated, in some inner debate. 'My mother's health was bad in those days – she was in and out of sanitariums. But she's fine now.'

Kara remembered the rumors about Sandra Cameron's battles with alcohol and prescription-drug addiction, though her husband spread reports that she was suffering from a rare disease she'd picked up on a trip to Morocco.

The parking area of the restaurant – The Magnolias – was already fairly crowded. Why did she always feel intimidated by crowded restaurants? Anita and Laura used to tease her about that.

'It looks fine from outside,' Jonathan said while they headed for the sprawling white colonial building framed by towering magnolias. 'And tonight I'll be able to enjoy good food. I didn't really taste a bite out there at Adam's Mark – though I'm sure it was great. My stomach was all tied up in knots.'

'Mine too.' No pretenses about Jonathan, she thought with pleasure. Most men tried so hard to play the macho scene.

They were seated at a table in a private corner of the large room. The air fragrant with the scent of fresh flowers. The illumination soft. The tab would be high, Kara thought – a place chosen by most local residents to celebrate important occasions.

For a few moments they focused on the elaborate menu, made their choices with mock seriousness. It was amazing, Kara thought, the way their moods seemed to blend. They were both still uptight from the exams and now the trauma of waiting for results. But Jonathan knew he had a substantial job. She didn't know what lay ahead of her.

'I have to start looking around for an apartment,' Jonathan told her. 'Of which there are few in Eden.' His smile rueful. 'But my parents understand I need a place of my own.' He seemed disconcerted for a moment. 'I mean, after all the years of sharing digs – all through boarding school, college and law school – I'm kind of overwhelmed by the big family house.'

'I don't have that problem.' A hint of laughter in her voice. 'Ever since I can remember, my grandmother talked about adding another bathroom to our house. If I latch on to a super case, I might be able to swing it.' She sighed. 'Right now my grandmother is on my back to look around for office space. She and my mother are already out there drumming up business for me. I have to keep reminding them I still haven't become a member of the bar.'

'You will,' he said quietly. 'So will I. We'll worry a lot in the next four or five weeks, but we'll make it.'

'You sound like my grandmother. The only reason she hasn't insisted on my ordering business cards – so she can hand them out among her church friends and the local groups she belongs to – is that I don't have an office address or phone.'

'I never knew my grandparents. I never knew my birth parents. I was adopted by the Camerons when my mother abandoned me. I was just a few months old—' He stopped short. 'But you probably know that. Everybody in Eden knows.'

'It's our local fairy tale.' *He doesn't know about Mom and the annulled marriage. What would Roy Cameron think if he knew Jonathan was seeing me? Would he try to stop him? But then Jonathan wouldn't say, 'I'm dating Kara Jamison.'*

How much time does the busy Mr Cameron spend with his adopted son?

'I was damn lucky.' Jonathan brought her back to the moment. 'But there was a time when I would have hocked my soul to come face to face with my real mother and father.'

'I never knew my father,' Kara said softly. 'He died before I was born.' Her eyes met Jonathan's. This was another bond between them, she thought with a sense of pleasure.

'I even secretly tried to find my birth parents through a private investigator – I never told anybody about that until now.' A new depth was entering their relationship. They could share anything, she thought recklessly – then retreated. Almost anything. 'I felt so guilty at trying to track them down.'

'It was a natural instinct,' she comforted him. 'You read all the time about people doing that.' *How will Jonathan feel if I can prove that Roy Cameron hired Joe to kill Eric and Gerry – and somebody else to kill Mattie? Will he hate me for that?*

'My parents – my adoptive parents – have been so good to me.' *Why does he feel troubled?* 'They gave me everything they would have given their own son, had he lived.' *My father. But he doesn't know that.* 'Five years ago – when I fractured my ankle skiing at Aspen – they sent a doctor and nurse on the company jet to bring me home. Back in high school, when my class was chosen to make a trip to Washington, my father arranged for the whole class to stay at the company condo at the Watergate.'

'That must have been exciting for your classmates.' She struggled to keep her voice casual. *He's on a guilt trip because he feels a lack in his relationship with Roy and Sandra Cameron.* A scrap of conversation with her grandmother filtered through her mind: *'Oh, Roy and Sandra didn't adopt out of a great feeling of sympathy. They needed a child to complete the happy-family picture.'*

'Will you be doing some preliminary work on your *pro bono* case?' Jonathan asked. 'That's a hell of a lot more exciting than what I'll find myself doing from Monday morning.'

Admonishing herself in a corner of her mind for this, she told Jonathan about her grandmother's experience with

Mattie, about their going to talk to Harvey Raines about Joe's confession – and their brush-off.

'It wasn't an auspicious beginning for my career as an attorney in Eden,' she conceded.

'You're right in the middle of it,' he said with candid excitement. 'You're sure your clients are innocent.' He hesitated. 'If there's anything I can do – in whatever time I have free –' he amended, 'I'd like to help.'

'That'll be wonderful.' She felt a fleeting surge of pleasure. He wouldn't say that if he knew her main suspect was his father. 'But I realize you'll be terribly busy.' *I don't want to drive Jonathan away from me. Am I insane to think there might be a future for us?*

Jonathan grimaced. 'Busy with my dull corporate work.'

'This may be my *only* work for the next five years.'

'That's the wrong attitude, counselor,' he scolded. 'Think positive.'

'If I'm lucky, I'll be doing wills and real-estate closings.' Kara sighed. 'When I'm dying to be involved in civil-rights cases, important environmental cases – and saving poor innocent suspects from undeserved prison sentences.' She struggled for lightness.

'Kara, I don't mean to rush you—' All at once he was serious. 'But I'd like to see a lot of you.'

'I'd like that, too.' Her face was luminescent.

'What about dinner on Tuesday? It'll be hard to push past Sunday and Monday without seeing you – but I'll sweat it out.'

'Tuesday would be lovely,' she agreed.

'All right.' His voice was joyous. 'Now, what mad dessert shall we order?'

A faint drizzle had begun to fall by the time they left the restaurant, but they sprinted to the car in high spirits. Reluctant to part, they lingered in the car before the house, exchanging law-school incidents. The drizzle was becoming a downpour.

'I'd better run for it,' Kara said at last. 'It's been a great evening—'

He reached to pull her close for what was meant to be a

casual good-night kiss. But all at once it was much more. She sensed he was as shaken as she was.

'See you Tuesday night.' Her voice unsteady. 'No need to walk me to the door in this rain—'

'May I call you?' A hand momentarily detained her.

'By all means.' Her smile was radiant. 'Night.'

She hurried up the path to the door – conscious that Jonathan was waiting to see her inside the house. How was Mom feeling about this? Was she upset? *But how can I stop seeing Jonathan?*

She let herself into the house, heard the sound of voices in the living room. Grandma and Mom were listening to the news.

'Did you get drowned in this downpour?' Edie appeared in the living-room doorway.

'Not too bad, but I'll change into something dry.'

'I have fresh coffee up,' Edie said. 'It'll be ready in a couple of minutes.'

Kara hurried to change into nightie, robe and slippers. How was she going to make Mom understand that there was nothing wrong in her seeing Jonathan? There was no way that he could hinder their efforts to solve Mattie's murder. And she mustn't even think about how Jonathan might feel when he found out – even though Roy Cameron denied it – that Tim Cameron was her father. And that she meant to flush out the truth about Roy Cameron's part in Mattie's murder.

She walked into the living room as Daisy switched off the television news. 'I can't bear the way the police are saying they have no motive for Mattie's murder,' Daisy scoffed. Despite their questioning of Hank and his friends, they gave no public report of this. 'You and Mom go there and lay it right in their laps – and they won't believe you!'

'Val called after you left.' Edie came into the room with the coffee tray. 'She's a nervous wreck—'

Karen tensed. 'Something new?'

'The police called Hank down for questioning again. When he came home, he told Val they just asked him the same questions.' Edie grunted in disgust. 'What do they expect to get from that?'

'They hope to catch him contradicting himself.' He was upset – he could do that, Kara thought uneasily. 'They're looking for evidence strong enough to bring him before a grand jury.'

'There's more.' Edie was grim. 'Hank discovered that they'd brought his boss down for questioning. He's worried he might get fired.'

'They want to wear Hank down.' In truth the police had nothing at this point. Only the fact that Mattie and Hank had had a nasty verbal fight. 'They're hoping for a confession.'

'But Hank didn't do it!' Edie exploded.

'We know that – but they're not accepting what you told them,' Daisy reminded her.

'I'll call Val and Hank in the morning and talk to them,' Kara promised. 'The police can't bring Hank before a grand jury without some real evidence.'

'How was your evening?' Daisy derailed the discussion. Her eyes full of questions. 'I hear the Magnolias is beautiful and the food superb.'

'Right.' But Kara sensed her mother's distress that she'd spent the evening with Roy Cameron's adopted son. She sought for words to alleviate this feeling. 'I didn't pick up anything useful from Jonathan.' Stress that he might drop some important kernel of information. 'But then I didn't expect that on the first go round.' That let Mom know she would be seeing Jonathan again. 'He's working on some new deal for the company.' He'd said this earlier, but she hadn't mentioned it before. 'I suspect it has something to do with the hospital takeover.'

'How will that help you solve Mattie's murder?' Daisy asked accusingly.

'Mom, I don't know what I'll pick up from Jonathan – but I have to gamble that something important will come up.'

'He's living and working with Roy Cameron,' Edie said urgently. 'Without even knowing it, he might reveal something important.'

'Mom, you read too many suspense novels.' Daisy sighed. 'What chance do we really have to solve Mattie's murder?'

'Together we'll do it,' Edie insisted. 'Kara's going over to

Salem on Monday. She'll read up the background in the Salem newspapers. She'll talk with Eric's father.'

'Eric's father may know why he and Gerry were rushing to Eden,' Kara pointed out. 'He may provide us with a motive for their murder.'

'We *know* the motive!' Daisy's voice was strident. 'They wanted to stop Roy Cameron from annulling my marriage to Tim!'

'We suspect that,' Edie said gently. 'We don't have proof.'

'Right now I'm concerned about Hank,' Kara admitted. 'Harvey Raines is fighting like mad for some little hook that'll allow him to bring Hank before a grand jury. I just wish I knew what Hank's friends – and his boss – have been saying . . .'

'Can't Hank ask them?' Edie demanded.

'He'll never get a verbatim report. People are too uptight at questionings to remember exactly what they said – and sometimes there's some little tidbit they don't even remember that can be interpreted in a bad way.'

'What can we do for Hank?' Edie was fighting for calm.

'All we can do is watch and wait,' Kara said tiredly. 'And pray we come up with a strong lead before Raines moves in.'

Is there something Hank didn't tell me? Something I should know?

Twelve

At 9.30 a.m. on Monday Kara was in the car and bound for Salem. She surmised that the library would open at ten. She would arrive there at a few minutes past. In her mind she went over her conversation with Hank and Val yesterday morning. They were close to panic. Fearful of an indictment. She'd laid it on the line with Hank. 'If there's something you haven't told me that could be incriminating, tell me now.'

'*Val and I were at the hospital emergency room when Mattie was killed. And there's no way I woulda hired somebody to do her in. Mattie was all the family we both had.*'

Kara felt slightly sick each time she remembered that Hank and Val's lives – Betsy's future – were in her hands. But they couldn't afford 'dream team' representation. She doubted that a local public defender would fight anywhere as hard as she. This might be the most important case that would come her way. It was the case that could give Mom her life back.

All right, focus on what I have to do in Salem. The public library or the local papers will have old newspapers on microfilm. Start there – then, with luck, locate Eric's father. Grandma thinks he still lives in Salem – but she's not sure. Please, God, let Eric's father still live in Salem. Let him be willing to talk with me.

Arriving in Salem, Kara sought out the library. Pulling up before the small white frame structure, she was assailed by apprehension. It was such a tiny library. Would they have microfilm of newspapers that dated back twenty-five years?

She left the car, walked to the entrance – for a moment fearful that it might not be open today. Then she saw a sign that said OPEN. She walked inside, approached the counter and asked the librarian about old newspapers on file.

'Oh, we go back forty years on microfilm,' the librarian said proudly. 'Just fill out a slip, and I'll get the film for you.'

Churning with anticipation, Kara sat at a table and threaded microfilm into the machine. As she'd expected, the murder of Eric and Gerry slightly more than twenty-five years ago had been front-page news. TWO LOCAL TEENAGERS BRUTALLY MURDERED. She read the long initial article, the expansive – but uninformative – coverage for the next few days. The Eden police, in whose jurisdiction the murders occurred, couldn't come up with a motive. The families of both were distraught, unable to help the police. The police concluded the murders were a savage act by a psychotic vagrant passing through town. It remained on the Eden police books as a pair of unsolved murders.

The newspapers reported, too, on the accident a day earlier that had killed Eden teenager Tim Cameron, who had been Eric Hamilton's college roommate and best friend. 'A tragedy reminiscent of a Shakespearean play,' one reporter mourned. Three friends dead within twenty-four hours.

Nobody saw any connection between the accidental death of Tim Cameron and the murder of Eric and Gerry. It appeared just a painful twist of fate. But now the link was clear. And for that Mattie had died.

Kara rewound the last of the microfilm, replayed in her mind all that she'd read. Nothing that she hadn't already known, she told herself in frustration. She returned the microfilm to the librarian, located a local telephone directory. Her heart pounding, she sought a listing for David Hamilton. He had two phone numbers – one residential, one business. He was a Certified Public Accountant.

She left the library and searched for a pay-phone. Would he be angry at being approached about his son's murder after all these years? Not angry, she decided. Upset. Like Mom, he'd be thrown back into that traumatic period in his life.

It was lunchtime. She was conscious of faint hunger. *Have a sandwich and coffee. Then phone Mr Hamilton.*

She found a pleasant-appearing coffee shop not far from the library. A friendly hostess led her to one of the few still-unoccupied tables. She ordered a chicken cutlet on rye toast and coffee, then leaned back and tried to form words in her mind that would persuade Mr Hamilton to agree to an interview. Surely he'd want to track down his son's killer – even after all these years.

Half an hour later she approached the phone at the rear. The noise level would provide some privacy, she comforted herself. With an unsteady hand she punched in Mr Hamilton's office phone number. A woman she presumed was his receptionist or secretary responded. She asked to speak to him 'on a personal matter'. For a moment she suspected she was about to be rebuffed, then she was put through.

'Hello, David Hamilton.' He was polite but brisk.

'Mr Hamilton, this is Kara Jamison. I'm Daisy Jamison's daughter. I—'

'Yes?' he interrupted with a tension in his voice that told her she'd evoked painful memories.

'I know this will come as a shock to you,' she said softly, 'but my grandmother has knowledge of a man who's confessed to killing Eric and Gerry. May I talk to you about this?'

'When?' He was terse. 'Not over the phone—'

'I'm here in Salem,' she explained. 'Whatever time would be convenient for you . . .'

'Can you come to my office now?'

'I'll be there in five minutes.'

At his storefront headquarters, she was ushered into his private office.

'Please sit down.' A slight, gentle man with sad eyes, he was visibly shaken.

'I know this comes as a shock,' she apologized.

'I want to know everything you've learned.' He leaned forward with an air of urgency. Kara remembered that, in addition to losing his only child, he'd lost his wife. She'd committed suicide on the first anniversary of Eric's death. 'Please tell me.'

Kara briefed him on what she knew.

'And the Eden police refused to believe this?' He was indignant.

'The District Attorney brushed us off. But Mattie Mason was murdered so that Joe's confession would never reach them.

106

They're convinced my grandmother was lying – probably to promote publicity for me. I'll shortly be opening a law office in Eden.'

'She should have taken the confession to the police as soon as her husband died. Why did she wait?'

'She was too distraught after Joe's death to go to the police – and later she was afraid she'd be prosecuted for not reporting it right away. She was about to take the confession to them when she was murdered. Mr Hamilton, I know the Eden police claim they could find no motive for Eric and Gerry's murder – but was there anyone you ever suspected?'

'At the time I was totally in the dark. Later I had suspicions that – that were too bizarre to voice.'

'Whom did you suspect?' Kara asked urgently.

'I knew I was groping in the dark – but later I asked myself, *Who knew Eric and Gerry were on that stretch of road to Eden?*' He took a deep breath, gearing himself to continue. 'I remember Eric's shock when he heard about Tim and Daisy's accident. That Tim was dead and Daisy hospitalized. He was devastated. Then in the morning – none of us slept much that night – Eric turned on the TV for the nine a.m. news. He was outraged when the newscaster reported that Tim's parents were conferring with a judge about having the marriage annulled. The station always keeps the time and the weather in a corner on the screen.' He was struggling for calm. 'It was exactly 9.04 a.m. when Eric called and spoke with Mrs Cameron. He said she was incoherent. He attributed it to shock. He decided that he and Gerry would drive to Eden to convince the Camerons not to ask for an annulment.'

Kara's mind was in turmoil. *Mom was right. Roy Cameron knew they were coming to Eden. He knew why. He wanted to stop them – at any cost.*

'Mr Hamilton, how did Eric and Gerry expect to stop the annulment?' Kara pursued. 'What did they know?'

'They knew that Tim's father was lying when he claimed Tim was heavily into drugs. That Tim hadn't known what he was doing when he married Daisy. That was a damned lie!' His voice was strident. 'Tim wasn't into drugs. It was Tim who got Eric *off* drugs. His mother and I were so grateful to him. And

107

that spring Tim and Eric started an anti-drugs campus group – to fight drugs among college students.'

'Mom was sure he wasn't into drugs – but nobody believed her.'

'I couldn't believe Roy Cameron would besmirch his own son's name that way.' Mr Hamilton's voice was scathing. 'But he'd do anything to have the marriage annulled.' He paused, seeming in inner debate. 'I suspect,' he said gently, 'that Cameron couldn't bear to see his son marry into a family that wasn't rich, like himself.'

'My grandmother took in roomers, clerked to raise her daughter. She fought a constant battle to survive. That wasn't the background he expected for his son's mother-in-law.' *But there's proof that my father was not on drugs. Why wasn't that brought out?*

As though reading her mind, Mr Hamilton explained. 'I know Eric's mother and I should have taken steps to point out that no way could Tim have been on drugs when he married Daisy – but we were devastated by Eric and Gerry's death. We couldn't think of anything else. And then – a few months later – Roy Cameron established a fund in Eden to fight drug addiction among teenagers. Leaving no doubt in anybody's mind that Tim was addicted to drugs. It made me sick!'

'It was great for his image,' Kara interpreted. And this monster of a man was her grandfather – even though he would never acknowledge this.

'That's all that matters in Roy Cameron's life.' Mr Hamilton's face exuded contempt. 'The glorified image he presents to the public. But I'll do anything I can to bring to justice the man who ordered Eric and Gerry's death – no matter how powerful that man may be. Even if it was Roy Cameron.'

Driving back to Eden, Karen replayed in her mind the turbulent encounter with Eric's father. She clung to the knowledge that she and Mom and Grandma were not alone in suspecting Roy Cameron. But how – *how* – could they prove that Roy Cameron had hired Joe to kill Eric and Gerry? And someone else to kill Mattie.

Jonathan sat in his father's huge, ornately furnished office along with Bill Hoffman and Bart, and tried to appear engrossed in the discussion, though much of what was being said disturbed him.

'Everything's going to plan,' Bart said smugly. 'I've checked on the doctors who'll bring in the most business. We'll work out stock deals for their wives, and—'

'That's dangerous,' Jonathan broke in. 'Twenty-six years ago Congress passed an anti-kickback law. In 1989 and in 1993 the Stark laws were passed – which bar doctors from referring their patients to medical institutions where they own stock. We know that right now the federal government is investigating deals that hospitals are making to recruit doctors who'll bring in business. We can't—'

'Grow up, buddy boy,' Bart drawled. 'Laws are meant to be circumvented.'

'Relax, Jonathan.' Bill Hoffman smiled reassuringly. 'We can arrange deals with the wives that will be legal.'

'We have to do that,' Roy pursued. 'Not only to have the most successful doctors steer patients to our hospitals, but to compensate them for the low fees our insurance policies will provide. And the fees must be low so that the bottom line on fiscal reports look good. That way our stock prices will soar,' he finished with a flourish.

'To sell health insurance and to own hospitals is a natural tie-in.' Bill Hoffman was complacent. 'Bart, maybe you ought to talk to the promotion people about trying for a story in the *Wall Street Journal* and *Fortune*. Kind of set the stage for what's to come.'

'The government may scream conflict of interests,' Jonathan warned, unhappy with this initiation into business. Why couldn't Dad be satisfied with Cameron Insurance? But he knew the answer to that. It wasn't just the money involved. It was the power.

'We're pretty squared away for the moment.' Roy glanced at his watch. 'And I have those people from the Berlin division coming in soon.'

'Sandra's due in today,' Bart reminded him.

'Cassie will see that Brooks picks her up with the limo.' Roy dismissed this.

'I'll drive over to the airport and bring her home,' Bart said. 'You know Sandra – she'll be put out if one of the family isn't there with the welcome mat.'

'Tell Cassie,' Roy said.

Bart hurried out to his reserved parking spot, slid behind the wheel of his Mercedes. Ever since they had set up the branch in Germany, Roy had had this thing about their driving German-made cars. He chuckled. That didn't stop Sandra from driving her red Jaguar.

God, he was pissed at Roy for bringing Jonathan into the company. Roy would push Jonathan up so fast his head would swim. *That hospital deal should have been mine!* Roy had some hell of a nerve throwing a plum like that at a twenty-five-year-old kid.

He'd been pissed at Roy since the day Sandra said she was marrying the buzzard. How could she have married out of her class that way? They were Old Family. Sixth generation here in Eden. Hell, he'd warned her they'd be ignored by the other Old Families. Pariahs – both of them – because she'd married that redneck. It didn't mean a thing – once she'd married Roy – that the family included judges, state senators, a grandfather who was Mayor for twenty-eight years.

Sure, he and Sandra both knew how desperate they were for money. They'd been living on capital since the day the old man had his massive stroke. The house had fallen into disrepair – their capital low enough to scare the hell out of both of them.

But it wasn't just the money. For a while, at least, she'd been totally infatuated with Roy. It had made him sick to visualize his gorgeous sister in bed with that redneck. She'd come down to the cottage and talk – in lurid detail – about how it was with them in bed. Sometimes he was sure she did it just to torment him.

But soon the infatuation evaporated. Roy was all tied up with the business. He had no time for his bride. Once she was pregnant – and Roy anticipated the heir he needed to satisfy his soaring ego – she moved into her own bedroom suite, spent a fortune on redecorating.

For a while – after Tim was born – she'd seemed satisfied with life. Despite their lowered social standing, her photograph appeared regularly on the society pages of the local newspapers. She was the rich and beautiful new mother – and, of course, Roy was becoming the town's most influential businessman. His rise phenomenal.

Bart's mind shot back through the years, to the days when Sandra was being pursued by every horny young boy in town. He used to hate every one of them. With their mother dead and their father wheelchair-bound after his stroke, there was nobody to rein her in.

Even now – all these years later – he was aroused, remembering how she'd parade around the upstairs floor of the house in sheer black chiffon panties and black lace bras. Their father isolated to a downstairs bedroom. She'd been hot as a pistol. For a little while Roy was all she wanted. But those times were long gone. Now she relished hearing his racy accounts of his own sexual encounters. But what did she do on all those trips out of town, out of the country? Close as they were, she never said a word – but he was sure she had her share of macho young studs. And he could kill each and every one with pleasure.

Bart arrived at the local airport just as Sandra's plane began to disgorge its passengers. He hurried forward to greet her as she passed through the security check.

'I gather you enjoyed the cruise,' he murmured with a brotherly kiss on her cheek. 'You look marvelous.' Nothing was overlooked in keeping her beautiful and elegant, even at sixty-six. The best plastic surgeons, the most expensive designer clothes, a masseuse who came in three times a week. And at regular intervals the trips to the best sanitariums, to be dried out.

'It was fun the first ten days.' Her smile was inscrutable. Had she indulged herself with young studs? Bart made a point of hiding his annoyance at such a prospect. 'After that it was a bore.'

A pair of porters carried Sandra's collection of Louis Vuitton luggage to the car. She settled herself on the front seat beside Bart, crossed her legs. A wide expanse of thigh displayed by the high slit in her newly fashionable long skirt, though the young still favored short skirts. She still had great legs, Bart thought with cynical amusement. The legs were always the last to go.

'How was your social life while I was away?' Sandra asked with mocking good humor.

'Oh, sugar, you don't want to know,' he drawled.

'I want to know,' she said imperiously. 'In every ugly, crude detail.'

'There's this luscious new cocktail waitress at the Golden Dove – just past the age of consent.' He whistled eloquently. 'She's got a pair of tits and an ass that set my teeth on edge . . .'

He felt a surge of heated pleasure. He was glad Sandra was home. He hated the way she was always running off on trips. His imagination went berserk. But now she was home and maybe – just maybe – he could persuade her to fight for him with Roy. Jonathan was adopted for window-dressing. *He* was flesh and blood.

Roy owes me the hospitals deal.

Thirteen

Kara spoke with deliberate slowness – so that Edie could digest every nuance of her report on the encounter with David Hamilton. She could feel the kaleidoscope of emotions that inundated her grandmother.

'I called Mom at the shop,' she concluded breathlessly. 'I couldn't wait to tell her.' Here was confirmation of what Mom had declared – to no avail – twenty-five years ago.

'I can see her now,' Edie whispered, 'in her hospital room, telling the conniving lawyer that Roy Cameron sent, that Tim never touched drugs. That their marriage was legal. But all he would say was that annulment proceedings were in progress – she could never call herself Mrs Timothy Cameron. But Daisy wasn't thinking about that—' Tears welled in her eyes. 'She couldn't bear having such an ugly thing said about Tim when he wasn't there to defend himself. She couldn't bear your being denied the right to your father's name. I felt so helpless. I couldn't afford to hire an expensive attorney to fight for her.'

'You have your own lawyer now. Well, almost a lawyer.'

'I never told Daisy – but in a strange way I was relieved that Roy and Sandra Cameron refused to believe you were Tim's child. Because if they had, they might have fought for your custody – and what chance would we have had against their wealth and power? You were what held your mother and me together all the years ahead. You were the shining light in our lives.'

'You and Mom were all I needed.' Kara fought back tears. 'You gave me all the love any child could want.'

'Your mother grieved that you couldn't bear your father's name. She felt she'd let you down.'

'No way,' Kara insisted. But she understood how Mom and Grandma had felt. This was a small town, and even in 1973 unmarried mothers were made to feel morally inferior.

'Daisy was such a warm, sweet, fun-loving teenager,' Edie reminisced. 'She never smoked pot or experimented with LSD. A few kids in Eden did. A few boys let their hair grow down to their shoulders and a few girls wandered around in crazy-colored, long dresses. But not most of them. They watched TV, listened to records, went square-dancing. The last two months of school – with Daisy so eager to go to college – I'd been fighting with the bank about increasing the mortgage on the house so that I could send her—' She sighed. 'Instead, that money went to pay her hospital bills.' She shuddered in recall. 'They were horrendous.'

Kara was startled. 'Did Mom know you were trying to send her to college?' Never once had this been mentioned.

'I didn't tell her because I wasn't sure the new mortgage would come through. The first bank turned me down. It just broke my heart – knowing how much she wanted to go to college – and graduating at the top of her class the way she did. And the weirdest thing – on the day of the accident the second bank notified me that the mortgage had been approved.'

'I wish you'd tell Mom,' Kara said tenderly. 'Let her know that you tried.'

'The way she withdrew into herself after Tim was killed – I didn't think I should. There never seemed a right time.'

All at once Edie seemed disturbed. 'Kara, you don't think that with what Mr Hamilton told her she'll want to try to go to court and resurrect all that ugliness?'

'Mom couldn't bring herself to go through that. And even with Mr Hamilton's testimony we don't know that the ruling would be rescinded.' Kara strived for a casual air. 'I don't want to be a Cameron.' But Jonathan's face leapt into her mind. *He* was a Cameron.

How would Jonathan react if he knew what his father had done to Mom? How will he react if we prove that his father was responsible for Eric and Gerry's murders, and for Mattie's murder? Can there ever be a future for Jonathan and me? I want that. I want it so much—

114

'I wouldn't care to fight Roy Cameron in court.' Edie punctured Kara's introspection. 'He owns too many people in this town. But why didn't David Hamilton go to that judge Roy Cameron had under his thumb and tell him Cameron was lying?' Edie erupted in fresh rage. 'He could have stopped the annulment.'

'Mr Hamilton's only child had just been murdered. His wife had a total breakdown. He couldn't think of anything else.'

'We knew Eric had called the Camerons and was heading to their house to confront them. Who else knew that?' Edie challenged. 'Nobody!'

Again, Kara ordered herself to think like a lawyer. 'We don't know that. We believe that's how it was. And at the same time,' she pursued, her mind charging ahead, 'we must place Roy Cameron in Eden between the time Dad and Mom had the accident and the time Eric and Gerry were murdered.' Through the years Mom and Grandma had woven Dad into her life. It was as though she'd truly known him. The few snapshots from Mom and Dad's precious summer together were cherished as though they were priceless masterpieces.

Edie grunted in exasperation. 'We *know* Roy Cameron hired Joe to kill Eric and Gerry!'

'All we know is that Joe confessed to the murders, and that he was hired by somebody in Eden.' Kara fought for a dispassionate approach. 'We don't know that Roy Cameron hired Joe. We're guessing he did.'

'Everything points to him. David Hamilton thinks so too!'

'He has a motive – but our first step is to place him here in Eden on those specific days,' Kara insisted. 'Then we'll—'

'Kara, any day now Hank may be indicted for Mattie's murder.'

'But we must realize that Roy could have hired Joe without being here in town,' she conceded. 'He could have phoned from Washington or Los Angeles or Shanghai – or wherever.'

'He called one of his henchmen – those creeps he uses for his rotten deals – to steal Joe's confession! Mattie walked in and caught the guy – and was murdered!'

'Grandma, you sound like one of those mystery novels you're always reading,' Kara joshed. 'But yes, somebody

115

wanted Joe's confession. And instinct tells me he was hired by Roy Cameron.' But a lawyer shouldn't work on instinct. 'Tomorrow morning I'll start digging at the library.'

Both Kara and Edie started at the sound of the phone.

'I'll get it.' Kara rose and crossed to the phone. 'Hello?'

'Kara, they're doing it again—' Valerie's voice was shrill with alarm.

'What are they doing?' Kara tensed. 'They' meant the police.

'A friend who works with Hank just called to tell me. The police picked him up for questioning again. He'll lose his job if they keep this up. How many times can they keep asking him the same things?'

'Val, they don't have enough to hold him,' Kara soothed her. Hank had a right to be represented by a lawyer, she thought uneasily – but he and Val couldn't come up with a retainer. Even if they borrowed on the house – which should be possible – the bank would take weeks to put through a loan. 'They're trying to trick Hank into contradicting himself – that's the reason for all this questioning.'

'He gets flustered easy. He might say the wrong thing,' Valerie wailed. 'Not meaning to—'

'Have Hank call me when he comes home,' Kara told her. Sure he wouldn't be held. 'I'll—'

'How long before you'll be able to practice law?' Valerie asked plaintively. 'I'm so scared—'

'Val, I just took the bar exams last week,' Kara reminded her. 'It'll probably be the end of the month – or close to it – before the results come in.'

She was more worried than she let Val know. The police were looking for contradictions in Hank's story. Sometimes a little thing could be misinterpreted, throw everything off. Harvey Raines was dying to close the case. One little slip in Hank's testimony, and he'd be headed for arraignment and a grand jury.

Jonathan drove with the real-estate broker to the garden apartments that she'd described with such enthusiasm.

'The architect designed the structures so that each apartment has side windows as well as front and rear. And there's a large parking area at one side. And all apartment living rooms face the south, so there's marvelous day-long sunlight.'

Now she was pulling up in the parking area beside the red-brick, pleasantly landscaped units. She'd seemed surprised that he was planning to move out of the 'ancestral home' into far less pretentious quarters. Her eyes had displayed avid interest when he'd indicated he'd require a two-bedroom apartment.

'I'll need a room to serve as my office,' he'd explained – reading her mind.

'Oh—' She seemed disappointed. 'I don't think this could be used as a professional apartment.'

'My home office,' he explained, and she smiled in approval. An office he hoped to share with Kara. Sure, they'd only known each other a few weeks, but why must they play this waiting game? They both realized they were meant for each other. It was as though they'd known each other for years.

'This apartment wouldn't be available,' the broker effervesced as they left the car, 'except that the family living in it inherited a house when her mother died and they moved before their lease expired.' Censure in her voice now. 'Of course, they're responsible for the rent until we sign a new tenant.'

The vacancy was a ground-floor apartment. The rooms were of fair size, the kitchen adequate.

'All the rooms will be repainted,' the broker reminded him. 'That makes such a difference.'

Jonathan gazed about at the vacant apartment with little enthusiasm. But face it – there were few apartments in Eden. Vacancies were grabbed up by senior citizens eager to move down here.

'The place has a lot of possibilities,' the broker said persuasively. 'And it's available immediately. Of course, vacancies don't stay long on the market.'

'All right, draw up the lease,' he capitulated. 'Could I move in by August the fifteenth?'

'Oh yes. But the lease will have to start from August the first. It's routine,' she assured him – anticipating an argument.

'August the first,' he agreed, surprising her. 'Draw up the lease. I'll stop by your office tomorrow to sign it.'

He left the apartment and returned to the white Mercedes, to be replaced by Friday with a Mercedes from the lower end of the line. A company car, but at his total disposal. Sometimes he was disconcerted by Dad's generosity.

Thank God, Mom was carrying on about the hot weather. She was flying in a couple of days to Sea Pines on Hilton Head. So she wouldn't be here to insist on having a decorator come in to furnish the apartment for him. He could pick up the basic stuff here in town. His face brightened. *Maybe Kara will help me.*

He was conscious of a flurry of excitement at the prospect of seeing her again tomorrow night. They'd had a long talk on the phone last night – and they'd talk again tonight. It was as though they were trying to make up for all the years they hadn't known each other. *When I'm with Kara I just want to hold her in my arms.*

During the college years he'd played around a bit. Not like his overheated roommate, he thought in retrospect. But nobody had affected him the way Kara did. He'd known almost from that first moment that he wanted her to be part of his life forever. And he kept remembering how he'd felt when he'd kissed her on Saturday. It was meant to be just a casual good-night kiss – but something happened. It happened for both of them.

In the four years he'd roomed with Bob – the first year at John Jay College of Criminal Justice, then the apartment at 104th and Broadway – Bob had had brief, hectic affairs with dozens of women. Always sure he was wildly in love with each one. In law school they'd had little time for socializing. The grind was too rough.

Jonathan's mind shot back to that last night before law-school graduation. He'd sat with Bob and Clay in their favorite booth at the West End and rehashed their plans for the years ahead . . .

Bob, of course, was going back home – with a job that was paying him a bundle right from the start. Clay was excited about his coming job as a public defender in the small town where he was born.

'Sure, the money stinks,' Clay conceded. 'But that's what I've wanted to do since I was ten years old.' He'd sat in a courtroom with his mother while his father was represented by an impassioned public defender on a false charge of embezzlement. At the time an ill-paid bank teller. But in eight years his father had worked his way up to the point where he could manage – with hefty college loans – to see Clay through a good state college and Columbia Law.

'Tell the truth,' Bob joshed. 'You just want the law background so you can break out as a hot-shot novelist, like John Grisham.'

Clay grinned. 'That too.'

Bob turned to Jonathan. 'You've got nothing to worry about.' A hint of envy in his eyes. 'You'll be running all over the globe, representing your old man's business. We should be so lucky.'

'I'm not mad about the prospect of running all over the world.' Jonathan was self-conscious, reading the minds of the other two. As the son of Roy Cameron, CEO of Cameron Insurance, his future was guaranteed. 'I've had enough of the big-city life, too. I want to settle down in Eden, South Carolina, get married in five or six years – raise a family. I want a life – not just a career in law.'

'That sounds good to me,' Clay said, almost wistful. Jonathan knew he was conscious of the $56,000 in school loans on his back. As a public defender, he'd spend a lot of years paying those off. And Clay was conscientious – he wouldn't try to dodge his debts.

Their waiter arrived with the food. They began to eat – conscious that this would be their last dinner at the West End. Now they fell into a nostalgic mood, replaying crucial occasions during the past three years. But in a corner of his mind Jonathan tried to deal with the relationship with his parents. They were so good to him – yet sometimes it seemed as though he hardly knew them.

Maybe four times in my life Dad took me to a baseball or football game. Dad was always busy with the company – and

119

Mom's health not good. Early on I knew my life wasn't like other kids' lives. I loved sleepovers with friends – but Mom made it clear she couldn't handle having kids at our house. I remember the time I was eight and I slept over for the first time at Ronnie's house. Ronnie's mother came in to tuck us in – and she kissed us both good-night. I thought I was in heaven.

Sitting at dinner with her grandmother and mother, Kara listened to the conversation between the other two with a sense of satisfaction. Mom was radiant. Mr Hamilton confirmed what she had always maintained. Dad was not into drugs. Their marriage should not have been annulled.

'I wish Mr Hamilton had come forward then,' Daisy admitted. 'I wanted to kill Tim's father when he set up that foundation to fight against drugs! It was as though he was deliberately tainting Tim's memory.'

'But Tim would have been pleased that the foundation has done some good in this town. Not that we've had a lot of teenagers into drugs,' Edie conceded. 'But the few involved have been helped.'

'Kara, will this be useful in tracking down Mattie's killer?' Daisy was ambivalent.

'It strengthens our suspicions,' Kara said thoughtfully, 'but we have a long way to go. I still think we have to tie Roy Cameron to Eric and Gerry's murder before we'll know who killed Mattie.'

'It burns me up,' Edie said, 'the way the police keep saying that "Mattie Mason's murder appears to be a robbery gone wrong" – but they're harassing Hank like mad!'

'Tomorrow I'll start trying to pin down Roy Cameron's whereabouts the afternoon Eric and Gerry were killed. First we must prove he was in town and—'

'You're back to that,' Edie scolded her. 'You said yourself – he could have phoned or faxed somebody here in town even if he was away—'

'He wouldn't fax – he wouldn't want a record of that,' Kara began.

'Right.' Edie nodded.

'But before we probe further, let's find out if he was in town that night. If we can, that'll save trying to track down calls – which could be rough. It's back to the microfilm.'

'Won't the librarians get suspicious at your poking around?' Edie was uneasy. 'Remember Sandra Cameron is on the library's board of directors. Of course, all she does is lend her name.'

'Nobody's going to connect what Kara's doing to that day,' Daisy said with conviction. 'That could have been a problem if Mrs Gordon was still head librarian, but the current librarians were little kids when all that happened.'

'They could be curious,' Kara acknowledged. 'But nobody will guess I'm trying to pin murders on the great Roy Cameron.'

At 10 p.m. – while the three women were watching the local TV news – the phone rang.

'I'll get it,' Kara said quickly. 'I'll take it in my room.' Thank goodness Grandma had had that extension put in last week. 'It may be for me.' She tried to sound casual.

When Jonathan called last night, she'd told a white lie. She'd said it was Anita. Instinct told her they would be upset that she was becoming so close to Jonathan. It astonished *her* that he'd become important to her life in such a short time.

In her bedroom she closed the door and darted to pick up the phone. 'Hello?'

'I suppose I'll survive until I see you tomorrow night,' Jonathan said. 'Oh, I rented an apartment this afternoon. I'm hoping you'll help me pick out the furniture. One day later in the week when you can spare the time.'

'Sure thing. I hope you don't want stark, plastic modern? I'll be useless.'

'I want warm and comfortable,' he told her.

'Then I'm your woman,' she laughed – and stopped short.

'I'm hoping for that,' he said softly. 'But no rush. We'll take our time.'

Kara hurried into conversation about furnished apartments she'd shared during college and law-school years, and he reciprocated with stories of his own. Safe conversation.

But her heart was pounding.

Fourteen

Kara awoke on Tuesday morning with a sense of falling through space. This was almost immediately replaced by a surge of joyous anticipation. *I'll be seeing Jonathan this evening!*

Now reality intruded. *I must be at the library when it opens. Read through microfilm, track down Roy Cameron's whereabouts on the day Eric and Gerry were murdered. Don't think about Jonathan's reaction to this if he knew.*

A smile lit up her face as she heard the usual morning sounds in the kitchen. Comforting sounds. Both Grandma and Mom were early risers. She left her bed to prepare for the day.

When she arrived in the kitchen – the air fragrant with the aroma of coffee brewing – she found Edie on the phone and listening intently to the caller. All at once she was tense. A phone call a few minutes past 8 a.m.? Had the police picked Hank up again?

'It's Peg,' Daisy said, reading Kara's mind. 'She knows we're always up early.'

'Now Peg, calm down,' Edie ordered, pantomiming to Kara and Daisy that this was of no urgency. 'Just call the doctor's office and tell his secretary. I'm sure it was just a mistake.' She listened again for a moment. 'Oh, sure, I'll be going to the meeting tonight.' She put down the phone with an indulgent sigh.

'What's Peg upset about now?' Daisy exchanged a good-humored smile with her mother.

'She got one of those things from Medicare – about an office visit to her ophthalmologist. It listed her as a diabetic,' Edie explained, heading for the range to prepare the blueberry pancakes she'd promised for breakfast this morning. 'I told her it was just some silly mistake.'

'But you don't believe that,' Kara surmised, studying Edie's expressive face.

'No.' Edie was blunt. 'I think whoever made out the Medicare report wanted to set her as a diabetic to alibi all the tests he's ordered for her.'

'Mom, you're so skeptical,' Daisy scolded.

'Come with me to tonight's meeting, Daisy,' Edie said. Kara knew Edie carried on a constant battle to coax Daisy into socializing. 'We need everybody we can get.'

'I should do some ironing tonight,' Daisy hedged.

'Leave it – I'll do it in the morning. This is important.'

'Okay, I'll go,' Daisy agreed, but with reluctance.

'You come too, Kara,' Edie prodded.

'I can't,' Kara said self-consciously. 'But what's this meeting about?'

'A couple of nurses from the hospital called it to discuss the impact on the community of its becoming a for-profit deal. They've contacted a few people to spread the word. Peg told me about it last night.'

'The takeover is a done deal,' Kara warned, but she was sympathetic. How was Jonathan involved in all that? *He said he'd be working in a new venture for Cameron Insurance. It* has *to be the hospital takeover.*

'Why can't you come?' Edie clucked in reproach.

'I'm having dinner tonight with Jonathan Cameron.' Kara saw her mother's shocked expression. 'The police are doing nothing except harassing Hank and Val,' she excused her seeing him. 'We have to try anything that might be useful.' *I can't let them know how I feel about Jonathan – not yet. Mom would be devastated. I'm not lying – it's just not the time to tell them.*

Edie turned to Daisy. 'We'll have an early dinner. Peg says they want to start the meeting at seven thirty since it's a midweek night.'

'I'll have a sandwich at the shop. I have to be there until close to seven thirty – I'm redoing one of the sales tables.' Daisy avoided Kara's eyes. 'I'll meet you at the school.'

123

Mom doesn't want to be here at the house to meet Jonathan. She's making up that business about working late.

'The library opens early on Tuesdays, doesn't it?' Kara glanced from Daisy to Edie.

'Yeah, it's a ten a.m. day,' Edie confirmed. 'And don't worry about either of the women there being suspicious about your research. Neither of them knows you. They know me,' she conceded, chuckling. 'I'm the one who puts in a reserve for each new Elizabeth Peters.'

Twenty minutes after Daisy left for the shop, Kara and Edie climbed into the station wagon.

'You should have a car of your own,' Edie fretted. 'Instead of driving this old wreck, shuttling me around the way you do—'

'I'm grateful for this old wreck. And once I land some paying clients, I'll lease a car. You'll have the "old wreck" back.' *When will that be?*

Kara dropped Edie off at the pharmacy and headed for the library. Driving slowly because of the dense fog that hung over Eden this morning. The aura of serenity that fog always provided for her at odds this morning with her turbulent emotions. Mom was so upset that she was seeing Jonathan – and she could understand this. But the day would come when Mom and he must meet.

Familiar landmarks told her she was approaching the library. Not the old, familiar library that had been her 'home away from home' in her growing-up years. Six years ago that small building had been demolished to make way for the large, white-brick structure of which Eden residents were so proud. The Cameron Library, she thought with distaste, built with the aid of government grants and a major donation by Roy Cameron.

Fighting self-consciousness, she made out slips for microfilm for the local newspapers she needed – requesting an entire week rather than specific days, to disguise her quarry. The rolls of film in hand, she crossed to the alcove where the microfilm machines were located, settled down to thread the first roll of film.

Scanning the headline of the evening *Ledger* on that fateful day, she felt her heart begin to pound. Endless times, of course, she had heard about the accident – but reading the headline, she was catapulted back into a time before her own. TIM CAMERON KILLED BY HIT-AND-RUN DRIVER.

With soaring anguish she inspected her father's photograph, centered in the news story. A tiny photograph of her mother – from her high-school yearbook – appeared further down. How young they both were. Dad so young to have his life taken away.

In her mind she heard her mother's voice. '*It didn't matter that we were still in our teens – we knew we wanted to spend the rest of our lives together.*' She remembered her grandmother talking about that summer, how beautiful the two of them were together. '*It was so sweet to watch them, their love shining from their faces. I admit I spoke against their marrying until Tim graduated college, though his father was determined that he would go to law school – and that meant another three years of waiting.*'

Slowly Kara read the long article about the accident. Visualizing the horror of those moments when a drunken driver had left his lane and hit them. The car had been Tim's high-school graduation present. She felt as though she was there, a witness to the tragedy that had robbed her of her father and dealt her mother such anguish through the years ahead.

She forced herself to focus on the purpose of this visit. Had Roy Cameron been in Eden on the day of the accident? No mention in this edition of the *Ledger*, she discovered after careful search. All right, move on to the morning *Enquirer*. She rewound the *Ledger* microfilm, threaded the *Enquirer* film of the following morning.

Arriving at the proper date on the film, she began to read the front-page news. She gaped at this morning's headlines in a wave of shock – though she knew every grim detail. LOCAL TEENAGER PROFESSES TO BE TIM CAMERON'S BRIDE. CAMERON ATTORNEYS SAY MARRIAGE TO BE ANNULLED. Tears blurred her vision. She was grateful that she was alone in the microfilm area. Why did it hurt so much to read what she already knew? Cameron's lawyers claimed Tim had been into hard drugs, had been inveigled into a secret marriage by a greedy young woman he'd known a few weeks.

Mom and Dad had known each other over a year, had corresponded all through his freshman year at college – but it was that last fateful summer that they realized they wanted to be together for the rest of their lives.

All at once Kara tensed. Roy Cameron had *not* been in town the day Eric and Gerry were murdered. He'd arrived home the following afternoon from a business conference in Brussels. Summoned home because of his son's death. The whole town stunned by the tragedy.

So, Roy Cameron wasn't in town, she reasoned. There were telephones and faxes in Brussels. He could have hired Joe as a hit man in a phone call. All right, more work to do. She stared at the microfilm without seeing – her mind charging ahead. She must dig into telephone-company records of twenty-five years ago, check calls that may have come into town from Brussels. They would be few. Not a call to Cameron Insurance, she reminded herself. A call to Joe Mason.

Brushing aside her apprehension at the formidable task ahead, she returned the microfilm to the librarian, asked for copies of the two newspapers for the month of May 1998. As long as she was here, she could look to see if Roy Cameron was in town the day Mattie was murdered.

Minutes later she was reading a brief item that placed Roy Cameron in a town a hundred miles away on the day Mattie died. He was the speaker at a Rotarian dinner and was the house guest of the local mayor on that night. But he could have arranged the murder from there, she rationalized. Or arranged it before he left town.

Where do I go from here?

In the ornate, darkly furnished Cameron Insurance Company conference room Roy Cameron sat at his usual place at the head of the table. Jonathan on his right, Bart on his left, the two men flanked by the handful of company executives assigned – along with Jonathan – to the Eden General takeover team.

In the past few days Jonathan had steeped himself in statistics plus the legal aspects of for-profit hospitals. He'd worked with Bill Hoffman to set up the legal papers that established Eden General as the first in a chain of hospitals to be a subsidiary of Cameron Insurance Company. He was uncomfortable in the knowledge that some local residents were loudly unhappy at the takeover of Eden.

With an effort he pulled himself out of inner mental debate to listen to his father.

'Damn it to hell, locals ought to be thrilled we're coming in to take over the hospital,' Roy harangued. 'It was on the verge of going under.'

'I heard rumors about a group forming to fight the takeover,' Bill Hoffman said uneasily. 'Some of the nurses are up in arms. They—'

'Bullshit,' Roy interrupted. 'The takeover is effective already. Too many highly paid nurses are doing menial jobs like bathing patients, giving back-rubs. Eden pays nurses twenty-five dollars an hour – let a seven-dollar-an-hour aide do those things. And we'll cut back the number of RNs assigned to a unit. Put it on a team basis – like Kaiser does. Instead of three RNs, we'll set up a team of one RN, a licensed vocational nurse, plus a nurse's aide. We'll save twenty-five dollars an hour on every unit. In the course of a year that's a bundle.'

Jonathan sat in grim silence while additional savings were plotted. His mind told him this was smart business, tested and proved in other hospitals. Yet he was disturbed at these cost-saving devices.

'And look at what Eden General has been paying its administrators,' Bart pointed out with disdain. 'Greedy guys there. We'll cut back.'

'We'll cut out unnecessary beds,' Roy picked up. 'Dispose of duplicated equipment – that's a major waste today in the whole hospital system. How many elaborate burn units does a town the size of Eden need?'

'We're dropping Eden's burn unit?' Hoffman was disconcerted.

Roy chuckled. 'Not just yet. When we take over Farraday Hospital – that's next on the agenda – we'll eliminate unnecessary departments. Cut out duplications.' He chuckled. 'We may even close Farraday. Of course, we aren't ready to deal with that just yet. But we can run a competent hospital – one this town can be proud of – and make a sharp profit for the company at the same time. It's all a matter of efficient operation.'

Kara waited impatiently for her grandmother to return from the pharmacy. Grandma knew so many people in town through her volunteer work and her church groups. With luck she would know someone with connections at the phone company. Yet her mind warned her this was a long shot.

She struggled to focus on more realistic approaches to connect Roy Cameron with the three murders. She was instantly alert at the sound of a car pulling up before the house. Grandma's ride home, she thought in relief, and hurried to the door. Again, she felt such guilt at taking Grandma's car the way she did – but it was temporary, she promised herself. She'd lease a car as soon as she could handle the expense.

'How'd you make out?' Edie asked, approaching the door.

'I need some help,' Kara apologized. 'It won't be easy—'

'Darling, what's easy in life?' Edie clucked. 'Tell me what's happened.'

While they settled themselves in the living room, Kara briefed Edie on what she'd discovered on the newspaper microfilm.

'Maybe we're chasing after the wrong quarry,' she conceded reluctantly. 'Roy Cameron was not in Eden when Mattie was murdered. He wasn't here when Eric and Gerry were murdered.' She paused, took a deep breath. 'But—'

'You found something out,' Edie pounced. 'What's the problem?'

'Roy Cameron was in Brussels,' Kara said. 'There's a chance he could have phoned Joe from there and made a deal. But how can we dig into telephone-company records of twenty-five years ago?'

'The company will have a record of all international calls . . .' Edie frowned in thought.

'We can't just go over there and ask for records.' A note of desperation seeped into Kara's voice. 'Only the police could do that.'

'I may have a connection.' Edie frowned, searching her

mind. 'Yes!' Her face brightened. 'Donna Aikens worked there for thirty years. She retired five months ago. She's a member of my reading group.'

'What can she do for us?' Kara was puzzled.

'She's got friends who're still there. Mildred Cannon,' Edie recalled with an air of triumph.

'Will she help us?' Kara was doubtful.

'You bet. Mildred and her sister both hate Roy Cameron.'

'Why?' Kara asked. Did they hate him enough to take chances?

'About seven years ago a cousin of theirs and her husband out in Texas had just built this gorgeous home, and it was almost destroyed by fire. They had a fire insurance policy with Cameron – but Cameron refused to pay. They claimed it was a case of arson. Mildred's cousin sued, and it got real nasty. Finally – they were out of money and exhausted – they settled out of court with Cameron Insurance for piddling damages. But Mildred says that even today some people in that town aren't sure it wasn't arson – after all the dirty rumors Cameron circulated. It was a big claim – for almost half a million – and they were determined not to pay.'

'Mildred could be fired if she was caught messing around with telephone-company files.'

'They hate Roy Cameron so much they'll go out on a limb to cause him trouble. They'll never realize why I'm asking questions about Roy Cameron making phone calls from Brussels twenty-five years ago – but they'll hope it means big trouble for him.'

'When?' Kara probed. 'When can you talk with Donna?'

'I'll call her tonight. She won't connect it with Mattie's murder. It may take a while before she comes up with answers. And I know,' Edie said, 'we don't have much time, with Harvey Raines trying so hard to nail Hank.'

'Call her,' Kara ordered. 'Tonight.'

'Before I leave for my meeting.' Edie smiled. 'I've got a good feeling about this.'

Kara fought panic as she prepared to dress for her dinner date with Jonathan. Would he hate her if he knew what she was trying to do? This was his father! *How else can I expect him to react? But Hank's life hangs in the balance. I have to do this.*

She'd been disappointed that Grandma hadn't been able to get through to her friend, Donna Aikens. '*I forgot she's away on vacation – and I don't know Mildred well enough to approach her directly.*' But Grandma expected Donna back by the end of the week.

Edie's voice filtered down the hall into the bedroom. 'Come over and have a quick dinner with me before we leave for the meeting. I have last night's leftover chicken, and I made a big salad to go with it. I'll throw the chicken into the oven and—' Silence on this end for the moment. 'Peg, I'll use the toaster/oven – it won't heat up the whole house.'

A few minutes later – while Kara debated between a turquoise linen shift and a dressier print, Peg came into the house by the kitchen door as usual.

'I'm so tired of cooking for myself,' Peg declared, then laughed. 'Of course, I cook one night and eat for three.'

'I know you'll feel deprived without dessert,' Edie joshed, 'so I'll put two apricot Danishes into the oven while we're eating.'

'Did I tell you, the two nurses who drummed up this meeting have persuaded Dr Callahan to come?' Peg was impressed. 'I suppose you'd say he's on the side of the enemy – but he won't go back and report to Roy Cameron,' she said with conviction.

'From what Val has said about him, I don't think we have to worry about that,' Edie reassured her. 'And I hear he's not exactly happy about the takeover.'

'Did you persuade Daisy and Kara to come to the meeting?' Peg asked. 'Daisy needs to get out more.' A familiar litany.

'Daisy will meet us there – she'll be working at the shop until past seven. Kara's having dinner with a friend.'

All at once Kara was apprehensive. *Grandma and Peg will have left for their meeting by the time Jonathan arrives, won't they? How will Peg react if she knows I'm seeing Jonathan?*

She deliberately dawdled in her bedroom – all the while listening for sounds from the dining area. Grandma would make a point of prodding Peg away from the house, she guessed instinctively.

'You don't need a second cup of coffee,' Edie scolded Peg. 'We want to be there early, hear if anything new has developed at the hospital. After the meeting some of us will go somewhere for coffee.'

A few moments later Edie called down the hall. 'Kara, we're leaving for the meeting now.'

'Promise me, no duels at dawn,' Kara called back.

'No problem,' Peg trilled. 'Neither of us get up that early.'

Kara sighed with relief. Peg wouldn't meet Jonathan arriving to pick her up. But how long could their relationship be secret?

Fifteen

Edie and Peg left the house in Peg's car. When they arrived at the elementary school's meeting room – loaned out at intervals to local groups – they found a dozen people had already arrived.

'There's Nan Logan.' Peg pointed to one of the two nurses from Eden General – still in uniform – who had organized the meeting. 'She's pissed as hell about the takeover.'

Surrounded by a cluster of retirees who'd taken up residence in Eden, Nan Logan was in vigorous debate with a quietly handsome man in his mid-forties.

'Let's not rush to judgment,' he said with a blend of caution and compassion. 'We know Eden General was in a financial mess. We have to sit back and watch how this situation develops.'

'Is that Dr Callahan?' Edie asked Peg.

'That's him. Nicest guy on the staff, everybody says. The hospital was thrilled when he agreed to come here. He's one of the finest pediatricians in the country. Val can't praise him enough for what he's done for Betsy. And,' her voice dropped to a whisper, 'he's single.'

'Peg, stop trying to fix Daisy up,' Edie scolded, but her eyes were wistful.

'Isn't this a case of conflict of interests?' a well-groomed woman with the air of a retired schoolteacher asked. 'I mean, a health insurance company moving into "for-profit" hospitals?'

'If it was, the government would have stepped in.' A brusque, florid-faced man who towered above the others jumped in before Dr Callahan could reply.

'There are other HMOs that own hospitals,' Dr Callahan conceded.

'I don't like what I suspect we'll see happening at Eden,' the other nurse who had called the meeting said defensively. 'First thing, they'll start firing nurses. We need every nurse on our staff!'

'Nurses will be replaced by LPNs and aides,' Nan Logan said with distaste. 'And by clerks and janitors,' she added with a derisive smile. 'That's what happens when for-profit groups take over. Think of how much money they'll be saving.'

'Next they'll cut back on testing,' a retiree in her late sixties warned, and her husband nodded in agreement. 'That means Cameron Insurance will see an improvement in their bottom line.'

'Aren't HMOs forever crying about how doctors over-test?' someone else picked up. 'They do MRIs today the way they did a simple blood test twenty years ago. Wow, what that does to billing!'

'No ethical doctor will allow needed tests to be eliminated,' Dr Callahan insisted. 'There *are* instances of over-testing—'

'Begging your pardon, Dr Callahan,' a rather timorous young woman whom Edie had known since birth broke in, 'but not every doctor is as ethical as you.'

'Necessary tests must be done.' Dr Callahan was firm. 'But,' he emphasized, and paused for a moment, 'doctors on staff must not be shareholders in laboratories. That can bring about dangerous over-testing. In fact, there are laws against that now.' But his eyes indicated some skepticism about this being respected.

'Mr Cameron's done so much for this town. I can't see him going into anything that would be harmful to us,' a modestly dressed woman of about forty said.

'What's she doing here?' Peg whispered to Edie, while latecomers joined their circle. 'Her husband is a mailroom clerk at Cameron Insurance.'

'I hear things—' A recent retiree to Eden cleared his throat with an air of self-consciousness. 'A neighbor back home carries Cameron Insurance. Her family has a history of skin cancer, so she's super-cautious. She had one of those single-cell skin cancer lesions on her nose removed, but Cameron Insurance refused to pay. They said it was cosmetic surgery.'

'I don't believe that!' the mailroom clerk's wife flared. 'There's always some troublemaker spreading rumors.'

'Some people in this town think Roy Cameron's some kind of god,' someone at the edge of the group scoffed. 'Let's dig in and come up with facts.'

'I realize there's some anxiety around town,' Dr Callahan soothed them, 'but let's withhold judgment, sit back and see what develops. There are for-profit hospitals that provide excellent care. I admit I'd like to see federal health insurance for every resident – with dental care as well. Like in England. But this isn't the time for that yet. We—'

'Dr Callahan, what can we do to protect ourselves?' another woman who'd just joined the group broke in. 'I mean, do we just sit back and watch our hospital turned into a profit-making machine?'

'For everybody's peace of mind, I suggest this group be built into a watchdog organization.' He hesitated, seeming in some inner debate. 'As a member of the Eden General staff, I can be no more than an onlooker,' he apologized. 'I suggest you form a committee to go out and solicit membership. A committee that will approach the hospital administration at any point when the group feels action at the hospital is detrimental to the welfare of local residents.'

'Let's call it "HWG". The Hospital Watchdog Group,' Nan suggested, and there was loud vocal approval.

'There's Daisy,' Peg whispered, and beckoned her to join them.

'You seem to think we won't be the losers with Eden General becoming a for-profit hospital,' another woman challenged Dr Callahan. Clearly skeptical.

'Cameron Insurance is known for efficient management. We must assume this will carry over into their management of Eden General. That should mean Eden can deliver top-notch care in a less expensive manner. Its financial situation up till now has been precarious. It couldn't have remained in operation for much longer under those circumstances.'

With a flicker of pleasure, Edie saw Dr Callahan's eyes linger on Daisy for a moment. She knew that several unattached women in Eden had tried to bring him into various social groups. He always evaded this. His life was medicine, Edie surmised. Yet she'd recognized a startled interest when his eyes encountered Daisy. She sighed. Daisy wouldn't be interested. She'd staved off half a dozen men in the past twenty years.

A dozen others arrived in Daisy's wake. Surveying the crowd and then the wall clock, Dr Callahan suggested that Nan call the meeting to order.

The conversation became super-charged. Edie couldn't remember anything eliciting so much concern in town. And the host of retirees that had taken up residence, she thought with satisfaction, were not blinded by the local adoration of Roy Cameron.

'All right,' Nan summed up briskly. 'Let's form a "watchdog committee" tonight.' Her eyes strayed about the room, lighted on Edie. 'You know more people in this town than even me. Will you form the committee?'

For a moment Edie was startled. Then excitement welled in her.

'I'll be happy to do it,' she agreed. She'd been on many committees through the years. But none that could bring her such satisfaction as this one.

Maybe – just maybe – she plotted, she could bring Daisy into this one. She brushed aside guilt that she was eager to bring Daisy and Dr Callahan together. Nothing would happen, she derided herself. Dr Callahan was married to his profession. Daisy emotionally tied to the memory of Tim.

Edie forced her mind back into the volatile exchange of ideas charging about the room. This would be a long, heated evening.

Kara loved dining at The Magnolias. The damask-covered tables set far apart, the vases of fresh flowers, the soft illumination, the quietness of the room provided an atmosphere of serenity. But she was faintly intimidated by its tabs. No doubt, though, she consoled herself, Jonathan was drawing a handsome salary.

'You've been pensive tonight,' Jonathan said when they'd

ordered and their waiter had left their table. 'It's this awful wait to hear about the law exams.'

'It's kind of scary,' she admitted. 'And my grandmother keeps after me to start looking for office space. Tiny space,' she added with a light laugh.

'How's your *pro bono* case going?'

'He hasn't been arraigned.' Her eyes were serious. 'But I'm sure it's a matter of time.' *Unless I can dig up concrete proof that Jonathan's father hired Mattie's killer.*

'No real leads?' His eyes were compassionate.

'Suspicions. I'm working on those.'

'You don't believe it was a robbery gone wrong?'

'No way.' She was startled that the words came out so strongly.

'I wish I could do something to help.' His smile was wistful. 'Actually, all through law school I wanted to practice criminal law. Like you,' he joshed, 'fighting for the innocent caught in legal problems they can't afford to handle. I can't believe how many hours I'm putting in at the office. All grunt work. Research. Bottom-line financial figures.' Pain infiltrated his voice. 'Only a segment of it's legal. Sometimes I feel more like an accountant than a lawyer – but I still don't know if I've passed the bar exams.'

'You'll pass,' Kara said confidently. But she understood the uncertainty that nagged at him.

'I could function in my present capacity without a law degree.' He hesitated. 'I suspect some local residents are upset about the takeover at Eden General—'

'It's been a non-profit hospital for almost fifty years.' *Mom was born there. I was born there.* 'They're scared about changes that might be made.' *How would he feel if he knew that Grandma is part of the opposition group?* 'They hear frightening reports.'

'Eden General was on the verge of bankruptcy.' Jonathan was somber. 'Only a takeover could save it. There'll be a series of articles in the *Enquirer* and *Ledger* in the weeks ahead that should reassure people. Everything out in the open. Times are changing, Kara.' He was almost defensive. 'Sometimes the old ways aren't effective any longer.'

'That won't sit well with longtime employees who're fearful of being fired.' *He has to know that will happen.*

He was startled. 'I haven't heard about any firings.' He paused. 'But there's some fat that will have to go. Dad's sharp. He knows it's urgent to cut medical costs.'

'Have you thought about putting a time limit on the company job?' she asked impulsively. 'I mean, that's not what you want to do with your life.' He shouldn't have to stay in a job he hated.

'I'll have to stay with the company for a while. But it won't be a lifetime commitment,' he said with sudden intensity. His eyes searched hers – seeking reassurance that she would go along with this. 'I want to see a shingle that reads "Cameron and Jamison".' Unexpectedly he grinned. 'You won't object to second billing?'

'I'll consider that.' Her tone light to match his own.

'You do understand, don't you?'

'Of course I do.'

'My parents have done so much for me.'

Have they? Oh, the money thing yes – but what about love? Mom says they wanted a son for window-dressing. That's what my father was – a part of the Cameron picture of the 'perfect family'.

'I won't be able to walk out after just a few weeks – or even months. But I'm not irreplaceable. Anybody with a degree in business administration or public health could do a better job. I'm hoping that in time Dad will realize that he's causing a lot of animosity in the company by pushing me ahead this way. Over guys who've been with the company twenty years – and are twice my age. Bart's livid.' She stared back blankly. 'Mom's brother,' he explained. 'He's been with the company forever. He figured one day he'd take over. It's going to be rough to tell Dad that I don't want to run his empire when he decides to retire.'

'Jonnie, nobody has the right to try to rule somebody else's life.' Her special name for him, that he said nobody had used since he was ten. 'Not even your father.'

An awkward silence engulfed them for a few moments.

'Oh, I signed the apartment lease this morning.' He seemed relieved to be on safer ground.

'Congratulations. That means you're settling in as a permanent resident.'

'You'll help me choose furniture?' he asked, his eyes tender. 'You said you would.'

'It'll be fun.' This was the mood for tonight. Yet she realized that once he had his own apartment their relationship could move into another phase. *Am I ready for that?*

'What about Saturday?'

'I'll mark it on my calendar,' she flipped.

All at once his eyes fastened on a group of new arrivals. He focused on trying to capture the attention of one among them. Now he broke into a brilliant smile, waved. His wave – and smile – were returned.

'That's Cassie Bates, my father's executive secretary. The tall woman in the flowered print dress. I've known her since I was a toddler. She was so good to me when I was a kid.' His voice was warmly reminiscent.

'The boss's son.' Kara chuckled. But it was more than that, she surmised. Cassie Bates saw a child reaching out for love. In her own household, Kara mused, they had little money, but so much love.

'Cassie has three sisters and a brother and a bunch of nieces and nephews and grandnieces and nephews. Her family comes here for special occasions.' Jonathan sent an indulgent glance towards the table where the large party was being seated. Kara felt a surge of unease. She didn't know Cassie Bates – but did Cassie Bates know the Jamisons?

If she's been with Roy Cameron for many years, she knows about Mom and me – and Grandma. Will she wonder who's having dinner with Jonathan? Will she ask someone in her party if they know me? Maybe I should have been up-front with Jonathan in the beginning – but that would have been so awkward. I don't want to lose him.

Now Jonathan focused the conversation on the apartment he'd shared on West 104th Street with law-school classmates.

'It must have been a great place seventy years ago,' he reminisced, 'but by the time we moved in we had battles with rats. Not mice,' he emphasized. 'Rats. We dealt with constantly bursting pipes, electrical problems, inadequate heat.

'Thank God one of the guys had a father who was a contractor, and the other's dad was an architect, so we had professional help. By the time we left, it was fairly respectable. And I'd learned a lot about apartment repairs.'

'You won't have to worry about repairs in this rental?' But with so many retirees coming to town landlords were independent.

'They're doing the routine paint job – but I can see changes I'd like to make. How do you feel about jacuzzis?' he joshed.

'I think they're great . . .' Was he harboring thoughts about her moving in with him? She felt hot color tinge her cheekbones.

'I don't foresee a long history in that apartment,' he said quietly, as though reading her mind. 'I see a comfortable house with at least one wood-burning fireplace and four bedrooms.' His eyes were making love to her. 'Our bedroom, a home office we could share – and bedrooms for the kids. I know,' he added quickly. 'We agreed not to rush – but that's my vision for us.'

'It's a beautiful vision.' Unexpectedly tears stung her eyes. The lonely little boy yearning for a real home and family. 'But you know I plan a career as a lawyer.' Flippant again because her heart was beating so insanely.

'I'll have to remain with Cameron Insurance for a year or two.' He was somber now. 'I owe that to the family. But later we'll form our own firm – Cameron and Jamison. Of course, once the kids are old enough to ask questions, it'll be Cameron and Cameron.'

'Like you said, let's take it slowly,' she reminded him. *Can it ever be that way?*

'Did I tell you? My mother's footing the bill for the furniture. Though it means we'll have to drive over to Augusta to this store where she has an account. She'd ordered them to give me anything I want.' He chuckled in anticipation. 'Sometimes it pays to have loaded parents.'

'No problem.' She felt a rush of relief. If they'd gone shopping for furniture in Eden, the word would be all over town. 'Did you hear? Jonathan Cameron and Kara Jamison are buying furniture together. What her mother couldn't do, she did.' 'So we'll drive over to Augusta on Saturday and shop for your furniture.'

All through a long, leisurely gourmet dinner Kara remained conscious of Cassie Bates's presence across the room – fearful that someone at that other table would recognize her and comment to Cassie about her being with Jonathan. It was a relief when Jonathan suggested they leave. It wasn't quite ten o'clock, but Jonathan made a point of being in his office by 8 a.m. – not long behind his father.

'What happened to our gorgeous night?' Jonathan reached for her elbow and steered her towards the car. The moon had disappeared behind ominous clouds. A drizzle was beginning to fall.

'It'll be pleasant for sleeping,' Kara comforted him. But then the Cameron house was centrally air-conditioned.

'I'll think about you when the rain plays a gentle lullaby on my window panes,' he said whimsically, 'and wish you were with me.'

'I love falling to sleep to the sound of rain.' *I'd love falling asleep in his arms. How did this happen so quickly? I first encountered him in late May – and it's only August. But I feel I've known him forever.*

She was pleased to see the house was dark when Jonathan pulled to a stop. The meeting at the school would go on late, even though it was a midweek night. Darkness enclosed the car when he reached to draw her close.

How will we ever scale the wall between us? The wall he doesn't know exists. Not yet.

Sixteen

Prepared for the night, Kara waited up for Edie and Daisy. Her mind still full of the hours with Jonathan. Reliving those exquisite moments in his arms in the darkened car. It was as though she was living in two worlds.

Restless, she crossed to a window, glanced out into the night. The earlier drizzle had become a downpour. She heard a car pulling into the driveway, ran to open the door and switch on the outside light. There was always an umbrella in each of the two cars for such emergencies, she remembered.

'Oh, nobody expected this!' Edie complained as she and Daisy – only slightly protected by the umbrella she carried – swept into the foyer.

'I have decaf up,' Kara told them. 'Or did you go out for coffee after the meeting?'

'It was too late,' Edie pointed out. 'We came straight home.'

'I want to hear all about the meeting.' Kara prodded Edie and Daisy towards the dining area.

'It was a good turn-out,' Daisy said with obvious satisfaction while she and Edie settled themselves at the dining table and Kara went to pour decaf into generous mugs. 'There was a lot of enthusiasm.' But in her mother's eyes she read anxiety about her own meeting with Jonathan.

'I think Jonathan's disturbed that some people are upset about the takeover.' True, but that wasn't what Mom wanted to hear. Mom wanted to know if he let anything slip that might lead to nailing his father. 'Still, he feels the new team can bring about more efficiency. You said Dr Callahan would be there,' she recalled. 'Isn't that bringing in someone from the enemy camp?'

'Dr Callahan is determined to be bipartisan.' Edie was emphatic. 'Val's right – he's special.'

Daisy frowned, seeming ambivalent. 'I don't think he'll go running back to the Camerons and report everything that was said. At least, I hope not.' Now she turned her gaze to Kara. 'What about the heir apparent? Did he say anything useful?'

'Nothing,' Kara admitted. *I don't expect Jonathan to lead us anywhere. But I can't break off with him – not the way we feel about each other.*

'I talked to Donna's neighbor at the meeting,' Edie said. 'Donna's due home from Myrtle Beach sometime Saturday. I'll see her at church on Sunday morning. I'm sure she'll talk to Mildred for us. Oh, I volunteered you for our grass-roots group.' Her expression apologetic. 'I mean, for whatever legal advice we may need.'

'Sure.' Kara forced a smile.

How would Jonathan react to her taking sides against the hospital? Yet instinct told her he would be for what was right. He didn't know what Roy Cameron was really like. All he knew was the man who'd provided his fancy boarding schools, an Ivy League college and Columbia Law. All he knew was the image his father created here in Eden. He didn't know about his father in the outside world.

Last night he'd talked about the time when he could break away from the company and go into private practice. With her. *Oh, I want that. He isn't concerned about building up a fancy, high-paying clientele. He's eager to make a contribution to the town. To have time to lead a real life.*

'I talked with Dr Callahan about the way the police are hounding Hank,' Daisy said, surprising Kara. Usually, Mom was so reticent with strangers. 'He was very sympathetic. He's convinced Hank couldn't be involved. He's been through some critical times with Hank and Val, when Betsy was having one of her asthma attacks.'

Edie sighed. 'Val's a wreck. It was hard enough to lose Mattie that way – but now this craziness with Hank.' She paused. 'And I suppose it could reach out to include Val.'

'We've come up with an iron-clad alibi for Hank and Val at the time of the murder,' Kara reminded them. 'Still, we can be sure the police suspect a third party's involved. Somebody Hank – and Val – brought in as a hired killer.'

'*Not* Hank and Val,' Daisy said passionately. 'Roy Cameron.'

Edie lay wide awake, too wired to sleep. She couldn't blame August heat tonight, she thought wryly. She heard the slipper-softened steps in the hall that told her Daisy, too, was awake. Heading for the bathroom for one of the pills she took on occasion to thwart insomnia, Edie surmised. Daisy – so conscientious – was determined to be fully alert on her job.

After a few moments Edie tossed aside the sheet and went out into the hall. Daisy was in the bathroom, at the medicine cabinet.

'You can't sleep either,' Edie said tenderly.

Daisy managed a weak smile. 'Too much going on in my head.'

'Come out to the kitchen with me. I'll make us hot chocolate.' Daisy needed to talk. Not about the hospital takeover – she was upset that Kara was seeing Jonathan.

'Mom, I worry about Kara,' Daisy confirmed, flipping on the kitchen light. 'This craziness of her seeing Jonathan Cameron.' Edie brought out a container of low-fat milk from the refrigerator while Daisy reached for two packets of hot chocolate. 'I know she's anxious about Hank's situation – but what are the odds that Roy Cameron's son will be useful?'

Edie poured milk into a pot on the range. 'Kara feels she must follow any possible angle that might be helpful.'

'She likes him.' Daisy blurted out. 'A lot. I don't want to see Kara hurt.'

'I met him.' Edie was searching for reassuring words, even while she understood Daisy's anguish. 'He's a bright, charming young man. He's not a Cameron,' she emphasized. 'He just happened to be adopted by Roy Cameron.'

'There's a kind of glow about Kara when she mentions him. I'm scared. What future can there be for her and Roy Cameron's adopted son? Tim's replacement,' she added bitterly.

'Daisy, don't jump the gun,' Edie scolded her. 'They've just met, discovered common ground. You know, both of them

143

waiting to see if they've passed the bar exams.' But weeks ago he'd found her stranded in the car and rescued her. There'd been something special even then when she talked about him. They met again at a crucial time – staying in the same motel when they were taking the bar exams. 'But they'll probably go their separate ways . . .' In her heart she wasn't sure of that.

'Do you know what Roy Cameron will do to her if he finds out his son is seeing Kara? He'll drag out the whole ugly story. He'll make her look like dirt.' Daisy closed her eyes in pain for a moment, as though to blot out a horrific image. 'Does Jonathan know about Tim and me?'

'I doubt it. I can't imagine Kara bringing it up.' *Poor baby, she must worry about that.*

'But somebody will see them together – and the word will get around. You know how it is in this town. She's had dinner with him twice. Suppose somebody from Eden was in Columbia for the bar exams and saw them together?' Daisy took a deep breath. 'She was on the phone forever on Sunday night and again last night. Do you suppose she was talking to him?'

'Daisy, you're getting fixated on Jonathan.'

'I couldn't bear to see Kara hurt,' Daisy reiterated. 'He's probably a neurotic mess after growing up in that house. He—'

'He spent most of his life away, at boarding school, college and summer camps,' Edie reminded her.

'Tim realized he didn't have a normal family. His father forever chasing after success. All he cared about was making money, grabbing power. His mother was happy only when she was on the society pages. Tim used to love to come to our house because he felt there was real love here. Oh sure, at odd moments his father and mother focused on him almost obsessively – but then it was over.'

So many times Daisy had talked about this, Edie remembered. Perhaps Jonathan – like Tim – was searching for what he didn't find at home.

'Kara hardly knows him,' Edie tried again. Weakly.

'She's in love with him,' Daisy insisted. 'How can there ever be anything good for her with someone who's part of that family?'

'Let me get the milk before it boils—' Edie rushed to take the pot from the stove. 'And Daisy, stop your imagination from running away. Kara's main concern right now is to get Hank off the griddle. She'll do whatever it takes to clear him.'

At her grandmother's insistence Kara spent Wednesday and Thursday mornings checking on possible office space – shocked at the way rents had escalated in Eden. She made notes, promised to get back to the brokers shortly. And on Wednesday and Thursday evenings she closeted herself in her room for long conversations with Jonathan.

'I miss you,' Jonathan said plaintively when he called on Thursday. 'Saturday seems so far away.'

'Not really,' she scolded. 'Only about . . .' she glanced at her watch, 'about thirty-six hours.'

'Maybe you should see the apartment before we go shopping.' An anticipatory lilt in his voice. 'Just a quick drive over—'

Kara hesitated. No, that would not be a good idea, though the prospect was appealing. *No.* Not the way they both felt.

'Draw me a diagram.' A garden apartment in Eden would be fairly traditional. 'We'll work from that.'

'Let's make it a day's outing in Augusta,' he cajoled her. 'An early lunch, shopping, some sightseeing. Do you know the Riverwalk?'

'I've heard about it—'

'I'll show it to you. It's this magnificent garden esplanade on top of the levee along the Savannah River. It's a huge tourist draw – and living thirty minutes away, you haven't even seen it,' he joshed.

'Remember, our main objective is shopping,' she warned.

'We'll do that, too,' he promised. 'And then an early dinner?' His voice a charismatic plea.

Kara hesitated a moment. Neither Grandma nor Mom would be home before ten. Grandma had a surprise party to attend. Mom wouldn't be home because she'd agreed to a dinner meeting with the watchdog committee in Grandma's absence. 'Why not?'

But she felt uncomfortable lying to her grandmother and

mother about the trip to Augusta. She'd spoken vaguely to them about more library research there. *'I'll pick up something from the Chinese place for dinner.'*

On Friday morning – minutes after Edie and Daisy left the house – Kara received a phone call from Val.

'Hank's been arrested!' Val's voice was shrill with terror. 'They read him his rights and all – and they took him away.'

'I'll be right over. As soon as I make a phone call. Don't panic, Val. I'll get Hank a lawyer to handle the case until I can take over.' Her mind leaped into high gear. 'It won't be expensive,' she promised. *Please God, let me pass the bar exams.*

'What do they have on him now?' Val was close to hysteria. 'You know how crazy he talks when he's nervous!'

'We'll find out.' She struggled to sound calm, confident. 'Val, you must stay cool – that's important.'

Off the phone she sat immobile for a moment – plotting her next steps. *Call Seth Rogers. He owes me – I dropped the clearance of that drifter right in his lap. And he probably needs extra cash. His clients are few, and Eden pays little for a part-time public defender.*

She reached for the phone book, found his number, dialed.

'Seth Rogers, attorney-at-law,' he greeted her. 'How may I help you?'

'Hi, this is Kara Jamison.' She strove for the casual approach. 'Remember me?'

'Sugar, how could I forget the woman who'll be the most beautiful attorney in this state?' he drawled. 'Still waiting for the results from the bar exams?'

'Still waiting,' she confirmed, and took a deep breath. 'That's the problem. My client has just been arrested on murder charges. The Mattie Mason case.' She paused as he whistled eloquently. 'Of course, I can't represent him until I'm admitted to the bar.'

'And you want me to handle the case until you're available.'

'It's a matter of three weeks at the most. His name is Hank Thompson. He was taken into custody this morning. I'd like

146

you to go down there and present yourself as his attorney. Harvey Raines will be after a fast arraignment – and that's all right. But he'll stall on a grand jury hearing date.'

'Yeah, Harvey likes to go fishing in August.' Seth chuckled. 'I don't know how successful I'll be in pushing for an early jury trial—'

'I don't want an early trial,' Kara told him. 'I need every minute I can salvage to dig into this case before we go to trial.'

'So this poor guy Hank Thompson will sweat it while you dig.' A faint reproof in his voice. 'No chance he'll get out on bail if he's up for Murder One.'

'He's facing life in prison,' Kara shot back. 'I need time to prove his innocence.'

'You're convinced he's not guilty?'

'Absolutely.'

'What has Harvey got on him?'

'Only circumstantial evidence. No proof that'll hold up in court.' *Unless Raines has come up with something I don't know about.*

'Harvey wouldn't have brought him in if he didn't think he had a chance at conviction.'

'Right. But all I want you to do,' Kara emphasized, 'is to represent him through the arraignment. I'm sure I'll be there by the time Hank faces a grand jury. His wife will pay you a flat fee of . . .' Kara hesitated. 'Three hundred dollars.'

'Come on, Kara, that's peanuts. I could do as well slinging hamburgers at McDonald's!'

'You'll put in maybe three hours, including traveling time. That's all she can afford. I'll handle the case *pro bono.*' *He won't turn down a flat fee – not with what he earns from his practice. Will he?*

He emitted a long sigh. 'Okay, so I'm working practically *pro bono*, too. Haven't you heard? That's fast going out of style.'

'I'll have Val – his wife – call the precinct and explain you're his attorney. Please, get on the case right away. And find out what motivated his arrest. What new evidence have they dug up against him?'

Kara put down the phone, contemplated what she'd arranged. This was the best deal she could put together for now. Val couldn't afford Condon & Jenkins or Rogers & Langley. Seth Rogers would have to do until she could take over.

The only way to clear Hank was to bring in Mattie's murderer. Why did Donna Aikens have to be on vacation just this week? No chance of tracing a Brussels call of twenty-five years ago without her friend's help.

But if Roy Cameron called Joe Mason from Brussels, we'll know it was to set up a hit on Eric and Gerry. Why else would a man in his position call a maintenance man at Cameron Insurance?

All right, call Val, tell her what's happening. Valerie picked up on the first ring. Kara explained the deal with Seth Rogers.

'I know this is rough on you and Hank,' Kara said gently. 'But we have to hang in there.'

'Why did they arrest Hank? What did he do or say that made them bring him in?'

'Seth Rogers will dig that up for us.' Kara sought in her mind for words of comfort. 'Remember, we have absolute proof that you and Hank were at the emergency room at Eden General when Mattie was murdered.'

'But they think Hank – or Hank and me – hired somebody to do it!' Val's voice was strident. 'We loved Mattie. How could we have done something like that?'

'They've got the slimmest of chances of proving Hank was involved,' Kara soothed. Masking her own anxieties. *What* had motivated Hank's arrest? 'Seth Rogers will get the facts for us. I'll call you as soon as I have word.'

Off the phone, Kara paced about the small living room – impatient for word from Rogers. *Please God, let there be no hitch in Grandma's enlisting Donna Aikens's help. A phone call from Roy Cameron in Brussels to Joe Mason here in Eden will be the first major step to his conviction.*

Almost two hours later Seth Rogers called.

'Hank was kind of wary of my representing him,' he said with dry humor. 'I made it clear I was a stand-in until you're admitted to the bar. I told him that—'

'What developed that led Raines to have Hank arrested?' Kara broke in impatiently. 'What new evidence do they think they have?'

'A new witness.' Rogers was blunt. 'Just a few days before Mattie Mason's murder Hank Thompson was at Eden Lumber buying material to patch up Mattie's roof. When the witness – the clerk serving him – said it was great that he bothered to help his wife's aunt that way, he shrugged and said, "Hey, I gotta protect my wife's interest. When Mattie croaks, my old lady inherits the house."'

'That means nothing!' Hank shooting off his mouth again, Kara thought painfully. 'He was embarrassed – he didn't know how to respond to that kind of compliment. We all know people like that.'

'But it'll be enough to indict him,' Rogers pointed out. 'Sure, it's circumstantial evidence – but all the little things are adding up to tie a noose about his neck. You've got a tough case on your hands, counselor. Not the best way to start a career.'

This was not something to discuss with Val over the phone, Kara cautioned herself as she digested what Rogers had reported. Drive over to drop this latest bombshell. *How does Hank always manage to say the wrong thing?*

At the Thompson house Kara found Val folding clothes in the living room while Betsy sprawled before the TV set. With synthetic calm Kara reported what had happened.

'Oh, that louse Greg Jones!' Val trembled with rage. 'He's mad because Hank discovered a couple of months ago that he was over-billing us for all the stuff Hank was buying to repair Mattie's house. His father and his uncle own the company.'

'It'll be some help if we can discredit him. I'll dig around.' But how was she to prove something like that?

'Folks are beginning to act weird towards us.' Valerie prodded Kara across the room, out of Betsy's hearing. 'Neighbors saw the police cars come up this morning. They saw Hank taken away in handcuffs. Why did the police have to do that? He wasn't going to run anywhere.'

'He'll be arraigned in a few days.' Kara struggled to sound matter-of-fact. 'Then he'll be held for the grand jury. Seth

Rogers indicated Raines is in no rush to go to the grand jury – which is to our good. He—'

'Do you know what happened this morning?' Valerie's eyes swung to Betsy, engrossed in *Sesame Street*. 'I called my neighbor across the way to see if she wanted to bring her little girl over here to play, like on most days – or if she wanted me to bring Betsy over there. She said she didn't think it was a good idea for her little girl to play with Betsy right now.' Her voice was choked. 'It'll be all over town by the end of the day! Everybody will know Hank has been arrested for Mattie's murder!'

'Val, you must be strong, for Betsy's sake. You can't afford to fall apart.'

'Kara, you have to clear Hank! He's innocent! The police are so impatient to close the case they'll do anything to pin this on him.'

'We won't let that happen,' Kara vowed. 'Keep telling yourself that.' But everything depended upon her pinning Mattie's murder on Roy Cameron. The most powerful man in this state.

Can I bring this off? Suppose I don't pass the bar exams? Hank will be left with Seth Rogers. Harvey Raines will make mincemeat out of him.

Seventeen

Jonathan was sweating through his second conference at Cameron Insurance. He presented the facts he'd collected on the Eden General financial history. Dad was right, of course. The chief administrator had been grossly overpaid – and grossly inefficient. He didn't need to be a CPA to know that.

'You're sure we won't be facing problems from the State Attorney General if we go ahead with other planned takeovers?' Bart needled him.

'I've seen no indication of his blocking takeovers of non-profit hospitals. But I'll be researching at the law library at the University of South Carolina sometime next week,' Jonathan said. 'Looking for similar cases. I don't anticipate any problems as long as we're above-board on everything.'

'In six months we will have completed negotiations for Farraday,' Roy began, and Jonathan fought to conceal his astonishment. That meant the company would control all hospital business in Eden. 'Not a word about this outside of this room,' Roy warned. 'But once we have control of Farraday, we'll close it. Occupancy at Eden will jump to ninety-five per cent. That's running at top efficiency. And with healthy profits.'

Jonathan intercepted Bart's smug smile. Bart would enjoy seeing Dad's image in this town tarnished. He loathed the way local residents idolized Dad. Bart was so damned jealous – he'd realized that since he was a little kid. Dad must know that. Still, he made no bones about it – Bart was good at his job.

'One thing more,' Bart picked up. 'My spies tell me there's a group forming in town. They call themselves the "HWG".' He allowed himself a sardonic smile. 'That means Hospital

Watchdog Group. A couple of the Eden nurses pulled it together. But it'll die aborning.'

'Enough of the Hospital Division,' Roy dismissed this. 'We've got a serious problem to face.' He paused for dramatic effect. 'If you've read the new report, you'll know we're showing no profit in specific areas. We won't renew either Medicare or Medicaid contracts except where we're making money. In rural areas,' he said, grimacing, 'we're taking a bath.'

'That's a lot of business.' One executive at the conference table was apprehensive.

'From a public-relations standpoint it might backfire,' another worried.

'Bullshit!' Roy shot back. 'Hell, states are cutting reimbursement rates down to peanuts. We can't deal with that. Other major companies have reached this same conclusion. In the few areas where it pays, we'll renew. The others we drop. And don't worry about public relations,' he said drily. 'Aetna, Oxford, Kaiser, Blue Cross – among others – aren't worried. They're getting out of Medicare and Medicaid in states where they're not showing decent profits. Why should we be suckers? We're not a philanthropic organization.'

When the meeting was over, Roy summoned Jonathan to his side. 'Come to the house for dinner tonight. Be there early. Around six or six fifteen. I'm flying in four division heads from Europe along with their wives. We'll have an all-day conference tomorrow. You don't need to be there,' he said indulgently. 'But I want you at the dinner. You know, welcoming them into the family scene. We'll discuss what you need to know before they arrive.'

'Sure, Dad.' Maybe the dinner wouldn't run late, he comforted himself. He phoned Kara every night around ten.

Sandra sat before her dressing table – a sheer black negligée over her black lace bra and black satin bikini panties – while Bart sprawled on the chaise longue and Lulu coaxed Sandra's silver hair into becoming elegance.

'Lulu, is it getting thin up there on top?' Sandra asked, squinting at her reflection in what Bart liked to call her 'kind mirror'. Despite her near-sightedness Sandra refused to wear either glasses or contact lenses, though she submitted to reading glasses since this was regarded as normal for the 'over-forties'. She preferred to ignore how long she'd been past forty.

'Miz Sandra, it's as heavy as when you wuz a girl.' Lulu supplied the expected – untrue – reply. Lulu had been her personal maid for forty-one years – since Lulu's fifteenth birthday. Her adoration of her mistress was linked to the extensive wardrobe she inherited at gratifying intervals – much of which was transferred into cash at a flourishing second-hand shop. The full-length white mink she'd inherited seven years ago remained in her personal wardrobe – to be worn to Sunday church services at the first hint of winter weather.

'I'm so sick of these stupid business dinners,' Sandra fretted. 'Bart, remember the wonderful dinners when we were children? Daddy had such a talent for bringing exciting people together.'

'Cassie said to tell you to expect a photographer from the *Ledger* over tonight,' Bart drawled. 'They like to brag about how international Eden has become because of the company.'

Sandra's usually petulant mouth lifted at the corners. Tomorrow evening's paper would carry her photograph on the front page of the society section. The Old Families might ignore Bart and her these days – but the whole town knew *they* were real society.

'Lulu, tell Mr Bart what you told me a little while ago.' Lulu was her cherished source of local gossip, via a large family and many church-member friends. 'You know, about that woman who tried to open up that old murder case—' One heavily veined, multi-ringed hand gestured in irritation.

'What old murder case?' Bart's smile was indulgent.

'Bart, you can be so stupid sometimes!' He enjoyed needling her, she thought with recurrent annoyance. He'd never got over being the 'baby brother'. 'Those two friends of Tim's.' It was ridiculous of her to worry about that. It was history.

'Well,' Lulu began, as always enjoying her role as informer, 'that Miz Jamison and her granddaughter – she got herself a law degree . . .' She paused in respect.

'So what have they been up to?' Bart's tone was contemptuous.

'Miz Jamison – the old lady,' Lulu specified, though Edie Jamison was a year younger than Sandra Cameron – 'she done went to the po-lice and told them Mattie Mason – the woman who was murdered last May and—'

'Bart, you know,' Sandra interrupted Lulu. 'The poor white trash who were after Tim.'

'Anyhow,' Lulu continued, 'Miz Jamison told the po-lice that Mattie Mason told *her* that her husband left a written confession when he died – that he killed that boy and girl from Salem. She said Mattie was murdered by somebody after that confession.'

'Which the police have never found,' Sandra said triumphantly, 'or the newspapers would have been full of it.'

'So what does that mean to us?' Bart challenged. 'We didn't know those kids from Salem.' He ignored Sandra's agitation.

'Tim knew them. They died the day after his horrible accident. If the police start to dig into their murders, we'll be thrown back into that awful period again. Haven't I suffered enough?' *Why is Bart so dense? He knows why I'm upset.*

Bart shrugged. 'It's only talk. That case is dead and buried. And if the police start to dredge it up, you know what'll happen. Roy'll step in and squash the whole thing.' His eyes held hers for a pregnant moment, then trailed over the length of her on display beneath the sheer black negligée – lovingly and expensively preserved via plastic surgery and liposuction.

'Miz Sandra, what you wanna wear tonight?' From habit Lulu ignored the tableau of brother and sister in silent, erotic contemplation.

Sandra pondered a moment. 'Lay out that new gray chiffon,' she ordered. 'Though why I waste a gorgeous Oscar de la Renta on Roy's new Foreign Division managers I don't know.'

'You can't resist looking beautiful,' Bart taunted her. 'Nobody would ever dream you're going on—'

'Bart, shut up!' In her mind she was still twenty-two. When Bart looked at her the way he was looking at her now, she

154

knew she was still desirable. 'Now get out of here so I can dress.'

Did that idiot man actually leave a confession when he died? And who had that confession now?

Jonathan heard his father and Bart in argumentative conversation as he approached the library. It was usually the same story – Bart complaining that Dad was almost 'giving away the store' when he set up new subsidiaries.

'After all these years, Bart, when are you going to learn to play the game? I won't allow the Eden General Burn Center to be closed. We can afford to carry it another six months or a year. We take over Farraday – we close *their* burn center.'

'There'll be people in town who'll be pissed when we take over Farraday,' Bart needled him. 'We've got a load of senior citizens in this town – they'll be livid when they discover Cameron Insurance will be dropping Medicare.'

'We only drop it in areas where we're not showing a profit – not here in Eden,' Roy emphasized, then broke off to greet Jonathan. 'How's your French these days?'

Jonathan managed a wry smile. 'I can handle a simple conversation. Is that the language of the evening?'

'Not for your mother and me.' Roy chuckled. 'Nor for Bart. Thank God, they all speak some English. And I gather they're all fluent in French. You know Europeans – most of them are linguists. Sprinkle in a bit of French from time to time. That'll make a big hit with them.'

Already Jonathan felt uncomfortable about the evening. He could handle the French with no sweat – he'd spent two summers studying at the Sorbonne. But he never truly felt comfortable in the company's business environment. How would he ever make Dad understand that the prospect of one day running a Fortune 500 company left him cold?

'Bart, fix me a drink this minute,' Sandra ordered, sweeping into the library with an air of expensively perfumed martyrdom. 'If you expect me to survive another of these horrible business dinners.' The glance she bestowed on her husband blended hostility with condescension.

'Oh, you know that crap Lulu was spewing out earlier?' Bart

seemed amused. 'Well, it looks as though the cops have the Mason murder almost tied up.'

'What do you mean?' Sandra gazed from Bart to Roy and back to Bart again.

Oh God, Jonathan thought with inner consternation. That probably meant Kara's client had been charged.

'Look at the headlines on tonight's *Ledger*.' Bart pointed to a newspaper strewn across the magnificent antique writing table that Sandra had bought on a trip to Spain.

Jonathan's eyes sought the headline: LOCAL LABORER TO BE ARRAIGNED FOR THE MURDER OF MATTIE MASON. Why hadn't Kara called him at the office and told him? But he knew the answer. They had a tacit agreement not to talk from his office. For now they both wished to keep their relationship private. She might have tried his cellphone, but the battery was run down.

Now Jonathan made a point of appearing engrossed in his father's instructions about how the four of them were to ingratiate themselves with his guests. But he was anxious about Kara's reaction to this latest development in the Mason murder case. The evening would seem endlessly long. But how could he manage to call Kara before it was over?

Kara sat with Edie and Daisy before the TV set – waiting for the late local evening news. It would be all about Hank's being charged with Mattie's murder – just as the early local news had been. Her eyes sought her watch at frequent intervals. Why hadn't Jonathan called tonight? He must have heard what had happened.

'They've got no real evidence against Hank,' Edie said impatiently. 'It's all circumstantial. I think Harvey Raines jumped the gun, bringing him in that way.'

'I did some checking today on Greg Jones.' Kara fought against frustration. 'He's not exactly a solid citizen.'

But Hank had a furious fight with Mattie. Val inherited the house. The small insurance policy – which Cameron Insurance refused to honor because Mattie didn't die a natural death – listed Val as beneficiary.

Both Hank and Val were at the emergency room at Eden

General when Mattie was murdered. Raines was sure Hank had made a deal with somebody to kill Mattie. He'd never be able to prove that, Kara told herself with shaky defiance – no matter how many times he questioned Hank's friends, the people he knew on the job. Yet instinct warned her that Hank would be held for a grand jury hearing – and indicted.

'I talked to Donna's sister at the store today,' Edie comforted Kara. 'She said Donna's sure to be back from vacation on Sunday. She'll talk to Mildred about getting the phone information you need.'

'She'll wonder why you want it,' Daisy worried.

'She won't care. She and Mildred both hate Roy Cameron,' Edie reminded her. 'Mildred will dig up the information – hoping it'll be bad for Cameron.'

'Make her understand we need to do this fast.'

'As fast as she can,' Edie promised. 'Sugar, you're going to clear Hank. My mind and my heart both tell me this.'

'It's time for the news.' Daisy reached for the remote to turn on the local TV station.

It's eleven p.m. – Jonathan won't call me this late. Does he know about me? Did Cassie Bates remember – and tell him? If he knows, he'll never call me again. I've been living in a fairy tale all this time. How can there be a future for Jonnie and me? But that's what I want – more than I've wanted anything in my whole life.

Eighteen

Kara awoke on Saturday morning with an instant realization that this was the day she was to drive to Augusta with Jonathan. A whole day together, she thought in joyous anticipation. For a moment.

Why didn't he call me last night? Has somebody told him about the old scandal? He can't know that we suspect his father was behind three murders. Why didn't he call me last night?

In a surge of apprehension she tossed aside the sheet and left her bed. Grandma was working a full shift today, she remembered – covering for somebody on vacation at the pharmacy. Mom always left early on Saturday morning in anticipation of a hectic day at the shop. And right on schedule, she thought hopefully, Jonathan would be here to pick her up for their day in Augusta. *He'll explain why he didn't call last night.*

They'd have lunch in Augusta, then head for the furniture store. It wasn't likely anybody there would know her. Nobody would call friends in Eden and say, 'Guess what? Jonathan Cameron was here in Augusta for hours with Kara Jamison. They were choosing furniture for an apartment.'

With guilty relief Kara saw Edie and Daisy off to their respective jobs. She vacillated in her feelings. Jonathan knew about her and would never call again. Jonathan had been caught in some family matter and wasn't able to call. Preparing to shower, she glanced out of the bathroom window. The day was overcast and gloomy – reflecting her own mood.

At a few minutes past ten the phone rang. Her heart pounding, she rushed to respond.

'Hello?' Faintly breathless. Hoping that it was Jonathan – fearful that he was calling to cancel the trip to Augusta.

'I couldn't call last night,' Jonathan apologized. 'I was drafted to sit through a long business dinner at the house. It didn't break up till way past eleven – I wouldn't call that late.'

Relief swept through her. 'I figured something like that.'

'I missed not talking with you. I had trouble falling asleep.'

'You mean you talk to me, and I put you to sleep?' *He wanted to call me – but he couldn't.*

'My day isn't complete if I haven't at least spoken with you.' His voice was a tender caress. 'In such a little while you've become so important to my life.'

'I missed talking to you, too,' she said softly.

'Bring along a sweater or jacket. The weather report talks about a sharp drop in temperature later in the day.'

'Sure thing.'

'I have to stop by the office to pick up some material I need to study over the weekend.' *About the hospital takeover? What'll he think when he finds out Grandma and Mom are part of the watchdog group?* 'I should be at your house in about an hour. Is that okay?'

'Perfect. Would you like coffee before we head for Augusta?'

'No need – we'll have an early lunch before we start the shopping spree.'

'See you in an hour. I'll bring a pair of umbrellas in case we run into rain.'

'I like driving in the rain,' he said whimsically. 'Even in a thunderstorm.'

'I like that too.' Another small bond between them.

'Oh, I forgot to tell you. I picked up a new car yesterday afternoon. Actually, a company car – but it's for my use. Hope you won't mind riding in a brand-new black Mercedes.'

'I think I can handle that.'

'See you soon.'

'Right.'

Off the phone, she sat immobile for a few moments. Where was she heading with her life? On a collision course, for sure. But wouldn't Jonathan understand that, if his father was guilty of murder, he ought to pay? He wouldn't want Hank to be jailed for a murder he didn't commit.

In a burst of uncertainty she hurried into her bedroom. For the third time she was changing her outfit for the day. Jonathan liked her in blue. Wear the blue pantsuit with a matching blouse. The temperature was already dropping. She'd need the jacket.

She went into the living room, sat on the sofa and picked up a magazine, flipped the pages without really seeing. Jonathan had talked about the house he meant to have some day – to share with her. '*I see a comfortable house with at least one wood-burning fireplace and four bedrooms. Our bedroom, a home office we can share – and bedrooms for the kids.*'

She was living a lie – letting him believe she just needed time to be sure they were right for each other. *Oh, I'm sure.* The phone rang, jolting her back into the moment. She left the sofa to respond.

'Hello.'

'Kara, have you heard anything yet about the arraignment?' Valerie's anxiety lent a huskiness to her voice.

'There won't be any decision until Monday.' Just what she'd told Val yesterday. 'I suspect it'll be scheduled for Tuesday or Wednesday evening. I'll call you as soon as Seth Rogers gets the word.'

'I'm so scared. I mean, Hank sitting there in the jail – not knowing what's going to happen.'

'We know Hank is innocent.' Kara forced herself to sound calm. 'The evidence against him is all circumstantial.'

'How long before you'll be able to go into court as his lawyer?'

'Another two or three weeks,' Kara surmised. 'By the time he goes before the grand jury,' she said with an effort at conviction, 'I'll be on the case.' Val's belief in her capability was unnerving. The little experience she had had during summer vacations had hardly prepared her for a murder case. 'I'll be there beside him at the trial.'

'I pray every day that this will all go away. Betsy's so upset – she can't understand why she can't play with Jennifer across the way. And she misses her daddy.'

'We'll see this through together, Val. It's a nightmare, but

Hank will be cleared.' *Do I truly believe that?* 'How's Betsy's asthma? Under control?'

They talked a few minutes longer, then Kara heard a car pull up before the house. 'Val, I have to go now. A friend just arrived. I'll talk to you later.'

Kara reached for her purse and the pair of umbrellas she'd brought out earlier, headed for the door. Jonathan was coming up the walk. 'It isn't raining yet, but any moment it'll probably start coming down.'

He prodded her back into the foyer, shoved the door closed behind them, and pulled her into his arms. 'There's something about rainy weather that makes me passionate,' he murmured. 'If we're in for a rainy season, you'd better marry the guy fast.' His eyes searched hers – pleading for a positive reply.

'Once the Hank Thompson trial is over,' she said after a moment of heated internal debate – astonishing herself. 'Then we'll set a date.' *Will he still want to marry me then?*

'May it be the shortest trial on record. With the defendant cleared, of course.' His mouth reached for hers, and they clung together in mutual hunger.

'We'd better get out of here.' Her voice was tremulous. 'We have shopping to do.'

'We have the whole day for ourselves,' he reminded her in triumph. 'I feel as though I have one foot in heaven.'

Jonathan took the key from Kara, locked the door, and hurried with her to the car. For an instant – waiting for Jonathan to circle the car and slide behind the wheel – she was unnerved. Was that Peg backing out of her garage? Did she recognize Jonathan?

'We'll have an early lunch,' Jonathan said in high spirits while he switched on the ignition. 'Annie Mae told me about this great diner right outside of town. And we'll have dinner,' he plotted, 'at the Partridge Inn. My mother says it's real gourmet food.' *But his mother doesn't realize he'll be sharing dinner with* me.

'You're making me hungry already.' She contrived to duplicate his convivial mood. 'How are you surviving on the job?' Her tone compassionate now.

'The legal aspect is small.' He sighed, radiating frustration.

'The major issue here – as in hospitals all over the country – is to operate them in a way that keeps them out of the red. I just wish I had some background in health management. That I knew where we could cut corners without lessening service. I'm trying like hell. I'm listening to the nurses, the doctors, even the aides. I know there's a segment of the population that's terrified of what could happen to Eden General. A group of locals have banded together to form a "watchdog committee"—'

Kara hesitated an instant. 'My grandmother is on that committee.'

He appeared startled. Only for a moment. 'From our very brief acquaintance I'd say she has her feet on the ground. If the group sees something that they feel we're doing wrong, I hope they'll approach us.'

Unexpectedly Kara laughed. 'If Grandma feels something is wrong, you'll hear from her.' She paused. 'You'd be the one for them to approach?' Were battle lines being drawn already?

'That's right.' But he seemed disconcerted. 'We may step on some toes. Some of the nurses who've been around for a lot of years are prickly. They don't take to change. But there must be change.' His hands tightened on the wheel. 'Medical care in this country is in crisis. It's imperative that the hospitals become cost-efficient.'

Kara listened while Jonathan expounded on his father's theory about how to correct the problems in the health-care system. He offered all the right phrases, she thought uncomfortably – accelerated-care nurses, team systems, computerization of patients' records. She'd read it all – and had heard the opposing arguments. It all sounded, she thought with soaring anxiety, as though Eden General would be managed by accountants rather than doctors and nurses.

Traffic was light this overcast morning. They arrived at the diner Annie Mae had recommended in record time. With most booths already occupied, they decided to order the 'Saturday special brunch'. Mounds of grits, satin-scrambled eggs, juice, and tall hot rolls, along with fragrant coffee in over-sized mugs, arrived.

'You know what I missed in New York?' Jonathan became

reminiscent when they'd made deep inroads in the array of food. 'Grits for breakfast. And fluffy biscuits.'

'More coffee?' Their friendly waitress approached. 'More biscuits?'

'Thank you, no,' Kara replied. 'Everything was fine.'

'Any more and I'll fall asleep right here,' Jonathan told their waitress with a warm smile. 'It's time for us to hit the road.'

With no difficulty they located the elegant furniture store that Jonathan's mother had chosen. Pricey, she suspected – but then Sandra Cameron wasn't on a budget. When they'd parked, Jonathan had brought out the diagram of the apartment – its design and dimensions similar to millions of apartments through the country. In her mind she'd pinpointed Jonathan's basic requirements.

Right away Kara sensed the glint of personal interest in their cordial salesman's eyes. No doubt in her mind that he was aware of the Cameron wealth and power. If he had friends in Eden, she thought uneasily, he'd be phoning to talk about 'Sandra Cameron's son and his girlfriend shopping for furniture'.

Don't think about all the obstacles ahead. Just focus on furniture for Jonathan's apartment. The apartment that one day might be ours. Jonathan won't allow his parents to come between us – he means to live his own life. But what'll happen if his father is indicted for murder – and I'm responsible for that?

A remark by the salesman brought Kara back to the moment. She explained that they were interested in floor samples.

'That's right,' Jonathan picked up. 'We don't want to wait months for delivery.' Unconsciously he'd used the plural.

As they were shown items available for immediate delivery, Jonathan deferred to her choices. This could be furniture that would one day grace that house he'd talked about for them, she mused in a corner of her mind. Beautiful – expensive – furniture, paid for by his mother. *Don't think about that now – just choose with care.*

'A queen-size bed.' Jonathan made one stipulation, and Kara saw the indulgent smile of their salesman.

She was amazed at the amount of time they spent in the

furniture store. But Jonathan seemed so happy. The furniture would be delivered to his apartment on Tuesday. His mother had instructed Annie Mae to shop for linens, towels, and kitchen necessities – not that she expected him to be involved in cooking. What would his mother say if she knew sheets and blankets must be ordered for a queen-size bed? But single people slept in queen-size beds too, she told herself defensively. Jonathan would be sleeping alone in that bed – for now. *Will I ever share it with him?*

They headed now for the levee and the Riverwalk. The weather remained unseasonably cool, but the clouds had evaporated, replaced by dazzling sunshine. Kara had heard about this destination of thousands of tourists since it was first built back in the 1980s.

'I discovered the Riverwalk about six years ago when Ralph – my roommate at Columbia – came to Augusta to see it,' Jonathan reminisced as they left the car and walked towards the river. 'Ralph's family lived in Jacksonville. I was home for a few days after floating around England and Ireland for the summer – and we meant to drive up to New York in the car he'd just inherited from his parents.'

Hand in hand they approached the Riverwalk – a charming four-block stretch of exquisite gardens and an amphitheatre, along with attractive shops and restaurants and the luxurious Radisson Hotel.

'Oh, Jonnie, it's lovely!' *Enjoy today – don't think about tomorrow.* 'I'm so glad you brought me here.'

They strolled along the magnificently landscaped Riverwalk, then sat on a bench at Oglethorpe Park at its end.

'We're here,' Jonathan said in a burst of exuberance, 'so let's do the whole tourist scene. Remember,' he said with infinite respect, 'Augusta is eighty years older than Eden. It was founded in 1735 by Oglethorpe.'

They walked about the historic Old Town district. They saw the Queen Anne and Second French Empire architectural gem that was the Cotton Exchange, functioning now as the Augusta Welcome Center. They visited the Augusta Artists Exchange – the 200-year-old renovated structure used as offices by brokers in an earlier century. They saw the King George, an authentic pub that had been brought over – piece by piece – from England. They saw the Row Café, which was once a cotton-grading room, and wandered through a thoroughly modern general store named Fat Man's – which Jonathan said no tourist ever missed. And at last Kara conceded to Jonathan that she was ready for an early dinner.

Daisy closed up the shop at the scheduled time, hurried to the bakery where she'd reserved a strawberry shortcake. Her contribution to tonight's dinner meeting at Nan Logan's house.

Arriving there, she found dinner preparations in high gear. Peg had brought a huge salad, another committee member salmon steaks – being grilled on the patio, Nan reported.

'And that cake looks luscious,' she crooned. 'My summer-time weakness. I have yams and Idahos ready to come out of the oven so we can sit down to eat as soon as Paul says the salmon steaks are ready.' She smiled at Daisy's blank stare. 'Dr Callahan. No formality around here, he insists. He's Paul.'

Feeling self-conscious and inadequate at standing in for her mother, Daisy offered to help set the picnic table, in place on the patio. She noted the wooded lot behind Nan's property – which provided pleasing privacy.

'Hi.' Paul Callahan glanced up with an exuberant smile as Daisy approached. 'Why does food always seem so much better outdoors?'

'It does if you're not eaten up by mosquitoes.' But she pantomimed approval of the mosquito-repellent candles that Nan had set up around the perimeter of the patio.

'I think these are ready,' Paul decided. 'How about a large platter?'

'I'll get one.' Daisy darted into the house and back to the kitchen. How did he manage to make a serious committee meeting seem like a party? Was he here to be helpful – or was he reporting to Roy Cameron? Instantly she felt guilty. Mom was forever scolding her for being suspicious of people. Mom liked Dr Callahan a lot.

In minutes the seven members of the committee had settled themselves around the table. Daisy was conscious of the way Paul Callahan had rushed to take the chair next to hers.

She was disconcerted by her pleased reaction to his obvious interest.

Not until the table had been cleared and they were sipping tall, frosted glasses of iced tea did they launch into discussion of the situation at Eden General.

'I'll be offered a severance package,' Nan predicted bitterly. 'But I'm not due for retirement for another five years.'

All eyes swung to Paul.

'I've heard nothing about this,' he conceded. 'It may be that they haven't studied Pediatrics yet.' He was somber. 'I like Jonathan Cameron – the young man who's heading up the Board of Directors now. He's young for the role – but he seems intelligent, and anxious to do what's right for the hospital.'

'Jonathan Cameron fell into that position because he's the old man's son,' a male retiree said drily. 'How old can he be? Twenty-five, twenty-six?'

'He wasn't born a Cameron,' Daisy said without thinking. 'He was adopted.' *Why did I say that?* 'But of course, that gives him the same perks,' she added, her face hot.

'Three nurses have been made redundant so far.' Nan was grim. 'And we don't know how many more will go.'

'How do the other nurses feel about this?' Peg exuded hostility.

'How do you think they feel?' Nan was impatient.

'First let's consider the packages,' Paul soothed. 'If they're good, Nan, you can be ahead of the game. You'll have that, your pension in time – and I'm sure you'll have calls for private-duty nursing.' Yet he didn't seem happy, Daisy thought.

'We'll get our pensions at the time they're due,' Nan admitted. 'I hear the son and heir insisted on that. But not the full pension. Just what we'd get at early retirement.'

'What about the patients?' Daisy was uneasy. 'So far the hospital will be short three nurses. And we don't know how many more will be excessed. Won't the patients suffer?'

'We must be realistic.' Paul seemed to be choosing his words with care. 'Some duties can be handled by lower-paid staff.' His smile was apologetic. 'Medical care in this country requires

166

serious cost-cutting. And by the same token nurses will be given more responsibilities, I suspect. This is happening in a lot of hospitals. Specialists aren't required to draw blood, for example – or give EKGs. Nurses can assume these duties. They're already doing it in some private groups of doctors. In some hospitals.'

'In a way,' a woman retiree from middle management offered, 'that should make a nurse's job more rewarding.'

'But what'll be missing,' Peg said, 'is the nurturing. That's what brought my generation into nursing. I know,' she smiled, 'today young women see it as well-paying compared to working at a checkout counter or flipping hamburgers, or as a receptionist or bank teller.'

They battled until darkness descended on the patio. Now the committee members retired to Nan's small but comfortable living room. At last Paul Callahan summed up the situation.

'We have to realize it's a changing world, and as with everything else in life there's a price tag for all the new benefits we acquire. With medical care being insured for more and more people – though there're still huge gaps – costs become an urgent problem.'

But he was troubled, Daisy decided. 'How can we be sure people aren't paying too high a price?' Again she surprised herself by questioning him.

'We must be watchful that we keep a fair balance. I don't know what'll happen in my department. But when I know, you'll hear about it,' he promised.

Kara and Jonathan drove up to the Partridge Inn's five-story, pink Victorian structure and inspected the endless expanse of porches and balconies with avid admiration. In the sprawling dining room they were greeted with charming cordiality and seated at a corner table that provided privacy for a pair of young romantics. Dinner – as Jonathan had predicted – was superb. They both chose the stuffed trout and for dessert a pecan tart with a marvelous whisky sauce. Over coffee Jonathan reached beneath the tablecloth for Kara's hand.

'I don't remember ever enjoying a day as much as this one.'

'It's been beautiful,' Kara whispered.

Their eyes clung. Her heart began to pound.

'I don't want today to end—'

'There'll be other days—'

'I want so badly to make love to you.' An eloquent question in his eyes.

'We shouldn't . . .' But she knew he read her ambivalence. *Today might be all they'd ever have.*

His face glowed with anticipation. 'We'll call it a dress rehearsal. Nobody will have to know it's not truly our wedding night.'

'Where?' she stammered, managed a shaky laugh. 'Your furniture won't be delivered until Tuesday.'

'We'll find a small, pleasant motel along the road,' he said. 'I'll go in to register while you wait in the car. Nobody will know us—'

'How will you register?' She tried for flippancy. This wasn't happening – but she knew it was. No stopping now. Not the way they felt.

He thought a moment. 'Mr and Mrs Alexander O'Neill. That has a nice ring to it.'

In the car they sat with thighs touching, her head on his shoulder. Like Jonathan said, this was a dress rehearsal for their wedding night. For tonight, let them live in a fairy-tale world where love conquers all.

Nineteen

Jonathan lingered at the door of the Jamison house – as though unwilling to leave her, Kara thought tenderly. A feeling she shared.

'You realize you have a commitment,' he murmured. 'You have to make an honest man of me now.'

'Soon,' she promised. But in a corner of her mind the old fears tormented her. *Will Jonnie want to marry me when he knows the whole truth?* 'When I've cleared Hank.' *Please, God, let me clear him.*

She watched from a living-room window while Jonathan strode to the new black Mercedes and slid behind the wheel. She smiled as she saw him lean forward to gaze at the house for an instant – as though knowing she was there watching him. The whole day seemed unreal yet beautiful. *Three months ago I didn't know Jonnie existed. Now I want to build my life around him.*

The flashing red light on the answering machine caught her attention. She crossed to press the 'message' button.

'Hi, Seth Rogers,' he identified himself. 'I ran into Harvey Raines earlier today. He said Hank Thompson's arraignment will be on Wednesday evening. Drop by tomorrow around one p.m. and let's go over the facts. See you then.'

She turned off the answering machine, pondered the situation. She shouldn't be at the arraignment, she reinforced her earlier decision. Let Raines believe he would be dealing with Seth. And now her mind went back to Jonathan and his eagerness to be helpful in Hank's defense. Thank God, he was too busy to pursue this.

Mom would be so upset when – if – she learned about Jonnie. Already she suspected something more serious than an effort to dig up incriminating evidence against his father. *My grandfather, even though he'll never admit this. I've never thought of Roy Cameron as my grandfather. Why now?*

In a burst of restlessness she decided to change into nightie and robe. Hanging away the blue pantsuit, she hugged it to her for a moment of blissful recall. She'd never wear it again without remembering today. In her mind their wedding day.

She tensed at the sound of a key in the front door. Grandma was home. She hurried out to greet her – suffused with guilt that she must dissemble about her day with Jonathan.

'How was the party?' She struggled to sound casual.

'Oh, it was great. Ronnie was totally surprised.' Edie's eyes searched hers with silent questions. 'How was the Riverwalk?'

'Fabulous.' She'd said she'd been sightseeing after a stint of library research. 'So beautiful. I can't believe it's so close to home and I'd never seen it.'

'You're all aglow,' Edie said with a sudden blend of affection and unease.

'It was an exciting day.' Kara struggled to appear casual. 'I know now why tourists flock to—'

'You look the way your mother used to look when she came home from a date with Tim,' Edie broke in. *She knows I was with Jonathan today.* 'Kara, does Jonathan know about your mom and dad? About what the Camerons did to her – and to you?'

'No.' Kara was defensive. 'How can I tell him?'

'If you're both serious – and it's clear to me that you are, my darling – he'll have to know.' Edie hesitated. 'And if you dig up facts that incriminate Roy Cameron, you'll both be facing agonizing problems.'

'I know,' Kara whispered. 'I haven't been able to bring myself to face that. Not yet.'

'You can't drop Hank's case . . .' Edie was troubled. 'You're all he and Val have.'

'I know that, too.' An edge of desperation colored her voice. 'Grandma, you'll like Jonnie so much you when you get to know him.' *If she gets to know him.*

'If you love him, then I know he's special.' Edie managed a shaky smile.

'Let's not say anything to Mom about this. Not yet . . .'

'Not yet.'

But Kara felt her grandmother's anxiety.

As the meeting broke up and the HWG members began to head for their cars, Paul Callahan contrived to linger with Daisy.

'It was a good meeting,' he said, 'but what I'd like to have is a clear profile of Roy Cameron. Even this early I'm getting vibes that disturb me. But I know I must be fair.'

'Most folks in town think Roy Cameron deserves sainthood.' Her tone was derisive.

'You don't.'

'No.'

'Could we discuss this over dinner? I need an unbiased opinion.' Yet the radiance in his eyes hinted at a more personal interest.

'I'm not sure I'm unbiased,' she warned. All at once her heart was pounding. What was so appealing about Paul Callahan?

'Monday evening?' he pursued. 'What would be a good time for you?'

'Seven,' she said after a moment. *This is unreal.* 'Let me give you my address.'

Driving home, Daisy tried to dissect her emotions. She was always self-conscious, uneasy on those occasions when Mom dragged her into local groups. Mom scolded her for not opening up to people. '*Daisy, you need a life beyond the shop and home. Give people a chance.*'

She'd asked questions tonight. She'd made contributions. Because the hospital was so important to this town, she rationalized. But in a corner of her mind, she acknowledged that Dr Paul Callahan was the catalyst for this. Why had he chosen *her* to explore a profile of Roy Cameron? Did he know what happened between her and Tim's family all those years ago? Again, logic interceded. It was unlikely that he knew.

Had he concocted that approach so he could ask her out? No, she reproached herself. He was truly interested in the future of Eden General. He cared about people – that was a trait that drew her to him. But even at the first meeting she'd

171

been conscious of the way his eyes sought her out. *Oh, this is insane thinking! Why would he be attracted to me?*

'The committee meeting must be running long,' Edie commented when Kara returned to the living room with mugs of freshly brewed decaf. 'Daisy's not home yet and Peg's house is dark.'

'Here's Mom,' Kara guessed at the sound of a car pulling into the driveway. 'I'll get coffee for her.'

She was glad Grandma knew how she felt about Jonathan, was uneasy about her mother's reaction. But for now that wasn't to be discussed. Still, she struggled with guilt that her relationship with Jonathan must be hidden from her mother.

'How was the meeting?' Kara heard Edie ask Daisy. 'Any new developments at the hospital?'

'Nan Logan and Peg were steaming,' Daisy reported. 'The hospital's already starting with severance packages. They're not about to waste time—'

'Peg's home.' Edie said at the sound of a car turning into her driveway.

'She was right behind me,' Daisy said.

'She'll be over any minute. Kara,' Edie called, 'another mug of coffee for Peg. I know,' Edie told Daisy, 'you've been guzzling iced tea at Nan's, but for some people the day's not over without a cup of coffee.'

'You're addicted,' Daisy scolded her good-humoredly. 'But since it's decaf, it's allowed.'

With her usual burst of speed Peg strode into the house, launched into a diatribe against Eden General.

'Now maybe folks in this town will knock Roy Cameron off his lofty pedestal.' She reached for the mug Kara extended. 'Oh, I need that. Even if it is the phoney deal,' she derided in a routine that was familiar.

'Are we protesting against the severance packages?' Edie asked. 'And to whom do we protest? The Board of Directors?'

'Jonathan Cameron.' Kara forced a smile. 'He's the man in charge. The one who'll deal with the Board.' She exchanged a fleeting, apprehensive glance with her grandmother. This was going to be sticky.

'We'll take that up at the general meeting on the eighteenth. We can't afford to let them steamroller the hospital operation,' Edie decided.

'Yeah, we can't sit back on our haunches and do nothing.' Peg was emphatic. 'Kara, I need some legal advice.'

'Sure.'

'Well, I'm worried about my house. I was talking with Carol Ramsey – you know, the retired schoolteacher from New York who's on the committee. Anyhow, her mother died down in Florida over a year ago – and her house down there is still tied up in probate.'

Kara smiled compassionately. 'That's a frequent complaint.'

'I'm leaving my house to my two nieces,' Peg picked up. 'Oh, I hope to be around another twenty years – but for my peace of mind I want to be sure they get the house without waiting forever. One's always having health problems and the other has a husband who can't seem to hang on to a job for more than a few months. Is there some legal way to make sure they don't have to wait two years after I die to get their inheritance?'

'Sure. You can—'

'I can't bring myself to turn over title now,' Peg broke in. 'I mean – that would be bad for my morale.' She was apologetic but firm.

'You don't have to do that,' Kara soothed her. 'You put the house in trust for your nieces. A revocable trust, so you can change it if you decide otherwise. All they have to do is take their "in trust" papers to the county clerk's office at the proper time, and the deed is recorded in their name.'

Edie's face lit up. 'Kara, let me do that with this house. Put the house in trust for you and Daisy. I want to know that when I'm gone, you'll always have a house. By then – with a little luck—' she crossed her fingers, 'it'll be paid off.'

'One good year for me, and we'll pay it off,' Kara promised. Grandma never stopped being concerned for Mom and her.

'My dream was to add another bedroom and a second bath – maybe two,' Edie said in a burst of exuberance. 'And of course, air-conditioning. I know,' she reminisced, 'what having

173

the house meant for my mother and then for me. And each generation wants a little better for the next.'

'We'll do that,' Kara vowed. 'Another bedroom, at least two baths, and air-conditioning. Your dream house, Grandma. Just let me pass the bar exams.' Life was made up of 'if's.

'Did you tell Edie and Kara about your conquest?' Peg asked Daisy archly.

'I don't know what you're talking about,' Daisy refuted, but her sudden high color betrayed her.

'Paul Callahan – you know, Dr Callahan from Eden General – is smitten,' Peg said with relish. 'He couldn't take his eyes off Daisy.'

'He's troubled by what's happening at the hospital,' Daisy stammered. 'He realizes that Roy Cameron is calling all the shots.' She paused a moment. 'He asked me to – to have dinner with him to talk about Mr Cameron.'

Kara and Edie exchanged startled – and pleased – glances.

'Peg, what came up about the rumor that Cameron Insurance is thinking about taking over Farraday Hospital?' Edie made a point of derailing the conversation. 'Any truth to that?'

'Nothing that we can pin down,' Peg admitted. 'You know how gossip circulates around this town. But we'll keep our eyes and ears open.'

'Peg, remember you're talking to Donna Aikens tomorrow about those telephone calls Kara wants checked out,' Edie reminded her. 'That's very important.'

'I told you – if Donna's not back in time to go to church tomorrow, I'll call her at home. She'll get Mildred on track right away. She says Mildred's always bragging about the phone company's computer system and their microfilm files. It may take time,' she cautioned, 'but Mildred will come through.'

'We don't have a lot of time.' Edie was grim. 'Tell her to move fast. She won't be sorry.'

Sunday morning Kara slept late. She heard Edie and Daisy moving about the house, then was vaguely conscious that they left for church. When the phone rang, she guessed the caller would be Jonathan.

'Hello . . .' A lilt in her voice.

'I miss you,' Jonathan mourned. 'What can I do to help you push the trial forward?' Meaning Hank's trial, she understood.

'He hasn't even been arraigned yet.' But her heart sang at his implication. 'It'll be Wednesday evening.'

'Rush for a grand jury hearing,' he urged. 'I'm hungry to claim my bride.' He hesitated a moment. 'Have you talked about us to your family?'

'Grandma suspects. I haven't told Mom yet.' Why couldn't he be the son of somebody they'd never known? And in a corner of her mind she realized that, in truth, he was. Why did he have to be adopted by Roy and Sandra Cameron? 'Have you talked to your parents about me?' *If he had, I'd know about it!*

'I won't until you give me the okay. I figure until your family knows, I'd better keep quiet. But about the trial. I'm tied up with this business at the hospital, of course – but if I can be useful, I'll manage to squeeze in the time.'

'I'll remember that.' *I hate being dishonest with him.*

'We haven't talked much about the case.' Jonathan was somber now. 'I know you feel the only way to clear him is to pin down the real murderer. You have somebody in mind?' Half-question, half-statement.

'I'm fishing.' *How can I say, 'I'm convinced your father is the murderer'?*

'I'll find time to fish with you if you believe I can help,' he reiterated. 'But for now, it's a beautiful morning. What about breakfast at that diner at the edge of town, where they make great biscuits and matching coffee? And if you're good to me, I'll bring along a loaf of bread and we can feed the ducks.'

'It'll take a while,' she apologized. 'I'm still in bed.'

'Don't torment me,' he chided. 'Pick you up in about thirty minutes?'

'Forty,' she compromised. 'I linger in the shower.'

'I'd love to linger with you.' He sighed extravagantly. 'But I suppose that'll have to wait.'

'See you in forty minutes.'

'I love you.'

'I love you, too.'

Dressed and waiting for Jonathan to arrive, Kara was assaulted by fresh anxieties. Eager to help her – to see the trial over so they could bring their relationship out into the open, as she'd promised – he would be probing into the case, she warned herself. *I've made a commitment I wasn't free to make. We agreed to take things slowly – but we haven't.*

On schedule Jonathan arrived.

'In a few years,' he drawled, 'we'll have to go to church on Sunday mornings. To set a good example for the kids.'

'That's where Grandma and Mom are now.'

'Aha!' His smile was dazzling.

'No,' she read his mind.

'You're a temptress,' he chided amorously and pulled her into his arms in the foyer. The door kicked closed behind them. 'In our private Eden.'

For an exquisite few moments their mouths clung. Passion ignited in her. Reluctantly she pulled her mouth from his.

'Jonnie, we mustn't be greedy—'

He sighed in mock despair. 'I suppose I'll have to settle for a sumptuous breakfast. Meager comfort food.'

'I have to be back home by one,' she told him. 'I'm meeting with Seth Rogers. The attorney who's standing in for me until we get the bar exam results,' she reminded him. 'He'll be with Hank at the arraignment.' She sighed. 'We know he'll be held for a grand jury hearing.'

'Where are you in the case so far?' He took the house key from her and locked the door. 'You said you were fishing . . .'

Kara fought for words that wouldn't lead her onto a dangerous path.

'We know that Mattie Mason was murdered to stop her from going to the police with her late husband's confession of murder back in—'

'Whoa, honey! Let's backtrack.' Excitement seemed to spiral in him. 'Be specific. What murders did Mattie's husband confess to?'

'Two teenagers from Salem – twenty-five years ago. They were killed on that strip of road between Salem and Eden.

Mattie's late husband, Joe, was hired – blackmailed, he told Mattie – to kill them. He—'

'How do you know this?' Jonathan broke in, caught up in this revelation.

'Mattie told my grandmother.' *Why am I telling this to Jonnie? Am I out of my mind?*

In a few succinct sentences she brought Jonathan up to date – avoiding any mention of whom they suspected of hiring Joe.

'I'm convinced I have to go back to those two murders to know who killed Mattie.'

'You need the motive for the first murders.' Jonathan was thinking aloud. 'Who wanted those two teenagers dead?'

Alarmed that she would stray into dangerous areas, Kara tried to change the subject. 'This is a glorious morning – no more shop talk. I'm starving. How about you?'

'Me too.' He opened the car door on her side, closed it behind her when she was settled on the front seat.

'How're things going at the hospital?' she prodded when he slid behind the wheel. 'Tell me what's happening.' No more unnerving talk about the murders.

'Everything's still in the beginning stages.' His tone was somber. 'I need to do a lot of cramming before I can get a handle on the situation. Of course,' he said wryly, 'my father's the one who's calling the shots. My title sounds important – but I'm just bringing facts together for him, checking out the legal implications. He's one of those CEOs who keep a finger in every pie. Not that I blame him,' he added with a note of apology. 'Everybody says he's close to being a genius in running companies. But you said no shop talk,' he reminded her.

'Right.' Didn't he understand that turning Eden General into a for-profit hospital was bad for the town? And were the rumors true about Cameron Insurance taking over Farraday?

'My furniture's being delivered on Tuesday. What about your coming over Tuesday night and deciding what belongs where?' His smile charismatic. 'Maybe we can have dinner there. You know, the take-out stuff we learned about in those years at school. The electric is on – we can have music with dinner.'

'Let me check my appointment book.' She pantomimed beguilingly. 'Yes, all clear. Dinner Tuesday evening – and then we move furniture.'

How can I be so light-hearted about this? By Tuesday – if we're lucky – we'll know if Roy Cameron called Mattie's husband from Brussels the night before Eric and Gerry were killed. Maybe right this minute Grandma's talking with Donna Aikens about Mildred checking the phone-company records. And that could mean the end for Jonnie and me.

Twenty

E die looked forward to Sunday mornings in Eden. She loved the air of serenity that descended upon the town. Many families made a habit of attending their respective churches. The occasion required their 'Sunday best' – though a certain element rebelled at this tradition and arrived in jeans or even shorts. Sometimes three generations walked or drove to church together. For a little while anger, cynicism, domestic battles were in retreat. For a little while – on Sunday mornings – all seemed right with the world.

The weather this Sunday morning was storybook perfect. The sky a dazzling blue, untouched by clouds. No hint of summer heat in the air, though sunlight provided a happy atmosphere. On every side late-summer flowers sprouted in colorful fragrance. But, arriving at their church with Daisy, Edie was disappointed that Donna was not in attendance.

'Donna always tries to be home for Sunday-morning church,' Edie whispered. 'She's a real creature of habit.'

'Maybe she ran into traffic,' Daisy suggested.

'But we'll catch up with her,' Edie vowed. 'Today.'

Edie was restless during the service. Her mind churning. Donna would be home today, wouldn't she? It was so important to check out those phone calls. She felt a surge of relief when the service was over – guilty that she was rushing Daisy to the door. On normal occasions she relished joining in the lively conversations of departing churchgoers.

She prodded Daisy towards the car. 'We'll go over and see if Donna's home.'

'Do you think we should?' Daisy was doubtful. 'Maybe we ought to give her a chance to settle in after her vacation.'

'Kara's dying to learn if Joe received a phone call from Roy

Cameron that night.' Edie's tone was ominous. 'Remember, Hank's being arraigned on Wednesday evening.'

Daisy slid behind the wheel of the car while Edie settled herself beside her.

'Just where does Donna live?' Daisy asked, and Edie gave her directions.

'She's home,' Edie said in triumph as they approached Donna's small frame house. 'There's her car.'

They walked up the short path to the door. Edie rang the bell. 'Don't be nervous,' Edie soothed Daisy. 'Donna won't mind. She'll understand this is urgent.'

The door swung open. Donna smiled in welcome. A tall, spare woman close to retirement age, she had a local reputation for being feisty and independent – and on occasion profane. 'I just got back from Myrtle Beach about half an hour ago. From my sunburn I guess you know where I've been.' She chuckled. 'I wore a sun block, but it happened anyway. I should stop looking for bargains.' Her eyes were bright with curiosity now.

'I hope you don't mind our bursting in on you this way,' Edie apologized, 'but something came up and I thought, *Donna's the one to help us.*'

'What's up?' Donna led the other two into her modest living room.

'Your friend Mildred is still with the phone company?' Edie's anxiety crept into her voice.

'Oh, Mildred will stay there till they throw her into retirement. And that's not far off,' she said with affectionate humor. 'You'd think she owns stock in the company, the way she's always bragging about the perfect set-up they have. Would you like some coffee?' Donna asked while Edie and Daisy sat on one of the pair of love seats that faced each other.

'No, thanks – we'll be having lunch soon. We need some help from Mildred,' Edie explained. 'And I don't know her well enough to approach her on something like this—'

'What's the problem?' Donna sat on the other love seat, leaned forward expectantly.

'We can't come out and give you particulars – not just yet,' Edie went on. 'But it's a big deal.' She took a deep breath.

180

'We need to know if a party here in town received a phone call – from Brussels – during a twenty-four-hour period some twenty-five years ago—'

'Sounds like a mystery novel.' Donna was intrigued.

'Like I said, we can't give you any particulars just yet.' She paused for dramatic effect. 'But it involves a serious threat to Roy Cameron if what we suspect – and can prove – is true.'

'Nothing would make me happier than to see Roy Cameron in deep shit.' Donna's face brightened. 'You have the phone number you're trying to trace? It's here in town?'

'It's in Eden,' Edie assured her. 'We've got the number. I have it right here.' She reached into her purse for the envelope that contained the pertinent information. In a corner of her mind she realized that Mildred would be able to connect the name that belonged to that phone number. 'We need to know what calls were received during the time period on the sheet of paper here – and specifically, if one of the calls came from Brussels.'

'Like in Belgium?' Donna pounced and Edie nodded. Not many calls from Belgium would be coming into Eden. 'I'll get in touch with Mildred today. I'll buzz you as soon as I talk with her.' Her eyes were wistful. 'I don't suppose you want to tell me anything else?'

'As soon as we can, we'll tell you. And it'll be a shocker,' Edie promised.

'Edie, shut me up if you think it's none of my business – but I heard something around town a few weeks ago . . .' All at once Donna seemed uneasy.

'What did you hear?' Daisy prodded her.

'Well, it's so nutsy. It leaked out from the District Attorney's office – you know how that happens in this town. Everything's supposed to be hush-hush in the DA's office – but not for long. Anyhow, somebody said that after Mattie Mason was murdered, you went to the District Attorney and claimed Mattie's husband had confessed to some murder twenty-five years ago – and that Mattie was killed to get his written confession.'

Edie took a deep breath. 'I went to the District Attorney and I told him that – because it's true.' Why had nobody brought up the rumor to her before? Did they think – like Harvey Raines – that she was after publicity for Kara? 'Mattie was going to the police with the confession – but you know how nervous she was after Joe died. She wanted to wait until Kara came home and could go with her. She was scared of being implicated. You know Kara's just out of law school.'

Donna nodded. 'Mattie wasn't just making it up? I mean, she wasn't out of her head or something like that?'

'Mattie meant it – and that's why she was murdered.'

'You think Roy Cameron hired Joe to kill somebody?' Donna's face radiated satisfaction. 'Wow, would I love to see him knocked off his fancy perch!'

'Donna, we can't prove anything yet! Don't say a word to anybody about this. If we're ever to make a case, nobody must be suspicious.'

'I won't say a word. Not even to Mildred. Most people would never believe it of Roy Cameron. They don't know him the way Mildred and I do.'

'Convince Mildred to check out the phone calls to this number,' Edie urged her. 'That may be just what Kara needs.'

Back home and conscious of passing time – she had to be with Seth Rogers by one o'clock – Kara brought out cold cuts from the refrigerator, set two plates at the table. She checked the rolls warming in the oven. Time to take them out. The coffee was done.

She heard a car pulling into the driveway. Grandma and Mom were home. She hurried to the door, pulled it wide.

'Was Donna Aikens at church?'

'No, but we went to her house,' Daisy told her. 'She's going to talk to her friend Mildred.'

'When?' Kara was breathless with anticipation.

'Sometime today,' Edie picked up. 'Donna's sure Mildred will help us. She's been with the company forever – she'll know how to check out their records.'

'Thank God!' Kara walked with the other two into the dining area, where lunch awaited. 'I know,' Kara forced herself to be realistic, 'I still won't have a real case. But things are beginning to add up. What Mattie told you, Grandma – and

182

with more evidence coming up, they'll have to believe you. And Mr Hamilton's testimony backs up your insistence, Mom, that my father was not into drugs. And if we can prove that Roy Cameron called Joe from Brussels, that's a strong point. Why would the CEO of Cameron Insurance make a phone call to a janitor at the company?'

'I want those murders avenged,' Daisy said with painful intensity. 'I want this town to know my marriage was illegally annulled. I want the town to know that my daughter is Tim Cameron's child.'

Kara met with Seth Rogers, went over the necessary details. The arraignment was a formality. No doubt in the mind of either Kara or Seth that Hank Thompson would be arraigned.

'The way I hear it, Raines is in no rush to go to trial,' Seth told Kara. 'And that's the way you want it,' he recalled. Questions in his eyes about whom Kara suspected, but that she wasn't revealing.

'Absolutely.'

'You don't plan on being at the arraignment?' Seth checked.

'I don't think that would be a wise move.' Her eyes were non-committal. She owed Seth Rogers no explanation. But she knew she was *person non grata* with Harvey Raines.

Seth shrugged. 'I gather that Valerie Thompson understands what she paid me covers just the arraignment.'

'She understands. By the time the case comes to trial, I will have been admitted to the bar.' *Please, God, let that be true.*

'Raines will be coming up for re-election,' Seth warned. 'He'll fight hard for a conviction.'

'He won't get it.' She managed a confident smile. 'Hank Thompson didn't kill Mattie.'

Kara hurried back home – hopeful that some word had come from Donna.

'Sugar, she'll call as soon as she talks with Mildred,' Edie soothed her.

'You're sure we gave her the right information?' Kara probed. 'I mean, the phone number where Joe lived at that specific time.'

'You know what a pack rat Mattie was. Val went through

an old address book of Mattie's – from the days when she first began to see Joe. He was living with his father then. His father was an alcoholic – almost a recluse. Any phone call that came in would have been for Joe. And that's the right number.'

'Val called a few minutes ago,' Daisy told Kara. 'She's anxious about the arraignment.'

'I'll call her.' Kara crossed to the phone.

She spoke briefly – reassuringly – with Val, then settled in a lounge chair to read a segment of the Sunday *Enquirer*.

'Kara, it's time you signed a lease for office space,' Edie fretted, glancing at the *Enquirer*'s classified ads. 'You said you saw something decent right on Main Street – and the price was right. Somebody's going to grab it up. Why don't you call the broker tomorrow and arrange for the lease to be drawn up? And don't tell me you have to wait for your letter from the bar admissions people.'

'I won't know until the letter arrives that I'll *need* office space,' Kara hedged.

'You know you passed,' Daisy chided. 'You were in the top ten per cent of your class. And you were never one of those who freeze at exams.'

'I could make the lease contingent upon my passing the bar exams,' Kara considered. 'It's just a matter of a couple of weeks now.' The office on Main Street was small – but spacious enough for one beginning attorney. And if – God willing – Jonnie decided to leave the company, the two of them could manage in that space.

But a tiny inner voice taunted her. What were the odds that Jonnie would want to be with her if she proved his father was guilty of murder?

Jonathan sprawled in a lounge chair in his bedroom and read the masses of photocopies he'd made at the library from recent newspapers and magazines. All dealt with the furor over HMO practices and controversy over for-profit hospitals. Dad was right, he conceded. Many HMOs were dropping Medicare and Medicaid contracts – claiming they were losing money.

He replayed in his mind what his father had harangued him about at dinner. '*Let's face the facts. It's the large corporations* who're screwing up health care in this country. They dictate the whole deal. Tell us what they're willing to pay. A corporation with tens of thousands of employees can ruin an HMO by refusing to renew a contract. The big corporations are calling the shots – not the insurance companies.'

What about the tens of millions of small businesses that couldn't make good deals with HMOs? Their costs – according to the figures he'd dug up – were soaring, to the point where many were giving up on providing health care for their employees. And then there were those who worked out a co-payment arrangement, to be split between employer and employee. But somebody on a small salary with a family to support couldn't handle that *and* put food on the table. *What's the answer?*

Deep in thought, Jonathan started at the knock on his door. 'Yeah?'

The door swung open. His father stood there. 'Bart's here. Come down to the library and join us. We need to talk.'

In the library – Roy and Bart fortified with bourbon on the rocks – the three men dissected the new reports handed in by Midwest district managers. Bart and Roy argued; Jonathan asked questions.

'Premiums have to go up.' Roy was firm. 'We owe it to our stockholders to show a comfortable profit.'

Figures tickertaped across Jonathan's mind. Dad said Cameron Insurance paid out less than 45 per cent of premiums – when other companies paid over 80 per cent. Couldn't Cameron afford not to raise premiums?

'There's going to be a hell of a lot of flak,' Bart warned. 'We could lose some of our biggest corporations.'

'If we keep our premiums where they are now, we have to cut a lot more fat.' Roy crossed to the bar to refill his drink. He meant to keep the premiums at their current level, Jonathan read. 'We're doing that with Eden General. That was the test – and it works. The way to survive today is to pick up more hospitals, make them cost-efficient. I want the Farraday deal sewn up, Bart. That's your job.'

'We can't move too fast on lining up hospitals,' Bart warned. 'We don't want the State Attorney breathing down our necks.'

'That's where you come in.' Roy turned to Jonathan. 'I want you to go over to the Capitol – talk to our man over there. No phone calls, no faxes, no e-mail,' he stipulated. 'Nothing on the record. But you let him understand we want no interference in buying up hospitals in this state.' Roy's smile was smug. 'We'll have three hundred hospitals in the next five years. We'll be able to control costs. We'll keep our corporations happy.'

'When do you want me to go to Columbia?' Jonathan fought to control his unease. He was disturbed by the back-room deals he suspected would be involved in these new acquisitions.

'I'll clear the time with George Ross in Columbia and let you know,' Roy said. 'And be sure you make the Eden General Board understand, I want no word around about the negotiations with Farraday. They're to keep their mouths shut.'

'I don't like what I've been hearing.' Bart grimaced. 'About that half-assed "watchdog group" that's been formed in town.'

Roy shrugged. 'They'll make a lot of noise – that's all.'

'What's Dr Callahan doing with them?' Bart challenged.

'Use your head, Bart,' Roy rebuked him. Almost supercilious, Jonathan thought. 'He's there protecting hospital interests. He knows the score.'

'I hear that damn Jamison woman is on their committee,' Bart said contemptuously. 'And a couple of nurses from Eden General.'

Jonathan tensed. *They're talking about Kara's grandmother.*

'Edith Jamison sticks her nose into everything in this town. Always did. Always trying to make out she's something more than poor white trash. It never did her any good.' Jonathan was conscious of a covert exchange between his father and Bart. 'And it won't do her any good now. As for the two nurses, I know about that. They'll be excessed.'

'You like to keep good relations locally, Dad.' Jonathan was apprehensive. 'Maybe I ought to meet with the group, try to reassure them about what's happening.'

'Fuck them. We've got most of this town behind us. We'll take over Farraday. Within a year we'll close it. I want to build up Eden General's Pediatrics Department. That guy Callahan has a great reputation nationally. He'll bring in patients from all over the South. Jonathan, whatever Dr Callahan wants in the way of innovative equipment, you see that he gets it.'

'I'll have a talk with him,' Jonathan promised. But he was uncomfortable. Dad was nursing a real vendetta against Kara's grandmother. *Why?*

Didn't Dad realize that closing Farraday – leaving Eden with only one hospital – was going to raise outcries in this town? In his mind he heard Kara's voice: '*If Grandma feels something is wrong, you'll hear from her.*' They'd be hearing from Kara's grandmother – no doubt about that.

How will I deal with Kara's grandmother? She'll hate what Dad means to do with the hospitals in Eden. And deep inside I know she'll be right.

Twenty-One

This Sunday seemed endless, Kara thought while she cleared away the dinner table. Each time the phone rang she raced to answer. So far there had been one wrong number, someone doing a survey, and a recorded message that was a sales pitch for retirement condos in Florida.

Just as she pushed the button to start the dishwasher, the phone rang again. She hurried into the living room. Edie was talking with the caller. Daisy pantomimed for silence, mouthing, 'Donna.'

'Oh, Donna, we understand it may take time,' Edie said, and Kara winced. *How long before Hank goes on trial?* 'Thanks so much for getting back to us.' She paused while Donna made some comment. 'But please, remind Mildred that all this must be kept under wraps.'

Kara felt a heady sense of relief. 'She's talked to Mildred.'

'Mildred is glad to help out,' Edie reported, off the phone now. 'We'll have to hang in there until she finds the right moment to search the company records.'

'She knows we need the information quickly?' Kara pressed.

'She knows, and she'll do her best to rush it through,' Edie soothed. 'She said that, hopefully, she'll have a report by the end of the week.'

Daisy was uneasy. 'She could be fired if she's caught looking up old records.'

'If it means bad news for Roy Cameron, Mildred's willing to take the chance.' Edie strove for calm, but Kara sensed her excitement. This could be the crucial link they needed. 'Daisy, what's on TV tonight?'

Kara made a pretense of joining Edie and Daisy in watching television. The images on the screen a blur. Voices background noise. In truth, she was impatient to receive her nightly call from Jonathan. But after the one from Donna, the phone remained silent. Always in a crevice of her mind was the fear that he'd learn about her connections to the Cameron family. That out of loyalty to his parents he'd feel he must stop seeing her.

Grandma had realized it was Jonnie who called every night. Surely Mom knew that, too – but she couldn't bring herself to face it. How was she to make Mom understand that there was nothing wrong in her loving Jonnie? *He's not a Cameron. He knows nothing about the past. We're two people who want to spend the rest of our lives together. Mom would like him – if she had the chance to get to know him. Will that ever happen?*

The phone rang. A jarring intrusion.

'It's probably for me,' Kara said. 'I'll take it in my room.'

'I'm sorry to be so late,' Jonathan apologized. 'I got involved in a business discussion with Dad and Bart.' He chuckled. 'After Tuesday – in the apartment – I should be able to avoid these impromptu conferences.'

'Problems?' she asked. They usually skirted around the subject of the Eden General happenings.

'I have to go to Columbia one day next week on company business. I planned on going anyway,' he reminded her, 'to do some research at the law library there. I don't suppose you'd be able to go with me?' It was a wistful appeal. Columbia would always be a special place to them.

'I don't think so.' But it would be beautiful to spend a whole day together.

'I don't think it'll happen before the end of the week. We have furniture-moving to do Tuesday evening,' he reminded her.

'What's taking you to Columbia?' she asked on impulse.

'I have to consult with the company's representative there. I suppose he's our lobbyist.' He paused. 'There's a possibility that Farraday may be on the auction block. But don't repeat that,' he said with sudden urgency.

'The rumor's been around town for weeks, Jonnie.'

'Kara, don't repeat this to anybody – not even to your

189

grandmother. I shouldn't have talked about it.' He sounded unhappy.

'I've told you,' she was faintly sharp: 'the rumor's all over town. Some people are disturbed.' The new people in town, plus the few who didn't belong to Roy Cameron's fan club. 'They're afraid Farraday will be closed. Except for the two private sanitariums in town, we'll be dependent on one hospital.'

'It won't happen right away. Maybe it'll never happen—' But he didn't believe that, Kara thought. 'Your grandmother will be upset.' It was a statement rather than a question.

'When the facts come out.' How could she not tell Grandma? And yet it seemed disloyal to Jonnie. But it wouldn't be news to Grandma – she already accepted the rumor as fact.

They talked a few minutes longer – both conscious of the confrontation between Cameron Insurance and her grandmother and the watchdog group that would come out once the Farraday sale was made public.

'I love you,' Jonnie said softly. 'None of this craziness will ever come between us.'

'Never,' she vowed. *But Jonnie doesn't know about the other craziness.*

Kara returned to the living room. Ignoring the 11 p.m. national news – a ritual in this household – Edie and Daisy were in tense conversation.

'Daisy, no, you can't do that!' Edie declared. 'You made a date to meet him for dinner tomorrow night. You have no reason to break it.'

'He'll just think I'm a vengeful woman.' Daisy's face was flushed. 'He expects an unbiased opinion. How can I give him that?'

'He wants to see the other side of Roy Cameron,' Kara interceded gently.

'He wants to hear it confirmed,' Edie picked up, 'that the man doesn't belong on that pedestal people in this town have put him on. He wouldn't be probing if he wasn't suspicious there was another – not so pretty – side.'

'All right,' Daisy capitulated. 'I'll have dinner with him tomorrow evening. But I don't know what good will come of it.'

'Tell him what we've read about Cameron Insurance,' Edie pushed. 'How everything seems to be above-board here in Eden, but ugly stories come out from other towns. Tell him about the national magazine exposés that nobody here in town would believe. Tell him what happened with Mildred's cousin – how when her new, expensive house burned down, the company tried to say it was arson, circulated all kinds of nasty rumors about her.'

'I'll tell him,' Daisy promised. 'But that doesn't mean he'll believe me.'

'He's a good person,' Edie said. 'He'll believe you.'

On Monday morning Kara went to the office of the real-estate broker handling the space she'd seen and liked. The broker brushed aside any qualms about including a rider that stipulated the lease would go into effect on September 1 providing Kara had been admitted to the bar.

'You'll pass the exam,' the broker predicted. 'You've got success written all over you.'

'From your lips to God's ear.' Kara borrowed one of Edie's favorite quotations.

'It's about time we had another woman lawyer in town. Marietta Logan is pushing seventy-five and goes into her office just two days a week. About all she does are wills and an occasional real-estate closure.'

Feeling isolated from reality, Kara drove back to the house. There was nothing constructive that she could do, she fretted – until Mildred came up with facts about phone calls to Joe's house all those years ago.

She heard the phone ringing as she parked in the driveway, darted to the house. *Maybe it's Mildred.* Breathless, she unlocked the door. The phone had stopped. The little red light on the answering machine was flashing. Churning with anticipation, she pushed the 'message' button. *Let it be Mildred.*

'Hello, this is David Hamilton. I'm just calling to see if there's any news yet. I'd appreciate some word.'

She should have been in touch with him before now, Kara scolded herself. He was as anxious as they were to see justice done. She checked his office number in her phone book, punched in the required digits. His receptionist put her through immediately.

'I thought you might have some word by now.' His voice held a wistful hope.

'Nothing concrete yet, Mr Hamilton – but I'm working on a strong lead.' She was careful in her choice of words. 'As soon as I have definite information, I'll get right to you. That's a promise.' Her voice gentle because she realized she had resurrected old grief.

'I know – as sure as I'm alive – that somehow Roy and Sandra Cameron are behind Eric's murder. Eric's and Gerry's,' he amended. 'And that poor Mattie Mason. You track it down to them, Kara!'

Off the phone with David Hamilton, Kara made her daily call to Valerie.

'It's awful, knowing Hank's in jail and folks here in town all thinking he killed Mattie.' Val took a deep breath. 'It don't seem right that they can't wait for a trial before deciding he's guilty. As little as she is, Betsy knows something terrible is happening. She keeps asking for her daddy – and why nobody wants to play with her.'

'You have to hang in there, Val. We've got some strong leads – but we're not there yet. I've talked with Hank. He knows we're fighting for him.' *How can I sound so confident when I'm a shambles inside?*

'I don't much like that Mr Rogers,' Val admitted.

'He's just covering for me until I'm admitted to the bar,' Kara consoled her yet again. 'He'll be fine for the arraignment. We know Hank will be held for a grand jury. We know he won't be allowed bail. Let him see that you're confident he'll be cleared – he needs to know that, Val.'

'I keep telling him how hard you're working for him. And I tell him to keep praying, like me.'

Kara and Edie were in the midst of dinner preparations. For the past twenty minutes Daisy had been pacing about the house, gearing herself for dinner with Paul Callahan. If Mom and Kara had not been so insistent, she told herself, she'd have found an excuse not to go out with him.

192

She tensed at the sound of a car pulling up before the house. She managed a swift glance in the foyer mirror before she opened the door, moments before he mounted the few steps to the entrance.

'Hi.' Her smile belied her unease. *This isn't a date. This is committee business.*

'Hi. You're looking lovely, as always.' He seemed almost shy.

'Thank you—'

'Paul?' Edie appeared in the foyer. 'I thought I heard your voice. Anything new at the hospital?'

'Nothing much.' He paused. 'Jonathan Cameron came to Pediatrics this morning. He talked about a serious expansion of the department, wanted me to advise him of any special equipment that I'd like brought in.' He chuckled for a moment. 'I warned him about the astronomical costs of new equipment just coming off the line, but he didn't seem fazed.' A glint in his eyes now. 'If the money's there – as it seems to be – we could make some real progress.'

'They want to make you a star attraction.' Edie repeated her earlier assessment. 'You came to Eden General with a lot of fanfare.'

'I just want to do my job.' He shifted self-consciously, turned to Daisy. 'Shall we head to the restaurant before the mob descends?' He grimaced. 'I hate waiting in line for a table. But I made reservations.'

'You're having dinner at the Magnolias,' Edie guessed. 'No other place in town requires reservations.'

'I hear it's quite good.' All at once Paul seemed anxious.

'Oh, it's great from what I hear.' Edie nodded in approval. 'I'd better get back to the kitchen and see what's happening in the oven. You two have a nice evening.'

Daisy was grateful that Paul kept up a running conversation about small incidents at the hospital today while they drove to the restaurant. This wasn't a date, she reiterated to herself. Paul was after information about Roy Cameron. But he was impressed that money was there to expand Pediatrics. He liked Jonathan Cameron. She remembered his remarks about Jonathan at their first meeting.

Kara had gone to dinner at The Magnolias with Jonathan Cameron. She didn't dare probe – perhaps she couldn't face having it confirmed – but she was convinced Kara was emotionally involved with him. Under the circumstances what could ever come of that? *I don't want to see Kara hurt.*

'Here I am talking your ear off about my work.' Paul intruded on her introspection as they approached The Magnolias. 'What about you?' he asked with lively interest. 'What about your work?'

'I don't do anything important. I'm the manager of a women's specialty shop.' *That must sound dull to a man like him.* 'I've been there forever.'

'Then you must be good,' he said, pulling into the parking area of The Magnolias. 'It takes skill to deal with the public.'

She was conscious of pleasure that he could believe this. All at once she was glad she'd come out to dinner with Dr Callahan – yet disconcerted that she felt this way. Paul, she corrected herself. That's what all the committee members called him.

Many of the tables were already occupied. The atmosphere convivial in a subdued fashion. Immediately the cordial hostess led them to their table. They focused on ordering. She struggled not to appear intimidated by the prices. She'd never once dined at The Magnolias. Paul coaxed her into following his lead, and she was grateful not to have to make choices.

When the waiter left their table, Daisy felt compelled to bring up the issue that had supposedly prompted this meeting. *This is not a date. It's a business meeting.*

'I want you to hear what those who don't belong to Roy Cameron's fan club say about him.' She took a deep breath, willed herself to be cool about this. Yet the way Paul looked at her was simultaneously exhilarating and intimidating. She saw in his eyes far more than an impersonal interest. 'Some of it is – not pleasant.'

'Please tell me what you've heard. I know you'll discard wild rumors,' he said gently. 'Just give me facts.'

Haltingly she embarked on what she knew must be said. All the while conscious of the intensity with which Paul listened. Mom said he'd been harboring some reservations about the hero-worship Roy Cameron enjoyed in Eden. Mom

194

was sharp about people. She'd sensed that in Paul right away.

'Those things don't match what you hear in town,' Daisy conceded. 'But from the early years Roy Cameron encouraged locals to invest in the company – and those who bought stock did well. That's all they seem to want to know.'

'Roy Cameron is a strange, complex man.' Paul frowned in thought. 'I suppose he considers Eden his little kingdom – and nothing must go wrong here. But what you've just told me turns me off. How did Cameron Insurance manage to survive national exposés? But he's canny as they come.' Paul didn't wait for a reply. 'Shrewd enough to beat the odds.'

They were silent for a few moments while their waiter served their chilled gazpacho.

'You've lived here a long time?' Paul asked.

'I was born here. My mother was born here.'

'I grew up in New York. Right in Manhattan.' His eyes were nostalgic for a moment. 'It seemed great for a long time. Then about three years ago I went over to Bosnia with a group of doctors. And something happened to me when I saw the suffering in those little towns. The anguish of families that were torn apart. Their grief for those who'd died without reason. I came back to New York and I thought there has to be a better life than the New York rat race. Both of my parents had been dead almost ten years. I was an only child with no family other than distant cousins scattered across the Middle West. Then I had this fabulous offer to come down to Eden and head up the Pediatrics Department. It wasn't just the money,' he said with disarming candor. 'It was freedom to pursue my research.'

'The way I hear it, nobody at Eden expected you to accept their offer,' Daisy recalled. 'They were thrilled when you agreed to come down here.' His respect in the medical field was awesome.

'I flew down and fell in love with the town. Everyone was so friendly, so eager to be helpful. People said good-morning on the streets.' He shook his head in eloquent astonishment. 'It was a whole different world to me.'

'It's not always that lovely—' Daisy tensed. *Why did I say that?*

'I'm sure it's not lovely to Valerie Thompson and her husband,' he said compassionately. 'I hope he's cleared soon.'

Daisy hesitated. 'You said you wanted an unbiased opinion of Roy Cameron. I – I'm not sure I'm capable of that.'

'I wanted to hear the other side. That's not being biased.' But his eyes were full of questions.

'You probably know about Tim Cameron. The son who was killed in a horrible car accident twenty-five years ago . . .'

'I know that it happened. That he was only nineteen.' He waited for her to continue.

'Tim wasn't alone in the car when he was killed.' She spoke compulsively now. 'I was with him. Tim and I had been married that morning. I survived. He didn't. His parents insisted I'd pushed Tim into marrying me at a time when he was heavily into drugs. Tim never touched drugs in his life! He'd founded a group on his college campus to fight *against* drugs.' She paused for a moment in anguished recall. 'Roy Cameron contrived to have our marriage annulled. He never recognized Kara as his granddaughter.' She was trembling now. The gazpacho abandoned by Paul and her. *Why am I telling him this?*

'I wasn't as young as you when I married. I was twenty-five and starting my residency. Probably the roughest period of my life. She was a nurse. We married seven weeks after we met. I knew almost from the beginning that it was a mistake. We stayed together – fighting constantly – for almost two years. She had huge plans for my career. Only they didn't match mine. I went into medicine because I wanted to be useful. I talked about going into rural America to practice – where even seventeen years ago there was a shortage of doctors. She wanted a condo on Park Avenue and a beach house in the Hamptons. She divorced me for a plastic surgeon catering to New York celebrities.'

'But you didn't go to rural America?' *Why did I say that? I make it sound as though he's a phoney.*

'I got caught up in research. I wanted answers for so many things. There's still so much to learn in the pediatrics field. That was one of the things that drew me to Eden General. They offered me a freedom I couldn't refuse.' He squinted

196

in thought. 'And now Jonathan Cameron wants me to expand the department, order expensive new equipment.' He gestured futility. 'I don't know what to think anymore.'

'The hospital needs you,' she said softly.

'But knowing what I know now about Roy Cameron, I'm not sure I can work with him. Because there's no doubt in my mind,' he said with deepening intensity, 'that this is a dangerous man.'

'You'll have to play it by ear,' she said after a moment.

'I'll fight for the hospital,' he promised. 'I'll do what I can to keep it the kind of operation this town needs. I'm glad you told me about Cameron. I'm prepared now.'

The waiter hovered at their table with a questioning smile. Paul gestured to him to remove the first course.

'There'll probably be a bloody war ahead,' Paul predicted when the waiter had left them. 'I'm ready to fight, but –' he paused, his tenuous smile ingratiating – 'but I'll be in a better position to do that if I'll be seeing you . . .'

'I want to be helpful.' She lowered her eyes, lest they betray the startling emotions that suffused her. Her heart was pounding. His eyes told her it was more than her help in the hospital fight that he wished for. 'Yes,' she said with fresh – almost defiant – strength, 'I'd like to know that we'll be seeing each other.'

Twenty-Two

Kara awoke to the sound of rain hammering a relentless tattoo against her bedroom windows. To an awareness of a dank cold in the house. She frowned, subconsciously remembered the light blanket that Mom had placed at the foot of the bed last night, after the TV weatherman predicted a sharp drop in temperature. She reached, pulled it up, emitted a faint sound of pleasure at the instant comfort it supplied.

She glanced at the clock on her night table. No need to get up just yet. She burrowed beneath the warmth of the blanket – for a few moments her mind in limbo. Then reality intruded. She'd waited all evening in the hope that Mildred would call. She'd even cut short her nightly phone conversation with Jonnie because their phone didn't have 'call waiting' and she was fearful of missing word from Mildred. Grandma kept reminding her – it might be days before Mildred came up with the information they sought.

But time is in short supply. Hank will be arraigned tomorrow evening. By the time he goes to trial, I must be prepared to clear him.

When would she hear from Mildred? Was she following the right course to clear Hank? Instinct told her she was, yet her mind shot up warnings that she must be prepared to change direction. But what other leads did she have?

All right, go over the facts. What does the prosecution have against Hank? The flimsiest of circumstantial evidence. He and Val inherited Mattie's house at her death. A small insurance policy – what Mattie considered her 'burial money' – listed Val as beneficiary. And that, she recalled, had not been recognized because Mattie had not died a natural death. A clerk – a vindictive clerk – at a lumber yard quoted Hank

198

as bragging that 'When Mattie croaks, my old lady inherits the house.'

No way could Hank – or Val – have personally killed Mattie. They were with Betsy at the emergency room at Eden General. The prosecuting attorney will claim Hank hired a hit man to kill Mattie. But he'll never find that hit man because he doesn't exist.

Harvey Raines has a flimsy case. Yet innocent men – and women – have been convicted by a hard-hitting prosecutor and a gullible jury. What else will Harvey Raines dig up – or concoct – against Hank before the case comes to trial?

The day ahead promised to be dreary, fraught with unanswered questions. But she felt a surge of tenderness as she remembered she would be with Jonathan this evening. They'd have take-out dinner in his new apartment and then they'd arrange the furniture that was being delivered today.

Poor darling – he was so uncomfortable in his working situation. A big office in the Cameron Insurance building, a smaller one at Eden General. *'Do you know how many people hate me for walking into the job this way?'* He knew he was being given a crash course to prepare him to succeed his father at some future date – over the heads of others who deserved this role. Including his uncle. *'Of course, Dad will still be CEO at eighty-five.'*

With a compulsive need to share his life with her, he'd talked about the long hours spent each day – sometimes extending far into the evening – when he struggled to absorb endless details of company business plus the workings of Eden General. He was too loyal to his father to come out and say, 'I'm shocked at what I'm learning' – but his feelings crept through. How much longer could he play this charade? No way, she thought grimly, could he remain for the two years he talked about. *Two years that belong to us.*

Reluctantly Kara left the coziness of her bed. Conscious that Edie and Daisy were in the kitchen, she hurried into the bathroom, closed the door and flipped on the electric heater. Always used with caution to keep the electric bills low. She stripped to skin, and stepped beneath the hot, stinging spray of the shower.

In the steamy heat of the bathroom she felt herself begin to unwind. Time to focus on the hours ahead. She'd drop by the real-estate office and sign the lease. *But I should be working to clear Hank. I should be working every waking moment. It's so frustrating to just sit back and wait to hear from Mildred. I should be working on other angles.*

Everything points to Roy Cameron as the instigator of the three murders. The motives are there. All right, suppose Mildred tells me today, 'Yes, Joe received a phone call from Brussels that night.' Where do I go from there?

Kara's mind moved into high gear. She knew how she would use today. She'd search the books she'd brought home from law school, track down precedents that were applicable. Decide how to approach the next step – if Mildred confirmed her suspicions about Roy Cameron.

It was past two o'clock when hunger persuaded her to take a break. The morning's labor had produced little that was helpful. Again, she was attacked by frustration. She had so little experience, she rebuked herself. This was a murder case.

She had just sat down with a grilled cheese sandwich and a mug of coffee when the phone rang.

'I just got some information that won't make you happy,' Seth Rogers said bluntly. 'From the DA's office.'

Her hand tightened on the phone. 'What information?'

'Our client,' he said drily. 'He hasn't been entirely truthful.'

'About what?' Hank shooting off his big mouth again?

'You told me Hank and his wife were at Eden General for two and a half hours on the night of Mattie Mason's murder. Clearing him of having been anywhere near Mattie's house at the time.'

'That's right.' Kara's throat tightened. 'Betsy – their little girl – was in the emergency room being treated for a bad asthma attack.'

'But he didn't tell you that he left the hospital for almost forty minutes. Plenty of time to have gone to Mattie's house and killed her. You still believe he's innocent?' A glimmer of condescension in his voice. 'Think again, counselor.'

200

'How did this develop?' Kara's mind was in chaos. All at once Harvey Raines's case against Hank had acquired teeth.

'A detective delving into the facts questioned staff at the hospital. An orderly remembered Hank had gone out for what he figured was about forty minutes. He remembered because he said the kid started a real ruckus in the emergency room when she realized her father wasn't there. With something that strong, the DA's office just might rush to trial faster.'

'I'd like you to go over to the jail and talk with Hank,' Kara said slowly. *I can't go and question him.* 'Ask him how long he was in the parking area. Did he see anybody there that could confirm this?'

'Look, our deal was for me to represent him at the arraignment. You're running up more billing hours.' His voice said he expected a battle.

'Another hundred dollars.' Kara suppressed her anger. 'I'll arrange it. Talk to Hank.'

'Hey, this isn't my only deal,' he balked.

'A hundred-dollar fee if you go down there and talk to him. Ten minutes in transit, another ten minutes with Hank. One hundred dollars.' Seth Rogers was money-hungry. His major practice was as a part-time public defender. In Eden that paid little. 'Immediately,' she stipulated.

'Okay, I'll do it. Stay by the phone. I'll get back to you in an hour or so.'

Off the phone, Kara sat motionless. Replaying in her mind the brief but unnerving conversation with Seth Rogers. Yet she clung to the conviction that Mattie had been killed for Joe's confession. She and Val had searched the house without finding it. Mattie's murder was linked to Eric and Gerry's deaths. No way could Hank be involved in the earlier murders. He couldn't have been more than ten at the time.

Kara checked her watch. Grandma would be home from the pharmacy in another hour. Let the two of them go over to Val's house. Grandma could distract Betsy while she talked with Val. Had somebody paid the orderly to lie about Hank's absence from the emergency room?

In just short of an hour Seth phoned.

'Hank claims he was in the parking area checking out the

201

car. He's sure it wasn't forty minutes – he just remembers being anxious that something was wrong with the transmission. And that would be a humongous bill.'

'Did he see anybody there?' Kara pressed.

'He didn't notice. He said people were coming and going – but he paid no attention. About my bill—'

'I'll mail you a check today.' Kara was terse.

'Look, we knew all along he'll be held for the grand jury.' A note of sympathy in his voice now. 'But the son of a bitch should have been honest with you.'

Taking refuge beneath one umbrella, Kara and Edie darted to the car as the downpour continued into early afternoon. At the Thompson house Kara and Edie discovered Valerie about to leave for visiting time with Hank. She was to drop Betsy off with the only friend who wasn't avoiding contact with her.

'It'll have to wait,' Kara said with uncharacteristic abruptness. 'We need to talk.'

'Betsy, your mommy told me you have a new doll,' Edie said ingratiatingly to the cherubic little girl. 'Can I meet her?' A doll that Daisy had dropped off for her several days ago.

Betsy's face lit up. 'Her name's Samantha.'

'All right, take me to Samantha,' Edie coaxed, and the two went off in a show of high spirits.

'Kara, what's happened?' Valerie's face was drained of color.

'You and Hank weren't entirely honest with me—'

'We were!' Valerie was struggling against panic.

'The District Attorney's office has learned that Hank wasn't at the hospital with you and Betsy that night. At least, not all the time.' Kara tried for a calm approach.

'But he was, Kara!' Then Valerie paused. 'Except for maybe ten minutes—'

'Almost forty minutes, an orderly at the hospital told a detective today.'

'It couldn't have been that long.' Valerie frowned in concentration. 'No!'

'The orderly says otherwise. Where did Hank go?' In forty

minutes he could have driven to Mattie's house, killed her, and rushed back to the emergency room.

'He went out to check on the car.' Valerie was searching her mind. 'It had been making strange noises when we drove over. Hank's always nervous about trouble with the car. You know how much any tiny thing can cost. But he never left the parking area!'

'It'll look bad that Hank didn't tell the police this,' Kara pointed out. 'And we'll have some problems with the length of time Hank was away. You say ten minutes, the orderly says almost forty. And Hank was unsure of how long.'

'Maybe somebody else remembered,' Val said with an air of desperation. 'Maybe somebody else will remember it was only ten minutes – or so.' All at once she appeared exhausted. 'Kara, Hank didn't kill Mattie.'

'No more surprises, Val,' Kara pleaded. 'If there's anything else you haven't told me, tell me now.'

'There's nothing else. I swear it. I didn't think that Hank running out to the car that way meant anything.' But her eyes mirrored her terror.

Not until Kara and Edie were in the car again did Edie voice her anxiety. 'Is this bad for Hank?' Her expression said she was sure it was.

'If Hank had left the emergency room for ten minutes it would mean nothing. In forty minutes he could have driven to Mattie's house and killed her,' Kara said flatly.

'He'll insist it was only ten minutes.' Edie was defensive now.

'His credibility isn't the greatest.' More frustration. And what else would show up to tighten the rope about his neck?

'Maybe somebody paid that orderly to lie,' Edie tried again. 'Somebody who wanted to frame Hank.'

'The orderly didn't offer this information,' Kara pointed out. 'Some detective went over to the emergency room and dug it out of him. If he'd been paid off, he'd have mentioned it when he was first questioned.'

'How do you handle this?' Edie was upset.

'I'll ask Val what mechanic she and Hank use. Then I'll go over and talk to him. Their car is old and beat up – I can imagine Hank being worried about it. All right, I'm fishing,' she admitted with a rueful smile. 'But tomorrow evening Hank's going to be arraigned, and the ball starts rolling. I know – we have no illusions about the case against him being dismissed. Just pray that Mildred comes up with something I can run with.'

'Let's have coffee.' Edie's solace in moments of stress. 'You won't be able to reach Val for at least an hour.' Right now she would be discussing the situation with Hank.

Minutes before Biff Monroe – Hank's mechanic – was scheduled to leave the service station for the day Kara caught up with him.

'Yeah, I do work on Hank Thompson's car . . .' He seemed wary.

'The car's not in the best of shape,' Kara pushed.

'Sugar, it's a heap. But Hank watches it like a baby. He's good with cars – he only comes here when he's kind of desperate. I mean, not sure what's wrong.' He cleared his throat self-consciously. 'Has this got somethin' to do with his bein' – bein' in jail?'

'It may have. I'm working with his attorney,' she lied. 'He asked me to do some checking. It would be natural for Hank to go out and start looking for trouble if he thought the car was making weird noises?'

'Look, Hank's a good guy. He works hard. Maybe he's not the sharpest guy in the world – and sometimes he's got a big mouth – but I don't believe he killed Mattie Mason. I hope they catch who did it – but that ain't Hank.'

Returning home, Kara tensed at the sight of an unfamiliar car parked at the curb. She hurried to the door, heard an unfamiliar voice in conversation with Edie.

'Kara?' Edie called, her voice telegraphing that her visitor was important.

'Yeah, Grandma—' She walked into the living room with an uncertain smile.

'This is Mildred,' Edie said. 'She's got some news for us.' But Grandma didn't seem happy, Kara noted. 'Mildred, you remember Kara? She's been away so much these last years.'

'Sure, I remember Kara. I watched her grow up through

the years. It's been a long time since I've seen you,' Mildred admitted. 'You sure grew up pretty. Like your mother and grandmother.'

'You have some news?' Kara tried to mask her impatience.

'I managed to get through to the dates Edie gave me. There was only one call to that number. I'm sorry – it came from a pay-phone somewhere on Main Street. We can't tie it to anybody.'

Kara's throat tightened in disappointment. 'What about calls from Brussels?'

'There were three to the Cameron house, plus four calls from the Cameron house to a hotel in Brussels.' Mildred's eyes searched Kara's face. 'That don't help you much—'

'Not the way I'd expected.' Donna and Mildred had hoped to incriminate Roy Cameron, Kara remembered. 'But it was wonderful of you to track down those calls.'

'Here's the time of the calls – from the pay-phone and to and from Brussels. At our time.' Mildred extended a sheet of paper with these notations. If you have any other lead—' Mildred hesitated. *She and Donna understand we're trying to link Roy Cameron to Mattie's murder. But they'll be silent. Still hoping he'll be trapped.* 'Any other numbers you want checked out, you just let me know and I'll go to work on them, you hear?'

'Thanks, Mildred. We do appreciate your help. I know you were taking a risk, and we're so grateful.' But she felt sick with disappointment.

'I'd better get going,' Mildred said. 'This is the night I volunteer at the nursing home. But remember, you want any other numbers, I'm your gal.'

'How are you going to track down that phone call to Joe?' Edie demanded in exasperation when Mildred had left. 'I'd bet my last dollar that the caller was acting for Roy Cameron!'

'We're up against a brick wall.' Kara began to pace. Her mind in turmoil. *We're back to square one. But I mustn't panic. I need a clear head to get Hank off the murder charge.* 'Somebody deliberately called Joe from a pay-phone – knowing the call couldn't be traced to him. Or her,' she added. She stopped pacing, reached into a pocket of her

205

slacks, brought out the sheet of memo paper Mildred had given her. 'The first call from the Cameron house was at nine twenty-three p.m. – three a.m. Brussels time.'

'Sandra calling Roy about the accident.' Edie tensed in excitement.

'Probably,' Kara conjectured. And reality took over. 'Maybe all those calls between the Cameron house and Brussels had to do with that.' Yet her mind refused to believe that these calls weren't related to Eric and Gerry's murder.

'Maybe – just maybe,' Edie persisted, 'Roy phoned Sandra with instructions for her to talk to Joe. On a pay-phone. Mattie told me – Joe killed those two kids because of something that was held over his head. Blackmail material. What did Roy Cameron have on Joe that demanded that kind of payback?'

Kara shook her head in anguish. 'We have nothing I can take into court.' It had been stupid to be sure they'd have at least a phone call from Roy Cameron in Brussels to Joe. Stupid to think she could build a case from there. She began to pace again – searching her mind for some sliver of knowledge that might lead to a breakthrough. Again she consulted Mildred's notes.

'Sandra's second call was at eleven twelve p.m., local time. By then she'd learned that Mom had been in the car and survived – and she'd been told about the marriage in Salem—'

'Mildred said there were four calls from the house to Brussels. When was the third?'

Kara consulted her notes. 'The following morning at nine eleven a.m.' At all once David Hamilton's words tickertaped across her mind: *'I remember Eric's shock when he heard about Tim and Daisy. A few hours earlier he and Gerry had been witnesses at their marriage. In the morning Eric turned on the TV for the nine a.m. news. He was outraged when the newscaster reported that Tim's parents were conferring with a judge about having the marriage annulled. The station always keeps the time and the weather in a corner of the screen. It was exactly 9:04 when Eric called and spoke with Mrs Cameron.'*

'Kara?' Edie snapped her back to the moment. 'What are you thinking?'

'Mr Hamilton was specific about the time Eric called the Cameron house. It was 9:04 a.m. Seven minutes later – at 9:11 a.m. – Sandra Cameron was calling Brussels. To tell her husband about the marriage.'

'And he gave Sandra instructions to call Joe, to order the hit. They knew Eric and Gerry were on the road to Eden.'

'The call to Joe was made at nine twenty-two local time.' The atmosphere was electric.

Edie reached for the memo paper. 'The fourth call to Brussels was two hours later – when Joe had reported the hit was accomplished.'

'It could have been that way.' Kara's voice was unsteady. *That meant* both *of Jonnie's parents were involved.*

'Then you have an angle to work on?'

'We have a possible scenario.' Kara was pensive. 'I'm not sure where we go from here. If I manage to bring those calls into the trial – and a thousand to one they'll be thrown out as speculation – how do I prove that they had anything to do with Eric and Gerry's murder?' She gestured futilely. 'Right at this moment the best I can do is to find somebody who can back Hank's claim that he never left the parking area at Eden General.'

'You said once you thought it was ridiculous that Harvey Raines would want to go to trial with such flimsy circumstantial evidence—' For an instant Edie exuded hope.

'That was in the beginning. Before the circumstantial evidence expanded.' Kara felt drained of energy. 'Raines is counting on the jury's being on his side – now that he has the statement from the clerk at the lumber yard and the one from the orderly at Eden General.'

Edie winced. 'Raines figures he has motive *and* opportunity?'

'He suspects there's a good chance that the jury will be on his side. It happens that way. It *shouldn't* – but it does. How many times have we read about innocent men and women spending long stretches in prison – then being proved not guilty?'

'Maybe somebody in the hospital parking area saw Hank tinkering with the car,' Edie offered.

'That's wishful thinking. He told Seth that he saw people coming and going – but he has no idea who they were.'

'Maybe one of them will remember seeing Hank there.' Edie was silent for a moment as Kara shook her head in dismissal. 'This is all so crazy! Hank didn't kill Mattie. No way.' Edie took refuge in indignation. 'Raines is willing to railroad him into prison.'

'Harvey Raines isn't interested in justice. He has an election coming up. He wants a conviction.'

Twenty-Three

'The rain's letting up,' Edie noted with an effort at cheerfulness while she poured a second round of coffee for Kara and herself. 'We may even have a nice sunset.'

But Kara was not diverted from her painful soul-searching. 'I know what the odds are against it happening, but I'm going to fight like hell to track down somebody who saw Hank tinkering with the car. I need to cause doubt in a jury's mind that Hank had the opportunity to kill Mattie.' *Because I'm getting nowhere with the Roy Cameron situation.*

'Hey, you could find somebody.' Edie exuded a shaky optimism now. 'It'll be tough – but it could be enough to cast doubt on Raines's meager evidence against Hank.'

Kara took a swig of coffee, squinted into space. 'According to the ER records Hank and Val were there from one twenty-five to four a.m. It's unlikely that anyone other than staff would be around at those hours. I need to know who was there on that specific night. Do you think Peg and Nan could manage to dig up a list of staff on duty then?'

'Count on it. They'll come up with names.' Edie was emphatic.

'I'll question every one.' A time guzzler, Kara's mind warned. 'I'll explain that I'm acting as a private investigator for Hank's attorney.' Tracking down someone who'd testify that Hank was in the parking area at those hours was no more than a Band-Aid. *But at this moment what else do I have?* Kara turned to Edie. 'I'll call Peg now—'

'It'll have to wait until later,' Edie told her. 'She's on a two-day private-duty case, at the patient's house. You know how fast they throw post-ops out of the hospital these days. Even at Farraday.' Edie was grim. Kara knew her grandmother was concerned about the rumor that Farraday would go the way of Eden any week now – and she herself knew from Jonathan that it was more than rumor.

She glanced at her watch. Jonnie would pick her up around six. Before Mom arrives home, she thought with guilty relief.

'I should put the chicken in the oven.' Edie rose to her feet. 'You know they keep warning people to make sure poultry's thoroughly cooked.'

'Grandma, I won't be home for dinner.' Her smile was contrite. 'I forgot to tell you . . .'

Edie was silent for a moment. 'Jonathan?'

Kara nodded.

'Darling, you're headed for big problems.' Edie's anxiety shone through her effort to appear cool about this.

'I know that. Why couldn't Jonnie have been adopted by somebody other than the Camerons?'

'But he wasn't. And you'll have to deal with it.' Edie's eyes were compassionate.

'Mom's suspicious, isn't she?' Kara's recurrent fear. *It isn't the time yet to tell her about Jonnie.*

The phone rang, disrupted conversation. Kara hurried to respond. These days every phone call evoked wariness, she thought, reaching for the receiver.

'Hello.'

'I'll be about twenty minutes late, sugar.' Jonathan was apologetic. 'I'm stuck here at the company. But it won't be longer than that.'

'No problem. See you then.'

'Jonathan doesn't know about your mother and Tim?'

'No.' Kara contrived a smile. 'If he did, I'm sure I would have heard about it.' His parents might reject her, but he wouldn't let that come between them. *But what if I unmask his parents as murderers?* 'I'd better change into something respectable.' Grandma assumed they'd be going to a restaurant for dinner. She didn't know about Jonnie's new apartment.

Jonathan strode from his office at Cameron Insurance to his father's for a last-minute conference. It would of necessity

210

be brief, Jonathan reassured himself. Dad was leaving on the company jet for Berlin in thirty minutes.

At his father's suite Cassie waved him into the inner sanctum. He pulled the door open, hesitated. His father was on the phone – castigating someone on the other end of the line in scurrilous tones. Without interrupting his tirade, Roy gestured Jonathan inside.

Feeling himself an intruder – and uncomfortable in this – Jonathan sat in the leather-upholstered chair before the huge executive desk. He was impatient for the phone conversation to be over. He covertly inspected his watch. Had he been cutting it too close when he told Kara he'd be only twenty minutes late?

'I don't want to discuss this on the phone,' Roy silenced the party on the other end. 'My son Jonathan will be in Washington tomorrow.' Jonathan's eyes widened in astonishment. 'He'll outline what we expect, present ideas we have about how this can be accomplished. He'll call you from the company apartment at the Watergate to set a meeting with you.' Roy slammed down the phone. 'Stupid, pretentious bastards!'

'I'm to be in Washington tomorrow?' Jonathan tried to sound amused – rather than startled.

'Sorry for this short notice, but it's important. Forget about the trip to Columbia for now. We're clients of a prestigious D.C. lobbying firm – one of the best in the field. Maybe they've got too many important clients. They have to learn that we rank with the best. I don't want to carry on these discussions by mail, phone, fax or e-mail.' His mantra, Jonathan thought. 'Nothing on the record.' Roy paused. 'Have you any idea how e-mail extends itself? When you sit down and send an e-mail, it goes to a server, where it's stored – and now you've lost control. Whoever receives it can do anything with it – even post it on the web.'

'I'd never given it any thought,' Jonathan confessed, his smile wry.

'I mean our discussions with the lobbying firm to be private. I pay a fortune to those bastards, listen to their advice. Most of the time. Hell, do you know how much they persuaded me to invest in Republican campaigns this year? You don't want to know.' Roy grimaced. 'And to play it safe I spent almost as much on the Democrats.'

'I'm not sure I know what I'm supposed to do.' *Am I to be an overpaid messenger?*

'I'm a rough son of a bitch with them. I want you to deliver my messages in that Ivy League manner of yours – which cost me plenty, too—' But with a wave of his hand he dismissed this. 'Cassie's at the computer setting up my notes – they'll tell you what I want. That overpaid firm has to understand that any "patients' rights" bill must be squashed before it comes to a vote. A bill with that potential could cost the company millions of dollars. Sure, we're not alone in this. The Health Insurance Association of America is powerful – way up there in the top lobbying groups. That doesn't mean we shouldn't fight, too. Make it clear our advertising budget will be high – Cassie's packet will have the figures. I expect their support against bills that hurt the company. They have access to the right people, favors to call in. I expect them to use that.' Roy reached for a notepad and pencil, began to scribble. 'This is who you call – the head of the firm. We deal only with the inner circle.' He pulled the sheet from the pad, handed it to Jonathan.

Jonathan inspected his father's rough scrawl, stared at him in astonishment. 'This is the ex-senator?'

Roy nodded. 'Hell, who better to push a deal? The top firm in the field has ex-senators Bob Dole and George Mitchell – plus Ann Richards. And they work together,' he said with relish. 'Haley Barbour – who used to chair the Republican Party – heads his own firm. Howard Baker – who was Senate majority leader and once Reagan's Chief of Staff – heads a lobbying firm. You scratch a lobbyist at the top of the line – and you find a high-level politician.'

'I'll be running with powerful names—' *How will they regard me, fresh out of law school and with no business experience?*

'Haven't you heard?' Roy jibed. 'This is the Age of the Young. Bart would give his right eye to go up there on this assignment.' His eyes glittered with malice. 'On *any* assignment to mix with our lobbyists. It'll never happen.'

'That's it?' Jonathan's mind was in turmoil. He wasn't unsophisticated. He was aware – on a surface level – of the machinations of Washington lobbyists. But he recoiled from being part of such deals. 'No other words of wisdom?' He masked his inner chaos with what he hoped was a cool approach.

'Cassie's at the computer with my notes – they'll give you all the material you need to talk with those guys,' Roy reiterated. 'She'll send them over to your apartment by messenger if she hasn't finished by now. She's made your reservations for the flight to Washington. Pick up your first-class tickets at the airport. Cassie will give you the time slot, arrange for someone to drive you to the airport in Augusta in the morning. Brooks will be traveling with me.' Jonathan remembered that Brooks wore a holstered gun, was bodyguard as well as chauffeur. 'Keys for the apartment, all information will be in her packet. Don't take any shit from the guys in Washington – as big as they are. They work for us – and we pay high.'

Jonathan managed a warm smile. 'Have a great trip, Dad.'

He lingered for a few moments with Cassie. Ever efficient, she had his packet waiting for him, explained the contents.

'Any problems arise in Washington, buzz me,' she said affectionately. 'I'll be in constant touch with your father.'

Waiting for the penthouse elevator, Jonathan checked his watch. He'd pick up Kara on time. How would she feel if she knew the real reason for this trip to Washington? There *should* be legal rights for patients. HMOs *should* have curbs. What would her grandmother – on the watchdog committee for Eden General – think? All he could tell Kara was that he was going to Washington on company business.

Sure, most people know about the financial deals lobbyists make with members of Congress, the arm-twisting. They know how lobbyists court voters – using whatever tactics will produce results. That's never been a secret. But it wasn't for this that he'd struggled through three years of law school. He dreaded sitting down tonight to study the packet Cassie had given him. This wasn't the future he'd envisioned for himself.

How do I muster the courage to tell Dad I can't stay on this track?

*   *   *

213

The rain had dissipated to a drizzle. The temperature below normal for August. Kara had changed into turquoise linen-blend slacks and a matching top that Jonathan had admired, then added a silver chain and her best earrings to provide a more festive appearance. Not for Jonathan – they'd have take-out dinner at his apartment. For Grandma – an outfit suitable for dinner at The Magnolias. *Oh, I hate this sub-terfuge. When will I be able to be honest with Grandma and Mom?*

She left the room and joined Edie in the kitchen. Hopeful that Jonathan would be here before Mom came home from the shop – and suffused with guilt that she felt this way.

'I'll buzz Peg around eight thirty this evening,' Edie told her. 'She's on duty from eight a.m. to eight p.m.'

'She'll contact Nan?' Another waiting period. 'I know we're asking a lot—'

'When Peg and Nan realize how important it is to Hank, they'll scrounge for names.'

'It's a long shot,' Kara reminded her. 'This happened back in late May.'

'Think positive,' Edie ordered. 'Sometimes a tiny thing pops up that solves a case.'

'We're asking for a small miracle.'

'You're going to clear Hank,' Edie insisted. 'I see it in my crystal ball.'

Kara heard a car pull up in their driveway. 'There's Jonnie.'

Purse slung over one shoulder, umbrella in hand, Kara rushed to the door. Jonathan was striding up the path.

'Hi.' Her eyes said what words must not.

'The rain's stopped. You don't need an umbrella.'

'Maybe for later.' She hesitated, eager to leave yet realizing Edie was approaching to exchange greetings with Jonathan.

'Hi there.' Edie appeared with a welcoming smile. 'How're things at the hospital?'

'Moving along.' Jonnie sounded uneasy, Kara thought. 'We're trying not to step on toes.' *He knows about the watchdog committee. He knows Grandma's part of it.*

'Eden General is so important to this town. It touches so many lives.' Edie was somber now.

'We want to make it efficient.' *Why was he frowning that way? Is some ugly business about to be revealed?* 'To know it serves the town in the best possible way.'

'That's what we all want.' Yet Edie's eyes were full of questions.

'We'd better hit the road,' Kara said with an effort at lightness. *Jonnie won't say anything about where we're having dinner, will he?* 'Before it starts to rain again.'

'Oh, here's Daisy—' Edie turned to Jonathan. 'You haven't met Kara's mother, have you?'

Kara's heart began to pound. *Grandma knows he hasn't met Mom.*

'No, I haven't,' he said with an aura of pleased expectancy.

Daisy approached the house with her usual small, swift steps. Kara saw her startled reaction to Jonathan's presence.

'Daisy, you haven't met Jonathan Cameron,' Edie said. As though this was an unimportant encounter, Kara thought. 'Jonathan, this is my daughter Daisy.'

'Hello, Jonathan.' Daisy extended a hand. *Mom was raised to be polite. She won't let on that she's upset to meet him.*

Jonathan smiled ingratiatingly. 'A beautiful lady, like your mother and daughter.'

Had it never aroused his curiosity that the three of them bore the same last name? Some malicious people in Eden – old-timers – liked to point out that three generations of women in this town bore the same last name. The scandal had never been put totally to sleep.

But Jonnie didn't know, she realized with sudden awareness while the other three exchanged small talk. She'd introduced Grandma simply as 'my grandmother'. And, of course, Mom would have the same name as she. But how long before he became aware of this?

Kara turned to her grandmother. 'You'll call Peg?'

'Sure thing,' Edie promised, and Kara saw instant alertness in her mother.

'Jonnie, we should get moving.' *Why am I so upset? Mom knows I've been seeing Jonnie. And when she gets to know him, she'll like him so much.*

215

In the car Kara sat beside Jonathan in silence for a few moments.

'What are you in the mood for tonight?' he asked, reaching for the ignition. 'In the way of food, that is.' His eyes gently teasing.

'Well, this isn't New York or Atlanta.' Her tone matching his. 'It's Chinese take-out or Italian take-out. Or we can go over to the supermarket, pick up a roast chicken, salad and dessert.'

'Sugar, as long as you're sharing it with me, I feel great about anything.'

'All right, let's head for the supermarket.' *He's so sweet.* 'You're sure your furniture arrived today?'

'I left a key for the driver with the "super", as planned,' Jonathan reported. 'They'll shove the key under the door when they lock up.' One hand left the wheel to reach for hers for a moment. '*Your* key.'

But he knows I can't move in with him. He knows we can't be married until this insanity with Hank is over. Will he want to marry me then?

'Oh, some annoying news,' Jonathan reported with a rueful grin. 'I have to leave in the morning for Washington. I'll be home by Friday,' he added quickly. 'And I'll call you each night I'm up there.'

'Why do you have to go to Washington?'

'Business for the company.' *But he doesn't look happy about it.* 'I'm an overpaid messenger boy. Anyhow, I'll be living in style.' *Hasn't he always?* 'I'll be staying at the company apartment at the Watergate.'

'Flying up on the company jet?' A good-humored taunt.

'Dad's using that for a flight to Berlin. I'll be slumming it on a commercial flight. But I'll call you every night,' he reiterated. 'Make sure you're not gallivanting around town in my absence.'

'Tomorrow evening Hank's to be arraigned.' All at once she was somber. 'I know – we realize he'll be held for the grand jury and that he'll be indicted. I'm chasing around for evidence to squash the District Attorney's feeble case.' Frustration in her voice.

216

'What about leads on the real murderer? You said you had a suspect in mind.'

'I still think I'm right about who's guilty.' She felt a rush of heat. 'But so far we can't tie him to the murder. I'm fishing around for another angle.'

'Look, if you think I could be helpful,' he said yet again. 'I know – between the company and Eden General I'm mired in the mud. Still, if you want to talk about it over dinner—'

'No. Tonight belongs to us. No business. Tomorrow I'll worry.'

The rush hour at the supermarket was past, Kara noted with gratitude. Along with Jonathan she headed for the rear. At the deli counter she ordered a herb-seasoned roast chicken.

'Split it in two, please,' she told the friendly clerk. *It feels so right to be shopping this way with Jonathan. As though we're just another young married couple.*

'Shall I get the salad while you're waiting here?' Jonathan pointed to the salad bar just behind them. 'Everything looks great.'

'A big salad,' she ordered. 'Frozen yogurt for dessert?'

'Low-fat, of course.' He grinned, aware of her insistence of a healthful diet.

'What else? "We have to set an example for the next generation."'

With dinner makings in tow they traveled the aisles in search of basics. Bread, butter, low-fat milk, sugar, salt, cereal, eggs, orange juice, fruit.

'Coffee,' Jonathan remembered. 'Regular and decaff.'

'Ditto tea,' Kara said. They were playing a game. A beautiful game.

Waiting in line at the checkout counter – Jonathan behind the shopping cart – Kara spied a neighbor, waved in greeting, then felt a twinge of unease. Did she recognize Jonnie? Was she remembering the old scandal? Would it be all over town tomorrow that she and Jonathan Cameron were shopping together in the supermarket? *I won't worry about that this evening.*

At Jonathan's apartment he unlocked the door, reached down for the key on the floor and handed it to Kara.

'Yours, Mrs Cameron,' he drawled. 'Oh, I know – it'll be Ms Jamison for a while yet. But I can handle that.'

The furniture had been placed in the appropriate area, Kara observed with approval, though not in its eventual destination. Several items would arrive later.

'Let's eat first, then move furniture.' Jonathan reached to pull her close. 'Our first home,' he murmured, pressing his face against hers. 'Suppose your car hadn't died there on the road that day – we might never have known each other.'

'Don't say that,' she whispered, then pulled away. 'Let's have dinner before the chicken goes cold and the yogurt melts. Oh, do we have a coffee-maker?'

'Right there.' Jonathan deposited bundles on the kitchen counter, pointed to the coffee-maker. 'That was Annie Mae's department, along with pots, pans, dishes and linens. Wow, am I spoiled!'

'Later we'll have to pick up a coffee grinder.' Kara reached to open a cabinet door, discovered attractive dishes. 'Oh, you're planning to entertain?' She lifted an eyebrow in mock astonishment. 'A service for twelve?'

'That's Annie Mae.' He chuckled. 'She probably figured I'd break a lot.'

'I'll get dinner on the table. You put up the coffee.'

'A bossy woman,' he clucked. 'Would you like some music, bossy woman?'

'How can we have a romantic dinner without music?' *We sound like a just-married couple. But I'm so scared this will never happen.*

While a CD provided music by Céline Dion, Kara and Jonathan sat at the dining table. They ate with relish – both conscious that this was their first meal together in the privacy of Jonathan's apartment. What he called 'our first home'.

'We won't move furniture for a while,' Jonathan decreed when they'd eaten and were lingering over coffee. 'I just want to wallow in being here with you.'

'I should clear away the dishes—' But she was reluctant to dispel the mood that held them blissful prisoners.

'Not yet.' He reached for her hand. 'How did I live all these years without you? Kara, suppose we'd never met?'

'Sssh.' *But what future lies ahead for us?*

He rose to his feet, reached out a hand to draw her to him. 'I want to make love. In our bed. In our home—'

'Me too,' she whispered, a pulse hammering away low within her.

Hand in hand they walked into the darkened master bedroom. The furniture arranged almost as though expecting their need for order here. Lamps as yet unconnected, no ceiling fixture. Not even a sliver of light infiltrating the blinds. *Just Jonnie and me and this wonderful feeling we share.*

'We should make up the bed,' she scolded, her throat tight with anticipation.

'Later,' he promised. 'That can wait. We can't.'

She was conscious of a frenzied fervor in her response tonight that Jonathan seemed to recognize, approve and match. Tomorrow Hank would be arraigned – she'd be thrown into the fever of clearing him as never before. How long before the ugly truth emerged? That she was convinced his parents were guilty of murder – and she must make every effort to prove that.

Don't think about that now. Cherish every moment.

Twenty-Four

R eluctantly Jonathan drove Kara home a few minutes before ten.

'You're taking an early flight to Washington – go to sleep at a decent hour,' she'd insisted.

But the apartment seemed painfully empty when he returned alone. Early in the day Annie Mae and Brooks had moved all his belongings from Cameron Manor to the apartment. Clothes had been hung away in the wardrobes or neatly stacked on shelves in the linen closet, to be transferred to the dresser and chest of drawers when they arrived. He focused on packing one valise for the trip to Washington.

Set the alarm clock for six a.m., he ordered himself – place it on the night table within easy reach. A company driver would arrive with the limo at seven. Now he reached for the packet Cassie had given him, propped the pair of pillows against the headboard of the bed – where just a little while ago he'd felt such rapture – and settled down to read. In a corner of his mind remembering how together he and Kara had made up the bed. It had felt so right.

Willing himself to concentrate on the business ahead, he studied his father's notes with soaring distaste. *All the company cares about is the bottom line. Will the company make a huge profit? Will company stock be strong? To hell with regard for decency, for the rights of the ordinary people of this world. God, does all big business operate this way?*

Now I'm to sit down with an ex-senator and some of the country's top-ranking attorneys to discuss Dad's demands. I'm twenty-five years old and haven't even been admitted to the bar. What kind of respect will they have for me?

But the answer jogged up in his brain. He was the figurehead for the shrewd Roy Cameron, CEO of Cameron Insurance. They would listen with respect. Yet the prospect of playing the role assigned to him was still intimidating.

Sleep eluded him. He was too wired to sleep, he thought, thrusting about in frustration until eventually he drifted into oblivion. He awoke before the alarm went off, with instant awareness of the torturous assignment ahead. He broke into a sweat despite the coolness of the bedroom. Kara would be outraged if she knew the message he was to deliver for his father, which went against everything she believed in. *What I believe in.*

He'd sit there in that fancy Watergate apartment and remind their lobbying team to fight against any 'patients' rights' bill. Fight against any federal regulations for HMOs. Forget about costs – results were what counted.

Up until this point Dad had glossed over the ugly manipulations of the top-level members of the Cameron team. Now everything was laid out with startling clarity. He understood why none of this was to be committed to phone calls, mail, faxes. Dad was sharp – nothing on record that could be used against the company.

Oh yes, that watchdog group had strong reasons to be concerned.

Kara awoke earlier than usual. Her eyes sought out the clock on her night table. Jonnie would be leaving for the Augusta airport in a few minutes. He wasn't happy about the trip. They talked about everything else but dodged discussing the nitty-gritty details about his activities for the company.

What kind of company business was taking him to Washington? Conferring with the company's lobbyists? What else would take him to Washington? He'd tried to appear amused by this trip. '*Wow, the pretentiousness of these big corporations. Dad keeps a staff at the apartment – the houseman will be at the airport to pick me up.*'

She lay back against the pillow – conscious of the stillness in the house. Grandma and Mom weren't stirring yet. They'd both be at Hank's arraignment this evening. She'd baby-sit for Betsy. Small towns were supposed to be supportive of their own, she thought in recurrent anger. So why was everybody all at once avoiding Val and Betsy?

Val was born in Eden. Her parents – both dead – had been born here. They'd never had much money, but Val said they'd had lifelong friends and that was important. Like her parents – like most people – Val and Hank struggled for survival. They'd had lifelong friends – they thought. Before he was even arraigned, Hank was judged guilty of killing Mattie. Friends – except for one family that was covertly sympathetic – had deserted. Part of the blame lay with the press, she conceded. The *Enquirer* and the *Ledger*, the local TV and radio stations all blasted Hank. At Roy Cameron's prodding, she was convinced. But people shouldn't have turned against Hank because of that. *He's supposed to be presumed innocent until proven guilty.*

Did anybody in this town believe what Grandma had told Harvey Raines? Did they truly believe Grandma had been lying? When she'd told Jonnie about Joe's confession, he'd believed her. But he didn't know the motive for Eric and Gerry's murders.

She kicked off the sheet. Another hot day ahead. Though the bedroom windows were open, not a hint of a breeze stirred the drapes. What could she do today to further Hank's defense? No word yet from Peg and Nan about staff on duty when he was tinkering with the car at the time Mattie was murdered. She couldn't forage for witnesses until names were available.

Every waking hour should be put to use, her mind taunted her. Hank's life – Val's and Betsy's – hung in the balance. What about the other line of defense – the important one? *How do I prove that Sandra Cameron made that call to Joe?*

Sandra was in town that night – there were the phone calls to and from the Cameron house. Now Kara was prodded into action. Her mind in high gear. Back to the library. Check on all of Sandra's activities during the period when she learned about the car crash – and that Eric and Gerry were coming to Eden to protest the annulment of Mom's marriage.

Fighting yawns, Jonathan arrived at the Augusta airport. Within minutes he was aboard the small plane that was to ferry its passengers to Atlanta. At Hartsfield he was able to salvage time for scrambled eggs and coffee at an airport restaurant before boarding the 10.15 a.m. for Washington D. C. All the while he tried to brace himself for the meetings ahead.

He hadn't been in Washington since the school trip years ago, but he remembered that August in the Capital was apt to be overbearingly hot. Still, air-conditioning made life comfortable. With a guilty twinge he remembered Kara's determination to provide the bedrooms of the family house with air-conditioners.

'*I remember on hot nights when I was little the three of us would sleep in the living room because it had this great air-conditioner.*' It was so easy to forget that not every family in America could afford air-conditioners. He'd been spoiled rotten – in some ways. But Kara had been rich with love.

He'd been touched by the beautiful warmth he'd felt between Kara and her grandmother. And then later between Kara and her mother and grandmother. Three people blessed with a wonderful closeness that shone from them.

His mind darted back through the years to the 'sleepovers' at Ronnie's house when he was in third grade. He'd been devastated when Ronnie and his family moved out to California. Even now he could remember his awe and pleasure when Ronnie's mother kissed them both good-night.

I never felt that kind of closeness with Mom and Dad. Would I have felt it with my birth parents? I'll never know. But Kara and I will have that closeness. Our children will know that kind of love.

At Dulles Jonathan was met by Oliver, the apartment's houseman/chauffeur. Now the lack of sleep caught up with him. He dozed at intervals on the long drive into town. He came fully awake as they arrived at the sprawling, ultra-luxurious Watergate complex – a curving riverfront conglomeration of office buildings, glitzy boutiques, expensive restaurants, apartments and the Watergate Hotel. For many years, Jonathan recalled his father saying, the company had maintained an apartment at the Watergate – home to many top-tier government office holders.

As for many Americans, the Watergate complex was associated for him with the downfall of the late President Richard Nixon. Here in June 1972 five men – involved in the Nixon re-election – were caught burgling the sixth-floor Democratic National Committee headquarters. It was incredible to realize, Jonathan thought whimsically, that more than 360,000 civilians held government jobs in Washington today. In 1800 – when the government first moved here – the whole workforce consisted of 130 people.

Moments after he walked into the decorator-furnished apartment, with its view of the Potomac, Mrs Stewart – the cook/housekeeper – prepared to serve him lunch. He remembered his father's exhortation: '*Make sure the staff is off-duty all day Thursday.*'

'That was a wonderful lunch,' he complimented Mrs Stewart. 'My father told me that eating at the apartment was like dining in one of the town's top restaurants.' His smile was ingratiating. Mrs Stewart glowed. 'Oh, and he suggested that the staff take off all tomorrow. The apartment will be serving as my office – no need for you to put up with us.' No witnesses to whatever discussions might one day be incriminating.

While Oliver unpacked his valise, Jonathan made a phone call as per his father's instructions. After a brief wait he was put through to the ex-senator whose name headed the firm. While they talked, Jonathan envisioned him from appearances on TV news programs. A courtly man with a faint Southern accent. Yet he suspected the ex-senator – who earned five figures for each lecture appearance – could wield a knife with the same skill as his father.

'It'll be a pleasure to work with you, Jonathan. I suggest we all meet for dinner tonight before we settle down to business. I'm sure the others on our team will be able to clear the evening. How does eight o'clock sound to you?'

'Fine,' Jonathan said.

'I'll make reservations at Lespinasse,' the ex-senator said, and Jonathan recalled his mother saying that this was the most expensive restaurant in Washington. 'At eight then, at Lespinasse.'

'*No business at dinner,*' his father had instructed. '*Dinner is just for the others to meet you. Save business talk for the apartment. They'll understand that. They'll bring their trophy wives – or their current women. It'll be a social occasion. You pick up the tab. Oh, whatever the scheduled time, you arrive ten minutes early. You be seated when they're brought to your table. Psychologically that's important.'*

Jonathan put down the phone, struggled against panic. *God, I feel inadequate in this situation. It's like playing a role in a stage production without knowing the lines.*

He settled down in a club chair and prepared to study Cassie's packet yet again. Despite the air-conditioning, he felt uncomfortably warm. Stage-fright, he mocked himself. Why was it so important to Dad for him to carry this off? And with sudden prescience he understood. Dad took malicious pleasure in making sure Bart realized that he'd never be number one at the company.

Everything he was to convey at tomorrow's meeting was abhorrent to him. Congress *should* pass a patients'-rights bill. Hospitals *should* be run by doctors, not by accountants. All the loopholes that the HMOs – including Cameron Insurance – were lobbying to push through Congress were obscene.

Dr Callahan – the head of Pediatrics, whom Dad called a 'star' in the medical profession – was enthralled with the lavish budget supplied for new equipment for his department. But he'd seemed disturbed at the meeting yesterday when Eden's new chief administrator – who clearly resented having to report to *him* – hinted that in six months the Pediatrics Department would be serving former patients of Farraday Hospital.

Wherever he went – at Eden General or Cameron Insurance – he sensed covert hostility at his presence. Still, he was accepted across the board as being in training as Roy Cameron's successor. They were sure that any infringement he observed would be reported to 'the old man'.

Kara wound up her phone call to Seth Rogers with a recurrent sense of his shortcomings as an attorney. But he'd be out of the picture after this evening, she reassured herself. She wouldn't allow herself to consider that she might flunk the bar exams.

She heard the sound of a car coming to a stop before the

house. 'Mom's home,' she called to Edie, and walked to the foyer to greet her mother.

'Another scorcher.' Daisy hurried into the comfort of the air-conditioned living room. 'Is dinner ready? Val will kill us if we're late getting to the arraignment.'

'We have plenty of time,' Kara soothed her.

'I'm putting dinner on the table,' Edie's voice drifted to them.

'I'll wash my hands.' Daisy headed for the bathroom. 'I closed the shop without straightening up. I'll have to go in early tomorrow morning.'

Kara went into the kitchen to bring out the salad bowl and a pitcher of iced tea. Edie transferred huge, paper-thin crêpes stuffed with last evening's leftover chicken in white wine sauce to dinner plates. Nothing was wasted in this household.

Daisy joined them at the dining table. 'Kara, you said you were going to the library today.' She was striving to appear calm. 'Any useful developments?'

'I reread all the newspaper reports but came up with nothing,' Kara conceded, her face somber. 'Then this afternoon I talked with Mr Hamilton on the phone. He's convinced Sandra Cameron made that call to Joe. But how do we prove that?' She gestured futility.

'Sit down and eat,' Edie ordered with determined cheerfulness. 'Crêpes are best while they're hot.'

'Grandma, nobody but you could make leftover chicken seem like a gourmet dinner.'

'Should we call Val and let her know we'll be there in plenty of time?' Daisy was solicitous.

'Buzz her while we're clearing the table,' Edie said. 'She's probably a nervous wreck.'

'She knows Hank will be held for a grand jury hearing. She knows there'll be no chance of bail.' But Kara exuded sympathy.

With a sense of urgency the three women ate dinner. Kara and Edie cleared the table while Daisy phoned Val.

'We'll be there in a few minutes,' Daisy promised.

They arrived at the Thompson house to find Betsy bathed

and in a frilly flowered nightie, and Val ready to leave with them.

'Hi, Betsy!' Kara dropped to her haunches to hug Betsy. How sweet, how vulnerable, she thought tenderly. 'Would you like me to read you a story before you go to sleep?' Betsy nodded, her eyes bright with anticipation.

'She'll be fine,' Val said, yet Kara sensed she was nervous about leaving her tiny daughter.

'Of course she will,' Kara agreed. 'And if there's any emergency' – meaning a sudden asthma attack – 'I know exactly what to do.'

'Will you tell me two stories?' Betsy's smile was beguiling.

'Two stories,' Kara promised. 'Now kiss Mommie goodnight.'

For a moment Kara was anxious when the door closed behind the other three women and Betsy stood immobile, her eyes fastened to the door. Then with an endearing glow she held one hand up for Kara's. How beautiful, the unquestioning trust of a small child, she thought, and in her mind heard her grandmother's voice: '*Your mother and I felt so rich each time you looked up at us and smiled. The whole world seemed beautiful.*' She envisioned herself with her child and Jonnie's in her arms, and tears stung her eyes. Would that ever happen?

Jonnie never had the kind of childhood with which she had been blessed. He'd never said that in so many words, but the truth seeped through. He was forever telling himself that the Camerons had been such wonderful parents. He dragged that out too often. The money was there – the luxuries, yes – but what about love? He had a voracious hunger for a real family. He talked with such affection about Cassie Bates and about the family housekeeper. What was her name? Annie Mae. That's where he found love.

How were Jonnie and she to muddle through this craziness to a life together?

'Kara, tell me *three* stories,' Betsy wheedled, a triumphant glint in her eyes.

'We'll see.' Kara's smile was indulgent. She'd take any bet that Betsy – already fighting yawns – would be asleep before she finished the first.

As she'd anticipated, Betsy's eyes closed in minutes. The heat of the day had subsided. Kara reached to pull the sheet about the small shoulders. But as she did so, her eyes rested on the arm that lay useless.

Maybe when this madness is over – and please, God, show me how to clear Hank – we can start a local fund to raise the cost of the operation that Dr Callahan said could correct Betsy's arm. Mom said he's so frustrated that the technique is available but beyond Val and Hank's reach.

At fourteen minutes before the appointed time Jonathan arrived at the Carleton Hotel, sought out Lespinasse, one of the most beautiful rooms in Washington – all blue and gold, with a high, hand-painted ceiling, fleur-de-lis upholstery, tables flanked by oversized armchairs. He was immediately seated at a choice table.

He was impressed by the elegance of the dining room, noted the Limoges china, the Riedel crystal, the bouquets of coral roses that adorned each table. Kara would admire it too, he thought with a sudden nostalgic tenderness.

On schedule the others arrived. Four couples, clearly patrons of the opulent restaurant. The men in expensive suits, the women in designer outfits and exquisite jewelry. Their attitudes a blend of conviviality and wary respect for the power Jonathan represented.

He was relieved that the other four men guided the conversation – all innocuous and requiring little from him. He was conscious of the careful name-dropping that was meant to remind him that their contacts were at the highest level.

At the conclusion of the evening Jonathan scheduled a conference for the next day at the Watergate apartment that would include luncheon sent up by a gourmet restaurant in the Watergate complex – as advised in Cassie's packet. None of the others suspected his unease, his inner reluctance to play this scene, he told himself in relief.

After cordial farewells he headed for the waiting limo. *I can't keep up this charade. I can't play Dad's game. But how do I tell him – after such a short run with the company – that I want out?*

Twenty-Five

K ara was relieved when she heard a car turn into the Thompsons' driveway. Jonnie said he'd probably call late tonight because of his business dinner. If he got the answering machine, he'd hang up and try again. He'd feel self-conscious about leaving a message when Grandma or Mom might get to it first. It was weird, the games she played with Grandma and Mom. Both must know her nightly late caller was Jonnie. Both avoided any inquiries.

She hurried to the door to greet the others. For Val tonight had been such a traumatic experience, she thought sympathetically. Val had taken fresh clothes to the jail this morning so Hank would look his best. Still, for someone who'd never been present at an arraignment it had to be painful. Petty thieves, drug dealers, prostitutes would be among those arraigned.

'Did Betsy give you any trouble?' Valerie's eyes reflected her anguish at tonight's occurrence.

'She fell asleep before the first story,' Kara reassured her.

'The arraignment was awful.' Valerie grimaced in pain. 'Hank looked so scared. And I couldn't do anything to help him.'

'Val, you have to take this in your stride,' Edie exhorted her. 'For Hank's sake and Betsy's.'

'I don't like that Mr Rogers,' Valerie said yet again. 'He was bored with the whole thing.' Her eyes searched Kara's. 'When will you take over as Hank's lawyer?' The oft-repeated question.

'As soon as the bar-exam results come through. No more than another ten days,' Kara comforted, battling a sense of anxiety. Yet she had vowed even before enrolling in law school to apportion part of her time to clients such as Val,

229

who couldn't afford high-priced representation. Always aware of what that lack had done to her mother and grandmother.

The women talked a few minutes longer, then Edie prodded Kara and Daisy to the door.

'Besty'll have you up by six thirty,' Edie reminded Valerie. 'Try to get a decent night's sleep.' But her eyes said she knew that would be difficult tonight.

Walking to the car, Kara managed a surreptitious glance at her watch. Had Jonnie called yet? Had he decided it was too late to call? *I want to talk to him. I wish I could explore the case with him – I feel so alone and lost. But I need to hear his voice. To know that everything is still all right with us.*

As Edie swung into the driveway Kara heard the phone ringing in the house.

'I'll get it!' Kara pushed open the door on her side even before the car pulled to a full stop.

'The machine will pick up,' Daisy called after her.

Kara unlocked the door, darted to her bedroom, reached for the phone as the answering machine went into action.

'Hi—' Breathless from her sprint, sure the caller was Jonathan.

'I figured you were still busy,' Jonathan said, relief in his voice. 'I was preparing a kind of impersonal message like "Hi, it's Jonathan for Kara. I'll call later."' Meaning that he was insecure in how much her grandmother and mother knew about their relationship.

'How's Washington?' How did people survive before telephones were invented?

'Hot as hell. But of course everything's air-conditioned.' He hesitated. 'It blew my mind to be talking to a former senator as though we were on equal ground.' Jonathan chuckled. 'But then he wasn't actually talking to me – he was talking to Cameron Insurance.'

'Wow, you're traveling in fancy company!'

'I had dinner with him and three of his associates and their wives at Lespinasse. This great restaurant.' *He's impressed by moving in high circles. Does that mean the job looks more interesting? Is he changing his mind about cutting out?* 'It was purely social – we talk business tomorrow at the Watergate apartment. At least,' he amended wryly, 'I'll give them the song and dance Dad prepared for me to deliver.'

'You'll be home Friday?'

'I was thinking about maybe trying for tomorrow night – but I suspect I'd better hang around in case they want to talk further. I miss you.'

'I miss you, too.'

'I wish we were back in the apartment. Just the two of us. I'll dream about us.'

'I'll consider that, too.' She strove for lightness. *Is he moving into that high-living world of his father's? He's always said he was no more than an onlooker. At boarding school, camps, college, law school for most of his life. Just at fleeting intervals had he been part of his parents' world. Is he being seduced by meeting senators and big-wheel politicians? Am I going to lose him, not because of three murders but because I can't compete with his parents' lifestyle?*

'Good-night, my love,' he whispered. 'Let me go to sleep and dream.'

'Call me tomorrow night, Jonnie. I'll be home all evening.'

Kara left her bedroom and walked into the living room. Her mother sat on the edge of a lounge chair and focused on the TV news. Her grandmother was in the kitchen.

'There's been nothing about the arraignment.' Daisy was tense. 'Just that Hank's being held for the grand jury.'

'I've got coffee up, and I'm putting in three of those peach and walnut muffins I had in the fridge,' Edie told Kara. 'They'll be ready in a few minutes.'

'You're determined to make me a butterball,' Kara joshed.

'You know me, Kara,' Edie scolded. 'They're not the commercial kind – I made them myself. No oil – I used my apple-sauce substitute.'

Grandma and Mom are trying so hard to be cool, but they're both upset about my relationship with Jonnie. Grandma knows how much he means to me. Mom guesses. And both wonder how there can be anything between me and Roy Cameron's adopted son.

Listening to Edie and Daisy talk about the watchdog committee – their fears about the way HMOs were pulling out of

Medicare and Medicaid programs – Kara told herself that she ought to be honest with them about her feelings for Jonnie. Tell them that she and Jonnie expected to marry as soon as the business with Hank was over. *Why is it so hard to say that? But how can that happen if his father is indicted for murder – and I'm responsible?*

Jonnie had sounded in awe of this whole Washington business. And he must be going along with his father's plans to take over Farraday. That was one reason why he was talking with the ex-senator – no doubt a lobbyist – because Roy Cameron was planning a hospital empire to tie in with his HMO operation. The lobbyist firm was to help clear the road for him. *That's not the Jonnie I know.*

'Paul Callahan came into the shop today.' The self-conscious undertone in Daisy's voice snapped Kara to attention. 'He wanted to buy a birthday present for the cleaning woman who comes in for him once a week. I thought that was so sweet. He wasn't sure about size or style – he asked me to help.' She paused. 'We're having dinner tomorrow night.' Her voice said she anticipated rejection, but she encountered none.

'Eden General is lucky to have him,' Edie said admiringly.

'He seems uncomfortable with the hospital.' Daisy sounded anxious. 'Up to a point,' she amended. 'He's euphoric about all the revolutionary new equipment he's been allowed to order, but I suspect some of the new hospital regulations really upset him.'

'Was he specific?' Kara asked. *Mom's worried he'll pull out, leave Eden. She likes him. She likes him a lot.*

'No, but I get that feeling.' They heard the *swoosh* that said the coffee was ready, and Daisy rose to her feet. 'I'll get the coffee.'

Kara awoke with an instant realization that she had overslept. That was because she'd had such trouble sleeping last night, she rationalized. So much chasing across her brain. She tossed aside the sheet and pulled herself into a sitting position. Was that Peg in the kitchen? Now she was wide awake. Had Peg come over with the list of names?

She left the bed, reached for the robe that lay across a chair and drew it over her ballerina length printed nightie. The shower could wait. Go see what had brought Peg here this early in the morning.

Peg was seated at the dining table where Edie was presenting her with a freshly heated Danish.

'Let's face it – we don't know if anybody saw Hank. We don't know if they'll cooperate,' Peg warned. 'They may—'

'You got the list!' Kara interrupted, the adrenaline flowing now.

'Nan worked the late shift last night – she was able to check out the computer files.' Peg seemed troubled. 'It looks like a wild goose chase to me. I mean, who'll remember what happened back in May?'

'It's amazing what people remember when you jog their memory.' Kara's mind was charging ahead. *If I can find one person who remembers that Hank was tinkering with his car in the parking area, I'll put a crimp in Harvey Raines's case. But that'll do nothing to link Mattie's murder to Eric and Gerry's – and that's what I have to do.*

'Sit down and have coffee while I make breakfast,' Edie ordered Kara.

'Did Mom leave for the shop already?'

'She said she had a lot of straightening up to do before opening.'

Fortified by coffee, Kara sat down with the list of the Eden General staff on duty the night Mattie was murdered. Nan had been efficient. Beside each name there was a home phone number and address. She'd present herself as working as Seth Rogers' private investigator – 'until I'm admitted to the bar and can practice law in this state.' That would add some validity to her efforts.

'Don't call people who work the night shift before afternoon,' Peg warned. 'They'll be pissed. I went over the names and marked the ones who're on days now – which means you can't contact them until evening.' She sighed. 'This gets real complicated.'

'Did you ever read a good mystery that wasn't complicated?' Edie countered. 'Kara, you take a crack at questioning them.

Like you said, even one person to back Hank up would be good.'

By dinnertime Kara had managed to talk with three of the Eden General staff who'd been on duty that night. She was startled at the hostility she'd encountered thus far. The general conception seemed to be that Hank had killed Mattie out of greed.

'He never had anything his whole life. He knew his wife would inherit the house when Mattie died.'

And this was the jury pool, her mind taunted her. But what could she do about it? Not a chance in the world of getting a change in venue.

Jonathan was astonished to realize it was almost 7 p.m. when the ex-senator and his team prepared to leave the Watergate apartment. His head was in a whirl from what he'd heard in response to his presentation of his father's demands. The four men – all shrewd lawyers – were candid about whose backs they'd scratched, what favors they could call in. And they had high respect – unlike his father – for the Health Insurance Association of America.

'Let's admit the clout that group has,' the ex-senator said with a grandiose gesture. 'They're up there among the most powerful. There're two ways of stopping a bill: powerful groups and powerful lobbyists.'

'My father feels we can't afford to lie back and ignore the threats that face the industry,' Jonathan repeated. 'Cameron Insurance has to take a major role in protecting our stockholders.' *How can I talk this way? I don't believe a word of this crap.*

'Oh, absolutely,' one of the attorneys said and the others nodded in agreement.

'There'll be a lot of noise about reforming HMOs – but when it comes time to vote, nothing will pass.' The ex-senator smiled indulgently. 'A lot of hysteria out there that will amount to nothing.'

Jonathan leaned back while the ex-senator summarized the firm's actions on behalf of Cameron Insurance. This was where the power was. Dad understood that. If he wanted a bill to fail, these were the guys to ensure that.

'Tomorrow we'd like you to spend some time at our offices,' the ex-senator added. 'Show you some of the campaigns we've been working on for the company.'

Jonathan intercepted a covert exchange between the others. One of the lawyers whom Jonathan had recognized from TV news shows cleared his throat, as though preparing for some controversy.

'We've given a lot of thought to Cameron's moving into the for-profit hospital chain subsidy. We feel that in planning this expansion the company must recognize the importance of catering for a set percentage of charity care. It's a public-relations necessity.'

Jonathan tensed. This was an area that unnerved him. Dad had been specific: '*Statistics prove that for-profit hospitals provide virtually the same amount of uncompensated care as non-profit hospitals. But we won't make any commitments. No need for this.*'

'We'll follow the norm in that area.' Jonathan broke the heavy silence. 'Just as we do with political contributions.' *I don't believe for a minute that Dad will allow any real commitment to charity care. He won't accept that it's company responsibility.* 'You know, of course, about the company's contributions to both political parties.' Because that's what the lobbyist team demanded. 'That will continue.' He was quoting his father almost verbatim.

'Oh, there's a party at one of the embassies tomorrow night,' the ex-senator resumed. 'I'd like you to come as my guest. It's time you began to meet people.'

'Thank you.' He made a show of anticipation. 'What time? Where do we meet?' *But I expected to go home tomorrow. Now I'll be stuck in Washington until Saturday.*

Kara doubted that she would hear from Jonathan tonight. But on the off-chance that he might call even this late, she sat up in bed and flipped through one of her grandmother's culinary magazines. He would call if he could. But he must be caught up in business meetings.

She started when the phone rang – shrill in the stillness of the night – reached to pick up. 'Hi—'

'Am I calling too late?' Jonathan was solicitous.

'No. I was waiting up – hoping you'd call. How did your meeting go?' It was weird, she thought. They talked about almost everything – even her frustration about Betsy's not being able to get the arm surgery that was so promising. But she couldn't bring herself to ask what specifically he was doing in Washington – and he didn't volunteer.

'God, I thought it would never be over.' He sighed. 'A lot of endless talk.' *About what? Cameron Insurance, or its new for-profit hospital plans?* 'And now it looks as though I won't get back home until Saturday morning. I'm being dragged to some embassy party tomorrow night. I'm representing the company,' he added with an attempt at wry amusement. 'My father would expect me to accept the invitation.' *Is he intrigued by being invited to glitzy embassy parties?* 'How're things going with your case?'

'I've got a list of staff members who might have seen Hank,' she said tiredly. 'But so far nothing positive.'

'And no other leads,' he commiserated. 'Kara, have you gone back and checked out those two earlier murders? You said you were sure they were linked to Mattie Mason's murder.' They'd discussed this, but she'd always shied away from any in-depth probing. Afraid of where that would lead.

'I've checked every angle.' Her voice all at once sharp.

'I don't have to tell you . . .' He was apologetic now. 'You need to ferret out a motive to connect the two.'

I know the motive – but how can I tell that to Jonnie? 'I don't want to think about it tonight – I'll never get to sleep.' *Somehow, I should have helped Val get a savvy lawyer – somebody with wide experience in murder trials. But even if she could sell the house quickly, how long would the money last with a top-notch criminal lawyer in a murder trial?*

'I'll take an early-morning flight from Dulles on Saturday,' he said cajolingly. 'Breakfast at our place?'

'Great.'

'I'll call you tomorrow night,' he promised. 'I'll manage to cut out of that embassy party at an early hour. Miss you, sugar . . .'

'I miss you, too.'

Jonnie doesn't know the horror hanging over our heads. How can I expect him to turn against his father even when he learns the truth? He feels he owes his parents so much. How could he marry the lawyer who's fighting to send one or both of them to prison?

Twenty-Six

Kara came awake with reluctance – subconsciously dreading the day ahead. She was aware of an unfamiliar stillness in the house. None of the usual morning sounds. She turned to the clock on her night table, was startled to discover she'd overslept by almost two hours. She'd lain awake until almost dawn – battling insomnia. Grandma and Mom had let her sleep, she realized in tender comprehension.

Her phone conversation with Jonnie last evening had disturbed her. He'd sounded so awed by meeting with the ex-senator and his associates. *Is he being swept up in that world of high-powered movers and shakers? Does he find it exciting?*

Don't think about that now. She had work to do. More phone calls to make to Eden General staff members. *Please, God, let there be one who'll recall Hank's presence on the hospital parking area the night Mattie was murdered.*

She struggled for optimism. *Harvey Raines's case is flimsy. Let me knock a hole in his contention that Hank was away from the ER long enough to have driven to Mattie's house and killed her.*

The day crept past with painful slowness. The two personal interviews she was able to schedule gave negative results. Arriving home – tired and dejected – she discovered Edie impatient to serve dinner.

'Nan called – we're having an emergency meeting of the watchdog committee this evening. That means an early dinner,' Edie apologized. Her face brightened at the sound of a car pulling up before the house. 'There's your mother. We can sit right down.'

Kara joined her grandmother in bringing food to the table. 'What brought on the emergency meeting?'

'The word's out that Cameron lawyers had a long session yesterday with the lawyers for Farraday,' Edie said grimly. 'You know what that means. We need to set up a campaign to warn people about what's sure to happen. Roy Cameron will close Farraday – we'll be left with one hospital. You don't count the two fancy private sanitariums,' she said with contempt.

'The *Ledger* ran several articles a couple of months ago about the empty beds in both hospitals,' Kara reminded her. Still, she was concerned about the town's losing Farraday.

'Oh, sure, there'll be no empty beds in Eden General.' Edie smiled in welcome as Daisy came into view. 'Darling, come right to the table. I have to leave early for a committee meeting that was just called this morning. We're meeting at the library at seven sharp.'

'What's up?' Daisy was anxious.

Edie explained the situation, urged Daisy to join her at the emergency meeting.

'Mom, I'm not on the committee,' Daisy protested. 'I went to the last meeting to represent you. No, it would look pushy for me to show up.'

'I'll probably bring them over to the house for coffee afterwards. Take that carrot cake from the freezer so it'll be defrosted,' Edie instructed. 'And put up coffee around nine thirty. I don't think we'll run past ten.'

Jonathan ate dinner in solitary splendor at the Watergate apartment. He was exhausted from the long day at the glitzy offices of the lobbyist firm. While it wasn't the largest in body count, he thought while he savored the cordon-bleu chicken Mrs Stewart had served him, its physical layout was impressive. Four floors of elegant offices in the most expensive part of town. Leave it to Dad to choose a powerhouse group to represent the company.

But it's worrisome that their sole objective is escalating profits for the company – to hell with how policyholders fare. And they agree with Dad about cutting hospital stays as short as possible, that it's smart to cut doctors' fees despite the uproar this will cause. The bottom line – that's all that counts.

239

Digging into a luscious bread pudding with bourbon sauce, Jonathan checked his watch. The ex-senator would be arriving soon in his limo. Damn, he hated the prospect of this embassy party! He loathed having to make small talk with people he'd never met before. He always felt so awkward.

Today had been more unnerving than he'd anticipated. Statistics had been laid out that – to him – were obscene. People were human beings – not just numbers. He remembered a favorite quote of the ex-senator, who spoke from long experience: '*It's easier to stop a bill than pass one.*'

God only knew what time he'd get out of that embassy party. *Try to call Kara now.* But no matter what, he promised himself, he'd be on an early-bird flight out of Dulles tomorrow morning. He'd made reservations.

In his room he phoned Kara, was tense when her mother responded.

'May I speak to Kara, please?'

'Surely – just a moment.' Southern politeness demanded courtesy – but had he been wrong, the one time he encountered Kara's mother, in sensing a kind of reserve in her? 'Kara, phone!'

When would Kara tell her family about them? Sure, they'd known each other only a little while – but they felt as though it was forever. Her family was upset about this business of Cameron Insurance taking over Eden General. And face it, this was reflected in their attitude to him.

But these takeovers were happening all over the country. Hospitals fought for survival because of too many empty beds, too much duplication of super-expensive equipment. Yet he felt uncomfortable with the entire Cameron Insurance operation – both the HMO scene and the planned hospital chain.

'Hello . . .' Kara's voice came to him with the lilt that said he was special to her.

'I figured I'd try to reach you early because I don't know when I'll be able to cut out from that embassy party. But we're having breakfast tomorrow,' he reminded her.

'Right. Jonnie—' She hesitated. 'People keep saying that Cameron Insurance is taking over Farraday. Is it true?'

'Like I told you, it's being considered,' he hedged. *How can*

I lie to Kara? Of course it's being taken over. 'I'll be glad to sit down with your grandmother's committee and discuss it – as soon as it's a fact.' *Dad's so sure he can merge the two and provide efficient service. But I don't like what I'm hearing at the hospital.*

'I'll tell her.' An uncertainty in her voice that disturbed him. 'It's just that – well, we read so much about how people are getting the short end when hospitals merge. So many horror stories.'

'Oh, Kara, I have to run,' he lied, fearing where this conversation was leading. 'I was just told the limo's downstairs waiting for me. See you in the morning – eleven sharp.'

Kara sat motionless by the phone for several moments – trying to deal with suspicions that had leapt into her mind. She'd cornered Jonnie – he'd reached for an excuse to cut short his call. He *knew* what was happening with Farraday. *He lied to me just now. He isn't happy about what's happening at Farraday – but he lied to me.*

Reluctantly she left the sanctuary of her room and joined her mother in the living room to watch the evening news. She was conscious of her mother's determination to be cool about Jonathan's nightly phone calls.

'There's nothing on the news about Farraday's going forprofit.' Daisy reached for the remote, switched off the TV. 'Nothing in the *Enquirer* or the *Ledger*.'

'They wouldn't dare until it's officially announced. Everybody knows Roy Cameron owns stock in both newspapers and local TV and radio.' She debated inwardly for a moment. 'Jonnie couldn't come right out and say that the company's dickering to take over Farraday—' She stopped short, startled to realize she'd used the affectionate diminutive.

'What did he say?' Daisy prodded.

'He said "it's being considered" – but his voice told me the deal was closed.'

'They'll shut down Farraday – or Eden General.' Daisy flinched at the prospect.

'Not Eden General,' Kara decided. 'Not when they're

buying all that super-expensive equipment for the Pediatrics Department.'

'The town has to take some action. We have to make people understand what's about to happen.' Daisy was indignant.

'We could go to the newspapers and—' But Daisy shook her head as Kara spoke. 'No, they won't print a word against the Cameron empire.'

'Let's put it out of our minds for a while.' Daisy reached for the TV remote. 'What shall we watch?'

Earlier than Kara anticipated, she heard cars pulling up outside. Grandma and the committee.

'I'll bring out the carrot cake.' Daisy rose to her feet with an eagerness that told Kara she expected Paul Callahan to be with the group.

Edie marshaled the committee members into the house. 'It was a good meeting,' she declared, radiating satisfaction. 'We're getting out circulars, making a lot of phone calls.'

'We've got a crew set to handle everything,' Peg said. 'We're delivering five thousand circulars right to residents' doors.' The others nodded enthusiastically.

'I'll have copy for the circular set by tomorrow afternoon,' Ralph Martins, the retired advertising agency executive, promised.

'Kara will go over it,' Edie said. 'To make sure we're not open for a libel suit.'

'Monday morning Nan and I will drive over to Augusta and have the photocopies made.' Peg was caught up in the excitement of the campaign. 'We don't want to do it locally – that'll kill the element of surprise. You know if we do it here in town the word will be all over before we get our teams to deliver the circulars. We'll have to man the phones to dig up enough people to hand them out.'

'I'd feel a lot better,' a longtime Edenite admitted, 'if we were sure that Cameron Insurance *is* negotiating to take over Farraday. We could end up with egg on our faces.'

'I'm sure the deal has been consummated.' Paul Callahan was somber. 'I've been picking up vibes at the hospital.'

'Do you think the bigwigs at Cameron know about our group?' another committee member asked uneasily.

242

'They know,' Kara said.

'They even know that I'm a member,' Paul added and chuckled. 'They're not quite sure on whose side. But they figure that – like a lot of doctors – I've cut my ties, and it might not be easy to join up with another hospital.'

'With your reputation any hospital would be thrilled to get you,' Peg said. 'But we want you to stay here in Eden.'

Kara intercepted his glance at her mother, saw Daisy's glow of encouragement.

'That's what I want, too,' he said softly.

'Everybody grab a mug from the table,' Edie ordered. 'Help yourselves to coffee.' She pointed to the dining table, where Kara and Daisy had set out mugs and other essentials. 'I'll cut the cake.'

Kara saw Paul Callahan focus on the group of watercolors that graced one wall.

'They're beautiful,' he told Daisy, and Kara saw the faint color that stained her mother's cheekbones. 'Should I know the artist? I'm not terribly bright about art . . .'

'You wouldn't know the artist,' Daisy told him. 'Nobody would. They're mine.'

'They're lovely.' He inspected them at closer range now. 'Painting was a kind of therapy for me in the years at med. school and during my residency. But I had no talent. Still, it saw me through rough times.'

'Kara, have you come up with anything to help Hank?' Nan approached with coffee and cake in hand.

'Not yet,' Kara admitted, her smile wistful. 'I'm praying someone on your list will come through. The grand jury hearing is scheduled for the middle of next month. That gives me a little time.'

But reality warned Kara – yet again – that she needed more than proof that Hank couldn't have been at Mattie's house at the time she was murdered. Raines would hang onto the motive of greed, and insist Hank had an accomplice. The attitude of the prospective jury pool was another cause of anxiety. Most people here in town were convinced that Hank was guilty – even before the grand jury hearing.

When their guests had left, the dishwasher had been loaded

243

and the kitchen restored to order, Kara settled in the living room with Edie and Daisy.

'It's late – we should go to bed.' But Edie seemed loath to do this just yet.

'Would you want to sit down and talk with Jonathan about what's happening at Farraday?' Kara asked her grandmother. 'He said he'd be willing to do that.' *Would it help?*

'Darling, let's be realistic. Jonathan probably has little to say about this. He's just his father's mouthpiece.' But Edie's smile was compassionate. 'I'll tell him our fears, and he'll try to comfort me. He'll go back to his father, tell him about the committee's feelings – and that'll be the end of it.'

'I think it's time to discount Jonathan as possibly being helpful in some way. I mean, in dropping clues we can use against his father.' *Her original alibi for seeing so much of him.* 'Maybe I'll – I'll phase out seeing him.' *Why does Grandma – and Mom – seem so startled?* 'Not all at once, of course—' *How can I kill our dream? But already he's forced himself to lie to me. His father will always be between us. His father will destroy us.*

'Let's go to bed,' Edie said again. Almost brusque, Kara thought. 'Tomorrow's going to be a busy day.'

Drowsy from lack of sleep, Jonathan boarded his flight at Dulles. The embassy party last night had been a colorful gathering – the guests representing many nations. Some of the men – like himself – in business suits, some in military uniforms, others in formal wear. The women beautifully dressed. Several in native garb lent a special air to the scene. He might even have enjoyed the party if he hadn't been concerned that Kara sensed he was avoiding talk about Farraday and was upset.

He slept until the plane was circling for a landing at Hartsfield. He was impatient now to be back at home, to be talking with Kara. Had he damaged their relationship by a stupid reaction to a question that disturbed him? Nothing must come between Kara and him – not even this troubling sense of loyalty to his father.

Shortly before 10 a.m. the small commuter plane that shuttled between Atlanta and Augusta landed and disgorged ts passengers. As arranged Jonathan picked up a rental car that he would leave at the branch in Eden. He'd be running close on time, but he'd manage to pick up Kara at 11.

He was relieved to discover east-bound traffic was light. Still, his mind was troubled by the confrontation with his father that lay ahead. No way could he deal with being part of Cameron Insurance. If there had been any doubts, they'd disappeared in his meetings with the Washington lobbyists.

Dad would be back from Berlin on Monday. Give him time to settle in, then face him with this. He and Kara would open their joint office as soon as the bar-exam reports came through. They'd both pass the exams – calm consideration assured him of this. Once Hank Thompson's trial was over, they'd be married.

Yet from time to time he worried about her insistence that they wait to go public with their relationship until the trial was over. Was Kara battling doubts? Was that the reason for this delay? *Is she less committed than I believe?* An unnerving possibility.

At the apartment he called Kara to say he was back in town and would be at her house in ten minutes.

'Fine. I'm starving.'

Did I detect an odd reserve in her voice? No, I'm on a guilt trip. Everything's okay with us. I think . . .

Twenty-Seven

Kara sat on the living-room sofa and made a pretense of reading the morning's *Enquirer*. Gazing at the pages without seeing. Waiting for Jonathan to arrive. It seemed as though he'd been away for weeks rather than three days. She longed to see him, yet dreaded the encounter because she knew this must be the beginning of the end for them. That little lie on the phone was the beginning of a big lie that would – in the weeks and months ahead – destroy what they felt for each other.

In these past weeks she'd been living in a fantasy world. Nor had she been honest with Jonnie, she taunted herself. Here she was, fighting to prove his father was guilty of three murders – and there he was, becoming more involved each day in a company that she despised for what it did to people. Already he was trying to cover up for his father.

How could I have allowed myself to become so derailed? The most important objective in my life is to clear Hank. Not just for Hank and Val and Betsy – for Mom and Grandma. Let this town know – after twenty-five years – that Mom's marriage should not have been annulled. That Mom was not some little floozy out to entrap a rich man's son. For Mom I must prove this.

'Kara?' Edie called from the hallway.

'I'm in the living room.'

'I'm leaving for work.' Edie walked into view. Despite her smile, Kara thought, she was upset. 'Will you be home for dinner?'

'I – I'm not sure.' She suspected Jonnie would expect to spend the day with her. She couldn't break off in one meeting – it would take a few days. 'I'll call around five if I won't be home.'

'Kara—' Edie seemed to be searching for words. 'Have you considered telling Jonathan about your mother and father?'

'What's the point?' Kara gestured her sense of helplessness. He'll hate me when he discovers what I'm trying to do.'

'I see the way you and Jonathan look at each other – and remember Daisy and Tim. What you and Jonathan share is precious – as it was for your mother and father.'

'I should have been realistic from the start.' For an instant Kara's mind shot back to that first encounter, when the Dodge broke down and Jonathan appeared. To that moment at Mattie's funeral when she turned and saw him staring at her with a smile that said, 'We have something special between us.' To the wondrous days in Columbia, when they were taking the bar exams. 'I know,' she said with agonizing resolve. 'We must follow separate paths. Better to end it now than to face ugly recriminations later. I don't want that to happen.'

'You won't need the car . . . ?' Edie retreated from a painful discussion.

'No.' Kara managed a faint smile. 'Jonnie's picking me up in a few minutes.' *He's going to be so hurt when he realizes I'm breaking off the relationship. But one day he'll understand.*

A few moments later Kara watched from window while her grandmother and Jonathan exchanged a few words in passing. *Grandma is a true romantic. She wants a storybook ending for Jonnie and me.*

'It's a scorcher again,' Jonathan greeted her as she arrived at the front door. 'The weathercasters predict another heat wave.' With a swift glance about to make sure they were unobserved, he reached to pull her close. 'It seems as though I've been away for weeks.'

'I know—' *Why did I say that? That's not the way to begin a breaking-up process.* 'But you sounded as though you were having a ball up there.'

Jonathan flinched. 'That's one ball I could do without.' He reached for her hand as he headed with her for the car.

'How was the trip home?' she asked when they were seated in the Mercedes.

'I slept most of the way. The flight from Atlanta to Augusta is a quickie, of course. All I could think about was seeing you

247

after that crazy hiatus.' He paused, pulling away from the curb. 'How're you making out with your interviews?'

'Striking out every time so far.' She took a deep breath. 'What about your deal in Washington?'

'I'm not comfortable with those people,' he admitted, all at once somber. 'I'm outclassed.'

Outclassed or at odds with what they mean to accomplish. Why can't he come out and tell his father he doesn't want to be part of the company? The year or two he talked about will be a prison sentence.

'I've got the lease on that office space,' she told him. 'If we both pass the bar exams—' she held up crossed fingers – 'we can hang out that shingle: Cameron & Jamison. Or maybe,' she tried for lightness, 'Jamison & Cameron.' *What am I saying? That won't smash the wall that stands between us.* The wall he didn't even suspect was there.

'I wish.' His face mirrored a wistful longing that blended with an acceptance of reality. 'But don't let's think about that today. After breakfast let's drive out to the lake and—'

'No.' She hadn't meant to sound so sharp.

'Why?' He was startled.

'I have work to do,' she said awkwardly. 'I have to be back at the house by one o'clock. The weekend is the best time to try to nail down people I want to interview. I've got to ferret out a witness to support Hank's claim about being on the hospital parking lot.'

'We'll have dinner. You have to take time out to eat,' he reminded her with the charismatic smile that set off sparks of arousal in her.

'I have to be at the watchdog committee meeting tonight.' *They're meeting, yes – but I don't have to be there. Mr Martin – the retired ad executive – is working on the copy for the circular. I'll meet with him on Sunday afternoon.* 'I'm their legal representative – even without my admission to the bar.'

'Kara, if I could talk to them,' Jonathan began, searching for words. 'Explain that the company wants what's best for the town.' *Does he truly believe that?* 'Both hospitals have been in serious financial trouble. You see this happening all over the country. All over the world. Computer companies, oil

248

ompanies, grain companies, merging to bring down costs. To
urvive.'

Not to survive – to increase profits. 'I don't think you
an change the committee's reaction to all this. I know you
an't.'

'If they'll give us a chance—' His hands tightened on the
vheel. 'It can work.'

*He's trying to convince himself. He isn't happy about what's
happening. Why can't he be honest and admit that? His father
doesn't deserve that kind of loyalty.* 'Thinking people here
n town read what's happening in other towns and cities.'
She strove for calm. 'Not just that non-profit hospitals are
becoming for-profit and developing horrendous problems. The
vhole HMO scene. Oh, sure,' she scoffed, 'we don't read about
t in the *Ledger* or the *Enquirer* – but pick up any big-city
newspaper and it's all there. Read the national news magazines,
onnie. The whole country is facing ghastly situations. Towns
ike this *must* sprout groups to fight for what's right.'

'My beautiful crusader,' he said tenderly. But his eyes were
troubled. 'Enough of serious talk. What are we having for
breakfast?'

At the diner at the edge of town – where they'd eaten before
– they found a long line waiting for booths. Nobody appeared
o mind. The atmosphere was Saturday-morning festive, the
oom comfortably air-conditioned. Kara was relieved – the
ine meant conversation was limited to casual talk.

A glance at those waiting, at those in the occupied booths,
eassured Kara that there was no one here she knew. She was
till wary of being seen with Jonathan by an old-timer who
night recall the scandal of twenty-five years ago and start
alk. 'What do you know! Daisy Jamison's daughter is going
vith Roy Cameron's son!' So how could she believe she and
onnie could ever have a life together?

'We're moving up.' Jonathan's voice zapped her back to
he moment. 'We just might get a booth before we collapse
rom hunger.'

Jonathan intercepted Kara's glance at her watch as they drove
away from the diner. It was close to one o'clock. She'd insisted

she needed to be home – manning the phone – by 1 p.m
He knew she was worried about Hank Thompson's defense
yet something else was bothering her today. He was gettin
crazy vibes.

It was this business with the hospital, wasn't it? He'd tol
her he wouldn't remain with the company forever. That thi
wasn't what he meant to do with his life. 'A year or two', he'
said. But he knew now he couldn't hang in there anywher
near that long.

'I know you're tied up tonight,' he began cautiously, 'an
you'll be chasing prospective interviewees tomorrow. But wha
about dinner tomorrow evening? Maybe a picnic by the lake,
he enticed her. 'There'll be a delicious—'

'We'll be working on committee business.' Kara kept he
eyes on the road.

'Monday night?' he pursued. *Why don't I come right ou
and ask, 'What's got you so uptight?' We need to talk, dam
it.* 'Tuesday?' A challenge in his voice now.

'Tuesday,' she agreed, her eyes still avoiding his.

'I'll call you tonight,' he said, pulling up before the house
People are around – I can't even kiss her goodbye. 'Lateish?

'I'll be tied up till all hours with the committee,' she sai
evasively. Now her eyes met his. Accusing, defiant. 'This wil
be a wild weekend of work. Call me Tuesday during the day—
She hesitated. 'We'll talk then.'

He drove away with a sense that his whole world had jus
been upended. *She's upset because I'm on the opposite side o
the fence on this hospital deal. I hate it as much as she does
Can't she understand I'm trying to break away from Dad an
the company?*

*Is this about the position she takes on the hospital problem
– or is Kara having doubts about our relationship?* All alon
she'd talked about 'going slow'. Had he been blind in believin
she had capitulated? That she knew – almost from the firs
meeting – that they were meant to spend their lives together
Was she struggling to get the message across that this wa
split-up time? He didn't want to face a world he couldn't shar
with her.

*   *   *

For Kara the weekend was nightmarish – endless phone calls, entreaties designed to provide Hank with a much-needed alibi, sleepless nights when she was haunted by the memory of Jonathan's anguished efforts not to betray his bewilderment at her sudden evasiveness.

The Jamison house became headquarters for the watchdog group's committee. Ralph Martin popped in and out at intervals – determined to make the circular they would distribute a dynamic call to arms. On Sunday evening – after a buffet dinner for the committee – Edie brought up the possibility of their drafting a letter to the Governor.

'An appeal for an investigation,' Edie pursued. 'Kara, you said something once about how a state attorney general might dig into Cameron Insurance's operation—'

'We can do that,' Kara acknowledged, clutching gratefully at this new demand. She needed to be thrust into activity every waking moment. She was haunted at unwary intervals by the memory of Jonathan's pained expression, his bewilderment that she was pulling away from him.

On Monday morning she accompanied Edie and Peg to Augusta to have the eloquent letter 'to all residents of Eden' photocopied. They'd wait to pick them up. Later in the day crews would hand-deliver the 5,000 copies. And every moment of the day she was conscious that tomorrow she would have dinner with Jonathan. She must make him understand that their relationship was dead.

On Monday afternoon Jonathan met with Paul Callahan to go over the equipment the head of Pediatrics was requesting. They sat in Jonathan's small office at Eden General for what was a mere formality. Roy Cameron had made it clear whatever Dr Callahan requested was to be approved. Yet today Jonathan sensed an odd wariness in him.

'This is a tremendous outlay for a small-town hospital,' Paul remarked while Jonathan cast a cursory glance over the list. 'But it'll help us build a magnificent pediatrics department.'

'That's what my father wants to see.' *What's bothering him? His eyes are full of questions.*

251

'But it'll mean little,' Callahan warned, 'if the pediatrics staff is slashed.'

'As you know, the new Board of Directors feels some downsizing is essential.' Jonathan hesitated. He had all the statistics at hand – as provided by his father. Yet instinct told him Dr Callahan would refute each one. 'Of course, we mustn't do anything that will lessen the effectiveness of hospital care.' *Damn, I sound pompous.*

'I'd like to be party to how the downsizing is achieved.' Paul was low-key, yet Jonathan suspected there would be some rough encounters ahead. 'That is, in my department.'

'Yes, of course.' Jonathan contrived to sound casual.

'Let me say how grateful I am for this new equipment. It'll be a tremendous asset.' Yet Jonathan felt his ambivalence.

Jonathan was conscious of the undercurrents that permeated the hospital. Nobody was taking well the early retirements that were being scheduled. Doctors would be up in arms once they learned about the new schedule of payments that Cameron Insurance was about to announce.

At regular intervals his mind dwelt on the sudden change in Kara's attitude towards him. Not even to allow him to phone her, he thought with anguish. He didn't buy that 'I'll be so busy' routine. Tomorrow night – when they'd meet for dinner – seemed so far away.

This all stemmed from his activity with the company, didn't it? All right, bring this out into the open. Make Kara understand that he meant to leave the company – soon. No way he could stay.

But I can't walk out overnight . . .

Twenty-Eight

Kara left the jail after a brief early-morning conference with Hank. She was able to see him on the premise that she was operating as Seth Rogers' assistant and would take over the case when her admission to the bar came through. Hank's morale was low, she worried – and Val lived on the edge of hysteria. Her efforts to place Hank at the hospital at the time of Mattie's murder were futile so far. Was she making a mistake in trying to convince both Hank and Val that Harvey Raines had the weakest of cases?

Driving back to the house, she allowed her mind to focus on seeing Jonathan tonight. It was incredible the way she missed his nightly phone calls. How was she to deal with what lay ahead? Maybe it would be best just to come right out and say, 'We've made a bad mistake. We steamrollered ourselves into a relationship that has no future.'

Jonathan wouldn't accept that. He'd demand to know why there was no future for them. *What can I tell him? About what happened with Mom and the Camerons? He wouldn't let that stand between us.*

She could hear him scoffing at this. 'Hey, that's history. What does it have to do with you and me?' He wouldn't let his parents stand between them – but how would he react to her fighting to convict his father for murder? No, she couldn't tell him that. End it now.

Checking the answering machine, she discovered David Hamilton had called again. He called almost every other day. She'd brought out his long-dormant frustration that Eric's murder remained unsolved. *Okay, call him.* She owed him that.

She reached Hamilton at his office. Knowing he wanted to hear every detail of her activities, she told him about the circular they had hand-delivered yesterday – and which from the flood of phone calls to the house, was creating consternation in Eden. She brought him up to date on efforts to clear Hank.

'That man had nothing to do with Mattie's murder.' Hamilton dismissed this impatiently. 'Roy Cameron's guilty. Of all three murders.'

Kara listened with compassion to his tirade – sharing his frustration as well as his convictions.

'Somewhere there's a hidden trail that'll lead right to the Camerons,' he insisted. 'Stay with it, Kara. You'll find it.'

Twenty minutes later Jonathan called.

'Hi.' He was trying to sound as though there was nothing wrong between them, Kara thought.

'Hi.' *Poor darling, he's so bewildered.* 'What time will you pick me up this evening?' Her instinct was to cancel – but she couldn't keep running away.

'Around seven?' he asked. 'Take-out dinner?' Hope in his voice.

'Seven is fine. But I'm beat – I just want to sit down and be served.' She was fearful of being alone with him in his apartment. All her resolve might evaporate. She hesitated. 'Did you see our circular?' Didn't everybody see it? Though it had been brushed aside quickly on last evening's and this morning's TV and radio news.

'A copy was under my apartment door.' He cleared his throat. 'It was great.' He was uncomfortable. 'I – I'm not for the Farraday takeover,' he admitted. 'You must know that. I'm just a puppet parroting what my father and the wheels at Cameron set up. Kara,' he said with fresh energy, 'we need to talk.'

'Oh, I have to go – somebody's at the door.' *So I'm lying. Didn't he do the same to me when he was in Washington?* 'See you later.'

Jonathan had known the moment he walked into the Cameron Insurance building earlier this afternoon that his father was back from the Berlin trip. When Dad was present, everyone radiated a kind of nervous tension. Now – at close to 5 p.m. –

254

he was impatient for the day to be over. To be with Kara. To break down this barrier that was popping up between them.

Maybe he'd cut out now, he decided in a flurry of anticipation. So it was early. He remembered days when he'd been here till close to midnight.

The phone was a jarring intrusion. He reached to respond. 'Jonathan Cameron.'

'Jonathan, I'm scheduling a business dinner at the house tonight.' His father's voice was brisk. 'Around seven.' *I'm supposed to pick up Kara at seven.* 'Have you seen the fucking circular that damn watchdog group sent around?'

'I heard something about it,' Jonathan hedged.

'We'll fix their wagon. Most of them are bored retirees from the north-east,' Roy scoffed. 'Too much time on their hands. And a couple of old bitches with a vendetta against the company.' Dad meant Kara's grandmother and that woman who lived next door, Jonathan surmised. 'Be at the house by six thirty.'

Fighting disappointment, Jonathan phoned Kara, explained the situation. 'It's rotten to call you so late, but Dad just got around to telling me,' he apologized. 'Tomorrow evening – I won't let anything get in the way.'

'Thursday,' she said. 'The committee's having an emergency meeting tomorrow evening. You know I'm their resident attorney.' She was trying to sound amused, he thought.

'Seven?'

'Fine.'

But she didn't sound fine, he analyzed. She sounded stressed out. Distant. All right, Thursday night they'd have a showdown. *I'm not allowing this craziness with the hospital to come between us. That's unacceptable.*

Jonathan left the office at twenty past six, headed for Cameron Manor. If it was a business dinner, then Mom would be served in her own rooms. Who'd be there? Dad and Bart, of course. Now he pinpointed the inner-circle members who'd be at dinner. *Why do they need me?*

But he knew the answer. He was the heir apparent, there to make the others realize they'd gone as far as they could in the company hierarchy. Even when Dad eventually retired, he'd still be running the show through his son. That's what he wanted them all to understand.

He arrived at Cameron Manor to find Bart and two company wheeler-dealers already there. His father was ranting about the castigating circular that had been distributed last evening – in time to be dinnertime reading matter.

'They're a bunch of weird nobodies trying to cause trouble.' Roy paused to swig down his bourbon. 'We'll take care of them.'

Jonathan knew the evening would drag on painfully. Once his father took the floor, nobody could break in. Only Bart allowed himself to ignore the outraged monologue and enjoy Annie Mae's superb dinner. Jonathan struggled to conceal his shock at some of the blatantly callous statements his father threw at them – and which elicited sounds of approval.

'We're not a philanthropic organization – we're in business to show a healthy profit. Our stockholders expect that of us. We're not providing free vacations for policyholders,' Roy finally concluded his tirade. 'It's time to institute short stays in hospitals – our own and others. And don't look so nervous about our new schedule of fees to doctors. In today's world the bastards have to be part of a health plan. If they don't play ball, they'll find themselves out in the cold.'

Back in his apartment, Jonathan sat staring at the phone for anguished minutes. Instinct said, 'Don't call Kara. She won't be in the mood to talk.' Instinct won.

He prepared for bed – knowing sleep would be slow in coming. He'd straighten out this ridiculous mess, he promised himself. He'd come right out and make the commitment – 'I'm leaving the company. I can't handle it.'

Kara would understand he couldn't walk out overnight. Wouldn't she?

By Wednesday morning Kara realized that they'd gotten through to residents who – up until this point – had considered Roy Cameron the best thing that had ever happened to Eden. The Jamison house had become a crisis center – the phone constantly in motion. Their own, Peg's and Ralph Martin's numbers had been given to all who had questions.

Some calls were vituperative. *'You're spreading ugly rumors. How can you do that to a fine man like Roy Cameron?'* *'There are people in this town with long memories – who know you're out to ruin Mr Cameron!'* But the truth would be out soon, Kara reminded herself. No doubt in her mind that Farraday Hospital would be taken over – and then closed.

How was Jonnie feeling about all this? Yesterday he'd called their circular 'great'. He said he was against taking over Farraday – which was an admission this was going to happen. Why did he allow himself to be used by his father? That wasn't the Jonnie she'd thought she knew.

Between incoming calls she tried to contact Eden General staff members who might remember seeing Hank in the hospital parking area on that fatal night. The odds were comparable to winning a state lottery, she scoffed.

The day was ebbing away. At close to five o'clock her grandmother phoned.

'Sugar, I won't be home until past eight,' Edie warned. 'A cashier called in sick. I have to cover for her. Don't wait dinner. And remember, your mother said she'd be working late at the shop – redoing the windows. Pick up dinner at a take-out – leave some for your mother and me,' she wound up.

'What would you like?' All at once the evening ahead seemed dreary.

'Whatever.' Edie was cheerful. 'If I don't have to cook it, it's always good. Calls still coming in?'

'They're thinning out,' Kara reported.

'I have to get back to work,' Edie said. 'See you later.'

In the kitchen of the Thompson house Val finished up the ironing – mostly Betsy's dresses and playsuits – scooped up the bundle and carried it into her small daughter's bedroom. From the living room came the familiar five o'clock sounds of *Sesame Street* on the television set.

'Mommie—' Betsy's plaintive voice brought instant terror to Valerie. She knew that wheezing sound meant an asthma attack was beginning.

'It's all right, baby—' She rushed into the living room – her

257

heart pounding. 'You're going to be all right.' When Betsy panicked, the attack grew worse.

'I hurt.' Betsy's breathing was labored. 'Mommie—' Painful gasps prodded Valerie into action. Too late for Betsy's medication to cut short the attack. This was a bad one.

'You'll be all right in a little while,' Valerie soothed, lifting Betsy in her arms while she tried to remember where she'd put the car keys. There! She reached for the keys while Betsy clung to her. 'We're going to the hospital, and they'll take care of you.'

Fighting panic – because some asthma attacks in Betsy's short life had been a race against death – she hurried with Betsy to the car, not bothering to lock the door of the house. Betsy's breathing growing more agonizing as fear clutched at her. Thank God, the hospital was only a few minutes away. Still, she drove with reckless abandon. At the hospital parking lot she brought the car to a screeching stop, ran with Betsy to the emergency entrance.

A few waiting patients sat in chairs along one wall. Valerie rushed to the counter where a nurse was stationed to receive incoming emergency patients. Not one she knew, Valerie thought as she rushed to the counter.

'She's Dr Callahan's patient,' Valerie gasped. 'She's having a bad asthma attack.' *Isn't that obvious to the nurse?*

'What health insurance do you have?' The nurse reached for a pad.

'None—' Valerie strove for calm. 'I'll pay—' She knew the routine for those minus insurance.

'That'll be seventy-five dollars plus costs for whatever tests the doctor orders.'

'Oh my God!' Valerie's throat tightened in shock. 'I came out without my purse!'

'We can't have a doctor treat a patient without payment,' the nurse said, with strained patience. 'Take her over to Farraday. They have a deal with the city—'

'At this time of day?' Valerie's voice rose to near-hysteria pitch. 'With all the traffic? It'll take me forty minutes! Betsy needs treatment *now*.'

'I can't have her seen without payment.' The nurse was

turning now towards a patient being brought in in a wheelchair. 'Move along, please.'

'She has to be seen by a doctor!' Valerie screamed. 'Call Dr Callahan.'

'He's not here. Move along, or I'll have to call security.'

With Betsy gasping in her arms, Valerie struggled for sanity. *I have some change in my pocket. Call Kara!* She charged towards the wall pay-phone, juggling Betsy in her arms – fighting panic. Her hand trembling, she punched in Kara's number. *Be there. Please God, be there!*

'Hello?' Kara's voice came to her with an edge of wariness.

'Kara, I don't know what to do!' Words tumbling over one another as she rushed to explain. 'I can't drag Betsy all the way over to Farraday in rush-hour traffic! She's having a bad attack!'

'Stay there,' Kara ordered. 'I'll be right over. Wait for me, Val.'

Kara's mind leapt into high gear. Take a checkbook, she told herself. First, call Dr Callahan. *He's not at the hospital, or he'd see Val. Try him at home.* She flipped through the phone book, found his number, called him.

'Callahan here,' he answered on the second ring.

She told him in succinct terms what was happening.

'I'm going over there with a check,' she said. 'But Valerie will feel lots better if you can see Betsy.'

'I'll be there in a few minutes! Damn that insufferable nurse!'

Kara left the house, drove to Eden General. She hurried inside to find Paul Callahan fighting with the ER nurse.

'Damn, I don't want to hear such nonsense,' Kara heard him say in low but firm terms. 'I'm seeing this patient.'

'Dr Callahan, it's against the rules.' The nurse's color was high. 'If she can't pay, she's supposed to go to Farraday.'

'She can't wait to go to Farraday!' he shot back. 'I'm seeing her.' He issued a stream of orders, headed with Betsy in his arms for an examining room. Val – frightened but in control – at his side.

'You heard Dr Callahan,' Kara told the nurse. 'Provide him

with what he asked for, or you'll have a million-dollar lawsuit on your hands!'

Kara watched while the nurse summoned an ER nurse to join Dr Callahan in the examining room. 'Pronto,' she barked, and repeated Dr Callahan's order for adrenalin and an IV.

Kara asked to use an inside phone line. She ignored the nurse's hostility. Jonathan must be told about this insane rule regarding treatment in the emergency room. No way would she believe he would condone this.

Wasn't Eden General supposed to be under his supervision in the handover from non-profit to for-profit? Yet his words crept into her mind: '*I'm just a puppet parroting what my father and the wheels at Cameron Insurance set up.*'

A crisp feminine voice picked up the phone in Jonathan's office.

'I'm sorry,' she said when Kara asked to speak to Jonathan. 'He's not in the hospital this afternoon. May I take a message?'

'Thank you, no.' Kara put down the phone. Call Cameron Insurance – he must be there.

Again, Jonathan did not pick up at the other end of the line. Again a feminine voice responded.

'May I speak with Jonathan Cameron, please.' Kara tried to sound casual.

'I'm sorry, he's in a meeting. May I have him call you back?'

'Thank you, no.' *Try him later – when he's out of the meeting.* But she churned with frustration at not reaching him.

Out in the parking area an ambulance screamed to a halt. Nurses, orderlies, an ER resident leapt into action. Two victims of a car smash-up were brought in on gurneys.

In the midst of all this frenzy Valerie emerged from the examining-room area. Pale and shaken but exuding an aura of relief. Kara hurried to meet her.

'Betsy's okay?' Kara needed reassurance. It was terrifying to see a tiny child fighting for breath.

'Dr Callahan wants to keep her here under observation for a couple of hours,' Valerie said. 'He'll hang around to keep an eye on her. But he says she'll be fine. I told you—' Tears filled her eyes. 'That man's a saint.'

'A dedicated doctor. We need more like him.' Her eyes searched Val's. 'Do you want me to stay with you?'

'You're so sweet, Kara. But you don't need to stay. I'm going back inside to sit by Betsy until Dr Callahan says I can take her home. Thanks for everything. I don't know what I would have done without you.'

'I'll call you later,' Kara promised. 'Thank God she's all right.'

Kara left the ER and headed for her car. She was still unnerved by the callousness of the ER nurse who'd refused to allow Betsy to be treated without a health insurance card or a check. Let Jonathan know about this!

At the house she went directly to the phone to try to reach Jonathan. He was still in the meeting. All right, she'd try again in twenty minutes. Jonathan must order that rule rescinded.

A few minutes past 6 p.m., Kara was finally put through to Jonathan. Skipping preliminaries, she launched into a graphic report of what had happened at the hospital.

'If Dr Callahan hadn't intervened, Betsy might have died. He insisted she be treated. Jonnie, what insane rules have they put into effect at Eden General?'

'I'll look into this right now.' Shock and rage ricocheted in his voice. 'I'll call you later.'

Twenty-Nine

Jonathan put down the phone, charged from his office and down the hall to his father's suite. Cassie was just leaving for the day.

'I have to talk with my father.' He was unfamiliarly brusque.

'It's not a good time, Jonathan.' Cassie seemed to sense this would not be a routine meeting. 'He's waiting for an important West Coast call. Can't it wait until tomorrow?'

'It can't wait,' Jonathan told her.

Moments later Cassie gave him the go-ahead. 'You may have to cut it short,' she warned. 'If his call comes through.'

'Sure.' Jonathan hurried inside.

Roy Cameron leaned back in his chair with an air of strained patience. 'How're you doing, Jonathan?' He made an effort at cordiality.

'I just heard some disturbing news from the hospital,' Jonathan began. 'I—'

'You have to be firm with those people when they get on their high horse.' Roy grunted in contempt. 'They—'

'That's not the problem, Dad.' Jonathan took a deep breath, reported on the incident in the emergency room. 'That child could have died if Dr Callahan hadn't intervened.'

'Some emergency rooms accept charity cases. They have deals with municipal governments. Ours won't. Jonathan, we're running a business. These rules are necessary. I—'

Jonathan stared at his father in disbelief. 'But it's wrong!'

'Come out of the clouds, Jonathan. That's one factor you've got to learn in business. If we're to be efficient, we have to know where to draw lines. Farraday accepts charity cases. So far . . .' Roy glanced at his watch. 'The ER nurse at Eden did what was expected of her. I suppose in the case of a special

262

patient we can overlook Callahan's impetuous reaction.' His smile indicated indulgence.

'Dad, suppose that little girl had died? We'd be responsible.'

'We're not responsible for the whole town.' Roy's tone was ominous. 'You've got to get one thing through your head. Cameron Insurance and its hospital subsidiaries comprise a business. We can't run a business as a philanthropic institution.'

Their eyes clashed. Jonathan felt sick.

'Dad, I don't think I can stay on in this job,' he said unsteadily. 'I can't deal with rules against humanity. I'll remain until—'

'Bullshit!' Roy shot back. 'What do you mean, you can't deal with rules against humanity? You're my son. One day you'll take over my empire. You need backbone! You can't be a bleeding heart and run a major corporation! I—'

'Dad, I can't handle working for the company.' Jonathan flinched before the rage in his father's eyes. 'I'm sorry. I just can't—'

'I did everything for you! You'd have grown up in foster care, out on your ass at eighteen! I gave you a fine home, a wonderful education. This is what you give me in return?'

'I'm sorry,' Jonathan said again. 'I'm grateful for—'

'I don't want to hear any more from you! You're no longer a member of this family. You're not an employee of the company. Leave the keys to the car on Cassie's desk. As far as I'm concerned you're dead. You don't deserve to bear the Cameron name!'

Feeling himself adrift in a strange world, Jonathan sought out the nearest pay-phone to the Cameron building, reached in his pocket for a quarter, and called Kara. At this hour in Eden it was impossible to get a cab without waiting at least an hour. But this was news – numbing though it was – that he was impatient to share with Kara. As though marking the moment for history, he checked his watch. It was 6.42 p.m.

'Hello.' A note of caution in Kara's voice told him she'd been encountering crank callers – the result of the watchdog committee's circular, he assumed.

'Kara, it's me.' He fought to sound casual. 'Look, I'm stranded at the office. Could you pick me up?'

'Sure,' she said after what seemed minutes but was only a moment, Jonathan realized. She couldn't figure out what was happening. 'Where will you be?'

'At the north-east corner of Maple and Fifth,' he told her. To wait in front of the Cameron building might mean another encounter with his father.

'Are you okay?' she asked with sudden solicitude.

'Kind of shaken up,' he admitted. 'I had a bad scene with my father. I told him about what happened at the hospital. I quit my job – and got thrown out of the family.' He tried for a touch of humor. 'I had to hand over the keys to the company car.'

'I'll be right there.'

This whole scene was unreal, he told himself while he waited for Kara to arrive. How could Dad be so upset because he didn't want to be part of the company? What was so terrible about quitting his job? Or was it, he probed, because Dad couldn't accept having his ethics questioned? His father's words charged across his brain: '*You're no longer a member of this family.*'

Mom would go along with Dad, he told himself. They never had any real battles – not since he was little. Just Mom's snide digs and Dad's biting retorts. Long ago Mom had decided life was less complicated if she followed Dad's lead.

He was no longer a member of the family. Not welcome at Cameron Manor. A stranger in Eden, in truth. But he was staying in this town, he told himself defiantly. The barrier between Kara and himself had just been obliterated.

Kara's mind was in turmoil as she drove towards the corner where she was to pick Jonathan up. She tried to piece together the facts. He'd been shocked – and outraged – about what had happened at the hospital with Val and Betsy. He'd gone to his father – and Roy Cameron must have told him the hospital rules were not to be broken. Jonnie couldn't accept that. He quit.

Now Jonnie believed there were no longer any barriers between them. He didn't know what she was trying to do. At this moment his father was furious at him, and he was shaken, hurt. But how would he react when his father was accused of murder? He'd rush to his father's defense. That would be natural, wouldn't it?

Her heart began to pound when she saw him standing on the corner. He looked so distraught. Not because his father had disinherited him. Jonnie wasn't concerned that he was no longer the heir to the Cameron empire. Roy Cameron was the only father he'd ever known. He was grateful for having been rescued from a future of foster care and little education. He felt such an obligation to the Camerons – that was why he'd allowed himself to be swept up into the company.

There, he saw her coming. She lifted a hand from the wheel to wave to him as she approached. She pulled up at the curb. He reached for the passenger-side door and opened it.

'I hope I didn't drag you away from something important.'

'You're important.' She leaned forward for a tender kiss. All her resolve about breaking up in eclipse at this moment. 'Fill me in, Jonnie.'

Returning to the stream of early-evening traffic, she listened while he briefed her on what had happened in the short while since they'd talked.

'Let's stop by for take-out Chinese.' She saw the startled, eager glow in his eyes. 'Grandma loves *moo goo gai pan*.' He understood – they wouldn't be going to his apartment. 'Both she and Mom are working late this evening, but we'll pick up enough for the four of us.' *Why am I chattering as though this is just another day in our lives?* 'Back in school we were big fans of Chinese take-out. You know, it was kind to our budgets.' But he didn't know. He had never had to budget – not in those days.

'I can't believe that in a few minutes my whole existence has turned upside-down.' He shook his head as though to thrust off a tightening band.

'That was your father's initial response – "Give him time to rethink the situation,"' she urged, because she suspected this was what Jonathan needed to hear.

'He meant it.' Jonathan was terse. 'He's not going to change his mind. If I don't toe the party line,' he said with unfamiliar bitterness, 'then I'm cast out.'

'Jonnie, it's not the end of the world.' But she understood his pain.

'I'd suffocate if I tried to stay with the company. You realized that, didn't you?'

'You know what you want to do with your life. That's a gift.' *He thinks all the craziness between us is over. I know how he'll react when he learns everything – even with the way his father is behaving. He's too decent and fine not to walk from me and rush to his father's side. But I can't break up with him right now. Not when he's hurting this way. This is the only family he's ever known – and they've kicked him out.*

They stopped at the Chinese take-out shop, made a pretense of lively interest in choosing. For the moment in a silent pact to ignore reality. At the house – while they ate – Jonathan began to face his future.

'I'll have to start worrying about money. That offer still open? Cameron & Jamison, Attorneys-at-Law. Or maybe Jamison & Cameron?'

'Let's wait until after Hank's trial.' *He can't understand why I'm stalling. He thinks I'm not sure about us. I was never more sure of anything in my whole life.*

'Okay,' he backtracked. 'I've got enough in my checking account to carry me for three or four months. In the morning I'll rent a small car.' His smile was eloquent. 'Not a Mercedes. And since I'm among the unemployed, let me help you with Hank's case. I'll be coming in fresh – I might be able to latch onto some tiny point that escaped you. Fill me in on everything you've dug up,' he persuaded. 'We'll work together to clear him.'

'For tonight let's try to relax,' she decreed. But her mind was charging ahead on dangerous roads. Was this the time to tell Jonathan about Mom and the Camerons? Let him at least understand that situation. 'Let me bring over more green tea.'

While Jonathan reminisced about the years at law school, Kara tried to gear herself for what she must say. She wouldn't be telling him she was convinced that his father – his parents – had the only motive for three murders. But she would make him understand that his parents would never have approved of her as his wife.

In a corner of her mind she asked herself with unguarded optimism if that mattered now. But only for an instant. That ugly scene between Jonnie and his father wouldn't erase a lifetime of loyalty. Of course he'd leap to his father's defense.

'Jonnie, there's something I have to tell you.' She managed to keep her voice steady. 'I should have told you months ago – but I guess I was afraid of driving you away.' *Why did I say that? It's a matter of time before I* do *drive him away.*

'Kara, that could never happen,' he reproached her. 'But what do you want to tell me?' He spoke to her as though to a much-loved toddler.

'This all goes back over twenty-five years . . .' She took a deep breath, told him about Tim and her mother, about the annulment. About her birth and the Camerons' refusal to believe she was their granddaughter. Conscious of his compassionate reaction, his shock that his parents could have behaved so callously. 'There's more,' she continued, and told him about Eric and Gerry, who were enraged about the drug charges. 'They were driving to Eden to protest when they were murdered.' She saw the pain in Jonathan's eyes as he assimilated that. *But he doesn't get the connection. He doesn't see the motive for their murder.*

'In a way it was your father who brought us together,' he said tenderly. 'I wouldn't be in Eden if his parents hadn't adopted me when they lost him.'

'I wanted to tell you so many times – but I couldn't bring myself to do it.'

He reached for her hand. 'You'll be a Cameron – doubly – when we're married.'

But how can that ever happen?

While they were making a pretense of gaiety over the predictions in their fortune cookies, the phone rang.

Kara rose to her feet. 'That's Val,' she guessed and hurried to respond.

'I'm home with Betsy,' Valerie reported. 'She's fine.'

'Once Dr Callahan arrived, I was sure she'd be all right.'

'I have to give her supper now and put her to bed. Kara, thanks so much. You came through again.'

'Val brought Betsy home,' Kara told Jonathan when she was off the phone.

'I still can't believe what happened at Eden General.' Jonathan flinched in recall. 'How could the ER turn Betsy away at a time like that? But they did,' he said grimly before Kara could reply. 'That's something that shouldn't happen at any hospital anywhere in this world.' His face radiated fresh rage.

'Dr Callahan was furious. He'll have plenty to say about that.'

'It won't matter,' Jonathan predicted. 'We're living in a world where too many people in strong positions consider only the bottom line.'

'But we have to fight against that – in the courts,' Kara pointed out. 'Jonnie, we're attorneys – we can help.'

'We'll help,' Jonathan agreed, then hesitated. 'You won't be angry if I cut out now?' His eyes pleaded for understanding. 'I need to think things through, get back on track. We'll talk tomorrow. Okay?'

'Sure.' Her smile was meant to be reassuring. He wanted to leave before Grandma and Mom came home. He wasn't up to discussing the encounter with his father. 'Come over here for breakfast,' she said on impulse, because he was so distraught – and was unnerved by this invitation. 'About ten o'clock.' Let him try to get a decent night's sleep.

Edie and Daisy arrived home within five minutes of each other. While Kara served them reheated Chinese take-out and tea, she told them about Valerie's experience with Betsy at Eden's ER.

'Val has no health insurance, of course – and in her panic she forgot to take her purse with her,' Kara wound up.

'A year ago – before Cameron Insurance took over – that wouldn't have happened!' Edie blazed. Dinner forgotten. 'How awful for Val and Betsy to have to go through that.'

'This isn't some TV program – this is real life. It'll be happening all over the country,' Daisy said. 'No health insurance, no cash – no treatment. Thank God, Kara, that you were able to get hold of Paul.'

'He was able to handle the situation this time.' Kara was pensive. 'I don't know about the future.'

'What do you mean?' Edie pounced.

'When Jonnie challenged his father about that hospital ruling, Roy Cameron told him the hospital wasn't a philanthropic institution. The ruling stands.'

Now Kara forced herself to report on Jonathan's confrontation with his father. 'Just like that, Jonnie's father disowned him. "*You're no longer a member of this family,*"' she quoted. 'Oh, Jonnie's not upset about not inheriting the Cameron fortune. He's young – he has a profession. He'll be all right financially. He doesn't have to drive a Mercedes or live in a mansion. But to Jonnie family has always been so important – perhaps because he'd been rejected by his birth mother and father. He's always felt such gratitude, such obligation to them. He never *wanted* to work for the company – he felt it was a duty.'

'Kara . . .' Daisy seemed to be weighing her words, 'you understand that this break with his father is very traumatic for Jonathan – but he'll still rush to his father's defense if you come out and accuse Roy Cameron of hiring hit men to commit three murders.'

Kara was startled. *Mom understands I'm in love with Jonnie.* 'I know there's no future for us.' She took a deep breath. 'I've told him about what the Camerons did to you, Mom. I wonder that – as sharp as he is – he doesn't see the connection to the three murders.'

'He'd never suspect anything so horrendous of his father. He may never believe it – even if you come up with solid proof. But you're young, Kara – with a great career ahead of you,' Daisy said defiantly. 'You'll survive this.'

Thirty

Kara awoke with an instant recall of the breakfast invitation she'd extended to Jonathan. Now she dreaded the encounter, even while she felt overwhelming compassion for his situation. His words of last night tickertaped across her mind: '*Since I'm among the unemployed, let me help you with Hank's case. I'll be coming in fresh – I might be able to latch onto some tiny clue that escaped you.*' But, like Mom said, he'd never believe his father was a murderer.

The morning was grey and dismal – reflecting her mood. She showered and dressed, joined Edie and Daisy in the dining area.

'I'll just have coffee,' she told Edie. 'Jonnie'll be over around ten – I'll have breakfast with him.'

'There's plenty of pancake batter for the two of you. You might want to add some peach slices.' Edie's casual tone was belied by the anxious glance she exchanged with Daisy. They knew she was hurting. 'And let the answering machine pick up. We're still getting a few crank calls about the circular.'

'Paul called earlier,' Daisy said, gazing from Kara to her mother. 'It was just a few minutes past seven – when he was on the way to the hospital to make morning rounds. He's upset about what happened with Val and Betsy. He's talking about resigning.'

'Leaving Eden?' Edie was shocked.

'No, he won't leave town.' Daisy's face was luminous. 'He says he'll try opening up a private practice.'

'Oh, patients will flock to him.' Edie exuded relief.

'He said that some prospective patients won't be able to come to him – he'll be off their hospital plan.' Daisy was anxious.

270

'Cameron Insurance isn't the only HMO serving this county,' Kara pointed out. 'Patients will follow him. They won't be so loyal to Roy Cameron when they realize what's happening with Eden General and Farraday. They'll join another health plan.'

'The situation will get a lot worse before it gets better,' Edie warned. 'But yes, people have such confidence in Paul. We won't lose him. You'll see.'

Daisy left for the shop. A few minutes later Edie prepared to take off also.

'I'll stop by at Val's for a few minutes before I go in to work,' Edie said. 'See if she needs anything from the supermarket. She won't want to drag Betsy around so soon after an attack.'

'It makes me furious that her friends – neighbors – are behaving as though she and Betsy have some horrible contagious disease!' Kara sighed in exasperation. 'People in small towns aren't supposed to behave that way.'

'Remember to add peaches or bananas to the pancake batter,' Edie said. 'That makes it special.'

'I'll remember.' Kara felt her grandmother's sympathy for Jonathan – for her. But there was nothing anyone could do to change the situation. Soon – very soon – Jonathan would look upon her as the enemy.

A few minutes before ten Jonathan arrived.

'Am I too early?' he asked with an air of apology.

'Jonnie, no—' She accepted his light kiss with a knowledge that he wouldn't go any further. Not here. 'Come out to the kitchen and let me fix breakfast.'

Over peach-laden pancakes and coffee, Jonathan talked about how he might be helpful to Kara in clearing Hank.

'I'm not trying to dismiss all the work you've done so far,' he insisted conscientiously. 'But I'm coming fresh to the case. You're so close to it. I want you to tell me every small detail you've turned up. Every faint suspicion that's entered your mind.'

'Right.' Her voice strained. *How do I tell Jonnie whom I suspect?*

'I think the best way to tackle this is to start at the beginning.

After breakfast let's go over to talk with Val. Show me the murder scene. Let's go over every tiny bit of information you've dug up. Who had a motive – besides Hank – for killing Mattie? And what's the connection between her murder and those two murders twenty-five years ago?'

'We'll go over to Val's house.' She battled panic. 'You'll see the murder scene.' *I'm convinced Mattie was killed because she was going to the District Attorney's office with Joe's confession. But I can't dig up one shred of evidence to prove this.* 'Maybe I have been blind to some tiny clue.' *What can we possibly discover at the murder scene? I've gone over that a dozen times – coming up with nothing. And if we find something, it has to incriminate his father.*

'One more cup of coffee,' Jonathan stipulated. 'Then we take off.'

Driving over to Val's house in Jonathan's rented car, Kara tried to gear herself for what lay ahead. How long could she play this insane game with Jonnie? They were leaping towards disaster. Thank God, Val was unaware of their suspicions about Roy Cameron – she wouldn't make some devastating comment. *But how long can I keep from blurting out what I suspect?*

'Who besides your grandmother and yourself knew about Joe's confession?' Jonnie probed as he pulled to a stop before Val's house.

'Nobody,' Kara said with fresh frustration. 'Mattie said she'd told nobody.'

'Not true,' Jonathan rejected. 'She told somebody. The person who went to the house – expecting her to still be at work – to steal that confession. Or—' He paused in thought. 'The person Mattie told passed the information – possibly without realizing it – to somebody else. The person who murdered Mattie. Who was her closest friend?'

'I don't know.' But a name popped into her mind. 'Alice Evans, I think. They both loved mystery novels and country music.' *Isn't that the housekeeper at Cameron Manor? Does that say anything to Jonnie?* 'We'll ask Val about that.' All at once a dizzying possibility assailed her. Had Alice Evans let it slip that Mattie had Joe's confession and planned

272

o take it to the DA's office? *That's a small point that I overlooked!*

Valerie was at the door as they walked up the path to the house – her eyes questioning.

'Val, this is Jonathan. He's just out of law school too – and he's going to be working with me.'

Val managed a wistful smile. 'We need all the help we can get.'

'Jonnie wants to go over the – murder scene.' Kara saw Valerie wince. 'He thinks I may have overlooked some small thing that could lead us to the real murderer. Oh, I told him that Mattie's closest friend was Alice Evans—' Val nodded. Kara turned to Jonathan now – her heart pounding. 'She's the housekeeper at Cameron Manor, isn't she?'

'No,' he said, surprising Kara. 'She's Bart's housekeeper – at his cottage on the estate. Valerie, let's go to the kitchen. I understand you found the body there.'

'That's right. The kitchen's this way.' Val led them from the tiny living room to the immaculate kitchen.

'I know this is painful,' Jonathan apologized, 'but I need you to tell me everything you can remember about that day.'

'Sure.' But Val was unnerved. 'I came into the house by the kitchen entrance.' She closed her eyes for a moment. 'And there she was – lying on the floor in a pool of blood. Her note beside her.' Val's face drained of color as she relived that traumatic encounter.

Kara digested each word that Val uttered – weighing each, searching for some hidden clue. Jonathan, too, was engrossed in her account.

'Was there any indication that Mattie fought with her killer?' Jonathan turned from Valerie to Kara. 'Anything that was discovered under her nails?'

'No indication that she fought him off,' Kara told him. 'Mattie was an avid mystery buff. Grandma keeps saying she can't believe Mattie didn't manage to leave some clue that would lead us to her murderer.'

'I've kept all her personal things in her bedroom.' Val struggled for calm. 'When I can bring myself to do it, I'll give away her tapes and her books and her clothes. But right now,' she said tenderly, 'it's like her shrine.'

'Could we see that room?' Jonathan asked, his voice gentle.

Val nodded. 'It's right at the end of this little hall . . .'

Valerie opened the door to the bedroom that had been Mattie's. The double bed that she had shared for a lot of years with Joe was covered by a much-washed comforter. A low bookcase crammed with paperbacks flanked one wall. A dresser at another wall was topped by a rack that once held Mattie's collection of country-music tapes – missing now. On a small, pillowed rocker sat a tote – as though Mattie had just returned from outdoors and had placed it there.

'Val, that's the tote you said was on the floor beside Mattie's body?' All at once Kara's mind was in high gear. 'The police didn't take it with them?'

'No.' Val appeared puzzled.

'Then it wasn't checked for fingerprints.' Jonathan's eyes met Kara's. 'If the murderer was looking for something—' He knew not to mention the confession to Valerie, Kara understood – at least, not yet. 'If he was searching for something his fingerprints would be on that tote.'

'My fingerprints are on it,' Valerie said wryly. 'I picked it up and brought it in here. There's nothing in it except a batch of Mattie's tapes that she used to take with her to work and her tape recorder—'

Kara felt prickles of excitement. 'Let me see the tape recorder.' She crossed to the tote. The recorder sat atop perhaps a dozen tapes. All at once Kara's heart was pounding. Jonathan's eyes – like her own – were riveted on the tape recorder. Val was bewildered.

'Rewind the tape,' Jonathan ordered, but already Kara's finger was there. 'Okay, now hit "play".'

'*Look, behave and you won't be hurt,*' an unfamiliar voice droned menacingly. Not Roy Cameron's voice, Kara noted. As was known to local people from his frequent public pronouncements. '*Just give me Joe's confession.*'

'Oh my God!' Jonathan whispered while the recording continued.

274

'I don't know what you're talking about,' Mattie hedged. *What confession?'*

'The one you told Alice about. Now find that confession and give it to me!'

'Put that gun away, Mr Bart.' Mattie was terrified but trying to conceal it. *'You don't want to—'*

All at once a radio blared loudly. Almost masking a loud report.

'He killed her!' Val screamed. 'Mr Bart from Cameron Insurance! He killed Mattie!'

Pale with shock, Jonathan leaned forward to switch off the tape recorder. Mattie had identified her killer.

'Kara, take the tape recorder to Harvey Raines. Explain how we found it. I'll go over later to confirm. First, I have to tell my mother before the word hits this town.'

'Jonnie, why?' Kara searched her mind for an answer. Why Bart?'

'Bart is a prime snob. That rules his life.' His eyes darkened in contempt. 'I remember when I was a little kid I heard him yell at my mother for having married someone he called "beneath us". Disgracing their family. When Tim married your mother – someone not rich and socially prominent – Bart's sick mind went berserk. Like my father, Bart wanted the marriage annulled. At any cost.'

'Eric and Gerry threatened to stop the annulment,' Kara added, 'so he hired Joe to kill them.'

'Hank will be cleared?' Valerie's eyes swung from Jonathan to Kara. 'They'll have to let him go now?'

'There'll be some formalities,' Kara explained, 'but, yes, Hank will be released.' And this town would understand that her father had married her mother because they loved each other – and he had not been under the influence of drugs.

'Okay, let's get this show on the road.' Jonathan strained for calm. 'Kara, take the tape to Harvey Raines, and—'

'My car's out front,' Val broke in. 'I'll give you the key, Kara.'

'Explain to Raines that Val and I were with you – we heard the tape together,' Jonathan stressed. 'I'll come over later and confirm that.'

'If they want you to give a statement, Val, I'll tell you,' Kara said.

'May I use your phone for a moment?' Jonathan asked Valerie. 'I want to see if my mother is home.' His face was taut. 'I have to go and tell her Bart has murdered three people. I can't let her find out from a TV or radio bulletin.'

'Go right ahead.' Valerie turned to Kara. Her face luminous. 'It's over – this whole awful nightmare is over.'

Jonathan waited while Lulu summoned his mother to the phone.

'Jonnie, you can't tell her just yet,' Kara whispered. 'Bart could take off—'

'I won't tell her before you've reached the DA's office,' Jonathan promised. He turned to the phone as his mother responded.

'I just wanted to make sure you're home,' he explained. 'There's something I have to tell you. It's about Bart—'

'What about Bart?' Kara could hear Sandra Cameron's shrill demand. 'Tell me now!'

'I'll be there in ten minutes. It's not something you'd like me to discuss over the phone. I'm leaving right now,' he said gently.

Sandra Cameron sat frozen beside the phone. Her eyes glazed, her face colorless. 'Lulu!' she shrieked. 'Lulu, fix me a drink this minute!'

'Yes'm,' Lulu called back. 'I'll jus' run downstairs for some ice.'

Sandra reached for the phone again, punched in Bart's private number at the company. Fighting hysteria. They had to figure out what to do. She'd been so scared – ever since that Mason woman died. Why wouldn't Bart ever let her talk about it?

'Bart Jennings here.' His crisp, arrogant voice came to her.

'Bart, you've got to get out of town! Fast!'

'What are you talking about?' But his voice was guarded.

'Jonathan's coming over here to talk to me. Something about you—'

276

'Nobody can prove anything.' But she heard fear in his defiant voice.

'Bart, they *know*. They'll prove it. You'd never let me talk about it, but I knew. Those two young idiots who were Tim's friends, and then that woman who died back in May.'

'Cool it,' Bart ordered. 'They'll never get me. I promise you that. Remember me, sugar. We were two special people.'

'Bart!' Terror welled in her. And then a shot rang out. *Bart!'*

Eden was besieged by media people when the District Attorney's office released the contents of Mattie's tape and announced Bart's suicide. Sandra Cameron was whisked away to a private sanitarium. Roy Cameron seemed to age overnight.

'I tried to talk to my father,' Jonathan reminded Kara when they returned to the Jamison house after the very private funeral for Bart. 'He walked away from me. You saw that. In some weird fashion he blames me for what's happened.'

'He's set you free,' Kara told him. 'You have no more obligations.' She struggled within herself for a moment. 'Jonnie, for the longest time I was convinced your father had hired Joe to kill Eric and Gerry and hired someone else to kill Mattie.' She saw comprehension break through in his mind. Now he understood her sometimes bewildering behavior. 'I was wrong.'

'Right ballpark,' he pointed out. 'Wrong player.'

'I was so scared. I couldn't see a future for us.'

The ringing of the phone was a harsh intrusion. 'I'll get it.' *I'm glad I told Jonnie. No secrets between us ever again.* Hello?'

'Kara, did you check the mail?' Edie's voice exuded excitement.

'We just got home from the funeral—' All at once she was tense. *The response from the bar exams?*

'It's on the table in the foyer. Go look this minute!' Edie ordered. 'I'll hold on.'

'What's up?' Jonathan asked while Kara darted from the phone to the foyer.

'The letter from Columbia—' She reached for the envelope

277

on the foyer table, ripped it open. Her eyes clung to the message. 'Yes! Jonnie, I passed!'

'I knew you would.'

'Let's go to your apartment and pick up yours.' Kara was radiant. 'Oh, first let me tell Grandma.' She darted back to the phone. 'Grandma, the lease on the office space is legal. I've been admitted to the bar!'

Jonathan prodded Kara from the house and to the car. Both confident that he, too, had been admitted to the bar – yet anxious for the sheet of paper that would confirm this. The letter was there in the mailbox. Jonathan tore open the envelope while Kara waited with towering impatience.

'You've got your partner,' Jonathan reported after a moment. Jubilant. 'Jamison & Cameron, Attorneys-at-Law.'

'It seems awful to be so happy in the face of what's happened.' Kara lifted her face to his. 'But congratulations counselor.'

'What would be a respectful length of time to wait before we're married?'

'Thanksgiving Day,' Kara decided after a moment's thought. 'We have so much to be thankful for. But let me call Grandma and Mom and tell them they have two attorneys in the family.'

'Family.' Jonathan spoke with reverence. 'Such a beautiful word.'